DESERT DREAMING

STEVE ELLIOTT

BALBOA.PRESS
A DIVISION OF HAY HOUSE

Copyright © 2021 Steve Elliott.

All rights reserved. No part of this book may be used or reproduced by any means, graphic, electronic, or mechanical, including photocopying, recording, taping or by any information storage retrieval system without the written permission of the author except in the case of brief quotations embodied in critical articles and reviews.

Balboa Press books may be ordered through booksellers or by contacting:

Balboa Press
A Division of Hay House
1663 Liberty Drive
Bloomington, IN 47403
www.balboapress.com.au
AU TFN: 1 800 844 925 (Toll Free inside Australia)
AU Local: 0283 107 086 (+61 2 8310 7086 from outside Australia)

Because of the dynamic nature of the Internet, any web addresses or links contained in this book may have changed since publication and may no longer be valid. The views expressed in this work are solely those of the author and do not necessarily reflect the views of the publisher, and the publisher hereby disclaims any responsibility for them.

The author of this book does not dispense medical advice or prescribe the use of any technique as a form of treatment for physical, emotional, or medical problems without the advice of a physician, either directly or indirectly. The intent of the author is only to offer information of a general nature to help you in your quest for emotional and spiritual well-being. In the event you use any of the information in this book for yourself, which is your constitutional right, the author and the publisher assume no responsibility for your actions.

Any people depicted in stock imagery provided by Getty Images are models, and such images are being used for illustrative purposes only. Certain stock imagery © Getty Images.

Print information available on the last page.

ISBN: 978-1-5043-2382-6 (sc)
ISBN: 978-1-5043-2383-3 (e)

Balboa Press rev. date: 12/09/2020

1
11 MARCH, 2014

THE SMALL KING Brown snake was warm, warmer than he had been for many nights. The nights had after all been unusually cool for this time of year, particularly taking into account the sweltering days. Less than three feet long he shimmered a coppery-brown colour in the early morning sun, or would have if he had been exposed to the sun. As it was he was comfortably curled in the dark beneath a large piece of canvas that he had discovered the previous evening.

Sharing the sleeping arrangements with the human had been a good idea, for a snake, although he had almost been crushed several times by the constant movements. Next time he would have to bunk with a human that did not toss and turn so much! Still, it had been a warm and mostly comfortable night and if he could find something to eat it would be a better day.

The flap of canvas above the snake suddenly disappeared as the swag was rolled up. In the blink of an eye the comfortable snake was exposed to the early morning sun.

"Fucking hell, a bloody snake! Theres a bloody joe blake under my swag!" boomed a voice.

"What's the problem Mick?" queried another voice.

"There's a fucking King Brown under my swag. I slept with the bastard!" yelled Mick, the owner of the first voice.

"You're a difficult bugger to please Mick", said Ben, "Last night you were complaining you had no-one to sleep with and now you find that you did you're not pleased. Make up your bloody mind!" "He hasn't bit you has he mate?" he added in a more conciliatory tone.

"Ha bloody ha mate", yelled Mick, "I was thinking more of a sheila, not a bloody joe blake. And no, the bugger hasn't got his fangs into me. Find me a waddy and I'll brain the bastard!"

"No you won't. You know it's illegal and we don't want the greenies coming down on us", said Ben firmly, "Just finish rolling your swag and let him be on his way. But be careful, I don't want to lose you to a snake bite!"

There were further curses and complaints from Mick's direction but he cautiously pulled his swag away from the still recumbent snake. He quickly finished rolling it and tied it before throwing it in the back of the nearby landcruiser. The snake, having been woken and its cover having disappeared, wiggled slowly into the nearest clump of spinifex and disappeared.

For those uncomfortable with the Australian idiom a joe blake is a snake, a Sheila is any girl or woman, whether or no their name is Sheila, and a waddy is a stick or club.

"Coffee mate?", said Ben handing a tin mug of sweetened black coffee to Mick.

"Thanks mate", said Mick, keeping a wary eye on the small spinifex clump into which the snake had disappeared. The spinifex was a brilliant dark green and Mick watched carefully for a flash of brown. He still wasn't certain that the King Brown wouldn't reappear intent on doing him harm. If it did reappear then he would dong it, no matter what Ben said. He took the coffee that Ben handed to him and took a healthy swig of the thick, black liquid.

"Anything for breakfast?", Mick asked, his eyes never straying far from the spinifex clump.

"Tinned spaghetti or baked beans", replied Ben, "That's all we have left until Ibrahim returns with the supplies. I guess he should get in about lunch time".

"I think I'll pass", said Mick, "Hopefully Ib will bring back something nice for lunch. And anyway, I don't want to spend any longer around here with that bloody snake!".

As Ben also was not hungry he too passed on opening a can. They had both had baked beans the night before and he didn't feel in the mood to repeat the experience. The two men quickly finished their coffees and packed the billy from the previous nights meal preparation and the mornings coffee into the large aluminium box which contained all of their catering equipment. The two mugs were quickly rinsed and joined the billy in the box, but not before Mick doused the spinifex to which the snake had retreated with the rinse water in a last fit of pique. There was no reaction from the bush, the snake either appreciating an early morning wash or having already moved on. In this dry country the spinifex undoubtedly welcomed the drink.

Both men then grabbed a handle at each end of the box and placed it behind the cabin on the tray of the land cruiser. Mick walked around the vehicle to the drivers door, and climbed into the cabin. Ben opened the passenger door and settled himself into the seat.

The sun was slowly emerging from the eastern horizon promising another hot day. But this was the East Pilbara region in Western Australia on the edge of the desert, and it was almost always hot here. Both men could already feel sweat beginning to form between their shoulders and under their arms. They knew that the day would be hot, the same as the previous day.

The two men who had been camped out for the night in their swags were exploring the East Pilbara for mineral deposits on behalf of a Perth based mineral exploration company, Major Minerals.

Ben Wilde, slumped in the passenger seat, looked rumpled but alert. He was dirty and his hair stood out from his head as though he had passed through a cyclone. But he was still an imposing figure. Standing six feet and two inches in the old money, one point eight eight meters in the new, Ben had a handsome face capped by thick head of black hair that reached to his shoulders. His eyes were a rich brown color. Having not shaved for several days he was starting to cultivate a short beard. Most women would have described him as good looking, although he never considered himself as being so. His clothes consisted of a pair of khaki shorts and a short sleeve shirt of the same colour, with pockets. Although after several weeks in the bush, and few changes of clothes, the khaki was almost obscured by the red dust. His feet were encased in RM Williams 'stockman' boots and, as far as he was concerned, all was right with the World on this beautiful autumn morning.

Mick Agostino was dressed in a similar manner to Ben. However, whilst Ben was tall and dark, Mick was short and dark, barely reaching five feet and seven inches in height. As well as coming second in the height department, Mick had also been short changed in the looks department. Where Ben was handsome, Mick was at best average with a broad face that hosted a large nose and was framed by an untidy mop of brown hair. His best facial feature were undoubtedly his bright green eyes. Moreover, where Ben was lean, Mick was stocky with the body of a professional weightlifter. The only thing the two men had in common was the deep brown tan caused by the relentless Australian sun. That and their common love for the Australian bush.

Ben was an exploration geologist working for a small publicly owned exploration company. As well as being his friend, Mick was his field assistant. Ben had been an exploration geologist for seven years and he loved what he did. Mick had been his field assistant for three years and he also loved what he did although he would occasionally grumble about the conditions. They were nonetheless firm friends. Mick would often tell anyone who cared to listen that it was his job to tie Ben's shoe laces and wipe his arse because he wasn't capable of doing it himself. In his opinion he was Ben's babysitter. Ben did not mind and laughed it off whenever Mick launched into a description of his duties. And in any case, whilst they were in the bush Mick had no shoelaces to tie as Ben always wore elastic sided boots without laces. So there!

"Where to boss?", asked Mick.

"I think we'll go to Blind Bluff today", said Ben, "The geology looks good there and I want to have a bit of a sticky-beak at that area. And don't call me boss!".

"Righto boss, on our way", said Mick turning the ignition key and turning a deaf ear to Bens instructions.

The motor came quietly to life and then roared as Mick pressed the accelerator, keeping his foot on the clutch. The motor quietened again as Mick lifted his foot and engaged the gears. The land cruiser rolled slowly forward over the dry and red loamy soil before coming to the track by which they had entered the previous day. The track was no more than two wheel ruts in the red soil although it could clearly be seen cutting a narrow swathe through the spinifex and stunted mulga trees to both the left and right with Spinifex growing between the ruts. Very few people ever travelled this way and most of them that did were geologists. Mick turned the steering wheel to the left and they were soon bumping over the uneven track at about fifteen kilometers per hour, red dust billowing up in their trail.

The track ran over fairly flat ground for about five kilometers before entering and winding up the slopes of some low hills. Ben could clearly see the hills looking red in the bright morning light with a thin, patchy covering of green spinifex grass. He knew that Blind Bluff lay on the far side of the Hills and that they would arrive there in about fifteen minutes. In the meantime they drove on in companionable silence.

Seventeen minutes later Mick bought the land cruiser to a halt in the shade of a large river gum tree which was situated on the bank of a small, dry stream. Blind Bluff rose from the plain on the other side of the stream. The bluff was a projection from the line of hills they had crossed, pushing away from the hills across the plain. Standing about thirty meters high, the bluff had steep slopes on three sides, the fourth side merging with a plateau formed by one of the hills.

"You wait here mate", said Ben, "Maybe you can fix that tire we holed yesterday. I'm going to go up and over the bluff to have a look-see and should be back within the hour".

Mick grunted, an indication that Ben took as an affirmation as he reached down to the cabin floor and found his geologists pick and then to the dashboard where he retrieved his Akubra hat and jammed it onto his untidy mop of hair. Stepping from the vehicle he grabbed his small backpack from the tray at the back and slotted the pick handle between his belt and the shorts that they supported. He crossed the dry pebbly stream and began walking upwards towards the top of the bluff.

The ground was at first the same red, loamy soil that was everywhere in the area. However, as he approached the bluff the loam soil gave way to a rocky soil with numerous small, flat rocks projecting through its surface. These rocks had fallen from the bluff which was composed of shale rock that formed irregular cliff faces near the top. Ben walked steadily up the hill towards the small cliff that formed the southern edge of the bluff. On arriving at the cliff face Ben squeezed through a narrow crevice and using the uneven rock surface as stairs clambered to the top of the bluff.

From the top of the bluff, one of the highest points of land in the area, Ben could see back to the south across the dry creek to where Mick was wrestling the punctured tire off the back of the vehicle. To the north and east the terrain was the ubiquitous red dirt with scattered spinifex and mulga typical of the area. To the west the bluff merged with the gently undulating hills that they had crossed on the way from their overnight camp.

Ben walked across the top of the bluff to the north on a relatively level surface with only a few rocky projections. Arriving at the northern cliff he eased himself over and down, once again using the uneven rocks as steps. The northern slope of the bluff was the same as the southern, red soil with numerous loose pieces of shale rock. Ben worked his way cautiously down the slope until it started to level out into the flat plain. Nearing the base he glimpsed from the corner of his eye a flash of bright green which he knew was not spinifex. Turning to the left he walked only three paces before he was looking down at a bright green rock. The small piece of rock was only about two inches long but he knew what it was instantly. Copper! Or, to be more precise, malachite, the bright green copper mineral that often forms from the weathering of copper ores. Already it seemed as though his little excursion had been a success.

Ben bent down and picked up the green rock and placed it in a small calico bag that he retrieved from his backpack. He also removed from the pack his small hand-held GPS unit and his notebook, turning the GPS on and placing it on the ground. Whilst the GPS warmed up and acquired satellites to fix its position he quickly noted the sample number, already printed on the bag, and described the rock and its surroundings in the notebook. The GPS having fixed the position he also noted this in the notebook and finally placed all of the materials, including the sample, back into his backpack.

Pacing back and forth over the area he searched for more of the green rock, unfortunately without success. He then turned to go back up the bluff in the hope of discovering the bedrock from which the piece of malachite rock had been dislodged. About five meters above the discovery site he found it, a small area of rock with patches of bright green, poking through the soil. Although the green coloured rock occupied an area less than a foot in diameter, Steve knew that this was the mother lode, the area where the copper lode breached the surface and the source of the small piece of copper that he had found lower down.

Once again Ben stopped, hunkered down and removed his

backpack. He also drew his pick from the belt and using the pointed end quickly dislodged a number of fragments of the rock. These fragments he placed in a new calico bag and using the GPS and notebook once again logged the samples description and location.

Not bad, thought Ben, not yet seven o'clock and he had already found some interesting mineralisation. And he knew from his previous research of the area that no previous prospector had discovered copper here. In fact, to the best of his knowledge no one had previously explored the area for copper. Gold yes – copper no.

Twenty minutes later, having circled around the east end of the bluff, Ben was approaching Mick and the vehicle over the flat.

"G'day mate", he said as he approached, "Finished that tire?"

"Yep, good to go boss, find anything?"

"Yeah, I got some copper on the other side of the bluff. Looks interesting".

"Good-oh! Where to now then?" asked Mick.

"Take us back to that line of hills near the main road and I'll have a bit of a gander around there", said Ben, "You never know, I might get lucky twice today. And then we can meet Ibrahim on the road after I've had a bit of a look around".

Both men climbed into the cruiser and Mick engaged the gears, setting of along the track again towards the north. An hour later they stopped at some gently undulating hills that ran off to both the east and west. Mick had stopped the cruiser on top of one of the hills and from there they could see about two kilometers away to the north the main bitumen NWR road. To the west the road terminated at the small gold mining town of Marble Bar, and to the east it terminated at the Nuclear Waste Repository (NWR) at Lands End, passing the turnoff to the homestead of Bright Downs station on the way. Marble bar was about eighty kilometers to the west, the homestead about fifty kilometers to the east and Lands End two hundred kilometers beyond that.

For the next three hours Ben quartered the hills for a two

kilometer radius around the vehicle. Like all good exploration geologists his eyes were constantly on the ground although he found nothing to match his earlier discovery. Everywhere he looked was either red earth or fragments of shale rock and dolomite. Occasionally he saw small pieces of quartz from veins but they were almost pure white and devoid of any indications of mineralisation. Certainly no gold. There were no indications anywhere of any type of mineralisation. Mick trailed along behind Ben constantly complaining about the "bloody spinifex".

Spinifex is a grass that grows in circular clumps that may reach heights of over a meter. The thin, needle-like leaves point upwards and outwards from the centre of the clump and can draw blood from the unwary wanderer. A brush against the leaves will result in numerous pinpricks which often results in an annoying rash. Wearing only shorts, some unwary steps by Ben and Mick had already resulted in both men having small dots of blood covering their legs.

Having discovered nothing of interest Ben opted to head to the main road to wait for Ibrahim who was bringing supplies back from Marble Bar.

Arriving back at the cruiser both men climbed in and Mick soon had the vehicle bumping along the track. Fifteen minutes later they arrived at the main road where Mick parked the cruiser in the shade of a large desert oak. Making themselves comfortable, each with a cold tin of coke extracted from the small Engel car fridge, they settled down to wait. Ben re-read the notes he had made in his notebook over the last two weeks whilst Mick re-read a girlie magazine he had stashed under his seat.

For half an hour they both sat quietly, each involved in his own study. At eleven thirty-six by the dashboard clock Ben glanced over his left shoulder to see a glint of light on the western horizon. He knew that the flash of light signaled the approach of a vehicle along the NWR road. Out here in the wilderness it could be nothing else.

"They're here mate", he said to Mick, knowing that the flash of light could only signal Ibrahims and Banjos vehicle. After all, the road led only to the isolated station homestead and the NWR facility and nowhere else. And no one travelled the road other than the station owner and workers, transport convoys with nuclear waste, and the occasional wayward geologist. It might be someone else but Ben doubted it. Ibrahim was expected and they knew from experience that the road was seldom travelled.

"Terrific, I'm starving", was the reply, "I'll put the billy on".

Ben and Mick both climbed from the cruiser and each quickly gathered an armful of small sticks and broken branches that had fallen from the desert oak. Retrieving a box of matches from the cruiser dashboard, and tearing a page from his magazine to start the fire, Mick soon had a small campfire going on the side of the road.

Fifteen minutes after spotting the flash of light a land cruiser identical to their own came to a halt on the side of the road a few yards from their cruiser. Both cruisers bore on the side doors the legend 'Major Minerals' and the company's logo, a stylized drilling rig. Two men climbed from the vehicle that had just arrived, a swarthy Arabic man from the drivers side and a black Aborigine from the passenger.

"G'day Ib, Banjo. What took you bastards so long?", complained Mick.

"We have only been absent for a day", said Ibrahim reasonably, the tall, dark haired and swarthy complexioned driver of the other vehicle, "And don't call me Ib please Mick. Can you not use my proper name, Ibrahim?"

"Come on Ib, don't get snotty. You're in Oz now so your name has to be only one syllable. That's why he's Ben, not Benjamin, and I'm Mick, not Michael"

"And what about Banjo?", replied Ibrahim, "That is two syllables. Ban–jo. Perhaps he should be called Ban?"

"Yeah, but he's a black fella so I've got to show him some

respect", answered Mick, "And besides, Banjo was a very famous Aussie!"

"You betcha", said Banjo who was indeed a black fellow, a full blood Aborigine, "Show respect or I'll put a bloody spear in ya". His words sounded serious but he had a huge grin dividing his face.

Ibrahim and Banjo were, like Mick, field assistants. Both were dressed in the same manner as Ben and Mick – grubby pocketed shirts and even grubbier shorts and scuffed and dirty work boots.

"How did you get to be named for a musical instrument?", asked Ibrahim, obviously intrigued. Ibrahim had known Banjo for over a week but only now seemed to be curious about the derivation of his name.

"Well, Banjo is my nickname, not my real name, you understand?", said Banjo, "My real name is Bert but tell anyone that and I'd have to kill you", he grinned, "My white surname is Paterson and my tribal name is Banjaman. My dad is a big fan of Banjo Paterson so when I was born he took our surname and my tribal name and came up with the nickname Banjo. I've been called Banjo ever since I was a baby".

Not completely happy with his explanation, Banjo began to recite:

> "There was movement at the station, for the word had passed around
>
> That the colt from Old Regret had got away,
>
> And had joined the wild bush horses – He was worth a thousand pound,
>
> So all the cracks had gathered to the fray,
>
> All the tried and noted riders from stations near and far
>
> Had mustered at the homestead overnight,

> For the bushmen love hard riding where the wild bush horses are,
>
> And the stockhorse snuffs the battle with delight.
>
> There was Harrison, who made his pile when Pardon won the cup,
>
> The old man with his hair as white as snow;
>
> But few could ride beside him when his blood was fairly up –
>
> He would go wherever horse and man could go.
>
> And Clancy of the Overflow…"

"Jeez, enough mate!", interrupted Mick, "That poem goes on forever. We'll be here all day reciting poetry at this rate".

"Why, that was beautiful Banjo", enthused Ibrahim, ignoring Mick, "you must tell me the rest later".

Banjo loved reciting the poetry of Banjo Paterson so Ben knew that Ibrahim would be sure to get his wish. Clearly Banjo was as much of a fan of the famous poet as was his father. And Ben did not mind Banjos recitations as he was also a Banjo Paterson fan.

Ben was pleased to have all the boys back together. He considered them all to be his friends, although he had only known Banjo for a week. They were all good men and he was proud to be working with them.

Ibrahim had been a refugee who had arrived in Australia by boat and after having spent over two years in detention was now free to start a new life in his new country. He had come from Iraq where he had seen and been through hell. In Iraq he had been a qualified engineer but here in Australia his qualifications were useless. It was something of a come down to go from engineer to field assistant. Nonetheless, he was usually cheerful and eager to please and had worked off and on with Ben for the past two years.

Steve had spoken to Ibrahim about taking engineering courses to gain qualification in Australia but he seemed happy working in the bush as an assistant.

Banjo was a full blood Aboriginal about eighteen years of age who Ben had picked up at the Mandandanja Aboriginal community near Marble Bar. On their way out into the desert, Ben, Mick and Ibrahim had called into the community to speak to the community elder, Jack, and let him know where they were going and what they were planning on doing. Steve always made a point of talking to the local Aboriginals so he didn't inadvertently do something to offend them. At Mandandanja they had met Banjo who was desperate for work and claimed he would do anything. Ben had phoned the Perth head office and easily obtained permission to put Banjo on the payroll. It made for a better working arrangement having four men in the two vehicles. The cynic in Ben also knew that if the company started a mine out here it would not hurt to have a contact with the local tribe of indigenous owners. Banjo was now their contact.

Ibrahim and Banjo had the previous day driven into Marble Bar to purchase more supplies as Ben was planning on being out in the bush for another two weeks. They had driven into the town the previous day, did the shopping, stayed overnight at the Ironclad Hotel, and driven back out into the desert this morning. Ben could make out the shape of three large cardboard boxes of supplies beneath the tarpaulin in the tray of the second cruiser. He also knew that the fridge in the tray held meat that they had purchased at the towns butchers. He hoped that they had bought something interesting to eat as he was sick to death of eating baked beans and spaghetti!

Mick had put the full billy of water on the campfire and it was already bubbling and producing a small cloud of steam. He had already dumped a small handful of tea into the billy and now, using his hat as a makeshift glove, lifted the billy from the flames. Holding tight to the handle he swung the billy several times around his head. This was the bush-approved way of getting the tea leaves to steep.

"Okay, who wants tea?", said Mick, placing the billy of tea on the ground, "And what do you got to eat? I'm starving and all we got left is bloody baked beans and spaghetti".

"Oh, I think you will like what we have bought you", said Ibrahim mysteriously.

All of them indicated that they would have tea so Banjo retrieved four tin mugs from the catering chest along with a container of sugar. Mick poured the black tea from the billy into each of the mugs, filling them almost to the brims. Each man then added his taste in sugar and gave it a quick stir with the teaspoon that Banjo had also retrieved. None of the men took milk with either their tea or their coffee.

Having settled his tea Ibrahim went to the fridge on his cruiser, lifted the lid and pulled out a fresh loaf of bread, a tub of butter, two tomatoes, a head of lettuce, a square of cheese and a paper package that Steve knew probably contained some cold meats.

Ben was proved right as Ibrahim unwrapped the package revealing slices of what looked like ham and polony. Mick retrieved a knife from the catering trunk and the men gathered around the front of Ibrahim's vehicle where the lunch components had been deposited on the bonnet. Each man quickly made himself a sandwich and settled on the ground under the shade of the desert oak, tea in one hand, sandwich in the other.

"I didn't think you Muslim buggers were allowed to eat pig", said Mick to Ibrahim, pointedly looking at the ham and salad sandwich that the latter was devouring.

"You are correct, Muslim's are not allowed to eat pig", replied Ibrahim, "But I am not a very good Muslim. As you know, I also drink beer and I am not supposed to do that either. I believe in Allah but do not believe that he would be so small minded as to deny man what he had himself provided".

"Yeah, well, good to see you've come to your senses mate", finished Mick, a huge grin creasing his face.

"You could say that", Said Ibrahim, "But I love my new country and want to fit in so I think eating pig and drinking beer is a small sacrifice. Allah will understand. And besides, I love pork!".

The lunch and tea were quickly finished and the three fieldy's turned to Ben for their next instructions.

"Where to now boss?", asked Mick.

Ben scowled sideways at Mick hoping he would get the message about using the word boss. However, as always Mick remained nonchalant, staring innocently at Ben. Ben had been thinking about where to go next and had come to a decision whilst eating. "We'll go to Bright Downs homestead and let them know we're in the area and see if they need anything. Did you bring back the latest papers Ibrahim?" Ben knew that the isolated stations only received newspapers with the mail about once a month. Fresh news was always appreciated by the isolated station people.

"Yes Ben, they are in the cruiser", replied Ibrahim.

"OK guys, lets go", said Ben climbing into the passenger side of his vehicle.

Mick also clambered aboard after brushing sand over the small fire with his boot and Ibrahim and Banjo returned to their cruiser and did likewise. Mick turned the key and the cruiser rumbled gently to life. Turning the wheel to the left he rode up onto the bitumen road before putting his foot down. It was only about fifty kilometers to the homestead, thirty on the bitumen and another twenty on a rough sand track. They would be there in about forty minutes. Ibrahim and Banjo, with Ibrahim driving, fell in behind and soon they were both cruising at about one hundred kilometers per hour across the desert.

The well maintained bitumen road was something of an anomaly in this part of outback Western Australia. Roads in this part of the World were usually dirt, or at best gravel. This road had however been constructed by the government to allow access to the Nuclear Waste Repository at Lands End with a gravel access road veering off to the right to the Bright Downs homestead. The mostly sand access track then meandered through sand dunes the twenty kilometers to the homestead.

After having travelled for less than twenty minutes Ben saw the sand road turning off to the south and marked by a faded sign, with numerous bullet holes, reading 'Bright Downs Homestead'. Some clown had been a good enough shot to pierce both 'o's in their centres. He instructed Mick to make the turn and they continued onwards down the sandy side road, albeit at about a quarter of their previous speed. Ibrahim and Banjo remained right behind as though welded, although they maintained a separation of about three car lengths to the rear.

The day had become hot, probably in the high thirties, but inside the air conditioned vehicle it was cool. The countryside had also changed to match the external temperature. Whilst travelling to the turnoff to the homestead they had been travelling over a fairly flat plain of red soil. Now they were travelling over yellow sand with huge yellow sand dunes rearing on either side of the road. Vegetation was limited to scattered clumps of spinifex and the occasional straggly salt bush. At its beginning the access road itself occupied a valley between two parallel sand dunes that each reared about thirty meters into the air and seemed to go on forever into the distance. They had entered the desert proper.

"Did you see that?", said Mick suddenly, shortly after they had made the turn onto the track.

"Did I see what", answered Ben, "All I can see is sand and a bit of spinifex".

"On top of the right hand dune – There was a tent"

"A tent? Why would anyone be camping out here on top of a dune?", replied Ben.

"Well, I'm sure I saw a tent up there, right at the top", Mick said somewhat belligerently.

"OK, we'll check it out on the way back", soothed Ben.

They travelled on down the gravel road, Ibrahim and Banjo following, until the dune on the left suddenly disappeared giving way to a flat yellow sandplain. About a half kilometer in the distance they could see the station homestead. As they drew closer they could see that the homestead comprised a large, single story wooden building with a tin roof and the typical Australian wraparound verandah. To the left of the homestead was what appeared to be a large tin machinery shed with a four wheel drive parked in the large open doorway. To the right was a long fibro and tin building with at least eight doors in the front. Probably shearers quarters, thought Ben, although it had been many years since this country had raised sheep, if ever. To the best of his knowledge Bright Downs was now a cattle station, although he could see no cattle and had not seen any on the journey in. Beyond the homestead was a long dirt airstrip next to which was another large tin building, possibly a hangar. Indeed, Ben thought he could see the front of a small propeller aircraft peaking through the open front doors.

Mick slowed the vehicle to a crawl as they approached the house. It was standing operating procedure to always approach a homestead at low speed so as not to drag in a column of dust which might settle on the manager's wife's washing line. It was not a good introduction to have an irate wife with filthy washing.

The cruiser finally halted in front of a small gate in the chain link fence that guarded the homesteads rather bedraggled front garden. The garden had once had a lawn and what looked like several rose bushes although now all were dead. The lawn was now mostly yellow sand. Ibrahim and Banjo pulled up in their vehicle directly behind the lead cruiser.

Ben opened the passenger door and stepped down onto the sandy soil, grabbing his Akubra hat and a geological map from the seat. He told Mick he would go in alone and gave Ibrahim and Banjo a small wave to indicate that they were to stay where they were. His strategy was simple. He had learned from experience that isolated station people could get a bit nervous when suddenly confronted by a number of strangers from out of the blue. He therefore always approached a homestead alone, usually with a map tucked under his arm to show that he was nothing but a harmless lost traveler. If things went OK with the station people then he would beckon for the others to join him. Things always went OK as the people in this remote part of the World yearned for the prospect of speaking with a new face.

Ben had only just stepped down from the cruiser when the homesteads front door opened and a tall man stepped onto the verandah. Ben reckoned he was a couple of inches taller than him with a thin but fit body clad in dark grey trousers and a collared grey shirt with work boots on his feet. The man was slightly darker complexioned than Ben with black eyes and a nose that had been broken at some time in the past. The man looked to be of European decent although it was difficult to be certain. The mans most distinguishing feature however was a scar shaped like the numeral 7 above his left eyebrow.

When the man spoke it was in perfect English without any trace of an accent, Australian or otherwise. "Welcome to Bright Downs. What may I do for you gentlemen?"

Ben was not used to being greeted so formally out here in the outback but he recovered himself quickly. "G'day mate, how are you. My name is Ben Wilde and the other blokes are my assistants. I am a geologist doing a bit of survey work to the west of here for Major Minerals and I thought we'd just drop in to say hello"

The tall man stared back at him, his face devoid of expression. "Very kind of you to do so. How far to the west?"

"About forty to fifty k" said Steve, "North and south of the NWR road".

"Ah, that is good. You will not interfere with us. Please be aware however that we are mustering so it would be best if you stayed off the station. You will be fine where you are as that is about ten kilometers beyond our boundary. I would appreciate it if you were to just stay out of our way."

Although not an extrovert Ben was usually fairly comfortable around people. This guy however seemed to set off all of his warning bells. The cold stare together with the formal manner of speaking was off-putting in this environment. It was as though the stranger was speaking from a prepared script and just wanted Ben and his men to be on their way. Although somewhat perturbed Ben continued with the traditional bush niceties.

"We have the latest papers if you want to catch the news", said Ben, "Shall I get them for you?"

"No thank you", said the stranger, "I am not particularly interested in the news but I thank you anyway".

Still confused by the mans attitude Ben nonetheless decided that discretion was the better part of valour. The man obviously wanted them gone and so Ben thought he had better oblige.

"Thank you sir. We will see that we stay out of your way. Good day to you"

With that Ben turned around and walked back through the gate to the cruiser. There was no reply from the stranger. Passing behind the vehicle he appeared to fumble and dropped the folded map he was carrying. The map landed on the sand at his feet and he stooped and picked it up, refolding it as he rose. Then, instead of going to the passenger side he went to the drivers and tapped on Micks window. Mick lowered the window so he was face to face with Ben.

"Whats up boss?" he said.

"Shove over Mick, I'll drive for a while", replied Ben.

"How did it go with the owner or manager or whatever he is?', asked Mick as he slid across the seat, "I notice that they didn't ask us in for tea and bickies".

"No. He's a strange bugger that one. Very formal and not very civil", said Ben quietly, climbing into the drivers seat.

Ben started the motor and pulled away from the homestead. Ibrahim followed slowly behind.

"Do you notice anything odd about this place?" asked Ben as they headed away from the homestead.

"Apart from what you say about the owner, no, not really", replied Mick.

"Well," answered Ben, "They've got shearers quarters that look like they're occupied for one"

Mick looked across at the shearers quarters which extended from left to right across their front. Now that he was taking notice he could see that the quarters appeared well maintained and through a couple of doors he could see what looked like made up beds. Several fresh vehicle tracks leading up to the quarters looked as though they had been made by vehicles previously parked in front of the building. From what he could see the quarters certainly appeared to be occupied, or had been very recently. The quarters certainly would not be occupied by shearers – There were no sheep up here.

"Maybe the station hands kip down there", said Mick.

"Possibly', replied Ben, "But have you seen any cows? He tells me that they're mustering but I haven't seen a single cow and if they're mustering they would have a chopper. I haven't seen one".

"Yeah, true, but the cattle and chopper could be way out back", Mick said, playing devil's advocate.

"OK then, what about the fertilizer", said Ben, "What would they need fertilizer for. They're certainly not going to be able to grow anything out here. Take a look in the map"

Without questioning him Mick picked up the folded map from the seat. Opening the first fold he saw that the folded paper contained a handful of sand with numerous white specks. He could see and smell at once that the white specks were indeed ammonium nitrate fertilizer. Odd indeed!

"I picked it up when I dropped the map", explained Ben, "I smelled it and then saw it when I got out of the bus".

"Granted, having fertilizer out here is a bit odd", said Mick, "But maybe they're taking it to another property down south?"

"Yeah, I suppose you might be right", said Ben, although he did not sound convinced. "But what would a cattle station be doing shipping fertilizer to farms to the south? Anyway, let's get the hell out of here. The owner or manager made it clear that we weren't welcome so let's oblige him and vamoose!"

The two vehicles had now entered the defile between the two large sand dunes. They travelled slowly over the rutted track for twenty minutes until they were less than two hundred meters from the main road.

"Whoah, stop here mate", yelled Mick, "I want to see if that was a tent up there or if I was imagining it".

Ben depressed the brakes and brought the cruiser to a halt in the soft sand. Ibrahim in the cruiser behind did the same. From where he was sitting Ben could see nothing on the top of the sand dune above him. They had however been a little higher up driving in so maybe the tent or whatever it was could only be seen on the way into the homestead, but not on the way out. Mick jumped from the cruiser and started to struggle upwards through the soft sand. Banjo in the meantime had climbed down from the rear cruiser. "Where are you going Mick", he yelled.

"I thought I saw something up there. I'm just going to have a look-see", yelled Mick back to him.

"Good'oh mate, I'll come with you", yelled Banjo, and he was of up the dune in Micks footsteps.

Ben climbed down from the cruiser and went back to Ibrahim's cruiser where he leaned on the window sill.

"Crazy bastards", he said to Ibrahim, "There's probably nothing up there"

"Yes, you are undoubtedly right Ben, but boys will be boys", replied Ibrahim.

For a while Ben and Ibrahim chatted about the trip so far and the prospects for the footy season which was nearing its end.

Although Ibrahim had only been in Australia for a few years he was a mad Aussie Rules fan. He went to every game that he could and barracked for the Fremantle Dockers. Ben was a West Coast Eagles fan but he still thought Ibrahim was a good bloke, although a little misguided.

Twenty minutes later Banjo returned to the vehicles with Mick trailing behind.

"I told you that there was a tent up there", said Mick, "Funny thing though. There were two sleeping bags in the tent and an old camp fire but no-one around. And they look like they've built some sort of bunker."

"Bunker?" said Ben.

"Yeah, well they've scooped a hole in the sand and surrounded it with dead spinifex like they were trying to camouflage it", he replied, "Maybe they've set up a blind to shoot roo's but it's a silly bloody place to do it. There's bugger all feed and no water so no self respecting roo is gunna wander through here. They'd be lucky to see one in a month!".

That is odd, thought Ben. Why set up a camp here near the intersection with the main road? Bloody odd! Still, his was not to reason why although he did wonder where the tents occupants had taken themselves off to. Ben looked around and noticed that vehicles had apparently been turning around on the track a little forward of where they were parked. It looked from the tire tracks that vehicles had come from the direction of the homestead, turned a tight circle on the track, and gone back the way that they had come. He could also see what looked like boot prints in the loose sand about twenty meters forward of where Mick and Banjo had gone up the dune. Although mostly infilled by the falling sand he estimated that they could not be more than a day or two old. Very odd, he thought.

Mick and Banjo clambered back into their respective cruisers and as Mick buckled his seatbelt Ben turned the key and depressed the accelerator. A few minutes later they were back at the intersection with the main road where Ben turned left, closely followed by Ibrahim. They headed west, back towards the turnoff to Blind Bluff.

"Well, what do you think of that mate?", asked Mick when they were well under way, "You reckon the owner or manager or whatever he is was not too welcoming yet someone's been camping next to his driveway. Bit odd if you ask me"

"Yeah mate, I think I'd have to agree", said Ben, "Certainly a bit odd".

2
11 MARCH, 2014

"Why would anyone put a cattle station out here in the desert", asked Mick suddenly, as they drove along the NWR road, "There's nothing for the poor buggers to eat!"

"Well, that's the thing", answered Ben, "When a cyclone crosses the coast they get bucketfuls of rain in this country. I mean that it really pisses down for days. And when that happens this country is green like you wouldn't believe. It can be excellent cattle country", he continued, "Provided it rains occasionally", he qualified.

Driving along the bitumen Ben kept his eyes partly on the road and partly on the flat plain to the right. Five minutes later he had seen what he was looking for. Something that he had glimpsed on the way out. About two hundred meters off the road he could see a small mound of black rock. Beyond that he could see several further small, black areas extending to the northeast towards a large sand dune. When he was level with the black rock he pulled to the side of the road and turned off the motor. The cruiser carrying Ibrahim and Banjo pulled to the side of the road behind them and their engine also went quiet.

"What are we stopping for boss?", asked Mick.

"Just some rocks over there I want to have a look at", replied Ben, waving a hand in the general direction of the rock that had interested him. "I'll just wander over and have a look. Won't be more than a few minutes".

Looking at Mick he added, "I can't see any cattle or a helicopter and there are certainly no signs of mustering so I don't think it will bother our mate back there. And what he doesn't know can't hurt him!".

Ben climbed down from the vehicle, jamming his hat over his untidy hair and retrieving his pick as he did so. He retrieved his small backpack from the rear tray and set off across the red earth. Mick, Ibrahim and Banjo had also exited the vehicles and were following him, joshing and laughing as they did so. Steve did not mind that they had also decided to go for a walk. After all, if he collected a lot of samples they could carry them back to the vehicles.

As he approached the pile of rock Ben saw that it was ironstone with the dark brown to black rusty colour typical of the rock. The small ironstone outcrop projected only a foot above the red soil with smaller pieces of the black rock scattered about. Ironstone was not rare but it was a little unusual out here. Ben's mind went into overdrive – perhaps he had discovered a gossan! A gossan was a mass of ironstone that forms on top of a sulphide orebody caused by weathering dissolving the majority of minerals and leaving only the iron. Many copper, lead, zinc and nickel orebodies had been found through the discovery of a gossan.

Having reached the rocks Ben crouched down and gave one of the loose rocks a sharp rap with the pick. The rock immediately broke into two pieces, the larger of which Ben picked up. Looking at the freshly broken face, with his hand magnifying lens suspended on a cord around his neck, Ben could see that it was indeed ironstone. More importantly, he could see that the ironstone was in fact a fine network of ironstone veins which intersected each other at angles. Ben was elated! It was a gossan, or at least looked suspiciously like one. Gossans often retained the structure of the original sulphide minerals as angular voids separated by thin ironstone veins. And the rock he held looked very much like other gossans he had seen.

"I think we have discovered a gossan boys!", gloated Ben, not bothering to hide his elation. He did not need to elaborate further as he had often discussed with the others what he was looking for and what a gossan was and what it meant. And he did not worry about calling the men boys, although two of them were older than him. The term boys was simply one of affection and had no undertones.

Ben knocked off a few more pieces of the rock until he had about half a kilogram. He unshouldered his pack and reached in for a sample bag, gathering the rock fragments and placing them in the bag. He then set the turned on GPS on the ground and drew his pen from the shirt pocket to commence describing the rock and its setting. He was almost immediately stymied. What should he call this new prospect? This was always one of the hardest jobs of an exploration geologist – naming of their prospects. There were no named geographical features in the area which may have given him a lead. The prospect he had examined that morning had been easy. It was situated on Blind Bluff so that was the name it was given. And then suddenly he had it! Bright Desert – They were after all on the edge of Bright Downs station on the edge of the desert. So the Bright Desert prospect it would be!

Ben wrote the name, which he underlined, and then a few lines about the prospect. The GPS had in the meantime acquired satellites so he added into his notebook the latitude and longitude displayed on the screen.

Ben looked up and noticed a similar small mound of black rocks a further fifty meters to the northeast and another mound about one hundred meters beyond that. Over the next thirty minutes he had visited, sampled and described the other two outcrops, each of which also appeared to be comprised of gossan.

About two hundred meters beyond the third outcrop his vision was halted by a large yellow sand dune standing over twenty meters tall. He could carry on to see what was on the other side but he thought that he had enough information for now. He turned and walked back towards the cruisers, the three other men tagging behind.

On arriving back at the road Ben threw his backpack into the lead cruiser and they all retook their seats.

"OK Mick, we're going back to Blind Bluff. I think we'll do a bit more work there before calling it a day. And what a day it's been!", said Ben.

Ben turned the key, waited for the motor to turn over and depressed the accelerator, gently easing them back onto the bitumen.

The two cruisers had only gone a few kilometers when they saw what looked like a small convoy of vehicles heading down the road towards them. As they got closer to the convoy Ben could see that it comprised three vehicles. A humvee with four men led the procession followed by an armoured car with two men which was in turn followed by a second humvee with another four men aboard. As they passed there were no weapons visible but he knew that all of the men in the jeeps were armed with the Australian infantry Austeyr assault rifle. The two men in the front of the armoured car were probably similarly armed. All of the men were dressed in jungle green army uniforms. Ben could never figure out why they wore uniforms camouflaged for the jungle when they were in a desert.

Although the convoy appeared out of place out here in the outback it was in fact a normal part of the scenery. This was the courier service transporting radioactive waste from the port of Port Hedland to the Nuclear Waste Repository at Lands End for burial or whatever it was they did with the stuff.

Although Australia did not have a nuclear industry, and therefore produced little radioactive waste, it had become the

World's dumping ground for the deadly material. Australia produced much of the uranium used by other country's nuclear reactors, had large areas of desert where nobody lived, was geologically stable with few earthquakes, and was politically stable. The Worlds leaders therefore had thought it fit and proper that Australia should take care of the waste generated by their nuclear power plants that used uranium obtained from Australia. The Australian government had finally caved to the pressure and five years previously had built the Nuclear Waste Repository in the middle of the Great Sandy Desert at a place they called Lands End. Since then the nuclear nations of the World had regularly been shipping their toxic waste to Australia for disposal, albeit at a cost. Out of sight, out of mind. And Steve thought the Australian government was out of its collective mind for allowing it to happen.

To most people the heavily armed convoy would have seemed a bit over the top. After all, spent nuclear fuel rods weren't worth anything, even to the average criminal. They were however worth a lot to terrorists who might use the material to make particularly nasty, dirty bombs. Not that there was much of a chance of a terrorist hijack in Australia but the government knew it kept the citizens minds at ease knowing the stuff was constantly guarded. And it wasn't as if the Australian army had much else to do!

By regulation, the convoy was travelling at a very sedate speed of only eighty kilometers per hour. After all, the authorities did not want a road accident spreading toxic waste across the countryside.

"What a shitty job", griped Mick, "Ferrying nuclear crap back and forth. I betcha they all glow in the dark"

"Oh, I don't know", replied Ben, "Nice drives in the country watching the scenery. No heavy work. And I think the stuff is sealed in lead containers so you could probably sit on it and not feel anything".

"Yeah, well, sooner you than me mate. I might want to have kids one day", returned Mick.

A half an hour later they were back to the turnoff and an hour after that they were back at Blind Bluff. Ben pulled the vehicle in under the shade of the river gum that Mick had parked under before and turned off the motor. He climbed down from the cruiser and using his hands instructed Ibrahim to park parallel to them about ten meters away across a small clearing. The three other men climbed down from the vehicles. Ben walked back to the cruiser and picked up the satellite phone from the seat where it had been recharging on the cigarette lighter. He turned it on and extended the aerial to acquire a satellite so he could make a call. It was time to report in to the head office. When he saw that the bars indicated that a satellite had been acquired he dialed the number of the office and placed the phone to his ear. The phone on the other end was picked up almost immediately.

"Major Minerals, how may I help you?", queried the melodious voice of Tiffany, the company receptionist.

"Tiff, Ben here, how are you?", said Ben.

"Great Ben, glad to hear you are still alive. How are things out there in the bush?"

"Good Tiff, can you put me through to Tim?"

"Sure Ben. See you soon and stay safe".

There was some clicking as Ben was connected to Tim's office. Tim O, Hallaran was the company's exploration manager and Steve's boss.

"G'day Ben, how goes it?", boomed Tim.

"Good Tim. Found some interesting stuff today including some copper and what looks like a gossan. I've got some samples and I definitely think they will be worth following up", replied Ben, "We'll be camping tonight at Blind Bluff. You'll see it on the maps. That's where I found the copper."

"OK, sounds good Ben. Take care and give me another bell tomorrow"

"Will do Tim. Speak to you then".

Ben pressed the disconnect and placed the phone back on the seat.

"OK, I want to do a bit of work up on the bluff," said Ben to his men, "and you buggers can help me. We'll probably camp here tonight so leave the cruisers where they are. Grab a couple of shovels and a pick and follow me up".

Ben grabbed his backpack from the tray, stuck his pick in his belt, jammed his hat on his head and set off across the dry creek bed. He made easy going of it and was soon standing on the other side of the bluff where he had discovered the copper outcropping. The other men were there within a minute. Ben paced off about ten meters to the west from the outcrop and made a mark in the soil with his boot and then did the same thing to the east. He made further marks with his boot above and below the first two marks.

"Dig me a couple of shallow trenches there and there between the marks", he said, "Let's see if we can find where this copper runs".

Mick and Banjo, who had bought shovels with them, set to digging the two trenches. Occasionally they would hit a displaced rock which Ibrahim would dislodge with the pick that he had bought. After about half an hour of grumbling and flying dirt the two trenches had been completed, each about three meters long and up to a foot deep. The walls of the trenches were compacted red dirt and shale, the floor uneven shale bedrock. Ben crouched down to inspect the western trench. The floor of the trench was composed almost entirely of the light brown shale, the same as composed the majority of the bluff. However, at the southern end of the trench was a band about thirty centimeters wide of the bright green malachite which probably continued on beyond the trench. Pleased, Ben walked the twenty meters to the eastern trench and again crouched down to closer inspect what had been unearthed. Here the trench floor was also mostly shale except for the end closest to the bottom of the bluff. Here the shale persisted but it was laced through with veins and masses of the bright green malachite over the full three meters of the trenches length. Much better, he thought. At least the mineralisation continues to both the east and west. He took off his backpack and repeated his routine. A few blows of the pick saw enough copper stained shale dislodged for a sample which he stuffed into a new sample bag. He also made some notes about the occurrence and logged its position using the GPS. He then did the same for the exposed copper in the western trench.

"OK guys", said Ben, "Mick, you and Ibrahim go back and set up camp. I know it's a bit early but we'll camp here tonight. Banjo and I are going out to have a bit of a look over the flat".

Ben was taking Banjo rather than Mick or Ibrahim to have a look for more mineralisation out from the bluff as Banjo, like many Aborigines, had incredible eyesight. Ben had seen him in action at another prospect a few days previously. The Aboriginal could pick out the smallest oddity from his surroundings that the majority of people would never see. It must be genetic, Ben thought, an Aboriginal thing. Whatever it was in the mineral prospecting game it was invaluable.

Mick and Ibrahim picked up the tools and tramped over the bluff back towards the vehicles. Ben and Banjo descended the remainder of the bluff and tramped off to the east across the flat dirt. It was not all dirt though, Ben noticed. Here and there small fragments of rock protruded through the surface. From what Ben could see these fragments were all shale similar to that comprising the majority of the bluff. About two hundred meters out from the bluff Banjo, walking ahead of Ben, suddenly stopped and dropped to his haunches. Ben rapidly caught up to where he was crouched.

"Copper I think Boss", reported Banjo in his childlike voice.

Steve looked down and saw a green flash between Banjo's feet. Definitely copper! I knew it, thought Ben, blokes got eyes like a bloody hawk. The small green rock fragment that Banjo had fixed on was about the size of a twenty cent piece. Ben knew that he would have walked straight over the top without seeing it.

"Any more mate?", he asked Banjo.

Banjo stood from his crouch and turning his head to and fro examined the area around them.

"No, I think that's it boss", replied Banjo, "Can't see any more anyway"

"OK, that's great Banjo. I'll just fix this and we'll do a run a bit further out", said Ben.

Once again the backpack came off while Ben mustered the tools of his trade. He quickly bagged the small piece of rock and noted its surroundings in his notebook and position with the GPS. He then set off further to the east, Banjo trailing behind and to his right. They walked out another two hundred meters from the bluff in the hot afternoon sun before Banjo again called a halt. When ben came up to him he saw that Banjo was almost standing on area of shale heavily laced with malachite that was about one meter square.

"Well done Banjo", said Ben, "You've got eyes like a hawk mate!"

"I dunno Ben. I think even you would have seen this lot", replied Banjo.

Once again Ben went through his routine with taking a rock sample. The prospect was looking better all the time. They had now traced copper mineralisation for more than four hundred meters, more or less in a straight line.

"OK mate", said Ben, "I think that's enough for now. We'll do a couple of loops back to the others and the camp. You go north and then back to the west and I'll go south, west and then north and meet you back at camp. Give me a yell if you find anything".

The two men set off in opposite directions, Banjo to the north and Ben to the south. Banjo's journey was shorter and he would be back in camp before Ben. Ben did not mind. He loved walking through the outback by himself. Although most people thought the outback bush was desolate and ugly, Ben thought that is was beautiful. As he walked his path scribed an arc of about five hundred meters centred on the bluff. Before he knew it he was tramping up one of the low hills that formed a line behind the bluff. He ascended and then descended the hill continuing to the west. When he was behind the line of hills he turned to the north, back towards the new camp. He walked on and was soon crossing the track that he and Mick had driven over that morning. He turned to follow the track to the right and climbed another of the low hills, at the top of which he could see the vehicles and the makings of the camp to the east. He descended the hill and strode towards the camp, crossing the dry creek on the way. It had been a long walk and he hadn't found anything, other than Banjo's two occurences of copper. He was nonetheless happy. The prospect looked good and would definitely warrant further work. Over the years he had spent countless hours tramping around the bush and finding nothing. This trip he had one, possibly two, good prospects that he had already reported to his boss.

As Ben entered the camp the sun began to sink into the west. The sky began to darken with orange and red fires marking the setting sun. The mulga shrubs and spinifex threw long shadows and the soil turned from red to purple. Ben loved this time of day when the desert took on new colours and textures. It would be fully dark within the hour.

Ben walked over to the blazing campfire that Mick and Ibrahim had built and were now sitting near in fold-out deck chairs. Banjo had also returned and was lolling comfortably in another chair. All three men were drinking beer from cans kept cold in the car fridges. Banjo was also busily puffing away on a roll-your-own cigarette. Ben sat down heavily into the chair that had been set aside for him and as he did so Mick threw him a beer that he had been keeping beside his chair awaiting Ben's return. Ben pulled the tab on the can and took a long drink of the beautifully cold beer.

Although most mining companies prohibited alcohol in the field Ben was of the old school. He had been able to convince his boss that a beer was good for the troops morale and as a result all of the men in the field were allowed three beers per night, and no more, paid for by the company. No alcohol owned only by the employees was allowed in the camp. No one had ever abused this rule. It simply wasn't worth it.

"My turn to cook, I think", groaned Ben, not happy with having to play chef tonight. He would not have it any other way though. Although he was in charge he pulled his weight and took his turn at all of the jobs, even the most menial. It was another reason he was so well respected by his men.

"Yeah, your turn all right mate. And make it good because I'm starving after having to exist on baked beans!", quipped Mick.

"No worries mate", replied Ben, "I'll make sure that you get some right good tucker".

Ben drained his beer, got up and walked to the catering trunk which had been placed near the fire. He opened the lid and pulled out the heavy steel barbecue plate, a large carving knife, a roasting fork and two billy's, placing them on the ground. He picked up the shovel and dug a shallow hole into which he placed, using the shovel, a mound of coals from the campfire. He pulled out the folding legs on the barbecue plate and placed it over the coals. Next he went to the fridge on the back of Ibrahims vehicle from which he extracted four partially frozen T-bone steaks. From one of the boxes on the same vehicle he obtained four large potatoes and a couple of onions. From the same box he took a large tin of mixed peas and carrots.

Returning to his small cooking fire Ben obtained a can-opener from the catering chest, opened the tin, poured the peas and carrots into one of the Billys and placed it on the edge of the main fire. He then pulled a roll of aluminium foil from the chest and used it to individually wrap the potatoes. These he pushed into the coals of the small cooking fire. Finally, he used the carving knife to slice the onions which went onto the barbecue plate to swiftly be joined by the steaks. The evening meal was cooking.

Ben left the meal to cook, the delicious aroma of the sizzling steak already filling his nostrils. He wandered over to the closest cruiser and delved for a beer in the car fridge.

"Anybody for another?", he called over his shoulder.

"Sure thing mate. Another three here", from Mick. The other three men had finished their first beers and thrown the empty cans onto the main camp fire. In the heat of the fire the thin aluminium cans would almost disappear by morning.

Ben pulled four beers from the fridge and passed them around. He then went back to his own chair by the cooking fire and turned the meat with the roasting fork. The peas and carrots were boiling busily and the potatoes were undoubtedly roasting in their aluminium coverings.

While Ben kept an eye on dinner the men talked and joked amongst themselves. The banter was innocuous, mostly to do with the days events and what they would do when they got home. Mick suddenly piped up, ready with one of his jokes or a funny story.

"You know that book you lent me about the gold rushes Ben. Well, I was reading some of it last night and I came across a story that will make you laugh. And it is true, at least according to the book".

"Go ahead mate, get it out of your system", said Ben.

"Well, it seems that in the early days of the gold rush at Coolgardie the local magistrate had arrested a couple of blokes for some misdemeanor and as there weren't many buildings then he put them in a tent. Now you must not leave this tent, he told them, if you do it will be the worse for you. So he left these two blokes and it was a bloody hot day and they were wondering how they could get a beer if they weren't allowed to leave the tent. Anyway, the magistrate returned that evening and the two blokes were rolling drunk. How did you get this way, he yells, you were forbidden from leaving the tent. We didn't, said one of the blokes, we just upped-stakes and walked under the tent to the pub. We were always inside the tent just like you said we should be, even when we were in the pub! Anyway, the magistrate was so impressed with their inventiveness that he let them go", Mick let out a huge belly laugh. The other three men also laughed. It was a good story.

"Yeah, they certainly made them tough and resourceful in those days", said Ben. He had often thought that he had been born out of time. He knew that he would have loved to have been around during the gold rushes one hundred and twenty years ago. The chaos and camaraderie would have suited him and he was sure that his prospecting skills would have led him to find something valuable.

Banjo suddenly piped up with "I've been reading a book about the stars and stuff and there was a bit about eclipses. You know I've never seen a eclipse". Banjo sounded forlorn at his lack of experience.

"Yes you have mate", said Ben, "You see one every night".

"No I haven't. And what do you mean I see one every night. Eclipses are supposed to be rare and I don't see one now"

"Yes you do", said Steve with certainty, "An eclipse is when a planet or moon passes in front of the sun. For example if the moon passes in front of the sun you have a full solar eclipse. But every night the Earth passes in front of the sun and stops you from seeing it. The only thing is that you happen to be standing on the eclipsing planet which is the Earth".

"Wow, I never thought of it that way. You're a clever bugger Ben", said Banjo, pleased that he had not missed out on one of life's experiences.

Ben slightly raised his hand to indicate that it was nothing. Nonetheless, Banjo continued to stare at him with undisguised admiration and respect.

Ben hoisted one of the drums of water from the tray of his vehicle and placed it on the ground. He then retrieved a small plastic bowl from the catering chest and half filled it with water from the drum. He placed the partially filled bowl on the hood of his cruiser and, with a small piece of soap, removed the days grime from his face and hands. Water was precious in the desert but the drums on the trays of both vehicles contained over one hundred and fifty liters. There was enough to spare to restore some humanity. The other men followed Ben and also quickly removed the days grime.

The dinner was ready now and Ben dished it out onto four tin plates. The potatoes were retrieved from the ashes and joined the meat and other vegetables. Banjo opened the catering chest and pulled out knives and forks for each of them. All four men were soon busy eating, the days work having made them hungry. In seemingly no time the meals were finished and the plates and utensils dropped into the large plastic washing tub. Ibrahim splashed in some water from a ten gallon drum and added some detergent from a bottle. With a scourer also obtained from the catering chest he set to scrubbing the plates. In a few minutes he had cleaned all of the plates, billy, barbecue plate and utensils, and laid them on top of the chest to dry.

The men all sat relaxed in their chairs, each with a third tinny in hand.

"You know Ben, that homestead we were at today, they are not good people", piped up Banjo.

"What do you mean Banjo?", queried Ben, "The bloke was a bit odd but he seemed OK".

"Well, about two months ago some of the brothers went hunting out that way. They weren't doing any harm but three of the blokes from the station saw them off with guns. And its not as though they have any stock left on the place. My people saw the last of the cattle go through on trucks months ago."

"Guns? You mean they threatened to shoot them?"

"No, not exactly. From what the brothers told me they were just waving their rifles around and they made it clear that no one was welcome on Bright Downs".

"That's a bit rough", said Ben, "particularly since you blokes own that land through native title. You have every right to go out there to do traditional stuff".

"Well, shooting roos with a three-oh-three is hardly traditional", added Mick, "Maybe if they had taken spears instead?".

"That's not the point", rejoined Ben, "They still have a right to be there. I thought that bloke was a bit odd. And you said all of the stock has gone Banjo?"

"Yeah, as far as we can tell. It looked as though the last few hundred were shipped out a few months back".

Odd, thought Ben. The homestead bloke had told them to stay clear because they were mustering. Mustering what though, if all of the cattle had gone? He supposed they could have been rounding up stragglers and strays but that didn't seem right. After all, if the last cattle had left months before they should have rounded up all the strays by now. Maybe the bloke was lying because he just did not want anybody snooping around his property. Still odd though.

Still deep in thought Ben walked over to his cruiser where he extracted a dolphin torch and a roll of toilet paper from behind the seat. He also pulled a shovel from the rear tray of the vehicle. He noticed that Ibrahim had done the same at his vehicle. Ben set off walking to the west into the dark, turning on the torch as he walked. Ibrahim set off on a similar mission to the east. About thirty meters out Ben stopped and placed the lit torch on the ground, illuminating a small area of red soil. Illuminated by the torch Ben dug a small hole over which he then squatted to finish his business. Having cleaned himself Ben backfilled the hole and walked back to the camp. Ibrahim was approaching from the other direction as he entered the firelight. He placed the shovel, torch and toilet paper back in the vehicle and returned to his chair.

The men chatted and joked some more for the next half hour before they all started to feel tired. It had been a long day. One by one they left their chairs and the campfire and rolled themselves into their swags. Before getting into his own swag Mick carefully lifted one end and peered underneath. He let the swag drop back into place and rolled onto it. Apparently he had no unwelcome bedmates this night.

Ben was the last to bed where he rolled into his sleeping bag and pulled up the zip. Although the days were hot out here, temperatures could approach freezing in the desert at night. Several times sleeping in the desert Ben had woken to find frost on his sleeping bag and in his hair.

Ben reached and unzipped his kit bag resting beside his swag. From the bag he extracted a rather dog-eared and dirty looking book. It was the latest Clive Cussler mystery and he could not wait to see the bad guys get their comeuppance. Dirk Pitt saves the World – again! Turning around in his swag he rested the dolphin torch on his boots, pointing at an angle in the air over the head end of the swag. He turned the torch on and laid back to read, finding his place in the book by the folded-over page. He read for about half an hour by which time all of the bad guys had either been killed or imprisoned. Closing the finished book he placed it on the earth besides his swag and turned off the torch. All was right with the World! He pulled the sleeping bag up to his neck and within minutes was asleep.

3

11 MARCH, 2014

At Bright Downs homestead Anwar Ashad was furious. The two men he was berating stood before him, their heads bowed and wearing expressions of shame mixed with fear.

"You were not supposed to be seen!", shrieked Ashad, "And yet you were! You are incompetent!".

Ashad spoke in Arabic. All of his men were fluent in that language.

"But sir", murmured the bravest of the two in the same language, "We were not seen. And we did not know the tent could be seen. We certainly could not see it from the road". Although he was supposedly a first amongst equals, Ashad insisted that the men call him Sir.

"Yes, but they did see your camp! You idiots! You have put us all at risk!".

"But all they saw was a tent. It could have been campers. They did not see us as we hid as soon as we heard them coming", explained the brave one, "We could have killed them!", he added with some vehemence.

"What, and bring the whole World down on us? Idiots!".

"We are sorry sir. It will not happen again", said the least brave of the two.

"No it will not! You will pitch the tent on the lee side of the dune where it cannot be seen. And if you are seen again I will have you shot! We have worked too hard and too long to be betrayed by incompetence!".

One problem solved, thought Ashad. Hopefully that mornings intruders would think nothing of their discovery. The tent had been pitched atop the sand dune as a watching post, both to observe visitors to the homestead and traffic along the road to the NWR to the east. Both were important to the successful completion of their mission. The watching post was manned by two men twenty-four hours a day and was in radio communication with the homestead.

When the two men had radioed that the watching post had been discovered Ashad had been apoleptic. He could have happily killed the men who had endangered the mission. However, all was not lost. After all, all that the intruders had seen was a tent with some sleeping bags. They would undoubtedly write it off as unimportant. Some campers out of their depth in the desert probably. They were after all only prospectors – Not police or military who might see something suspicious in the small camp. In addition, Ashad could not afford to lose any of his men so as much as he might want to he could not shoot them.

Ashad cast his eyes over the other seven men standing close to the walls of the homesteads large living area. All were watching him with undivided attention, some with a little fear. Several of the men had AK47 rifles slung over their shoulders.

Two of Ashad's men were not there. They had driven out to relieve the two men who now stood in shame before him. The two relieved men had driven the four wheel drive back to the homestead.

"Mohammed!", he yelled, pointing to the large swarthy man nearest the door. "You were responsible for the fertilizer and they also discovered that. What did you think you were doing!"

"But sir, they could not have seen the fertilizer! It is in the truck behind the hangar and they went nowhere near the hangar. I know, I was there when they came", protested Mohammed.

"Be that as it may", replied Ashad, "But I saw the geologist scoop some sand out front into his paper and when I went out to look at what he had seen I saw a trail of fertilizer at the front of this house. When you came back with the truck and parked it out front some of it must have leaked out".

"A thousand regrets sir. I should have seen", said Mohammed. Mohammed had driven the fertilizer up from the south where it had been obtained from a number of different sites, not all legally. When he had returned to the homestead he had parked the truck out the front, not moving it to the hangar until the following day. Clearly, some of the fertilizer had dribbled onto the ground through the tailgate.

"Yes you should, you idiot. From now on you all must be much more careful! Now get out and go about your duties. All of you idiots!".

The men filed slowly from the room leaving Ashad alone. He was still annoyed but he knew no real harm had been done. After all, they had all been here for nearly three months and he was confident no one knew of their presence. Or rather, they knew there were some men at Bright Downs but not how many or what they were doing.

What they were doing was training for the Jihad. Ashad acknowledged that his superiors had been brilliant with their plan. Back home in the Middle East training camps, terrorist camps as the Westerners liked to call them, were routinely identified from satellites or the American drones. And then they were destroyed by special forces or by cruise missiles. It was getting harder and harder to establish safe bases from which to operate. And then the leaders had come up with the idea of establishing a camp in the heartland of the enemy. After all, there were no satellites or drones spying on Australia. Here they could operate undetected and unmolested. It was a brilliant plan and there was not a chance that their mission could be stopped.

The original plan was that the men would train in Australia before leaving for missions in other countries, possibly even America. The leaders had then decided upon a plan to be completed within Australia. The men would no longer have to risk leaving the country and entering another.

Ashad was the undisputed leader of the eleven men at Bright Downs. He and eight of the men had entered Australia as ordinary tourists. Three of the men had entered Australia illegally by boat and had been confined in an immigration camp for nearly two years. That was how long the leaders plan had been in operation. Another two men had not made it. The illegal boat that had been carrying them had sunk off the Western Australian coast and they had drowned. Of his remaining men five were from Iraq, including himself, four were Saudi Arabians, two were Yemeni and one was a Pakistani.

Ashad and all of his men were cleanskins. None of them had previously been tagged by Western authorities as possible terrorists. Getting into the country had therefore been very easy. On landing, or release from detention, all of the men had made their way to the northwest where they had effectively disappeared. Now they all lived at Bright Downs. Ashad, his second in command Sameer, and two others in the big house, the remainder in the old workers quarters.

Ashad and his men had all that they needed. Radios and satellite phones had been purchased by Ashad in Perth and bought to Bright Downs. Two of the men went into Marble Bar once a month for supplies. The AK47's that each man carried had been supplied by an Indonesian gun runner who had dropped them at an isolated beach on the northwest coast from whence his men had collected them. They needed nothing else.

The room empty, Ashad turned and walked to the office at the front of the house. Sitting in the uncomfortable wooden chair at the small desk he picked up the satellite phone lying on the desk top. The phone was connected to an aerial positioned atop the house roof so he could make telephone calls from indoors. He dialed a long number he had committed to memory and waited for a response.

"Mastan here, is that you Anwar?", came the tinny query from the phone.

"Yes sir, it is Anwar. Calling to let you know that all is well".

"Ah, that is good. Is everything going to schedule?"

"Yes sir. All is in readiness".

"Good, call me again in two days".

The phone went dead.

Ashad's calls to his superiors were always brief and to the point. Longer calls with incorrect exchanges might invite unwelcome attention from the Americans who listened in to all phone calls made anywhere in the World, even Australia.

He placed the phone back on the table and sighed. It had been a long day with some unwelcome developments. He was not however going to tell his superior of the days lapses in security. They were in any case minor and would create no difficulties, or so he hoped.

Standing from the chair he stepped to the small window and looked out. Sand, sand and more sand. What a horrible place. His country too had deserts but this was truly desolate. Who would want to live in a place like this, he thought. He had however to admit to a sneaking admiration for the pioneers who had built this house in the wilderness.

Ashad exited the small room by the door he had entered. He strode down the short corridor and opened the door at the end. This door opened onto the wraparound verandah which cradled the house. A narrow table with benches each side stretched much of the length of the verandah. The majority of his men were now seated on the benches smoking and talking. As they became aware of Ashads presence the talk died until there was silence.

"As you were men", growled Ashad, "Let us not stand on ceremony".

For a moment the silence remained until a few voices took up the conversations that had been curtailed. The hubbub rose slowly but did not again reach the volume that it had had before Ashad's entrance. And there was no laughter. Ashad new the men feared him but that was as it should be. If they did not fear him and obey unquestioningly then the mission would fail.

Ashad took a seat at the head of the table and looked down its length. The men seated there looked like riff raff, most with long hair and beards. Their clothes were an odd mixture of army surplus military fatigues, jeans, checkered shirts and track suits. Nonetheless, he knew that they were all good men prepared to kill. And to be killed. Ashad new that by the time they were finished here most of his men would either be dead or in a cage. Ashad did not intend to be one of them. He intended to return to Iraq where he would receive the rewards owed to him.

One of the Yemenis was cooking tonight and Ashad sat alone whilst he waited for his meal. Once again he reviewed in his mind the events of the day. Some of his men had been careless. Carelessness might lead to discovery. However, overall he was content that the mistakes had been minor and there would be no repercussions. All was still going according to plan.

Fifteen minutes after he had taken his seat the Yemeni exited the kitchen carrying a large tray weighed down with barbecued steaks. A second man placed a large bowl of salad on the table together with two loaves of bread. All of the men were soon busy helping themselves to the food. As the tray and bowl were passed to his end of the table Ashad also helped himself, placing two steaks and a large mound of salad on his plate.

As he ate Ashad thought that the steak tasted like cardboard in his mouth. He knew most of the other men felt the same. They would have been happier eating Middle Eastern foods but he had prohibited the purchase of any foods native to their homelands.

He did not want to alert anyone to the fact that there might be a group of Arabs in their midst. The men would just have to eat the Western filth and hope their stomachs could cope.

Having finished his meal Ashad sipped from the glass of orange juice that had been placed before him. No alcohol in this house! At least none that the men might know about. He clapped his hands together once to get the men's attention.

"Men", he said in his deep voice, continuing to speak in Arabic. All heads and eyed turned towards him. "Tomorrow you will continue your combat training". This elicited smiles from most of the men seated at the table. "Tariq and Aziz, you will run the run". The two men previously the subject of Ashads anger groaned softly. "Mohammed, since you were also an idiot you will join them". Mohammed, seated near the far end of the table, also groaned.

The run, known by the men as 'The Run of Shame', was a twenty kilometer run through the desert behind the house. If it had been over flat ground it would have been bearable but Ashad had designed the course to go over at least ten of the mountainous sand dunes. Men returned from the run exhausted, their feet blistered and their boots full of sand. The run had been instituted by Ashad as a punishment for misdemeanors.

Having said his piece and finished his dinner Ashad rose from his chair and re-entered the house. He knew that the orders that he had given would be carried out without question. Ashads room was on the left at the end of the corridor. He walked down the corridor, opened his door and entered the room. Unlike most of the men, Ashad got to sleep alone. Closing the door he quickly undressed, flinging his clothes on another wooden chair, and entered the small ensuite bathroom. He climbed under the shower and turned both taps to their full. The water was nonetheless only tepid. Try as they might they had not been able to get the hot water system to function correctly.

Ashad scrubbed himself clean with a bar of rough soap that

felt like sandpaper. Having rinsed himself he climbed from the shower and looked into the small, cracked mirror set above the basin. In the reflection he saw a well muscled body with a flat stomach and bulging biceps. Nothing like the soft and flabby westerners he had seen. He was proud of his body, seeing it as a well honed fighting machine. He had dedicated that body to Allah to fight the holy war.

Stepping out of the bathroom he moved to a small wardrobe where he pulled from the top shelf a pair of boxer shorts and a T-shirt. These he donned before reaching under his bed for his prayer mat. He pulled the mat out and placed it on the floor facing to the north west, towards Mecca.

He dropped to his knees on the mat and leant forward until his forehead was touching the floor. In that posture he prayed to Allah to make him strong for the work ahead and to aid him in his mission. Having made his peace with his god he stood and rolled up the mat, placing it back under the bed.

Finished with his obeisance to his god Ashad moved to the small desk and opened the left hand drawer. He did not keep the drawer locked as he knew that none of his men would dare enter his room, much less touch his private things. From the drawer he took a small bottle of Johny Walker whisky, his one indulgence that was anathema to his faith. But he believed that his was a forgiving god who would forgive him his little weakness for all the good he was going to do for his faith.

Ashad unscrewed the bottle lid and took a long draught straight from the bottle. He then replaced the lid and replaced the bottle in its hidey hole in the drawer. He would have loved to have had more but his supplies of the illicit drink were limited. And he could hardly ask his men to buy him more when they went to town for supplies! Although the supplies purchasers were always instructed to buy at least two cartons of beer. It would seem odd to the people in the town to have men on an outback station not ordering or drinking beer. However, when the beer was bought back to the station all of the cans of beer were emptied into the sand.

He then climbed into the small single bed, punched the pillow into submission once, and within minutes he was fast asleep. Once again, as usual, he dreamt of wealth and power which he knew were his by right.

The first beam of morning sunlight slanting inwards from the small window in the opposite wall awoke Ashad from his deep sleep. He rolled over and looked at the small clock on the stand beside the bed. Five thirty in the morning. A new day and plenty to do.

Ashad rolled out of the bed and quickly donned the clothes he had been wearing the previous day. He then entered the small en-suite bathroom where he vigorously brushed his teeth. It would not do for the men to smell alcohol on his breath.

He opened his door and walked down the corridor to the common dining room and kitchen at the front of the house. Most of the men were already there sitting on chairs or benches eating their breakfasts. Some were eating bread and jam, others cheese and cold meats (no pig) and a couple were eating scrambled eggs. There were no women in the house. The men took turns cooking the evening meal but for lunch and breakfast they fended individually. Ashad helped himself to a coffee from the large urn and a plate of scrambled egg from the stove. The scrambled eggs obviously belonged to another of the men but there would be no complaints.

Having finished their breakfasts the men rose one by one to go about their duties and their training. Most would today go to the shooting range to improve their shooting ability. This afternoon Sameer would teach them how to fight with knives. Tariq, Aziz and Mohammed wearily set out to complete the run of shame.

4

12 MARCH, 2014

THE SAME SUN that had woken Ashad also roused Ben from his slumber. He rolled onto his back on the swag and stretched his arms above his head. Another day, another dollar, he thought.

Ben sat up and turned to the east where he could see the sun beginning to peak above the horizon. About five thirty, he thought. He had slept well and felt refreshed, ready for the day ahead. It never ceased to amaze him how he always slept better and woke up more refreshed on his swag on the hard ground than he did in his comfortable bed in Perth.

Around him the others were beginning to stir in their swags. They all yawned and stretched their arms and Mick farted, the brrrt sound carrying clearly. Mick farted upon waking every morning so it was no surprise. To Ben it was a sort of odorous alarm clock. Thankfully, however, they were not smelly or, if they were, they were confined to his swag. Mind you, none of us smell very fresh, thought Steve. Might see if we can get a tub today.

Ben stood up and stepped away from his swag. He pulled on his shorts and dirty shirt and walked over to the fire. The campfire had been reduced to a low mound of ash but he could still see a few red embers. Hunting around beneath the gum tree he soon found a handful of dry grass and small twigs that he threw onto the embers. He bent down over the embers to blow some life into them and soon had a small blaze going. He took some larger branches from the stockpile the boys had made the previous day and added them to the reborn campfire. It was soon blazing steadily.

"Come on guys, up you get", he said, loud enough to be heard by all. "Time waits for no man. Move your arses".

The other men were however already standing near their swags, having awakened with the sun as had Ben and immediately pulled on their clothes. They needed no more urging to move. Banjo picked up the billy from where it sat atop the chest and filled it with water from the large drum. He placed the now full billy on the side of the fire. He then fetched the tin mugs from the previous night and, from a jar in the chest, placed a large teaspoon of coffee in each. The billy soon boiled and Banjo slopped the boiling water into each of the mugs, passing one to each of the other men. The men all added sugar from the container in the chest, two spoons in Ben's case, and sat down on their chairs.

"What are we doing today boss?", asked Mick.

"I think we will head south. Looks from the aerial photographs as though there might be some interesting rocks down there", answered Steve. "And stop calling me boss. I might be in charge, be smarter, better looking and have a bigger dick but my name is Ben, not Boss", said Steve crankily. Mick was always calling him boss and he hated it.

"Well Beeeeen," replied Mick, "you might be most of those things but you certainly don't have a bigger dick! But if you want to be called Ben, boss, then Ben it is. Ben Little Dick if you like", he guffawed.

Ibrahim had retrieved some more supplies from the car fridge and was busy cooking bacon and eggs on the hot plate. These were soon done and each man again retired to his chair with his breakfast. Ibrahim in particular had helped himself to a mountain of bacon.

"I still don't get it", said Mick, "Here I am watching a Muslim bloke scoffing bacon. That's pig you know!"

"As I have explained before, Mick", replied Ibrahim, "I am a Muslim but not a good one. I believe in Allah, God to you. But I do not believe he would have been so pedantic as to deny certain foods that he had after all provided. I believe those prohibitions, indeed many of the things the Imams preach, were invented by man. Perhaps the first Emir loved bacon and wanted to keep it all for himself? And I do not believe that when I go to Heaven I will have fifty virgins. I have had one in my life and she has been all that I have ever needed".

"Furthermore", Ibrahim added, "If Allah sees fit to punish me for eating pork rather than rewarding me for being good then he is not the god I think he is".

Mick laughed heartily and was joined by Ben and Banjo. Ben was fairly sure that Banjo would not even know what pedantic meant. But it did not matter. He got the gist of the joke. Seeing the reaction Ibrahim smiled and then also burst into laughter. The laughter expanded out from the camp in jolly waves.

"Ah man!" said Mick, tears streaming down his cheeks, "You're a card Ib mate".

Ibrahim did not complain about the shortening of his name. He could see that it was a lost cause. He would forever be Ib to Mick, although thankfully both Ben and Banjo referred to him by his full name.

Although he had laughed Ben also thought about what Ibrahim had said. He respected Ibrahims belief in a god although it was not a belief that he shared. He was an atheist. As far as he was concerned there was no god. After all, he knew the Earth to be at least four billion years old, not the few thousand quoted by the bible. And if the Earth, supposedly created by god, was that old, why had the big man waited so long to complete his masterpiece – man. If the history of the Earth was compressed into a twenty-four hour clock civilized mankind had only been around since a few seconds before midnight. It did not make sense in Ben's mind. Also, as far as he was concerned, God had a terrible problem with low self esteem. Why else did he demand that everybody had to keep telling him what a good bloke he was. And what sort of god would have created a World so full of disasters and injustice, a World where kids and babies died. As far as Ben was concerned, if he met God walking down the street, he would spit in his face. And then he would call the cops on him. They would at least be able to book him with negligent homicide and failing to provide a safe work place! However, despite his own views Ben was tolerant of the views of others. If they wanted to believe in a supreme being then so be it. His friend Mick, for example, was a Catholic but like Ibrahim, not a very good one. But the choice of belief was theirs and theirs alone.

The men quickly finished their breakfasts and Ibrahim washed the dishes, drying them with a threadbare towel and depositing them in the chest. They then rolled up and secured their swags and threw them into the backs of the cruisers. Mick took a little longer securing his own swag as he had not forgotten his unwelcome visitor of two nights previous. This time however there was no snake under his swag waiting to wish him a good day.

Banjo and Ibrahim lifted the catering chest into its position on the tray of their vehicle. Ben took one of the shovels and swiftly buried the remnants of the camp fire.

Ben swung himself into the drivers seat of his vehicle and was soon joined by Mick in the passenger seat. Ibrahim and Banjo boarded their vehicle, Ibrahim in the drivers seat.

Starting the motor Ben lightly depressed the accelerator and both vehicles rolled away from their overnight camp. They climbed slowly over the tops of the low hills and accelerated slowly across the flat plain on the other side. The cruisers were soon passing Ben's and Mick's camp of two nights before although there was no sign other than a small mound of dirt over the old campfire.

Two kilometers further on and the rough track veered sharply to the south.

The two cruisers followed the track to the south over the flat earth and the occasional small hillock. There was however nothing to interest Ben so they continued on without stopping until they were about thirty kilometers south of their overnight camp. As they had continued to the south the sand dunes, at first not visible to the east, had encroached closer to the road. Ben finally stopped the cruiser, the nearest large sand dune less than a kilometer to the east.

As the cruiser rolled to a stop a large red kangaroo bounded in from the right and stopped only twenty meters to the front. It was a big male, a boomer, and he looked back at the strange object, tilting his head to the side. It looked to Ben as though the kangaroo was thinking. Probably along the lines of 'I know what I am doing here. I live here. But what the bloody hell are you and what are you doing here?'.

"Bloody big bugger isn't he", said Mick, "And there's another two over there", pointing to the left towards the sand dune.

Ben looked to the left and saw that there was indeed another two kangaroos, one about twice the size of the other. Probably a mother and her joey. The big boomer in front of the cruiser must be dad, thought Ben.

Ben opened the door and climbed down from the vehicle. Mick also climbed down and came around to join him as Ibrahim and Banjo got out of their vehicle and ambled over. The boomer looked at them one last time and then bounded off to the east, probably to join the mother and joey.

"See that opening in the dunes over there", said Ben, pointing to the east, "About seven kilometers beyond that there is something I want to take a look at". He placed an aerial photograph he had bought from the cruiser on the bonnet. "According to the photo there's a black coloured area I want to see. It might be some rocks poking through the sand or it may be nothing. Do you think we can drive along between the two dunes?" He pointed at a dark grey smudge on the photograph as he was talking.

"Yeah, looks to be pretty flat", said Mick, "And not much vegetation that I can see. We can give it a go".

"Boss", started Banjo, "Sorry, Ben, he said quickly amending himself to the correct form of address. You should know that this is poison country. Bad land"

Ben turned to look at Banjo. The Aborigine looked very serious and, for a full blood Aborigine, pale. Something was definitely bothering him.

"What do you mean Banjo?, asked Ben.

"Well, you see, the old blokes say this is poison country. Bad country where no one is supposed to go. Bad things happen here. My people are not allowed to come near this place. This has been a bad place for a long time".

"I am sorry", said Ben, truly contrite that he had forced Banjo into an uncomfortable situation. "If you like you and Ibrahim can go back the way we came, back to the camp, and we'll catch up with you".

"No, no. I don't believe all of the old fellas tales. I mean, I haven't been struck by lightning have I? We'll be OK", Banjo replied. He still looked worried but there were glimpses of determination. He did not want to look wanting in front of his new friends.

"OK, if you are sure?" said Ben, watching Banjo's face. Banjo nodded and set his face into a more determined mask.

"Good", continued Ben, "Mick and I will go first. You blokes follow in our tire tracks to avoid any stakes. And Banjo, if you have any concerns you and Ibrahim turn around and get out of here".

This was standard practice when bush bashing in a convoy. If the rear vehicles stayed in the front vehicles tire tracks only the front vehicle would get any punctures.

Ben climbed into the passenger side of his cruiser motioning Mick to get behind the wheel. He wanted to navigate by the aerial photograph whilst Mick drove. Ibrahim and Banjo walked back to their vehicle and took their places.

Mick turned the key and the motor rumbled to life. He pulled forward and immediately turned the wheel to the left Bumping over clumps of spinifex as he left the track and headed towards the gap between the two large sand dunes. He kept the speed low, around ten kilometers an hour, as they headed towards the gap.

"You know", he said, "That's probably why those roos are here. If the black fellas don't come here and don't hunt here they probably feel safe. This must feel like a sanctuary to the roos".

"Yeah, you're probably right", said Ben.

And Mick probably was right. The kangaroos had probably learnt over generations that here was a place that they did not get shot at, at least not by Aborigines. In its own way it was probably like a game reserve. The animals could go about their lives here without risk of being slaughtered.

The three kangaroos by the dune, seeing the vehicles headed towards them, turned and bounded away over the sand. In several long bounds, a few more for the youngster, they had reached the top of the sand dune and disappeared over the top. They certainly were not going to take any risks with these strange creatures, even if it was safe country.

Although the ground was relatively flat the spinifex clumps formed intermittent small hillocks. It was slow going as they crept towards the sand dunes and entered the steep sided valley between two of them. Travelling at only five kilometers per hour, barely walking pace, the journey seemed to take forever.

Part way through the journey a fawn coloured blur shot in front of the vehicle and out the other side. A quick double take and Ben saw that it was a young dingo pup which came to a sudden stop about twenty meters to the south of the cruiser, on the lower slope of the sand dune. In the meantime Mick too had seen the blur and jammed on the brakes.

"A little dingo pup", he said, "And look, that must be mum over there".

Steve looked where Mick was indicating and saw a much larger dingo stationary on the side of the sand dune to the south. The pup loped over to its mother, and both stood looking back at the strange vehicles. Mum and pup looked a symbol of something good and pure, standing on the sand in the middle of nowhere. Mother and her baby in the wilderness. The mother licked the pups face and gave another long look at the humans and then bounded off over the crest of the dune. The pup bounded after it and both had soon disappeared.

"Beautiful animals aren't they", said Mick, uncharacteristically sentimental. Although he said nothing Ben had to agree with him. He loved dingo's and thought of them as being quintessentially Australian. They were beautiful animals, far better than the average dog. He would keep one for a pet but that was prohibited by law.

Mick restarted the stalled vehicle and they continued moving.

Finally, after more than an hour of travelling Mick stopped the cruiser where the two sand dunes had come together to form one.

"This is as far as we go I think boss", said Mick, "I could have a go at driving over the dune but I don't fancy our chances".

"No, that's OK Mick. I can see on the photo we're only about three hundred meters short. We'll walk from here", replied Ben.

Ben and Mick dismounted from their cruiser and behind them Banjo and Ibrahim did the same.

"You blokes stay here", said Ben, "I'll just go and have a look-see".

"I'll come with you if you don't mind Steve", said Banjo. Whatever was happening at any time, Banjo always wanted to be a part of it. He would probably crawl over hot coals rather than sit still. And he knew that he was in bad country and wanted to stay with the man with the most power.

"OK, sure, come along for the stroll. Maybe you'll see some bush tucker".

Banjo nodded, pleased that he could go with Ben. He was still nervous about being in the 'bad country', but he felt safer with Ben. He did not fancy his chances of seeing any bush tucker though. Bugger all to eat in this type of country, unless maybe he spotted a lizard. Mind you, he had seen the kangaroos before and the dingos must be eating something.

Ben and Banjo paced up to the dune and, the loose sand moving beneath their feet, scrambled to the top and down the other side. The ground before them was again flat, loose sand. As they walked forward Ben cast his eyes left and right to see what had caused the dark patch on the photograph. All he could see however were the two sand dunes, redivided, on either side and the flat sandy valley between them. The valley was mostly clear with intermittent clumps of spinifex and the occasional saltbush. The sand dunes were even barer with only the occasional clump of spinifex. As they walked Ben could see nothing that might have produced the anomaly on the photograph. There were certainly no rocks. Then he saw blackened stems of saltbush protruding from the sand and some clumps of spinifex reduced to ash. He saw now what had produced the dark smudge on the aerial photograph. There had been a small fire here, probably the result of lightning. Since the aerial photographs had been shot most of the scant vegetation had regenerated, covering what had been a landscape burnt black.

He was about to call a halt and retrace their steps when he saw a small piece of rock protruding from the sand dune on the left. He walked over, grabbed the rock and pulled it from its resting place in the sand. The rock, composed of sandstone, was about half a meter long but less than ten centimeters thick, both sides appearing to be perfectly flat. Even more intriguing was that two of the edges of the piece were straight and met in what he judged to be a perfect right angle. Rocks came in all shapes but this piece was intriguing. It had two flat sides and two straight edges meeting at a right angle. To him it looked to be man made. But that was impossible. There had never been any European settlement out here in the desert, other than the station homestead to the north and the outstation to the northeast.

Ben dropped the piece of rock in the sand and continued forward for a few more paces. He suddenly realized that he was no longer walking on sand. He had firm footing beneath his boots which must mean rock. He looked down and saw that he was indeed standing on rock. The rock was a fawn colored sandstone, very similar to the piece he had just discarded. Crouching down to get a better look he saw that the rock under his feet was like a paved path about half of a meter wide and five meters long. He could also see that about every meter along its length there appeared to be a straight line cut through the path from side to side. And the sides of the path were also perfectly straight, marked by the sand falling away slightly on either side. If he did not know better he would swear that he was walking along the top of a buried wall. Impossible!

"Banjo", he called to the Aborigine about ten paces back, "Go back to the cruisers and bring the boys and a couple of shovels back here. And bring back my camera. Oh, and you had better bring the GPS too, it's in my backpack. In fact, just bring my pack".

He did not know what he had found but he was bloody well going to find out.

Banjo scampered back down the valley in the direction of the cruisers.

Ben sat back into the sand and took the water flask hanging from loops off his belt. Putting the flask to his lips he took a long drink and replaced it in its loops. He considered what he had found. Very odd, he thought. It could of course be bedrock but the pattern appeared far too regular. There was definitely something odd here. Leaning forward Steve used his hands to scoop some of the sand away from the side of the 'wall'. As he did so he saw that the edge of the 'path' fell away vertically. The blocks making up the path were flat on top and appeared to be flat and perfectly vertical on the sides. He kept shoveling with his hands until he had cleared an area about one meter long and twenty centimeters deep. Definitely a wall, he thought. Could not possibly be anything else. Could it?

Resting from his labors Ben could hear the boys talking and joking with each other as they headed his way. Looking up he saw Mick approaching, leading Ibrahim and Banjo. Banjo looked slightly embarrassed, as though he was being led somewhere that he did not want to go.

"Something bloody odd here boys", he yelled, "I want to dig a bit and see what it is"

"Sure thing boss", said Mick crouching beside him, "looks like you've found a bloody wall in the middle of nowhere", he added, looking at what Ben had unearthed.

Ibrahim and Banjo set to with the shovels. They did not need instruction as it was fairly obvious – Dig where there was sand and not rock. With the broad bladed shovels they had soon cleared an area about three meters long and one meter deep on one edge of the wall.

"Look here Ben", yelled Banjo, obviously excited and a little agitated by what they had found, "It looks like a door. This might be Burrums house!"

"Who the hell is Burrum, Banjo? He your uncle or something?" laughed Mick.

"No. Burrum is bad spirit. He cause all sorts of bad things. You don't want to cross Burrum or he will get you", said Banjo in a small voice, somewhat nervously. "We better get going I think".

"Hold up Banjo", said Ben reasonably, "If this is Burrums house he obviously don't live here anymore since it is full of sand. I don't think you need to worry about him".

"But you don't understand Ben", whined Banjo, "Burrum still live in house even if full of sand. Burrum can live in sand. He can live in the sky. He can live in rocks or even a tree. He bad spirit not like you or me".

"OK Banjo. Don't panic. We'll be out of here in a minute. I just need to document what we have found", said Ben.

With that assurance Banjo calmed down some but his eyes still flitted from side to side nervously. Ben however figured that he was OK for the moment.

Ben scrambled over to where Banjo had been digging and found what did indeed appear to be the top of a doorway. The sandstone dropped vertically for about half a meter and then, over a width of a meter or so, there was nothing but space other than sand apparently falling in from the other side. The rocks had been undercut in a straight line and the sides were also straight. It certainly looked like a doorway, disappearing into the sand below.

"I'll be buggered", breathed Ben, "It's a bloody doorway in a bloody wall in the middle of bloody nowhere. What have we discovered?"

"And where's my camera Mick?", he added.

"Here we are Ben", said Mick, holding the camera up from where he had safely placed it atop the stone wall.

Ben grasped the camera and began to take photographs. He photographed the wall from several angles and the apparent doorway. He also photographed the piece of loose rock he had discovered earlier. Finished photographing, Ben grabbed the GPS from atop the wall and wrote the latitude and longitude into the small notebook he carried in his shirt pocket.

Ben thought that they had done enough. It was not company business anyway. It was certainly not an orebody. Nonetheless, his curiosity had been aroused by this strange structure in the desert. He was going to follow it up, even if it was on his own time. For now however he was going to leave and get Banjo back to a place that he found more comfortable.

"OK boys, back to the cruisers", he said, "Time to earn our keep".

Desert Dreaming

Ben carried the camera slung around his neck whilst Ibrahim and Banjo carried the shovels. Mick did not have to carry anything since he was the senior fieldy, and being the senior had its advantages. Strung out in a short line they wandered back towards the vehicles, Banjo walking close besides Ben in case Burrum attacked.

5
13 MARCH, 2014

Anwar Ashad was doing one of the things that he did best, preening himself in the cracked bathroom mirror. His shirt was off and he was admiring the hard muscles on his chest and abdomen. His thoughts were interrupted by a tentative knocking on the door to his bedroom.

"Yes, what is it", he barked.

"Sir", came a small voice steeped in fear, "There has been an accident. You must come quickly".

Ashad smiled to himself. When would these idiots learn. He was the leader here, he must do nothing, quickly or otherwise. If they wanted to have accidents then it was their problem, not his. Nonetheless, he had better see what the accident had involved.

He quickly pulled on a shirt to cover himself and strode out of the small bathroom to the door to his room. He threw open the door to see Mahdi, One of the Saudi Arabians, on the threshold.

"Yes Mahdi, what is it that requires my attention", he growled at the hapless messenger.

"Sir, one of the men has been shot", said Mahdi, "It was an accident, on the shooting range", he clarified so that Ashad would not think that they had been attacked.

"Yes", muttered Ashad uncertainly, "And where is he now?"

"He still lies on the range sir. The other men are tending to him".

Well, if the idiot was being tended to it meant he still lived. Everything to do with the plan had been going so well. How could it go wrong now? Still, he must see to the wounded man and attend to what must be done. However, he said nothing. Actions always speak louder than words was a maxim that governed his life. And with that thought in mind he turned back into his room and grasped the webbing belt draped over a chair. The webbing belt had an attached holster and in the holster was a Smith & Wesson pistol. He wrapped and clasped the belt around his waist and turned to exit the room.

Walking forward and trailed by the uncertain Mahdi, Ashad crashed open the back door of the house. He strode quickly to the old four wheel drive that Mahdi had evidently driven back from the range. He pulled himself up into the passenger seat as Mahdi circled the vehicle and climbed into the drivers seat.

"Take me to the range, and be quick about it", Ashad said.

Mahdi turned the key and the motor rumbled to life. They were soon traversing a rough track that led from behind the homestead towards the sand dunes to the north. The track led over a sand dune and then crossed the NWR road. They then had to cross another sand dune and skirt the end of a third before the four wheel drive pulled out onto a flat area of land about one hundred meters wide between two large sand dunes. In the distance Ashad could see the butts from which the men fired and the man-shaped targets beyond them. They drove on past the butts and came to a halt about half way to the targets.

Several men were milling around the area, most with AK47's slung over their shoulders. Two men were kneeling on opposing sides of a third man lying on the ground. One of the kneeling men was trying to get the lying man to take a drink from a hip flask of water.

"What has happened here", barked Ashad as he stepped down from the vehicle. "Who is responsible for this?"

Ashads second in command, Sameer, stepped forward. "The man who has been shot is the Pakistani Afzaal", he said nervously, "He was going forward to check his target when he was hit by Hussein who was still shooting. It appears that it was a misunderstanding".

Misunderstanding my eye, thought Ashad. He knew that the Yemeni Hussein did not like the Pakistani. He would not be at all surprised if the Yemeni had done it deliberately to take out an enemy. He walked over and crouched beside the wounded man, the helper on that side shuffling to the side. He could see instantly that Azfaal was still conscious. He could also see the blood soaking through the right leg of the fatigues he was wearing. Some blood was also soaking into the sand beneath his leg. The men had not yet got around to exposing or bandaging the wound.

"Where are you hit?" he asked unnecessarily, "Are you in pain?"

"Yes Sir, croaked Azfaal. "I am hit in the leg and am in much pain. I need a doctor, Sir".

Ashad knew that the man would not get a doctor. There was no one with first aid experience in his group and he could not bring in an outsider. There was only one choice.

"We will get you some painkiller", he said, "hold steady and pray to Allah".

As he spoke Ashad shuffled around until he was directly behind Azfaals head. He drew the Smith & Wesson from its holster and placed the muzzle touching the top of Azfaals scalp. Azfaal felt the metal pressing against the top of his head. He knew what was about to happen.

"No sir!", he groaned, "I will heal…"

The rest of his words were shut off by the sharp report which echoed back from the dunes. Blood sprayed from his mouth as the bullet exited the bottom of his head and went on to bury itself in his chest. He died instantly.

"Bury him!", barked Ashad, as he hoisted himself back to his feet, "In the sand dune", nodding in the direction of the nearest dune.

All of the men looked at him aghast. He had just murdered one of their own.

"We had no choice", barked Ashad, deftly spreading the blame. "We could not take him to a hospital and we could not care for him. He got his painkiller and it is better this way. He is with Allah and with the virgins".

The men still stood rooted to the spot. If they had not feared Ashad before they all did now. He had shown himself to be merciless.

"Get to it!", he yelled, seeing no one was moving. "Bury him now and have done!".

The men suddenly stirred to life, two men running back to their vehicles to retrieve shovels. Those two men were soon back and busily digging a hole in the shifting sand. Two other men grabbed Azfaal's body by its feet and hands and carried it to the developing hole.

Ashad thought about what this development meant to his mission. He was now one man down, three if he counted the men lost on the boat. He had only ten men left. Would that be enough? Of course it would, he thought. Nothing could stand before the will of Allah.

"Hussein", barked Ashad.

"Yes Sir", said Hussein quietly, standing directly behind him.

"Hussein", continued Ashad more quietly as he turned, "Was this an accident?", staring deeply into the other mans eyes.

"Yes Sir. I was preparing to shoot when Azfaal ran in front of my position. I could not stop in time. It was an accident", said Hussein quietly.

"Well then, your marksmanship needs some work", said Ashad slyly.

"What do you mean Sir?", queried Hussein, "My shooting has been perfect", he added with some offence.

"Well, judging by the position of the body it would appear that you would have missed your target by a considerable margin", smirked Ashad. He had seen the look in the other mans eyes. He was convinced that Hussein had shot Azfaal deliberately.

"And if by some chance you were aiming for Azfaal your markmanship still needs some work since you only wounded him in the leg", he added.

Hussein did not know how Ashad knew which was his target or where he had been lying but he knew better than to dispute the observation which was in any case correct.

"I will continue to practice sir", he said.

"Do so. Let us go", said Ashad turning to Sameer, "I want to see the observation post".

Sameer stepped into the driving seat of the vehicle that Ashad had arrived in. Ashad hoisted himself into the passenger seat as Sameer turned the key and depressed the accelerator.

The vehicle had travelled only a few meters when Ashad said "Stop, I forgot". Sammeer bought the vehicle to a halt as Ashad unclasped the belt from his waist. "Hussein, see that my pistol gets back to the house", he barked. He handed the belt with the attached holster and pistol out the window to Hussein. "All right. Go", he commanded Sameer.

Ashad and Sameer were going to drive to the NWR facility on the NWR road. Ashad had handed over his pistol as he knew it would be disastrous if the vehicle was stopped and searched on the open highway by an overzealous policemen. No one was permitted to take a weapon onto public roads for that very reason. In fact, In Australia it was forbidden for any person to go armed in public other than policemen.

Sameer drove the vehicle slowly over the rough track until

they had reached where the track intersected the NWR road. He turned left onto the sealed road and increased the speed again until they were soon hurtling along at one hundred kilometers per hour. The trip to the NWR facility would take two hours.

"Sameer", said Ashad after a period of silence, "Hussein shot Azfaal deliberately. You do know that don't you?"

"I suspected sir", answered Sameer, "But I could not be certain"

"Tomorrow, Hussein does the run of shame. And he must know why he is being punished. I cannot lose any more men but neither can I have insubordination. See to it!"

"Yes sir. It will be done".

The remainder of the journey was completed in silence.

About two kilometers short of the facility Sameer pulled the vehicle off onto a small side track to the south. Less than half of one kilometer along the track it bent around a sand dune where they were now invisible from the NWR access road. It was necessary as they did not want to be caught spying on the largely secret government facility. Both men climbed down from their seats and stood on the rough track.

"About one kilometer that way", said Sameer, pointing to the east.

Their destination was an observation post that had been set up two days previously to observe the facility. Sameer had helped set up the post and so knew its location relative to where they were.

Both men set off walking through the sand towards the east. It was easy going on the flat surface with a large sand dune rearing on their left shoulders. Fifteen minutes later they had arrived at the base of another large sand dune.

"At the top", said Sameer succinctly.

The two men scrambled through the shifting sand of the dune until they were near the top.

Sameer grabbed Ashads arm and held him tight. "Down sir. We do not want to be seen", he said.

Both men dropped onto their stomachs and continued the

ascent in a crawl. Near the top they encountered an open topped tunnel that had been scooped into the dunes side. By this tunnel the observation post atop the hill could be approached from the rear without anyone being seen from the NWR facility. It had not been necessary to crawl for the last few meters but Sameer thought it wise to alert his leader of the potential hazard. Better safe than sorry. They scrambled through the tunnel entrance into a one and one half meter deep, round depression in the top of the dune. A third man awaited them there. He had undoubtedly been watching them for their entire walk from the vehicle.

In the bottom of the depression was a rolled up sleeping bag, a twenty liter container of water and some dry food bars. The eastern wall of the depression was capped by a spinifex bush that had been there before the depression had been dug. It was a smart move, though Ashad, anybody looking at the top of the dune from the facility would see no change, just a Spinifex bush where it had always been. The man charged with manning the post had cut some small holes in the spinifex to allow for an unobstructed view. Looking over the depression lip and through the spinifex towards the east, Ashad could see the NWR facility spread out below. It was like looking at a three dimensional map, he thought.

The facility covered a square area of about six acres surrounded by a two meter tall mesh fence with three rows of razor wire on the top. Within the compound, and to the right, a broad tunnel delved into the earth at a shallow angle. Underground the tunnel ended in a broad, cathedral-like space about fifty meters below the land surface. Although Ashad could not see into this space he knew that that was where the waste was stored. On the far side of the enclosure were twenty small buildings, each the size of a sea container. These were the accommodation quarters for the facility workers and the soldiers who guarded it. Each quarter was separated from the next by about one meter of open ground. This was to ensure the workers and soldiers privacy. To the left of the quarters was a larger building which Ashad took to be the kitchen and mess. That building formed an L shape with the long line of quarters. Close to the near fence were two larger buildings. These would be the administrative offices and workshops. To the left was the only gate into the facility. The gateway comprises two tall mesh and razor wire gates which could be swung inwards to let in trucks. Next to the gateway was a small building the size of Ashads bathroom. This would be the hut for the guards at the gate. Ashad could see one uniformed man sitting inside the small hut and a second leaning on the wall on the outside.

In addition to the buildings and the tunnel entrance Ashad could see two humvees and six four wheel drives parked next to the quarters. The humvees would belong to the soldiers, the four wheel drives to the facility workers. A fork lift was parked at the mouth of the tunnel.

In the far right corner of the fenced in area Ashad could see a large, wide diameter drilling rig. There were four men busy around the base of the rig which appeared to be working. Ashad knew that the drilling rig was there to drill deep holes into the bedrock, down which the canisters of waste would be lowered to depths approaching two kilometers. The holes would then be filled with concrete making it almost certain that there would be no escape of radioactivity.

"What have you seen Habeeb?", he asked the occupant of the post, a small man with strong Arabic features.

"In two days I have counted twenty-one men", answered Habeeb, "Four men work on the drilling rig, four are employees moving the waste around and underground, two are supervisors, two work in the kitchen, and eight are soldiers under the command of a Lieutenant".

"And what else?", continued Ashad.

"Two soldiers are usually on duty at the gates and every two hours two soldiers drive one of the humvees around the perimeter. The workers and supervisors come and go at odd times. The supervisors spend most of their time in the nearest building. The workers live in the quarters to the left, the soldiers to the right, and the two supervisors in the middle. When they are not on duty or not working the men spend most of their time either in their quarters or in the mess. The fence is electrified, as you can see"

Ashad looked closer at the fence and could indeed see at regular intervals small tin plates affixed to the fence with lightning bolt symbols, the universal symbol for electricity. That might make their job trickier, he thought, but by no means impossible.

"There is also a CCTV camera by the gate and another over the mouth of the tunnel", continued Tariq, "And I suspect that there is another camera on the administration building although I cannot see it from here".

Ashad scooped up the binoculars from where they lay atop the sleeping bag on the floor of the pit. Focussing the binoculars he peered through a gap in the spinifex. As the binoculars came into focus he could see the camera mounted on a pole inside the gate. Swiveling to the right he saw a second camera mounted on a similar pole above the entrance to the tunnel.

As Ashad continued to look down upon the facility he saw two uniformed men exit the mess and clamber into one of the humvees. Both men were wearing desert camouflage and carried Austeyr automatic rifles. He had seen the same rifles carried by Australian soldiers in Afghanistan so knew what they looked like.

The humvee backed away from the quarters and set of across the compound towards them. Ashad instinctively ducked and then cursed himself. They had not seen you fool, they were only doing their rounds! Sure enough, on reaching the fence the vehicle turned right and commenced its circuit of the site, passing between the fence and the administration building.

Ashad had seen enough. The facility was well set up and well guarded but he knew that he could take it.

"You are doing well Habeeb", he said to the small watchman, "You will be relieved tomorrow". Habeeb actually blushed and nodded his head appreciatively. "Come Sameer, let us return to the homestead".

Ashad slid down the west bank of the sand dune followed by Sameer. Both then trotted back towards their vehicle watched by Habeeb from his eyrie. Reaching the vehicle they both clambered in and were soon back on the main road heading west.

6

20 MARCH, 2014

As usual Ben awoke just as the sun was just beginning to clear the horizon. He rolled over in his swag, yawned and sat up, looking around the still quiet camp site. Mick, Ibrahim and Banjo remained sound asleep.

"Wake up boys!", said Ben loudly, "Time to hit the road!"

Mick snorted and farted as Ibrahim and Banjo jerked upright in their swags, Banjo rubbing the sleep from his eyes. Banjo was the first out of his swag, swiftly donning his shorts and shirt before rummaging in the catering box. He turned back to the others with two tins of baked beans in his hands.

"Sorry guys", he said, "But beans is all that we have left for brekky"

It had been eight days since they had discovered the strange wall in the desert and all their fresh supplies were gone. Ben had not bothered to resupply as today they were going home.

"Don't worry about it Banjo", said Ben, "We'll have brekky in Marble Bar. We should get there just about when the café opens, and we'll drop you home on the way. We will have coffee for the road though".

For the past week Ibrahim and Banjo had been collecting

stream sediment samples in the area around Blind Bluff. Ben was hoping that those samples would tell him how widespread the copper mineralisation that he had seen at the bluff was. At the same time Ben and Mick had been visiting and sampling various rock outcrops in the area. They had been very fortunate in picking up Banjo because otherwise Mick and Ibrahim would have done the stream sediment sampling whilst Ben explored the rocks alone. Ben had found nothing further but was still hopeful for the Blind Bluff and Bright Desert prospects. The previous night had been the first when all four men had camped together for the week.

Mick and Ibrahim were already out of their swags and dressed by the time Ben levered himself out and donned his field clothes. Banjo had returned the cans of baked beans to the catering chest and was now nursing the fire back to life. He soon had it burning brightly with a full billy can of water at its edge. He fetched the four clean cups, added coffee to each and then boiling water from the billy before handing each of the men their morning fix. Each man added sugar to the coffee as they preferred it.

Ben took his cup and blew on it until it was cool enough to take a sip. The others did the same except for Mick who downed his cup in one long swallow, apparently impervious to the heat.

"So home today Ben. Reckon we'll make it by tonight?", Mick asked.

"Yeah, I think so", replied Ben, "Provided we don't have any holdups. If we do then we'll overnight at Meeka". Meeka was the approved outback shorthand for the old gold mining township of Meekatharra.

They all quickly finished their coffees, eager to be away. All except for Banjo who seemed to dawdle, sad that the trip had come to an end and knowing that he was going to miss his new friends. He was however very pleased that he had not had to return to the bad country.

Having finished breakfast the four friends quickly rolled their swags which, along with the camping equipment, were deposited in the two cruisers. As a finishing touch Mick shoveled sand over the campfire to ensure that it was extinguished. Then Ben clambered into the drivers seat of his cruiser inviting Ibrahim to join him in the passenger seat. Although Mick normally rode with Ben, Ben thought a change of company would be good for everyone. Mick took the drivers seat of the second cruiser to be joined by Banjo.

Ben started the motor, put the vehicle into gear and began to slowly pull away from the camp site, Mick following in his tracks. For their final night they had once again camped at Blind Bluff so Ben knew that it was only a short trip to the highway.

"So what do you think Ibrahim?", asked Ben, "Been a good trip do you think?"

"Yes, I believe so Ben. You have made some finds which might turn out to be good and I have made a new friend in Banjo. I am much blessed to have such good friends such as you, Mick and Banjo", replied Ibrahim, "But I will be glad to get home to my wife", he added sheepishly.

"Can't say I blame you mate, although I've got no one to go home too I'll still be glad to get home for a few days. And the find that intrigues me the most is that wall we found in the desert. Where do you think that came from?", said Ben.

"I have no idea Ben. An ancient civilization?", replied Ibrahim.

"There ain't no ancient civilizations in Australia, mate. Except for the Aborigines of course. And they certainly didn't construct stone walls", said Ben.

"Well, maybe you can find someone in Perth who is an expert in these matters. Remember, Australia is a very young country and there are probably many things you still don't know about its history before the arrival of the white man", replied Ibrahim.

"Yeah, you're probably right", said Ben, "I'll see if I can consult an expert, maybe an archaeologist, when I get to Perth".

As Ben finished talking he noted that they had arrived back

at the sealed NWR road. He turned left onto the road, towards Marble Bar and home, with Mick and Banjo following close behind. However, a short time later he saw what looked to be a vehicle in trouble on the side of the road, facing towards Marble Bar. He could see that the vehicle was stopped on the verge, the bonnet was open and at least one man appeared to be peering into the engine compartment.

Ben eased his cruiser to a stop immediately behind the broken down cruiser and Mick slid in behind. Ben alighted from the vehicle and walked to the front of the broken down vehicle to see if he could offer assistance. As he arrived at the front of the vehicle he could see that there was not one but two men who lifted their heads from the engine as he approached.

Ben surreptitiously examined the two men as he approached. One man was short and stocky with a dark swarthy face largely hidden behind a large black beard with flecks of grey. About forty years old, Ben thought. The other man was younger, probably late twenties, taller and very thin. He also was dark but not as dark as the first man. He also sported a beard but it was very thin and looked as though it had been an appetizer for rats.

"G'day gentlemen, looks like you're having some problems. Anything we can do to help?", asked Ben.

The older man looked at Ben with an expression that could only be defined as suspicion and contempt. Nonetheless, he was prompt to answer. "The motor suddenly stopped on us. I do not know why", he said, delivered in a fashion that indicated that English was not his first language.

"No worries", said Ben, "What if Mick takes a look? He's pretty good with vehicles"

Mick along with Ibrahim and Banjo had now also arrived at the front of the broken down vehicle.

"Yeah, I'll take a look mate. Should be able to get you back on the road in no time", said Mick.

So saying Mick immediately bent to look inside the engine

compartment and started tapping some things and twisting others.

"My name is Ben. This here are Mick, Ibrahim and Banjo", said Ben, indicating the other three men as he spoke their names. "We're an exploration crew working for a Perth company. What are you fella's doing out here? There's nothing along this road other than the waste facility".

"I am John and this is William", said the swarthy man, "We are cowboys at Bright Downs station on our way into town for supplies".

"Cowboys?", laughed Mick, his head still beneath the bonnet, "You only have cowboys in America and this is Australia. Here we call you fellows stockmen!".

"That is what Yu… John meant", said the younger, thin man, "John used to work on a ranch in America and he thinks maybe he is still there", he added with a forced laugh. John did not look at all pleased that the younger man had spoken.

"Bright Downs station eh?" said Ben, How many of you are there out there?"

"Just William and I and the manager", said swarthy face with some reluctance.

"Hey, I think I've found and fixed your problem", said Mick from beneath the bonnet, "It was a fuel blockage but she should be right now. Give the motor a turn and see what happens", he added whilst he slammed the car bonnet.

The swarthy man, John, stepped around Ben and climbed into the drivers seat. He twisted the key and at first there was some grinding followed by a cough and finally the motor roared into life.

"Thank you very much", said John from behind the wheel, "We will bid you good day now. Come William", he added imperiously addressing the younger man who immediately scuttled around the vehicle to leap into the passenger seat. Without further ado John had put the vehicle into gear and slowly pulled back onto the road before roaring off towards Marble Bar.

"Well, that was interesting", said Mick, "Talkative buggers weren't they".

"Yeah, well, couple of strange blokes if you ask me", said Ben, "Suit their boss at bright Downs though as he's a strange bugger too. And I've never seen two blokes that look less like stockmen than those two. Still, better hit the road if we want to get home".

Mick and Banjo idled back and got into their cruiser and Ben and Ibrahim did the same in theirs. Ben turned the ignition and as the engine roared to life he put it into gear and crept back onto the main road, closely followed by Mick and Banjo.

Before long they were cruising down the highway at the posted eighty kilometers per hour. That was as fast as they could go on this road because of the waste disposal plant although on occasion Ben did have to admit that they exceeded the speed limit. There were no cops out here anyway. But they were closer to Marble bar now and getting closer by the minute. When they were cruising at the speed limit Ben partially turned towards Ibrahim and said "Those blokes weren't stockmen, I'd stake my life on it. At least they didn't look like any stockmen I've ever met. I doubt if either of them have ever ridden a horse in their lives!"

"I think that you are right Ben", replied Ibrahim, "Maybe they are wannabe stockmen come up here to get a taste of the life?"

"Maybe, but I don't think so. And they're foreigners too. I don't know where they come from but they weren't born here. No offence Ibrahim, I've got nothing against foreigners"

"No offence taken Ben. And I can tell you where they come from", said Ibrahim, "After all I should be able to recognize my own kin"

"What!" said Ben, astounded, "Are you telling me you're related to those blokes?"

"No, no Ben. I am not related, or at least I do not think I am. But I am an Arab and should be able to recognize my countrymen"

"What, are you saying that …"

"Yes Ben", interrupted Ibrahim, "They are Arabs".

7

22 MARCH, 2014

THE BRRRT! BRRRT! brrrt! woke Ben from a sound slumber. His arm darted out from beneath the covers and slammed down on top of the mobile phone on the cabinet beside the bed. The noise ceased.

Ben rolled over and sat up straight in the bed. At first he was confused and then he realized that he was back in his bed in Perth, not still out under the stars. They had driven back into Perth about eight o'clock the night before. After the discovery of the wall they had stayed out for another eight days prospecting, with no success. Ben had then called a halt to the expedition and they had driven the twelve hundred kilometers back to Perth, taking two days to do it and staying in the town of Meekatharra for one night on their way south.

His alarm had told him it was six o'clock in the morning. He clambered out of the bed and walked across to the wardrobe. From a bottom drawer he took out clean underwear, a pair of shorts and a T-shirt. He dressed quickly and exited the bedroom, grabbing his keys on the way to the front door of his apartment. Letting himself out he locked the door behind him and walked down the single flight of stairs. The apartment block had a lift but Ben always preferred to use the stairs.

Ben lived alone in a single bedroom apartment in West Perth, only a short walk from the head office of his employer, Major Minerals. Pushing open the double glass doors at the entrance to the complex he exited onto the street. He crossed the street taking care to avoid the morning traffic and was soon standing on the edge of Kings Park. Kings Park was a large area of native forest near the centre of the city and was the venue for his daily run, when he was in town.

Ben commenced jogging down a grassy trail leading into the park. As he ran he thought about his tasks for the day. He had a lot to do on his first day back.

Ben loved the park. He was surrounded on all sides by eucalypt and banksia trees and the occasional grass tree, or blackboy, with its long fronds waving in the air. It was possible to sit in the middle of the park, in the middle of the city, and pretend that you were out in the bush. Sure, the low murmur of cars and the occasional siren sort of spoiled the feeling but it was still possible if you closed your mind. Ben had done it many times. When things got tough it was his habit to go and sit in the middle of the park and switch off. It worked for him.

Ben continued on his run at a steady jog. He only wanted to get his blood pumping, not kill himself. He looped down to the south of the park and then north along the cliff tops bordering the river. He then turned for home and five kilometers later was pushing open the front door of his complex. He trotted up the stairs, obviously with energy still to burn. He unlocked his front door and entered the small flat going straight to the small ensuite bathroom adjacent to his bedroom. He stripped off his sweaty clothes, turned on the shower as hot as he could bear and ducked under the stream. Five minutes later he was clean and dry and in his bedroom hunting in the wardrobe for clean clothes. He found clean underwear, black trousers and a blue business shirt which he hastily donned. These were followed by a pair of black dress shoes. He was not going to wear a tie today, his first day back in the big smoke.

Ben decided he would walk to work. After all, it was only a ten minute walk to the office. He left his apartment, locking the door behind him, went downstairs and out of the front door. A left turn onto Kings Park Road, a left again onto Outram Street and five minutes later a right turn onto Colins Street. He walked ahead and a few minutes later was outside of the building that housed the head office of Major Minerals. He walked up to the front door and opened it. As the front door was not locked he was obviously not the first into work. Inside the spacious lobby he ran up the stairs, again ignoring the lift. On the second floor he opened another glass door and stepped into the reception area of Major Minerals. The reception area was a carpeted cube with photographs of mines and drilling rigs adorning the walls. The only furniture was several comfortable chairs, a small coffee table with some magazines and rock samples, and a long desk behind which sat Tiffany, the company's receptionist and general dogsbody.

"Morning Tiff", he said to the angelic girl behind the reception desk. Tiffany was, Ben knew, thirty years old but looked fifteen with her long blonde hair in pigtails and her elfin looks.

"Morning Ben", said Tiffany, "good to see you got back OK".

"Yep, here I am", replied Ben "Couldn't get rid of me that easily".

Tiffany giggled, adding to her youthful appearance. "We wouldn't want to get rid of you Ben", she smiled, "You are the horniest thing around here".

"Ah, Tiff. Flattery will get you everywhere"

Ben was actually quite attracted to Tiffany. She was quite beautiful and had a body to match. Today she was wearing a scallop-necked white blouse with ruffles at the sleeves and a trim black skirt together with black flat shoes, her 'beetle crushers' as she called them. Ben would like nothing better than to see what was under the skirt and blouse but he knew better than to let his imagination run away with him.

More importantly, Tiffany had a great sense of humour but Ben knew he would never do anything, no matter how many come on's he got from her. You never messed with someone you worked with. That way led only to disaster.

"I'll see you later Tiff. I'd better start putting my report together", he added.

Ben walked through the door behind the reception desk and down the short corridor to his office. The big office at the end was the Managing Directors. Ben's was the second door on the left.

He entered the office leaving the door open behind him. He never closed his office door, believing that everyone should have access to him whenever they wanted. He firmly believed that this was the only way to work. Those bureaucrats who fenced themselves off from their employees were just asking for trouble, in his opinion.

He sat down in his ergonomic chair behind his desk and switched on his computer. As it was booting he unslung the camera from around his neck, that he had bought from his home, and plugged it into the computer. The computer was soon humming and Ben accessed the software for photograph downloads and downloaded the photographs he had taken during the recent trip.

Ben scrolled through the photographs he had taken. These included photographs of the various prospects, some general scenery photographs for his own collection, and the photographs of the ruined wall in the desert. Stopping at a photograph of the wall with the partial doorway visible he enlarged the image. Very odd, he thought looking at the image. I still can't believe that we found an old wall in the desert.

Shrinking the image Ben opened his web browser at the Google search page. Using some well chosen key words he did a search for any known buildings in that area of the desert. He got numerous hits but scanning through them he saw that nearly all were irrelevant. The relevant hits insisted that there were no known buildings in that area, the nearest being the Bright Downs homestead thirty kilometers to the north. The other nearest known buildings were also station homesteads seventy kilometers to the west and ninety kilometers to the south. A small outstation of Bright Downs was situated about eight kilometers to the northeast of the wall. Ben's discovery was indeed an unexplained anomaly.

Thinking further Ben entered 'desert' and 'sand accumulation' into the Google search engine. He pressed enter and was rewarded with a list of thousands of hits. He flicked through a number of the more likely hits but found nothing of use. So, he thought, how long would it take to bury a two meter wall beneath sand in a desert? Having failed to find an answer in the digital World Ben as usual reverted to the old fashioned method of looking things up in books. He had a small bookcase which contained a number of texts devoted to geology, one of which on the science of sedimentology he withdrew and leant back in his chair to read. He turned to the section on aeolian sediments, those sediments created by wind, and began to read. Nearly half an hour later he was nowhere closer to an answer and, frustrated, closed the book and placed it back on its shelf.

He knew that deserts were very dynamic environments and it was possible that that much sand had built up in a few decades. However, he believed to have buried the wall as it had the sand must have been accumulating for hundreds, if not thousands of years. Still, it was another avenue that he could not prove.

Remembering Bright Downs Ben did another search on the station. From that search he learnt that the station had been purchased three years previously by a Saudi company. Why would the Saudi's want a marginal cattle station on the edge of the desert? he thought. Perhaps they thought there was oil under it? No, he thought, as a company they would know that even if there was oil it belonged to whoever held the petroleum lease for the area, not the station owner. And the station owner didn't even own the land. The station was a long term lease from the government. The government of Western Australia actually owned the land.

And in any case Ben knew the areas geology and knew that there was no way that the station sat on oil. It simply was not possible.

Ben closed down the web browser and bought up Microsoft Word. Using his notebook, which he had also bought from home, Ben began compiling a report on his latest field trip. The report came together easily, detailing what he had done and the results of that work. More time was spent on detailing the two prospects he had discovered, Blind Bluff and Bright Desert. With these two areas he went into greater depth summarizing his findings and what those findings might indicate. The descriptions of the prospects would not of course be complete until he had received the assay results of the samples he had collected. That reminded him. He picked up the telephone on his desk and dialed a number. It rang several times before being answered.

"Morning. Who is this?", came a rather strained voice. Micks voice with an edge of tiredness.

"Morning Mick, did you tie one on last night?", asked Ben cheerfully.

"Ben! Do you know what bloody time it is mate!" It was not a question.

"And good morning to you too mate. You did tie one on didn't you?"

"I had a couple of beers. You have a problem with that?", grumped Mick. "And it is my bloody day off!"

"Sure Mick, I know. I didn't want to disturb you but I just wanted to check that you would get those samples in to the laboratory today".

"Of course I bloody will, even on my day off!"

"Thanks mate. Speak to you later", finished Ben, hanging up the phone. He knew Mick would do as he promised.

Ben finished off the report and sent the result to the printer in the map room across the corridor. He then picked up the telephone to make another call. Checking a number from his filofax he dialled.

The call was answered almost immediately. "Good morning, Global Geophysics, how may I help you?", in a breathy feminine voice.

"Morning Sue, Ben Wilde. Is Guy there?"

"Oh, hi Ben. Sure, I'll put you through"

The telephone went silent and then there was a click and a gruff male voice. "Morning Ben, how are you mate?", said Guy Williamson, CEO of Global Geophysics. "I thought you were in the bush?".

"Got back last night", said Ben, "Listen mate. I have to clear it with the boss first but I might need a couple of IP surveys done. Are you available?".

An IP survey stood for induced polarization, an electrical method use for detecting sulphide orebodies buried at depth beneath soil and sand.

"Yeah, sure mate. Things are pretty slack at the moment so I could probably let you have a crew in about a week. How's that sound?", replied Guy.

"Perfect Guy. I'll speak to the boss and let you know tomorrow"

Ben hung up the telephone and swiveled in his seat. What next? His mind returned to the wall that he had discovered. Bugger, thought Ben, that wall will be the death of me. But what can I do about it? The thought came suddenly to him. He turned back to his computer and did a quick search for the Perth museum. He soon found a web page for the museum and noted down the listed phone number on a sticky note. Looking at the number he picked up the telephone again and placed the call.

"Good morning, Perth museum. How may I help you", came a feminine voice.

"Thank you, yes, do you have an archaeologist I might be able to speak to?"

"Might I ask what your query is regarding?"

"Sure. I have found something odd up in the desert in the East Pilbara and I thought one of your people might be able to help me. Can you?".

"Certainly sir, I will put you through to Dr Michaels"

Once again Ben heard silence and then a click as he was reconnected.

"Hello, this is Doctor Michaels. How can I help you?" came a breathy feminine voice.

"My name is Ben Wilde", said Ben, "I'm not exactly sure that you can help but I don't know where else to turn".

"Well Mr Wilde, try me and we'll see what we can do"

"Well, I am a geologist and I was recently in the desert in the east Pilbara where I found something very odd".

"Odd? What was odd Mr Wilde?".

"I found what looks like an old stone wall with what appears to be a doorway cut into it", said Ben, "The wall was mostly buried beneath the desert sands. The odd thing is that there is absolutely no record of any previous buildings in that area and so I am a little confused. I had hoped you might be able to enlighten me".

"Mr Wilde, just so you know my specialty is Aboriginal culture. And to the best of my knowledge the Aborigines built no walls. However, you have me intrigued. Do you have any photos?"

"Yes, yes I do", replied Ben.

"Well, I'll tell you what. Why don't you come into the museum this afternoon and I will see what you have. How does two o'clock sound?"

"Perfect. I will be there. And thank you again".

Ben hung up the phone. Maybe I'll get some answers, he thought. Worth a shot.

Whilst he was deep in thought Tim O'hallaran appeared in his doorway. Like Ben, Tim was dressed in a plain blue business shirt and black trousers. No tie. Ben knew that the absence of tie meant that there were no meetings with the Board or with shareholders today.

"Morning Ben, How did the trip go?", he asked.

"Good Tim. I found a couple of beaut prospects that are worthy of follow up, as I told you on the phone. Do you want to hear about them now?".

Tim answered in the affirmative and Ben launched into a condensed version of the report he had just completed.

Having given a detailed account of the two prospects, Blind Bluff and Bright Desert, he awaited Tim's comments.

"Yeah, they sound good Ben", he said, "What do you want to do now?"

"Well, we of course don't have the assays yet but Blind Bluff stands up by itself, there is definitely copper there, and I'm pretty sure that Bright Desert is a genuine gossan. Here, take a look", said Ben, throwing to Tim a piece of the gossan that he had bought in that morning.

Tim examined the nondescript looking piece of dark brown rock, turning it over in his hands to look at every side.

"I have to agree Ben", he said, "It certainly looks like a gossan".

"I know we don't have the assays", continued Ben, "But I am confident and we should look to see if we can generate some drill targets by a couple of IP surveys, Starting with the blind bluff copper prospect of course".

"I'll bite", said Tim, "You organize it but if one of the two doesn't come off then you owe me a beer".

"And if both don't come off?", queried Ben.

"Well, then you owe me two beers", said Tim, smiling.

"Fair enough. I'll get it done. It means I'll have to leave for the bush again next week. Is that OK?".

"Sure. Just get it done and we'll see what you come up with", finished Tim.

Tim turned and walked down the corridor to his own office,

leaving Ben alone. He turned back to the paperwork on his desk, including the expenses for the trip, and got to work.

At about twelve thirty Ben placed his pen on the desk and rose from his chair. He left his office, the company offices, walked down the stairs and out onto the street. Whistling as he went Ben walked to the small café on Hay Street where he always bought his lunch when he was in the city. At the café he bought a chicken and salad roll before returning to the office to eat his lunch at his desk.

At one twenty Ben again rose from his chair and left the office. He had not bought his car to work that morning so he walked back to his apartment to get his beat up old Landrover for the drive to the museum in Northbridge. He retrieved the Landrover from the car park beneath the complex and set off on the drive to Northbridge. Arriving near the museum he could not find a parking place. This was typical of the Northbridge area, there was never any free parking. Having done a lap of the block he finally found a single space behind the art gallery. Locking his car he set off on the one block walk to the museum.

As he walked Ben mused. Northbridge was where most of Perths nightclubs were situated. When he had been younger he and his mates were regulars in Northbridge on Friday and Saturday nights. Getting drunk and trying to pick up chicks. He had always been much more successful with the former than the latter. Ben smiled at the memories. He seldom came to Northbridge anymore. He was simply no longer interested in getting drunk or the opportunity for a one night stand. I must be getting old, he thought.

Arriving at the museum he entered the large foyer decorated with statues and various artworks. At the far end of the foyer was a diorama of an Aboriginal family, made of wax, at a mia mia. A mia mia was a rough shelter made of sticks and grass. The waxen Aboriginal man was balanced on one leg with a long spear in his hand, the butt resting on the floor. A waxen woman and a small child squatted by a representation of a campfire.

Ben approached the long desk manned by a young man with his hair in a ponytail.

"I have an appointment with Doctor Michaels", he told the young man, "My name is Ben Wilde".

The young man looked at the appointments book on the desk before him and finding Ben's name, smiled. "Up the stairs", he said pointing to a flight of stairs to the left, "Along the corridor to the end, turn right, second to last door on the left".

Ben thanked him and started up the stairs. The directions were easy to follow and he was soon standing in front of a closed door bearing a nameplate, 'Dr Michelle Michaels'. He knocked on the door.

"Come in", called a husky voice.

Ben opened the door and entered the room. Ben was not sure what he had been expecting but it was not what greeted him. He had expected Doctor Michaels to be an old crone with grey hair and glasses. The woman sitting at the desk was about Ben's age and, to put it bluntly, was a knockout! She had long auburn hair and, other than the hair colour, was the spitting image of actress Michelle Pfieffer. She even had the same first name! Ben was a little stunned and almost stumbled into the office. Michelle was dressed in jeans, a loose short sleeved green shirt and sneakers.

"Doctor Michaels, my name is Ben Wilde. A pleasure to meet you", he said in his most manly voice.

"Mr Wilde. Likewise a pleasure. Please have a seat", pointing to the chair pulled in before her desk. As Ben approached she leaned over the desk and offered her hand. Ben took it and shook it briefly. At the same time he surreptitiously examined her left hand and noted that there was no wedding or engagement ring. He had to fight himself to be able to let go of the lovely soft hand.

Ben sat on a wooden chair before the desk and examined the room. One wall was bookshelves crammed with various books, most of them on the Aboriginal people. The opposite wall held framed photographs of various Aboriginal people, one or two of whom Ben thought he recognised. One of the photographs appeared to be of Jack from the Mandandanja community nearby to where he had been working. Two spears and a didgeridoo leant in a corner and the floor behind the desk was stacked high with other books and loose papers.

"Please excuse the mess", said Michelle in her breathy voice, "I don't get many visitors. And please call me Michelle." she added whilst smiling.

"No problem. You should see my office", said Ben, smiling in return, "And please call me Ben".

"OK Ben, what can I do for you?"

Ben placed the file that he had carried from his landrover on her desk. He opened the file and drew out two printed photographs which he placed down in front of her. The photographs were general scenes showing the sand dunes and desert near where he had discovered the wall.

"These are just to put you in the picture", he said, "This is the country where I discovered the wall".

Michelle examined the photographs while Ben drew another photo from the file. This photograph showed the wall and underneath the top of what he had taken to be a doorway. He placed it on the desk with the others and turned it around so she could view it right way up.

"We were doing some prospecting in the area when I discovered an unusual rock formation", he said, "We dug some of the sand away and discovered what you see there. See how it looks like a made wall with a doorway?".

"Yes it does, doesn't it", said Michelle, "Can you tell me where this was exactly?"

Ben once again delved into the file and took out a map of the area. He unfolded the map and placed it in front of her. The map was of government issue and showed all tracks, roads and homesteads in the east Pilbara region. A small ink cross marked where he had discovered the wall. There was nothing on the map in that area other than parallel brown lines showing the positions of the sand dunes and a small black box showing the position of the Bright Downs outstation, eight kilometers northeast from the cross. A dotted brown line showing a track linked the outstation with the bright Downs homestead to the north.

"X marks the spot", said Ben pointing at the map.

"And", continued Ben, "I think that it is odd that it is so deeply buried in sand. I can't prove it but I get the feeling that it would have taken hundreds of years for that much sand to accumulate".

"It is certainly very unusual", said Michelle, "Although it's a bit outside my field of Aboriginal studies".

"Anything you can do to satisfy my curiosity would be appreciated", said Ben, "This anomaly is driving me crazy!".

"I'll tell you what I'll do", said Michelle, "I was actually planning to be up in that part of the World in a week or so to see some people from the Manyilyjarra people at the Mandandanja community. What if I were to meet you, say in Marble Bar, and you can take me to look at your find?"

"That sounds perfect", said Ben, "I know some of the people at Mandandanja as I often call in their when I'm working in the area. In fact one of the boys from Mandandanja works for me. I will look forward to it. Let me know when you will be in Marble Bar and we'll take it from there".

Ben took his wallet from his hip pocket and extracted his business card which he handed to Michelle. She in turn handed him her business card from a small pile on her desk.

"I will be in contact", said Michelle.

"I will look forward to it", replied Ben, "You can keep the file" he continued, tapping the cardboard file still on her desk.

They exchanged further pleasantries and Ben made his farewell, regretting that he had to return to his office. He certainly regretted having to leave such a gorgeous creature. Still, he would see her again in a week or so.

8

30 MARCH, 2014

BEN WAS SITTING at the bar of the Ironclad Hotel in Marble Bar. He had driven up from Perth and arrived that day and it was now early evening. The bar was buzzing with the conversations of the locals and a few tourists come in out of the sun for a cold beer. Ben had taken a week off work to meet Doctor Michaels, Michelle, and she was supposed to be here in Marble bar this evening.

Marble bar was an old gold mining town, first settled during the gold rushes of the 1890's. With a population of only a few hundred the place still had the feel of a frontier town. And he was in the cultural and entertainment centre of the town, the Ironclad Hotel. The hotel, clad in corrugated iron, had received its name from American airmen who had been based at a nearby airstrip during the Second World War. Those servicemen had named the hotel the Ironclad as it was constructed entirely of sheets of corrugated iron on a wooden frame. Everybody who lived in or visited the town had at least one drink in the Ironclad, most had many more.

Ben heard the door to the bar creak open on its rusty hinges and turned to see who had arrived. Michelle, dressed in boots, tight jeans and a pale blue shirt stood in the doorway scanning the crowd. She saw Ben and smiled, then walked briskly across the wooden floor.

"Mr Wilde, good to see you", she breathed in her sexy voice, "not been waiting too long I hope?".

"No, I just got here", lied Ben, "And please call me Ben".

By this time Michelle had attracted the attention of most of the men in the bar. Most were working men who had come in from the mines or other jobs for a beer after work. Although none were drooling, Ben could see that several were close. He hoped that he was not going to have to fight to protect Michelles honour. But if that was the way it went, then that is what he would do.

Ben stood from his stool and grasping Michelle gently by the arm guided her into the less busy lounge to the left of the bar. He thought that the further he could get her from the sex-starved locals the better.

"A bit quieter in here", he said, "We can talk and make our plans for the expedition".

They sat on plastic chairs at a small, round plastic table.

"Can I get you a drink?", asked Ben.

"Yes, a lemon, lime and bitters please", replied Michelle.

Ben walked back to the bar, noticing as he did that several of the ragged working men were eying him enviously. At the bar he ordered Michelles drink and another beer for himself. Returning to the table he sat down opposite Michelle and surreptitiously examined her. As far as he could see, she was perfect. And unmarried. No wonder the other blokes were jealous!

"I am ready to go tomorrow morning", said Michelle, "I have camping gear in my vehicle out front".

"Good, tomorrow it is", said Ben, "Cheers!', raising his glass.

Having finished their drinks both Ben and Michelle retired to their rooms to clean up for dinner. Ben had a quick shower and threw on a clean pair of jeans and a collared shirt that he had bought bush especially for the occasion. Michelle turned up in the restaurant in a clean pair of jeans and a white blouse.

Together Ben and Michelle had a delightful evening getting to know each other over a pleasant dinner in the hotels dining room. Although they were a long way from the coast Ben chose the fish with a light salad whilst Michelle had only a salad. She however seemed to be content with such a light meal.

Ben was surprised to hear that Michelle was a Western Australian, born and bred, like himself. From high school she had won a scholarship to the University of Western Australia where she had studied, appropriately, archaeology. In fact she had been at the university at the same time as Ben had, although he could not remember ever seeing her. And with a face and body like hers he surely would have remembered! Ben had spent the evening glued to his chair entranced by this lovely and intelligent woman. She was everything that he had ever imagined in the perfect woman and then some. And she was so self effacing, apparently unaware of her beauty or intelligence. Or rather, she knew that she was intelligent but chose to make light of it.

At about ten pm, both tired from the long drive, they had said good night and each retired to their rooms at the rear of the hotel.

The following morning, on waking, showering and leaving his small room at the rear of the hotel, Ben found Michelle in the dining room. She was tucking into fruit and some toast as Steve sat down at the table. The elderly waitress, having seen him enter, waited patiently at his elbow.

"Bacon and eggs on toast", said Ben to the waitress, "And a large cup of coffee".

Ben and Michelle had dined in the same room, at the same table, the evening before. It had been a pleasant evening, chatting about their work and reporting funny stories they had each been involved in. Ben had found that Michelle was a good and entertaining conversationist with a wicked sense of humour. He had thoroughly enjoyed the evening and had been disappointed when it had ended. He was even more disappointed to find himself in his small hotel bed alone by himself. Ah well, such is life, he had thought. Tomorrow is another day.

Sitting at the small table Michelle was dressed in the same clothes she had been wearing the previous day when she had arrived at the hotel. She looked bright and alert, not bad considering it was six o'clock in the morning and the three glasses of white wine she had demolished the previous night.

Michelles bright green eyes locked on his as she said, "Morning Ben, ready to hit the road are we?"

"You bet", said Ben, "I'll just get some fuel aboard and we'll be on our way".

They both ate quietly and, finished with breakfast, Ben went in search of the hotel owner. He found the grizzled old man in the front bar.

"Morning Dave", he said, "Just want to settle the bill"

Dave pulled from under the bar the receipts for the previous night, and for the mornings breakfast, and after some quick maths said, "If you are paying for you and the lady the total is three hundred and thirty two fifty".

"Yep, I am paying for the lot", said Ben, dragging his wallet from his hip pocket. He gave Dave his credit card who ran it through the machine and handed Steve a receipt.

"Did you just pay my bill?", came Michelles voice from behind him, "I can pay my own way you know".

"That's OK Michelle. You can get it next time", replied Ben.

"OK then. Lets go", said Michelle, somewhat annoyed at Ben's presumption. She had a dark green tote bag over her shoulder and hanging from her hand was a tightly rolled swag.

"Please Dave", continued Michelle, "I will be leaving my car here for a few days. Can you keep an eye on it?"

"The white Hertz hire car? Sure, no problems. Might take it for a spin if I get bored", he cackled.

Ben saw that Michelle obviously knew Dave.

As if reading his mind she said, "Dave and I are old mates, aren't we Dave?".

"You bet", said Dave, "Miss Michaels is always up here poking around with the abo's"

"Aborigines Dave, not abo's", corrected Michelle.

"Sorry ma'am, Aborigines"

"OK, lets go", said Ben, grabbing hold of Michelles swag, "Do you have everything?"

"Yep, ready to roll", said Michelle.

Ben took her swag and exited the front door of the hotel. His landrover was parked at the curb. He threw the swag into the covered back of the vehicle and threw his own kitbag after it. Michelle gently placed her tote bag in the tray of the vehicle and climbed into the passenger seat.

Ben started the engine and a few minutes later stopped at the towns only service station, pulling up adjacent to one of the pumps. He pressed the fuel cap button, climbed down and stuck the diesel nozzle in the fuel tank. He filled the tank to the top, replaced the nozzle, and went into the small service building to pay for the fuel. It had taken a few minutes to fill as Bens vehicle had long range tanks that could cover nearly one thousand kilometers between fuel stops. A few minutes after returning to the four wheel drive they were exiting the town and driving onto the sealed NWR road.

They had driven for about an half an hour, chatting idly, when Michelle saw the sign for the Mandandanja community.

"Do you mind calling in here Ben?", she asked, "I need to talk about some things with their elders".

"Sure, no problem", said Ben, turning into the gravel road leading to the community.

Only one kilometer later Ben pulled up in front of what was obviously the community's administration building. Ben had been here a number of times previously and therefore knew the layout of the camp well.

In addition to the brick administration building the community comprised about twelve fibreboard houses, a community centre, a small brick school and a small fibreboard shop. As Ben bought the vehicle to a stop a tall black man with a heavily lined face and grey hair and beard walked out from the administration building. He walked over to the stopped landrover.

"G'day Jack, How are you today?", Ben welcomed the Aborigine.

"Good thank you Ben. And how are you?", said Jack, "And you Miss Michaels?", he added, spying Michelle in the passenger seat.

"Good thanks Jack", they chorused. Michelle obviously knew Jack as well as Ben did.

Jack Bilbulum was an elder of the Mandandanja community. All of the Aboriginal people of the community, and most of the whites in the region, respected Jack Bilbulum. His word was law. His knowledge of his country and the laws and customs of his people was encyclopedic. Although he was a gentle soul people knew not to cross him. Ben too respected Jack. If for nothing else, Ben respected the fact that Jack, an Aborigine, spoke the English language better than he did and knew more about the country that they were in than he ever would.

"What can I do for you this fine day?", queried Jack.

"Well Jack, I need to talk to you about some artifacts I found on my last trip. You OK with that?", said Michelle.

"Sure, come on in and I will make you a tea".

Ben and Michelle both clambered down from the vehicle and followed Jack to the front door of the administration building. Jack pushed the light wooden door open and ushered them inside. They were standing in a small reception area with an unmanned desk with a single telephone and no other equipment that Steve could see. Jack ushered them through a side door into a slightly larger room which appeared to be a kitchen with a square table with seats in the centre.

"Have a seat", said Jack, as he began pulling out drawers. Having finally located three teabags and three mugs he put them on the small side table. He filled the kettle from the tap and switched it on to boil. He chatted amiably as he waited for the kettle, mostly about the weather and the Eagles chances for the football season. The water having boiled he made three mugs of tea which he placed on the table. Some more delving into the drawers produced a tin of biscuits which he also placed on the table.

"Milk is in the fridge", said Jack, pointing to the antique looking refrigerator against one wall. Both Steve and Michelle declined but both added a couple of spoons of sugar from the small canister in the centre of the table.

"So what can I do for you?", Jack asked, "It is not often you see a geologist and archaeologist travelling together".

"Oh, Ben and I are on another project", said Michelle, "But I wanted to ask you about some artifacts I discovered on my last trip", she added whilst withdrawing some photographs from her shirt pocket. She placed the photographs on the table so Jack could see them. Some photographs showed aboriginal carvings on a shear rock face. Other photographs appeared to show carvings in a shallow cave.

"Mundiwindy", said Jack without hesitation, "About thirty kilometers north of here".

"You know this area?", asked Michelle, surprised, "And I thought I was the first living soul to lay eyes on these. At least since the original artist", indicating the photographs.

"I go there a few times a year", said Jack, "That is kangaroo dreaming country. It must be respected".

"Certainly Jack, I understand", answered Michelle, "No one knows of it but me. And you of course!".

"Please keep it that way Michelle", said Jack, "As I said, that is kangaroo dreaming country. All of the elders know it and the youngsters are taken there when they come of age. One of your photos there shows a group of kangaroos in a circle. That is the kangaroos doing the sacred kangaroo dance. I'm sorry, but I told a lie when I said only I know of it. It is also on the Register of Aboriginal Sites. No one ever goes up that way but I wanted to make sure it would be protected so I made sure it was on the register".

"Thanks Jack. That is interesting. I will have to do a bit more research on it".

"No problems Michelle. And now where are you off to with Ben?"

"Ben here has found an interesting area about thirty kilometers south of Blind Bluff", answered Michelle, "We're going out to take a look".

"Be very careful", said Jack, "That is bad country down there. For generations my people have been forbidden to go there".

"We will Jack. I just want to have a look. But why do you call it bad country?"

"It just is. And always has been. We do not question the dreaming", said Jack.

"So it's a dreamtime story that it is bad country?", asked Ben.

"Yes" said Jack, "Bad spirits inhabit that country and my people are forbidden from going there. My people go there and they die!'".

Ben naturally did not mention that one of his people, Banjo, had been there with no apparent ill effects as he did not want to upset Jack. Nonetheless, he was curious as to why the ancient Aborigines had declared that area out of bounds.

Having finished their tea, and bypassed the biscuits, Ben and Michelle stood to leave. They said their farewells to Jack and exiting the building climbed into the landrover. They were soon back on the main road and heading east.

At the turnoff to Blind Bluff Ben took a right and they were soon bouncing over the rough track. They passed Blind Bluff and about three kilometers later Ben stood on the brakes and bought the vehicle to a halt.

"See that knoll over there", said Ben, pointing to a steep hill about one kilometer to their right, "I found some paintings there the last time I was here that I thought you might want to have a look at", "Unless of course you've already seen them", he added hastily.

"No, I did not know there was anything down here", replied Michelle, "I'd love to have a look".

Pleased, Ben turned the landrover off the rough track and drove across country. The spinifex clumps constantly jolted the vehicle but they made it to the foot of the knoll in about fifteen minutes following the tracks Ben had made two weeks previously.

Ben pointed up the slope to where a dark opening in the rock yawned. "There's a cave up there. The paintings are inside".

They both climbed from the vehicle and commenced the hike up the steep hill. Arriving at the mouth of the cave they both came to a halt. The cave was about three meters across and two meters tall, carved into the solid rock. Although the interior was black Michelle could sense that it did not go far into the hill. Stepping forward the light improved and she could see that she was right. The cave was no more than a shallow scrape into the hill side with the back wall visible less than two meters away. She stepped into the cave and crouched down.

Imprinted on the back wall of the cave were numerous primitive drawings painted with ochre. She could see stylized kangaroos, emus, turtles and men, all painted in the characteristic Aboriginal x-ray style. In each painting it appeared as though the artist had been looking at the insides of the animal, or man. What appeared to be bones and internal organs graced each of the drawings. Most had been painted with white and red ochre with the occasional splash of yellow. To the right were a number of handprints outlined in red ochre. These handprints were produced with the simple expedient of the artist filling his mouth with ochre paste and spraying it onto his hand positioned in front of the wall.

Michelle had bought her camera from the vehicle and with a flash took a number of photographs of the paintings.

"I told Jack about these", said Ben, "Although he already knew about them".

Michelle nodded in acceptance.

"Thank you so much for bringing me here Ben", said Michelle, "You have already made this trip worthwhile. These paintings are marvellous".

"I wonder why Jack had not told me about these paintings?", she mused.

"Old Jack won't tell anyone anything they don't need to know", laughed Ben, "He likes to keep his peoples business private".

"Oh!, look at that", said Michelle suddenly, pointing to the bottom right of the rock face.

Ben followed the direction she was pointing and saw something that he had not seen before. It appeared to be a drawing of two flat roofed houses, each forming a square, and each with a single doorway but no windows. However, instead of being painted in ochre this drawing had been carved into the rock. Above the carved squares were four carved concentric circles.

"I have never seen anything like that before", said Michelle, "I wonder what it means? Oh, I know the concentric circles mean resting place or shelter, but I have no idea what the square carving is. It is most unusual as the aborigines seldom drew or carved straight lines."

Ben was also nonplussed. He had seen many aboriginal paintings and carvings but he had never seen anything like this. He simply shrugged to Michelle to indicate his own confusion. Michelle took another photograph of the unusual carving.

Having seen enough they turned from the rock face and walked back down the hill. Michelle did not bother to take a GPS coordinate of the site as she knew its approximate location and also knew that she would be able to find the distinctive knoll on an aerial photograph or satellite image.

Nearing the base of the hill Michelle tripped on a jagged piece of rock and would have acquired scars had not Ben's arms shot out to hold her. Holding onto each other they looked briefly in each other's eyes before breaking apart. Michelle muttered her thanks with a small, winsome smile.

Reaching the vehicle they climbed in and continued their journey back to the track and then south. Eventually arriving at the turnoff into the sand dunes Ben could see more of his own tracks from about two weeks previous. He warned Michelle that the journey might get more uncomfortable and set off along the old tracks. He finally came to a halt at the sand dune that barred further progress.

"We have to walk from here", he said, "It's only a few hundred meters".

They dismounted from the landrover and continued on foot. Ben took a shovel from the back of the landrover and carried it with him. He soon saw the broken piece of stone that he had discovered and discarded before. He picked it up and showed it to Michelle.

"Don't you think the edges of this look man made?", he asked.

"Possibly", said Michelle, "It is difficult to say".

Ben dropped the piece of stone and they continued on. Before he knew it they were standing on top of the wall. The hole that he and his men had previously dug alongside the wall had mostly been refilled with the moving sand. The top of the doorway was however still visible.

"I'm going to try and clear some of the sand", he said, "Its fairly loose so shouldn't be too difficult".

Ben jumped down beside the old hole and commenced shoveling mounds of sand. He threw the sand as far as he could from the hole to avoid it falling back in. He dug and dug and, although he didn't appear to be getting anywhere, persisted. It was a hot day and sweat was soon pouring down his back and over his face. He removed his shirt and threw it up onto the sand dune.

Michelle had taken a seat in the soft sand of the dune. She was fascinated with Ben's rippling muscles as he continued to dig, deeper and deeper. She might in other circumstances have been bored but was fascinated by the desert country and by the site of a handsome and fit man toiling like a navvy.

Ben dug for almost two hours, occasionally exchanging comments with Michelle and also taking regular stops for a rest and a drink. Eventually he had cleared a hole two meters deep and about three meters long. The bottom of the hole terminated in what appeared to be brown clay. In addition to revealing the full extent of the doorway he had also revealed one end of the wall. This end terminated in a perfect square, turning at right angles to head back into the opposite sand dune.

Throwing the shovel aside and breathing heavily he said to Michelle, "This is definitely a man made wall with a man made door. Can you explain how it got here?"

"No I can't Ben. But look on either side of the door".

Ben looked and saw something that he hadn't seen when he had been busy digging. Carved into the soft sandstone either side of the door was a series of concentric circles in a vertical line reaching from the floor to the top of the wall. The circles were finely crafted and definitely the work of a human hand.

"I don't know what they mean here", said Michelle, "But in aboriginal paintings and carvings concentric circles denote either a resting or camping place".

Ben thought that that was appropriate. It looked as though this had been, at one time, a camping place. But surely not an aboriginal camp. Aboriginals were a primitive people not capable of building like this. Were they?

"Now that you have had your exercise I think we should look around a bit", said Michelle.

Ben agreed. Both set off walking along the valley between the dunes. Having found nothing more they retreated to the wall.

"Lets have a look over the top of the dune", said Michelle, already clambering up the slope. They reached the top and then did a controlled fall to a new valley on the other side. This depression was also confined between two dunes and Ben could see nothing of interest. They walked about one hundred meters in both directions but saw nothing but sand. They clambered back over the dune and again stood on top of the wall. Michelle began climbing the opposite dune and Ben followed.

The third inter-dune valley was much the same as the first two. However, about twenty meters to the south Ben could see something projecting from the dune wall. On getting closer he could see that it was a block of sandstone with three edges meeting at a perfect right angle. Although it projected less than half of a meter from the sand Steve could see that it had been crafted by hand. It was a part of the same mystery.

He pointed out the block to Michelle who crouched to examine it closely. She then turned away and scrambled up the sand dune to the top where she stood and did an ungainly pirouette. She thrust her hands into the air and screamed, "This is wonderful Ben. I don't understand it but there is definitely something marvelous here. We will solve this mystery!".

Ben scrambled up the sand dune to reach her but she had already disappeared down the other side. He caught up with her and they walked back towards the landrover side by side.

"I don't understand this", she said, walking briskly over the sand, "Europeans only reached Australia two hundred and thirty years ago, this area of Western Australia only one hundred and thirty years ago. There are no known records of Europeans building out here, other than the known station homesteads. No known civilizations were ever known to have voyaged to Australia before the Europeans. And if they had, and built a city, they would have built it on the coast and not over five hundred kilometers inland. The only people who have been here any length of time are the Aborigines. And they did not build stone buildings, at least none that we know of. This is truly a mystery which must be solved".

They talked further about what they had found as they walked to the vehicle. Upon reaching the landrover they had still made no conclusions. Michelle clambered into the passenger seat, Ben into the drivers.

As they drove back to Marble Bar they continued talking about the mysterious find. Finally Michelle said. "I don't know how but I am going to talk my bosses into doing an excavation out here but I am sure I can convince them. I mean, an unknown building in the middle of the desert – They will probably jump at the chance. And I am going to head it up if it kills me!".

Driving back to the main road over the Bumpy track Michelle suddenly sat up straight in her seat and cried, "The Aborigines knew about that place! They must have!".

"What do you mean Michelle? How do you know that they knew?"

"Remember those cave paintings you showed me earlier? That carving at the bottom seems to me like a drawing of your wall! Complete with the door!"

"If they know of it why do they call it 'bad country?'", asked Steve, "And why did they mark it as a resting place or shelter?".

"I don't think the modern Aborigines know about it", she said, "I think whoever did that carving knew of it. And he may have marked it as a shelter for those who lived there. And perhaps those people were not very nice to the Aborigines so they marked it as a bad place".

"Perhaps", said Ben, unconvinced, "But it still all seems very odd. You will just have to unravel it".

After a long drive with an almost continuous discussion of the possibilities, Ben dropped Michelle at the Ironclad Hotel and headed back towards Perth.

9

10 APRIL, 2014

Back in the saddle again, thought Ben. He was again sitting in the bar of the Ironclad Hotel in Marble Bar having a beer. Mick and Ibrahim were also sitting at the bar at either side also drinking beers. Ten days after arriving back in Perth from the trip with Michelle he was back in the country he loved. They had left Perth to drive north two days ago, arriving in the small outback town only this afternoon.

Ben and the boys were awaiting the arrival of the crew from Global Geophysics. Guy had promised him that they would be in town today but they still had not arrived. They had been there for almost two hours but had been drinking mostly squashes. Ben did not want to be drunk when the geophysicists arrived. They had changed to beers in only the last half hour.

"G'day Ben", boomed a voice from the main door to the pub. "Sorry we're a bit late"

Steve turned on his stool to see a large bear of a man at the door. It was Nigel Mackie, Global's chief geophysicist.

"Nigel mate, good to see you", said Ben over the noise of the bar, "Come and take the weight off and I'll buy you a beer".

"Cheers mate. I could certainly use one. It's been a long, hot drive from Port Hedland".

Nigel stomped over to the bar followed by two other men who he introduced as John and Alan, his assistants. They pulled up stools so all six men were in a line along the bar, Ben and Nigel in the middle. Ben ordered six beers from the bartender, he and his men having just finished theirs. A frothing schooner of beer was placed in front of each man.

"Cheers mate", repeated Nigel, raising his glass. His two offsiders added their own cheers.

"We're heading out tomorrow if that's OK with you blokes", said Ben to Nigel. "But tonight we're all staying here".

Steve had booked rooms at the back of the pub for both his and Nigel's crew.

"Sounds good Ben. We'll be ready to go", boomed Nigel.

The six men finished their beers and, Nigel having ordered another six, retreated to the dining room behind the bar. They sat together around a large circular table and perused the menu. All of them ordered steak, chips and salad which was soon placed in front of them. All of them tucked in as though they had not eaten in a month. Finishing off the last of his chips Ben spoke up, "We'll drive out tomorrow but we've got to call in at the Aboriginal community on the way to pick up another of my blokes".

"No worries mate. We've got plenty of time", said Nigel.

Having finished their meals the men returned to the bar where they took up their original stools. New beers were ordered and the men were all soon chatting amiably. Mick and Ibrahim had their heads together no doubt plotting some mischief, Ben thought. Still, it was good to see that they were getting on so well. Ibrahim did not even complain about Mick calling him 'Ib' anymore.

Another couple of beers and they had all had enough. They all finally left their stools and went out the pubs back door to their rooms. After a round of semi-drunken 'goodnights' they retired to their rooms and all were soon sound asleep.

The following morning all six men had breakfast in the dining room. They then returned to their rooms to get their kit before jumping aboard their vehicles. Ben and Mick had the same cruiser that they had the previous trip and Ibrahim had his cruiser. The three Global Geophysics men all squeezed into the front of their landcruiser. Seeing their discomfort Ibrahim yelled out. "Men, I have got this vehicle to myself. Why don't one of you drive with me".

Obviously happy with comfier travelling arrangements, John scrambled down from the Global Geophysics landcruiser and into the passenger seat of Ibrahims cruiser. The three vehicles were soon cruising out of town and down the highway to the east.

Fifty kilometers out of Marble Bar Ben pulled his lead vehicle onto a gravel side road adjoining the highway to the south. The other vehicles followed. The three vehicles travelled only one kilometer down the side road before entering the Aboriginal community of Mandandanja.

Once again, as Ben pulled up in front of the administration building, Jack walked out the front door. Jack had heard the vehicles approaching and slow as they turned into the community. He walked over to Bens stopped cruiser and leant into the window.

"I seem to be seeing a lot of you lately Ben. How are you", Jack said.

"Good thanks Jack", said Ben, "We're here to pick up Banjo if he's ready to go"

"Yes, here he comes now", said Jack, indicating the form of Banjo scurrying across from one of the houses with his kit bag over his shoulder and his swag dangling from one hand. As well as being an elder of the tribe, Jack was also Banjo's uncle.

"G'day Banjo, ready to go?", called Ben.

"Sure thing Ben", replied Banjo, hoisting his kitbag and swag onto the back of Ibrahims vehicle. He stepped to the passenger door which was opened by John. Ben expected John to step down and go back to the Global Geophysics landcruiser. Banjo however shooed him back with his hands saying. "Stay with us mate. With those big bastards in the other vehicles you will be a lot more comfortable with a couple of skinny bastards like me and Ibrahim".

Ben was impressed. Banjo did not even know John but he was already looking out for his comfort. Indeed, Banjo was already introducing himself to his new friend.

"Bye Jack", said Ben, idly waving a hand in Jacks direction, "We'll have him back in about two weeks".

Jack said nothing, simply standing by and waving as the vehicles pulled away.

The three vehicles drove along the bitumen NWR road to the east. It was a long trip out from Marble Bar. Ben and Mick regaled each other with stories of their time back in the big smoke. Whilst Ben had been working and exploring with Michelle, Mick had been on leave with most of his time to himself. From what Ben could gather he had managed to get himself into a bit of mischief, including bedding the girlfriend of another man. However, Steve could see no new scars so figured that it had all worked out OK.

Reaching the track turnoff to Blind Bluff, which he had marked with some yellow flagging tape, Ben turned right. The other vehicles followed. Bumping over the rough track they reached Blind Bluff by lunch time. Mick pulled the cruiser into the shade of the old gum tree and switched off the motor. The other two vehicles pulled in behind. Everyone climbed down from the vehicles and gathered around Ben.

"Lunch boss?", asked Mick.

"Lunch", replied Ben.

Banjo and Ibrahim pulled the catering chest off their vehicle and placed it on the ground. Ibrahim then dug a small hole in the ground into which Banjo threw a couple of handfuls of dry grass and twigs. Mick was collecting broken branches fallen from the tree. In no time they had a small fire blazing onto which Banjo placed a billy full of water. Ibrahim rooted around in the car fridge and emerged with some cheese, cold meats and tomatoes. From the freezer on the back of his vehicle he also pulled a loaf of bread. These he placed on the bonnet of his cruiser along with a sharp knife and four tin mugs. John fetched another three mugs from the Global vehicle.

A small flock of white cockatoos had settled in the branches of the old gum tree. One of the cockatoos, taking the opportunity presented, relieved itself, a small white blob speeding towards the earth. The cockatoos aim was true. Mick was still scavenging for wood beneath the tree and the blob hit his hat in the top middle. Banjo, the only one who had seen what had happened, burst out laughing. Mick, sensing that Banjo was laughing at him but unaware he had been used for target practice demanded "What are you laughing at Banjo. Is me collecting wood funny?". The other men stood around looking dumbfounded.

Banjo laughed louder. "Check out the top of your hat mate", he called.

Mick whipped off his hat and looked at the top. "You filthy bastards!", he yelled, looking upwards at the cockatoos. Seeing what had happened everyone else burst out laughing.

Mick grabbed a small stick from the ground and hurled it into the tree where it ricocheted off some branches, narrowly missing Mick as it returned to Earth.

The cockatoos, however, retained their perches, unperturbed by Micks histrionics.

"Bloody sods", said Mick, defeated, "How would they like it if I crapped on them?".

The men settled down and were soon drinking tea from their mugs. The Global men all added milk, the Major Minerals men all had their tea black. Each man also made himself a sandwich and set to munching contentedly.

After they had finished their lunch Ben said to Nigel. "Nigel mate, come with me and I'll show you where the survey is to be done".

"Mick, Ibrahim and Banjo, grab a few of those pegs and the crack hammer and come with us". The pegs were one meter long stakes each about two centimeters wide. These stakes were universally used for marking out survey areas. Ibrahim grabbed an armful of stakes as did Banjo and Mick picked up the crack hammer from the back of his vehicle. All seven men set off across the dry creek and up and over Blind Bluff. Arriving at the small copper outcrop Ben said to Mick "Bang a peg in here Mick". Mick took a peg from Ibrahim and banged it into the ground next to the copper showing.

Ben then paced out to where Banjo had previously found the small piece of copper.

"Bang another peg in here Mick", he said.

Mick took another peg from Ibrahim and seated it firmly into the ground.

Steve paced out another two hundred meters from that site past the furtherest copper occurrence that Banjo had discovered and had Mick set another peg there, in line with the first two. Returning to the copper outcrop he paced two hundred meters back the other direction over the low hills. He had Mick place another peg there, in line with the first three.

"OK Nigel", he said, "That line of pegs marks out roughly where I think the line of lode is. Do the survey over that and extend it for another three hundred meters in both directions. Can you figure out what to do from that?"

"No worries Ben. Leave it to us", answered Nigel, "Give us two days to do it just to make sure. And leave us a pile of those pegs if you would".

"And Nigel, from the way the shale dips I would say that if there is an orebody it would dip to the south. You might want to extend the survey further in that direction".

"Sure thing Ben", answered Nigel.

"OK Nigel. We have got some other jobs to do elsewhere. We'll leave you blokes to it but we'll be back here tonight to camp with you. Mick will also stay with you in case you need anything.".

Ben, Ibrahim and Banjo traipsed back over the bluff back towards the vehicles.

On reaching the vehicles the three men unloaded a tied bundle of stakes and placed them on the ground. They also lifted Micks kitbag and swag from Ben's cruiser and placed them in the shade of the tree. The men then climbed into the vehicle, Ben in the drivers seat, Ibrahim in the passenger and Banjo in the middle. Ben started and swung the vehicle around in a wide turn to follow the track back to the NWR road.

"We're going to have another look at the Bright Desert prospect", said Ben to his passengers, "I didn't have a very good look last time".

They reached the NWR highway, turned right and headed to the east. Some time later Ben saw the black rocks of the prospect and pulled into the side of the road. Looking over towards the small gossan outcrops he saw that the ground was relatively flat. He had also walked it a while back and new is was fairly free of bumps and stakes. He therefore decided to drive across country to the furtherest of the gossan outcrops to take up the hunt from there. He turned the vehicle to the left and took off at a crawl across the spinifex, arriving a short time later at the small outcrop of rock. He climbed down from the cruiser and was followed by Ibrahim and Banjo.

As Ben stood studying the outcrop he remembered the assay results he had got back from the laboratory. All four samples of the gossan that he had collected had assayed anomalous in zinc, copper, silver and lead. In fact one sample had contained nearly two percent zinc and another had contained just under one percent copper and still another had assayed eighty-two grams per ton of silver. It was indeed a true gossan probably capping a base metal sulphide deposit. Ben was very excited by the find.

"I want to see if this line of gossan extends any further that way", Ben addressed Ibrahim and Banjo, gesturing towards the large sand dune. "So I'm going for a walk. You blokes can come if you want".

"Sure thing", said Banjo' "We're with you".

The three of them set off towards the dune.

"Keep an eye open for black rocks", Ben told Banjo. He addressed Banjo specifically as he had by far the best eyes. He knew that Ibrahim would also be keeping his eyes open.

They had walked about one hundred meters when Banjo piped up, "Got one Ben", he said pointing about five meters to his left. Ben walked over to see what he had found. Where Banjo had pointed he saw a jagged black rock about fifteen centimeters across sticking out of the soil. He levered it out of its resting place with his pick and held it up to his eyes. He saw immediately that it was almost identical to the gossan in the outcrops.

"Well done Banjo", he said, "She's still going then". Ben placed the rock in his backpack, intending to log it later.

They continued walking until Ben heard some dull thumps. Those sound like rifle shots, he thought. Perhaps someone was shooting kangaroos. Still, they continued on until they reached the base of the thirty meter high sand dune. The rifle shots, which were almost continuous, sounded louder.

"OK guys, lets go over the top", he said, "But keep your heads down. It sounds as though someone is shooting roos and I don't want either of you getting your heads blown off".

They scrambled to the top of the dune and, mindful of the rifle shots, flattened themselves at the top with only their heads showing above. Looking down into a valley between sand dunes Ben saw seven men, all lying prone and aiming and shooting rifles at targets further up the swale. He saw that the targets were cutouts in the shape of men. There were four four wheel drives parked near the men.

"I don't like the look of this", he said to Ibrahim and Banjo beside him, "I think we'll retreat". He had no reason to believe that what he was seeing was suspicious but the sight of so many armed men made him nervous.

Ben suddenly heard a shout from one of the men below him. They had been seen. Several of the men began yelling at each other in a language that he could not understand. One of them yelled, in English, "You up there, come down here!".

"Lets go guys. I really don't like this", whispered Ben, pulling his head below the top of the dune. At that instant Ben heard several loud cracks and saw sand fountain up from where his head had just been.

"They're fucking shooting at us! Run!", Ben yelled.

The men scrambled down the dune and began running back towards their cruiser. As they ran Ben heard a roaring sound and turned his head in time to see one of the strangers four wheel drives crest a low point in the sand dune and come hurtling towards them.

"Run!', he yelled, "Get back to the car".

But it was too late. The four wheel drive had already cut them off and three men piled out, all carrying rifles. Two of the men went down on one knee, the third remained standing. All pointed their rifles towards the now cowering men. Ben, Ibrahim and Banjo came to a halt.

"Put your hands in the air and get down on your bellies in the dirt", bellowed the standing man.

Ben could see that it was hopeless. He raised his hands above his head and got down on his knees and fell forward into the dirt. Ibrahim and Banjo followed suit.

The three men walked towards them, all keeping their guns leveled at the prone figures. They soon had them surrounded in a loose circle. Ben saw that one of the men carried a length of rope. He pulled a wicked looking knife from his belt and cut the rope into three lengths. While two of the men kept their guns trained on them, the rope man quickly went between them tying their wrists behind their backs.

"On your feet", said the leader, a short man with a thick black beard. "Walk back towards our firing range. Give trouble and you die".

Not knowing what this was about but feeling it prudent to comply, Ben struggled back to his feet, followed by Ibrahim and Banjo. They walked back the way they had come and struggled up the sand dune. It was more difficult with their hands tied. They almost fell down the far side before regaining their balance and continuing walking towards the rest of the men and their vehicles.

The vehicle that the men had used to pursue them crested the low point in the sand dune to their right.

"In the back", demanded the leader, pointing at one of the parked tray back vehicles.

"We can't like this", said Ben reasonably, turning to show his tied hands.

"You men," barked the leader to two of the others, "Throw them in the back. Tariq and Mustapha, you ride with them. If they try to escape, kill them".

Tariq and Mustapha climbed onto the tray back and sat with their backs against the cab. Two of the other men grabbed Ibrahim by his feet and arms and swung him onto the tray. They repeated the move with Ben and then Banjo. Ben, Ibrahim and Banjo were left lying on their sides on the tray, their hands bound securely behind them. One of the men climbed into the drivers seat while the leader climbed into the passenger seat. The vehicle roared to life and the driver steered down the dirt track heading to the south. Three other vehicles with the rest of the men followed behind. A few minutes later they bumped over the sealed NWR road and continued following the sand track. As they continued on Ben could see between the two guards that the leader, in the cabin, was talking on what appeared to be a hand held radio. Ten minutes later they stopped in front of the Bright Downs homestead. Their driver and the leader stepped down as did the men in the other vehicles. All of the men, with the exception of the leader, were armed with AK47 rifles either carried in one hand or slung over their shoulders. Their two guards also jumped down from the tray, keeping their rifles leveled at the captives.

Ben, Ibrahim and Banjo struggled to their feet, hampered by their bound hands. As they did so the man Ben had spoken to a few weeks before appeared in the house doorway and stopped on the verandah.

"Well, Mr Wilde was it not? So nice of you to join us", he said, an evil smile creasing his face. "Get down from the vehicle".

One of the armed men was standing at the rear of the tray. Ben pivoted on one leg and lashed out with the other. As he had hoped his boot connected with the centre of the armed mans face. He dropped as though shot, blood from his busted nose spraying into the air. Ben was also pleased to see several teeth fly from his mouth. Before he could press his advantage another of the armed man had used his rifle to sweep his feet from under him. Ben dropped to the tray and over the edge onto the sand. Without his hands to cushion the fall Ben's head hit the sand with a sickening thump. He was at first groggy but came to his senses as the man on the verandah spoke again.

"Try that again and you will die. Right here, right now!", he barked.

Ibrahim and Banjo obediently jumped to the ground to stand beside Ben.

The remaining men formed a circle around the three captives with all of the rifles pointing inwards.

"Sameer", he continued, addressing the man Ben had taken to be the leader, "They will be missed if we do not stage a diversion. Take their vehicle and crash it about twenty kilometers back along the main road. Make it appear as though it was an accident. Take the black boy, kill him, and place him in the wreck. Remember, no bullets – It must appear to be an accident. Take the little black bastard away and make sure that it looks convincing!".

"No!", yelled Ben, "Why are you going to kill Banjo. He has done nothing!"

"Two dazed men walking into the desert to die after a car crash might be believed", said Ashad with a smirk, "Three? I do not think so".

"Take me then!", yelled Ben, not quite believing his own bravery.

"I think not Mr Wilde", said Ashad, "You, I need to question".

Two of the armed men grabbed Banjo by his arms and hustled him into the front seat of one of the four wheel drives. One man climbed into the drivers seat, another into the passenger, effectively imprisoning Banjo between them. The third man jumped into the back of the tray back four wheel drive.

"You sick bastard!", cursed Ben, struggling against two men who had seized his arms, "Let him go and we will do what you want!".

"But what makes you think I want you to do anything, Mr Wilde?", asked Ashad, "Bring them into the back empty bedroom", he commanded his men.

Ashad turned and re-entered the house unwillingly followed by Ben and Ibrahim, each followed by two men with aimed rifles. They were forced down a short hallway and to the right into a small room. The room had seen better days. The yellow paint was faded and the carpet had been torn up leaving uneven tufts at the edges poking out from beneath the skirting. The only furniture was a steel bed with a torn and stained mattress. A small window at the back of the room looked out on sand, and more sand.

"Sit", ordered Ashad, gesturing to the bed.

Ben and Ibrahim sat.

"My name is Ashad, Mr Ashad to you", Ashad began, "This will be your prison until I decide how to kill you", he added reasonably. "Untie them", he ordered one of the armed men.

"When I have from you everything I need then we will deposit your bodies in the bush where you will be found by the searchers.

Such a pity to be involved in a car accident and then to wander in the desert until you die", said Ashad with a smile.

The man who had received the order stepped across towards Ben taking a double edged knife from his belt. He gestured for Ben to turn around and then sliced through the rope in one quick movement. He did the same for Ibrahim and then all four armed men left the room, but stayed outside in the corridor, their guns pointed into the room.

"Mr Wilde", Ashad continued, "Why were you spying on my men?".

"We weren't spying", groaned Ben, "We were looking for rocks. I explained to you before that I am a geologist".

"I do not believe you", said Ashad, "First you turn up here uninvited and then you are caught some weeks later spying. Are you ASIO? Perhaps even CIA?".

ASIO, standing for Australian Security Intelligence Organisation, was Australia's equivalent of the American FBI. The CIA of course was Americas intelligence arm.

"What, you think I am a spy?", gasped Ben, "I told you that I am a geologist!".

"If that is how you are going to be, so be it", murmured Ashad, "We will see how you hold up under interrogation. Your people are very good at torturing my people at Guantanamo Bay. We are also very good at torture. I will leave you to think on that for a while".

With that Ashad turned and exited the room, closing the door behind himself. Both Ben and Ibrahim could hear him issuing instructions on the other side but in a language that Ben could not understand. Ibrahim, however, could understand. Ashad was talking in Arabic, the language that Ibrahim had been raised with. Ashad spoke for a few minutes and then there was only the sound of steps retreating away from the door.

"What the hell is going on?", Ben asked Ibrahim, "Are these arseholes terrorists or something?"

"Yes, I do believe that they are", replied Ibrahim.

"Well, we better get out of here. See if we can help Banjo", said Ben.

"I think that will be difficult", replied Ibrahim, "They have a guard at the door and another outside that window", gesturing to the small pane of glass.

"How do you know?", queried Ben incredulously.

"You forget that I speak Arabic", explained Ibrahim, "I could hear what Mr Ashad was saying outside the door".

"Oh shit!", exclaimed Ben as he stood up. "Look, we'd better get some rest while we figure out what to do. You take the bed first".

Ibrahim protested at denying Ben the bed but after some convincing laid down and was, surprisingly, soon asleep. Ben lay on his back on the floor staring up at the scabrous ceiling.

10
10 APRIL, 2014

THE THREE MEN who had been tasked with creating a believable accident had a problem. They had driven back to where the Major Minerals cruiser had been abandoned and found the keys still in the ignition. That part was OK. But how were they going to stage a road accident without injuring or killing themselves? It was Tariq who came up with the answer.

They first drove the cruiser to the side of the bitumen road where they shut it down. Using some rope they then tied the steering wheel to the door handles so the wheels were aimed straight and would not deviate. They then reversed their own vehicle up to the front of the captured vehicle and tied a thick rope between the two. Their vehicle was going to tow the other vehicle.

Banjo in the meantime had been left tied in the gunmens vehicle. One of the men roughly pulled him out and dropped him face down onto the unyielding tarmac. Banjo turned his head to see what they were doing only to see the butt end of a rifle descending rapidly towards his head. With not enough time to avoid the blow the butt cracked into the front of his skull. Banjo blacked out instantly.

"Is he dead?", asked one of the men.

"I don't know", said the man who had wielded the rifle, "But he will be after the accident", putting the emphasis on the last word. All of the men smiled.

Hoisting Banjos inert body from the ground they placed him in the cab of the Major Minerals cruiser, on the passenger side. As he was unconscious, and likely to stay that way for some time, they released his binds. It would not do to have an accident victim found with his hands bound! One of the men pushed his limp body across so it was in the centre of the bench seat. Banjo was left sitting upright, his head lolling onto the drivers side headrest.

The three gunmen climbed into their vehicle, one in the front driving and the other two in the rear tray. The driver started the motor and the four wheel drive pulled away, the rope to the rear growing taught. Seeing that the rope was holding he gradually increased speed. He drove steadily for about twenty kilometers to the west until he could see a gentle bend in the road in the distance. He stopped the vehicle, and leaving the engine running, climbed out.

"Tariq", he said, "We will do it at that bend up ahead. Be ready".

Tariq, sitting in the tray, nodded as the driver resumed his seat. The driver slowly pulled away and gradually gained speed until they were travelling at almost 120 kilometers per hour. Tariqs partner in the tray watched the bend approach and when they were just starting to enter it he turned and yelled at Tariq, "Now!". Tariq was lying flat out in the tray, the top part of his body protruding over the back of the vehicle. In his hand he held a very sharp machete and with the command of 'Now!' he swung it down with all of his might. The machete struck the towing rope and although several strands parted the rope did not break. Without pausing Tariq raised his arm and chopped down again. This time the rope parted cleanly and their vehicle began to pull away. The Major Minerals cruiser, no longer with the benefit of the tow, began to slow. However, it was still doing in excess of 100 kilometers per hour when it left the road. For a while it cruised serenely along until it hit a drainage ditch. The front wheels immediately skewed to the left, despite the restraint on the steering wheel. The rear end of the vehicle slid around until they too hit the ditch. Having lost traction and now almost side on to the direction of travel the vehicle abruptly flipped, bouncing onto the roof, back onto the wheels and then back to the roof again. For a moment it teetered there until gravity took command and the vehicle flopped onto its side, the passenger window pointing into the air.

The men had stopped their vehicle about five hundred meters down the road. They did a U-turn and drove back to the wreck being careful to park on the tarmac so they would not leave any tracks. Stepping out of their stopped vehicle they saw that they had done a good job. The cabin of the vehicle was intact but badly dented. The passenger window had blown out and the tray was skewed at an angle to the cabin. Camping equipment that had been in the tray was strewn around the crashed vehicle.

The three men walked over to the wrecked cruiser. Peering in the cracked windscreen they could see Banjos body lying hard up against the drivers window, which was itself resting on the ground. One of the men scrambled up the wreck and dropped into the cabin from the broken side window. He removed the ropes from around the steering wheel and accepted a ball-peen hammer which was handed to him by another of the men. With the hammer he hit the windscreen where the drivers and passengers heads would have hit had they been in the crashed vehicle. His efforts produced satisfyingly concentric fractures in the windscreen. Banjos head had already made such a pattern in the centre of the windscreen. One of the men outside then handed down to him a container half full of blood. The blood belonged to a kangaroo that they had shot and butchered earlier that day. Very carefully he splashed some of the blood onto each of the concentric fractures. Not too much but just enough to indicate serious head wounds. He straightened up, standing on Banjos body, and hoisted himself out of the cabin. One of the other men had detached the rope that had towed the car to its destruction.

Making sure that they had forgotten nothing they returned to their four wheel drive, got in and drove away, back to Bright Downs homestead. None of them had thought to see if Banjo actually was dead. He had been through a horrific crash and he looked to be dead. That was enough.

11

11 APRIL, 2014

Ben heard the door handle turn and he leapt to his feet. He had fallen asleep on the floor! The door opened to reveal three armed men, all with Kalashnikovs pointing inwards.

"You! With us!", barked the short man in the centre, pointing at Ben.

Ben shuffled to the door where he looked back at Ibrahim, who had also been awakened by the noise. Ben smiled weakly to be rewarded with a small smile from Ibrahim. "Back soon – I hope", he said grimly, and shuffled out with his guards. He was taken down the short hall to another, larger room where Ashad sat behind a rather worn timber desk.

"Mr Wilde", said Ashad in a friendly voice, "Have you decided to co-operate? Please sit down", gesturing to a rickety looking wooden chair.

Ben sat and one of the guards pulled his arms behind him. Before he knew what was happening his hands had expertly been tied at the back of the chair. He looked across the desk at the smiling face of the man who called himself Ashad. The scar in the shape of the numeral 7 was very prominent above his left eye. Ashad had received the scar when he was a boy of eight playing in an abandoned building in Baghdad. He had been playing alone because even then he had had no friends. He had tripped on a dislodged brick and his head had hit a piece of torn tin, creating a ragged tear. He had acquired the broken nose in the same fall.

On anyone else the scar would have just been a scar. On Ashad, the mark seemed to scream 'I am bad, I am evil, and I will hurt you!'. Ashad seemed to have a permanent smile fixed to his face but the smile never reached his eyes. Those eyes were dark orbs that showed absolutely no compassion.

"Co-operate how?", asked Ben in a nervous voice, "I am a geologist. I am not a spy. We were not spying on you. I know nothing other than that you are an arsehole!". His voice rising as his indignation momentarily overcame his caution and fear.

"Hit him", said Ashad in a bored tone.

The man standing to Ben's left stepped in front of him and, drawing back his arm, backhanded Steve across his face. The blow immediately drew blood from his nose and he suspected that his lip had been split.

"I know nothing!", he repeated.

"Hit him again".

This time the man to his right stepped in front and backhanded him across his face. Blood flew, a few speckles landing on the desk.

"Now, Mr Wilde, you are becoming boring. Have you told anyone else of what you have seen or suspect here?", said Ashad.

"Go to hell, you prick!", roared Ben through his bloodied lips. He was not sure why he had not just answered the question but he suspected that he just did not want to give Ashad the satisfaction. He also suspected he would probably get a beating for it. He was right, he did get a beating. The beating lasted for almost an hour. Finally, bleeding from his nose, his lip and two cuts above his eyes, not to mention the numerous bruises to his body, the ropes binding him were cut away and he was lifted from the chair by two of the guards. He was dragged back to the back room, the door was opened, and he was thrown onto the floor of what had become his and Ibrahims cell. On hitting the floor he passed out.

Ben woke to feel gentle tapping on his cheeks and a far away voice repeating "Ben, are you with me? Ben, are you OK?". He opened his eyes and saw Ibrahim staring down at him.

"Jesus Ibrahim", he groaned, "What the hell happened"

"They beat you Ben. You have been unconscious for about two hours", replied Ibrahim.

Ben's eyes flicked to the window. It was dark outside. Ibrahim lifted a paper cup of water to his lips and Ben took a few tentative sips. He could tell from the lumpy surface beneath him that he was lying on the bed.

"You put me to bed?', he asked, "Thanks mum". He grinned even though it hurt.

"They have bought us some food", said Ibrahim, passing him a plate with some muck on it.

Ibrahim felt around on the floor and came up with a plastic spoon. Ben took a closer look at the plate. The mess appeared to be a mound of rice and what looked like a tinned stew. Knowing he had to eat to keep his energy up he took a small spoonful. It tasted terrible but it was better than nothing. Without thinking about it he finished the entire plate although the chewing hurt his battered mouth. As he was finishing the door was suddenly thrown open for the second time that day. Three armed guards stood there, the same three that had come to collect Ben.

"You!", one of them barked, pointing to Ibrahim.

Knowing it was pointless to argue Ibrahim got up from where he had been kneeling beside the bed. He walked over to the door, two of the men grabbing his arms. The last guard slammed the door as Ibrahim was led away.

Reaching Ashads study one of the men opened the door and the other two ushered Ibrahim to the chair that Ben had used earlier. Ibrahim could see splatters of blood on the arms of the chair and on the desk. One of the guards removed a short length of thin rope from his pocket and bound Ibrahim's arms behind the chair.

"I do not know your name", said Ashad from his chair behind the desk, "Please introduce yourself".

"My name is Ibrahim Allawi", answered Ibrahim in perfect Arabic, "What do you want from me?"

"You speak Arabic", said Ashad, obviously surprised.

"Yes, of course. I am Iraqi", said Ibrahim proudly.

"What is a son of the prophet doing with the infidels?", questioned Ashad.

"I had to come to Australia. You must know how bad things were in Baghdad", said Ibrahim, "And I needed to work".

Ibrahim had devised a plan that he thought might just work. It would depend upon the man sitting opposite him. For an hour he and Ashad talked. Ashad asked questions and Ibrahim replied with the answers that Ashad wanted to hear. But he stuck with the story that ben was a simple geologist. There was no violence. After the first quarter hour Ashad had dismissed the armed men from the room and untied Ibrahims hands. He even gambled by taking his pistol from his holster and laying it on the desk within Ibrahims reach, although it lay closer to him.

At the end of the hour Ashad sat deep in thought. The Iraqi seemed to be genuine in his hatred of the west. It was not his fault that through unforeseen circumstances he had been forced to come to this den of iniquity. He had come to Australia as had some of his men, as a refugee. Like him, Ibrahim was an Iraqi. He even knew people in Baghdad that Ashad had known. People he trusted. He knew the Koran and appeared to be a true son of the prophet. He could have taken my pistol and killed me but he did not. He was one man down and this man could take his place. There was no risk. He would be constantly surrounded by his men and could not escape. He made a decision.

"Ibrahim, would you like to join me and my men? We are

here on a task for Allah. You can help us and partake your share of the glory!".

"Certainly Sir. I would be honoured to join your fight. Instruct me and I will obey".

Ashad did not tell Ibrahim what their mission entailed. He would not tell him the plan until he had to know, until he was certain that he could be trusted. After all, none of his men yet knew what the plan was and they would not know until it was time. In the meantime he would train with the rest of the men. Having taken him into the fold he came around the desk and, lifting Ibrahim from the chair, embraced him and kissed him on both cheeks.

"Welcome Ibrahim. Welcome to the army of Allah".

Ibrahim had also convinced Ashad that Ben was indeed a geologist and their stumbling across the shooting range had been nothing more than an accident. Ashad did not care. It was too late to take back what had happened. And he could not let the man go to spread word of the terrorists at Bright Downs. He would enjoy torturing Wilde for a few more days and then he would kill him. In fact he might have Ibrahim kill him.

Ashad himself escorted Ibrahim from the house and showed him where he could sleep in one of the workers quarters. Ibrahim entered the small room and threw himself onto the lumpy mattress. What do I do now? he thought.

12

11 APRIL, 2014

MICK WAS WORRIED. He had been worried the previous night when Ben, Ibrahim and Banjo had not returned to Blind Bluff. He had slept only fitfully, coming fully awake anytime he heard the slightest noise, thinking that it was the boys returning to camp late. It was now early morning the following day and he and young John were travelling east on the NWR road, towards Ben's last known destination. They had left Blind Bluff at daybreak, determined to find the missing men. Micks friends.

Mick was driving the car at about 100 kilometers per hour and was just about to enter a gentle bend in the road.

"There, on the right!", yelled John.

Mick swiveled his head and saw it too. A crashed cruiser lying on its side on the barren red dirt about thirty meters off the road. Swags, water bottles and other equipment were scattered around the overturned vehicle. It had to be Ben's vehicle! He pulled to the side of the road and shut down the motor. Both he and John exited the vehicle swiftly and ran to the wrecked cruiser. At first Mick could see no one either in or around the vehicle. Then he saw a form lying up against the drivers window which itself was pressed into the dirt. He could tell instantly from the dark skin that it was Banjo. But where the hell were Ben and Ibrahim?

"Is he alive?", yelled John.

"I don't know. Give me a moment", yelled Mick.

He hoisted himself up the roof of the vehicle, now the side, and looked down at Banjo's still form. Hoisting himself up further he then lowered himself through the window, being careful to place his feet either side of Banjo's body. Bending down he felt Banjo's limp wrist for a pulse. Feeling nothing, he tried his neck, just above his collarbone. There he could feel a weak pulse. Weak, but consistent. Banjos head was covered in blood but Mick could see no obvious wound.

"He's alive!", yelled Mick, "Call the RFDS. The satphone is on the seat!".

RFDS was the Royal Flying Doctor service, Australia's aerial ambulance and remote medical care specialists.

John raced back to the cruiser and retrieved the satellite telephone. "I don't know the number", he yelled to Mick despairingly.

Mick threw the small notebook he carried in his shirt pocket out of the window above him.

"Last page!", he yelled, "Call the Marble Bar cops and they will put you through!"

John picked the notebook up off the dirt and shuffled through to the last page where he saw a list of telephone numbers. He found the number for the Marble Bar police station and called. The small Marble Bar station had only two police and no other staff. John discovered straight away that he was talking to a sergeant of police.

"We are about 280 kilometers east of Marble Bar on the NWR road", he told the sergeant, "We have found a car accident. There is one man badly hurt. Please send a doctor immediately", he continued excitedly.

"Calm down lad. We will contact the RFDS and they will send

a plane. They should be there in about an hour and a half. Make the casualty comfortable. We will be there in about two and a half hours", said the sergeant.

"The RFDS and cops are on the way", yelled John, "RFDS should be here in an hour and a half".

Mick was still standing on the drivers window in the cabin. John ran back to the wreck and hoisted his head over to look down.

"I know we shouldn't move him", said Mick, "but at least we can make it easier to get him out when we have to"

And with that he started to kick at the windscreen. Already weakened by the crash and by the ball-peen hammer, a few hard kicks saw the windscreen crack and then pop out of its frame to fall onto the dirt.

"That's better", said Mick, hunching down and climbing through the hole where the windscreen had been. He ran over to his vehicle and returned a few moments later with an old sweatshirt that had been stashed behind the seat. Mindful of further hurting Banjo he balled up the sweatshirt and gently stuffed it under his head to act as a pillow. Standing up again he looked around. Where the hell are Steve and Ibrahim, he thought. Surely they can't have gone too far. Perhaps they were heading towards Bright Downs homestead for help?

"You stay here with Banjo, John. I'm going to see if Steve and Ibrahim are walking towards Bright Downs", he said.

Mick ran over to the cruiser and leapt behind the wheel. He was soon cruising down the highway at about 120 kilometers per hour, his eyes scanning left and right for two men walking through the desert. Reaching the Bright Downs turnoff he turned in and immediately saw a vehicle heading towards him. He pulled to the left of the road as the other pulled to the right and they were soon both stationary, drivers window to drivers window. Mick could see that it was the station owner. With both windows already down they could easily talk to each other.

"G'day mate', Mick said, "There's been an accident down the road and we're missing two men. Have you seen them?".

"Oh, I am sorry to hear that. No, there has been nobody here", replied Ashad.

Bugger, thought Mick. So they did not come this way. So which way did they go?

"Thanks", he said, still thinking furiously, "Sorry to trouble you".

"Do not worry", said Ashad, "We will watch out for your friends".

Mick mumbled, reversed the vehicle, did a three point turn, and was soon heading back the way he had come. He turned left onto the highway and within ten minutes he was back at the scene of the accident. For his part Ashad turned right onto the highway and went only a few kilometers before turning left onto the track to the shooting range.

Arriving at the scene of the accident Mick pulled the cruiser to the side of the road and dismounted. Nothing had changed other than John squatting in the poor shade of a stunted shrub. Banjo still lay unconscious in the wreck but fortunately was shaded from the worst of the sun.

"How did you go Mick? Find anything", asked John.

"No. Not a thing. I spoke to the station manager and he's seen nothing".

Mick walked over to the wreck and looked around for tracks. There were a number of barely visible boot prints in the hard red clay around the wreck, some of which were undoubtedly his and Johns. He scouted out from the wreck for further tracks but could see none on the baked hard red earth.

"John", he said, "I'm going to have a wander around to see if I can discover where they went. You stay here".

Mick walked ever widening circles around the wreck but could see no sign of any tracks. As he walked he continuously cried out "Ben! Ibrahim! Cooee!" in the forlorn hope that they might be lying nearby stunned and his calls would alert them. Of course he heard nothing in reply.

Well, they didn't go to Bright Downs, he thought. And they weren't heading towards Blind Bluff or we would have seen them. He returned to the wreck. Looking again at the windscreen he could see three blood smeared impact points marring the glass. That's not like Ben, he thought. He always wears his seatbelt, even if we're only tooling down some track at five k. But he wouldn't have been flung forward to hit his head if he had been wearing a belt. He crouched down and looked into the interior of the cabin. Everything appeared to be normal, for a wreck. Then he noticed the gearstick which was in neutral. Odd, he thought. Maybe it sprang out of gear when they crashed? Giving up on the puzzle for the moment Mick went and sat beside John in the meager shade.

For over an hour they sat until Mick heard the drone of an engine coming from the west.

"Hear that", he said, "Must be the RFDS".

He and John both stood and stared towards the west. For a couple of minutes they could see nothing and then John caught the glint of sun off a wing.

"There she is Mick", he said, pointing.

Mick saw it too.

The plane flew over them at about five hundred meters, continuing towards the east. It then did a gentle turn until it was facing back the way it had come, and down the length of the road. As it approached it gradually lost altitude and Mick could see that it was preparing to land on the highway. The plane finally touched down with twin puffs of smoke from its rear wheels and taxied towards them. Pulling up on the road about twenty meters from them the motors began to wind down. A door opened in the belly behind the wing and three people jumped down the short distance to the road. Two of them reached inside the plane and pulled out a folded up trolley. They quickly unfolded it and were soon pushing it ahead of themselves. As they approached Mick could see that one was an older man with grey hair. He would be the doctor, Mick thought. The other two were younger, one a man and the other a woman. And his nurses, thought Mick.

The older man went straight to the wreck and squatting down peered through the removed windscreen. For a few minutes he felt around Banjo's neck and shoulders and finally stood.

"OK, put a neck brace on him and pull him out of there", he said to his two assistants, "Gently!"

The woman nurse reached beneath the trolley and came up with a plastic contraption that looked to Ben like a wide horses halter. Leaning into the wreck she carefully wrapped the halter around Banjos neck and buckled it at the back.

The male assistant then pulled the trolley to the front of the wreck and lowered it so it was less that half a meter off the ground. They then each grabbed one of Banjo's arms and carefully pulled him from the wreckage. Moving slowly they laid Banjo on the trolley and jacked it back to its full height. One then inspected the neck brace to ensure that it was properly fitted whilst the other, the woman, carefully strapped him to the trolley. Finished, they started pushing the trolley, with Banjo, towards the plane.

"He is in a bad way", said the doctor, "I don't think any bones are broken but he has nasty head injuries. If we have the fuel we will probably fly him straight to Perth. Thank you for your help gentlemen".

"That's OK doc", said Mick, "He's our mate".

The doctor nodded in acknowledgement and walked back to the plane. The nurses had already loaded Banjo aboard the plane and then themselves climbed aboard. The doctor pulled himself up into the doorway and also disappeared. The door was slammed shut and a short time later the propellers began to spin and were soon a blur. The plane did a tight turn and lined up on the road heading to the east. After a wait of a few moments it began to move, increasing speed as it sped down the road. The plane lifted off, the wheels were retracted and it commenced a gentle turn towards the south, towards Perth.

Left alone again in the desert silence neither Mick nor John felt like speaking. John went and sat in their cruiser while Mick sat under the shrub and brooded.

Another hour later and Mick could see a glint of light off glass or metal on the road in the distance to the west. The cops at last, he thought. Five minutes later a police landcruiser pulled up beside Micks cruiser. Two men stepped down. An older man wearing sergeants stripes and a younger man, obviously a lowly constable. The two men walked over to where Mick was sitting.

"RFDS come and gone I presume?", said the sergeant.

"Yeah, about an hour ago", said Mick, "They took Banjo, the injured man, but two of our mates are still missing". Mick quickly explained the situation. How many people had been travelling in the cruiser, who they were and where they were headed. He also explained that the accident had probably happened the previous afternoon. Finally, he told the sergeant that he had already checked the road to Bright Downs.

"It seems that they might have busted their heads on the windscreen", said the sergeant stooping and peering at the windscreen laid on the ground, "Perhaps they are dazed and wandering in the bush somewhere?

"They must be", said Mick, "They're certainly not here and nor are they on the road".

"OK, I'll organize a search party. We'll find them in no time. Can't have wandered far in this heat", offered the sergeant.

The sergeant wandered back to his vehicle and was soon on the two way radio. He called his office in Marble Bar temporarily manned by his wife, and also called the police and SES in the larger city of Port Hedland. The SES was the State Emergency Service, a group of volunteers sometimes called in by the police to assist in searches.

While he was waiting for the troops to arrive Mick decided he would continue the search himself. He walked over to his cruiser where John still sat.

"Fancy going for a drive?", asked Mick.

"Sure, where are we going?", replied John.

"I want to start the search so I thought we'd do a bit of a circuit", said Mick with grim determination.

John merely nodded and climbed into the cruisers passenger seat whilst Mick climbed into the drivers.

Mick started the motor and was soon cruising down the highway. Five kilometers out from the wreck as measured on the speedometer Mick turned at right angles off the highway and began bouncing across the dirt and spinifex. Bouncing along, and hoping he didn't stake a tire, Mick completed a circle of five kilometer radius out from the wreck, keeping a wary eye out for anything that looked unusual. Finding nothing. Returning to the wreck he went to see the sergeant.

"Sarge", he said, "I'm going to pick up my swag and other gear and should be back here in about two hours. I am going to camp here until we find them!"

Mick traipsed back to his cruiser and headed it to the west. When he arrived at Blind Bluff he told John to join his mates and help with the survey they were still doing. Then he remembered that he had better tell head office what had happened. He picked up the satellite telephone from the seat beside him and dialed the head office number from memory.

"Major Minerals, How may I help you?"

"Tiffany, Mick here. Can you put me through to Tim".

"Certainly Mick. Wait one".

A moments silence and a click and he was connected.

"Mick. What can I do for you?", asked Tim.

Mick quickly explained the situation to Tim who was horrified. He offered all of the support that the company could provide and asked to be contacted at any time. Mick muttered his thanks and after promising to call to relay developments, hung up.

Mick loaded his swag and a small box of food and cooking utensils onto his vehicle, climbed into the drivers seat, and left Blind Bluff camp.

Arriving back at the wreck site Mick pulled his cruiser into a clear patch adjacent to the main road. He noted that three other landcruisers had arrived in his absence. They would have to be men from the Telfer mine, come to lend assistance. However, the men were all clustered by the vehicles. No one seemed to be actually searching. Mick walked over to where the police sergeant was examining a map spread on the bonnet of his car.

"How's it going sarge?", he said, "How come those buggers over there aren't searching for them yet?".

"I have organized to commandeer all of the trail bikes in Marble Bar", said the sergeant wearily, "They will be much better to search with and should be here shortly. The blokes from Telfer are waiting for the bikes".

The sergeant was correct as half an hour later four trail bikes on the back of two landcruisers arrived at the site. Three of the Telfer men commandeered three of the bikes. Mick commandeered the fourth. For the rest of the day Mick did ever widening circuits on the bike out from the wreck site looking for any sign of his friends. The three other men on bikes did the same. By late afternoon two small aircraft had arrived from Port Hedland and were searching a forty kilometer square in a grid pattern. More vehicles also arrived from Port Hedland with additional police and SES volunteers. There were also several more trail bikes on the Port Hedland tray back four wheel drives.

A half hour after Mick had arrived back at the wreck site from his latest search Nigel and his boys turned up anxious to help with the search. They were happy to leave their job to try to find the missing men.

As the sun sank into the west in a flare of red and orange, Mick had to concede that he had done all that he could for the day. There was no point in trying to search at night. He returned to the wreck site, stood the bike on its stand, and sat despondently on the side of the road. He noted that the planes had also retired for the night, flying back to Marble Bar.

A large camp including a number of tents had been established at the site. Mick estimated that around thirty people had joined the search.

"Want a cup of tea love. Something to eat maybe?", came a feminine but elderly voice to his left.

Mick swiveled his head and saw an elderly lady complete in a floral print dress. She must have come out from Marble Bar to assist with the search.

"Thanks, a tea would be terrific", said Mick, "I'll get something to eat later". He could see that an impromptu barbecue was already underway near the tents. All of the searchers were gathered around the fire eating sausages in bread rolls and picking at salads. All were drinking water or soft drinks. A search party is no place for alcohol.

While the woman went in search of a cup of tea, Mick went in search of the police sergeant. He found him chatting to some SES volunteers near the barbecue.

"No sign of anything?", he asked, already knowing the answer.

"Not a trace. Not even any tracks that we can follow", said the sergeant, "We'll widen the search radius out to thirty kilometers tomorrow".

"Great", mumbled Mick as he walked away to complete one last task. About fifty meters out from the main camp he gathered all of the spinifex, shrubs and fallen wood that he could find. This he threw into a large pile. He continued his search for wood venturing out as far as three hundred meters from the pile. The rest of the wood he threw in a separate pile to one side. Finding a box of matches in the cruiser he lit the first pile and watched as the flames caught and then danced in the air. Flames were soon shooting up to two meters into the air. That should do it, he thought. He had lit a beacon fire that would be visible for miles. It would guide Ben and Ibrahim to him, if they saw it.

Mick got his swag from the cruiser and laid it out close to the beacon fire. He then walked over to the barbecue where he was greeted by a few of his fellow searchers. Not interested in talking, Mick exchanged the minimum of pleasantries before grabbing a steak with his fingers straight off the barbecue. He also found the lady with the tea and took it from her, downing it in one giant gulp. Munching the steak as he walked he got back to his swag and through himself onto it, lying on his back. Finished eating, he threw the bone onto the dirt and drifted off the sleep, knowing he would wake several times during the night to stoke the beacon fire.

For four days they maintained the search, widening the search area every day. Still no sign was found of the missing men. On the fifth day the search planes did not reappear. All of the Port Hedland police and most of the SES volunteers drove away. Even Nigel and his boys had gone back to their work at Blind Bluff. The search was coming to a standstill.

Mick had contacted the Perth office to report on developments of which there were none other than Bens and Ibrahims continued absence. He did however learn that Banjo had been taken to Royal Perth hospital where he had been placed in an induced coma. Both Tim and Tiffany had visited Banjo in hospital and reported to Mick that he seemed OK, although still unconscious. Banjo had sustained a fractured skull but the doctors believed that he should make a complete recovery although it would take time. Mick went in search of the police sergeant.

"Eh sarge, it looks like you're scaling down the search?", a statement morphing into a question.

"Yeah Mick. Sorry about that but people have lives and work to get back to. And we've seen not a skerrick of your friends", answered the sergeant, "We'll maintain a small presence here for another couple of days but then we'll have to throw in the towel.

Hopefully they walked quicker and further than we thought and they'll turn up somewhere burnt and exhausted but OK", said the sergeant.

"Yeah, OK", conceded Mick. They had done all they could and there was still no clue as to where Ben and Ibrahim could have gone. He would just have to hope for the best.

13
11 APRIL, 2014

THE AFTERNOON AFTER he had been captured by the terrorists, for he was now sure that that was what they were, Ben heard footsteps approaching his door. Without any further warning the door was flung inwards, framing Ashad and two gunmen flanking him.

"Good afternoon Mr Wilde", said Ashad almost cordially, "I am afraid that we have visitors so I am going to have to inconvenience you. Please lie face down on the floor".

Not wanting to antagonize them, Steve got to his knees and fell forward onto his face.

"Bind him and gag him", he told the two men in Arabic.

Whilst one man covered him with a rifle the other knelt on his back and quickly bound his hands and legs. A filthy rag was then pulled into his mouth and tied behind his head.

"You two stay with him", he continued in Arabic, "If he twitches, shoot him".

Ben did not know what had been said but knew it was probably not good. He also knew that he was going to risk neither his life nor that of the visitors by giving the gunmen any excuse. He resolved to lie quietly and not move a muscle.

Ashad turned and left the room, shutting the door behind him. Ben was left face down on the floor. The two gunmen took up positions on either side of the door, leveling their rifles at him. Ben noted that one of the gunmen had the beginnings of two black eyes, a broken nose and a few teeth missing. This man glared at him with hatred. The other man stood stolidly, seemingly bored with his task.

Ashad reached the front door just as a four wheel drive with Western Australian Police markings pulled up at the fence. Two men, both dressed in the khaki uniforms of the outback police, emerged from the vehicle. One had sergeants stripes on his sleeve, the other was a constable.

"Good afternoon gentlemen, what can I do for you this fine day?", said Ashad.

"Well sir", said the sergeant, a large man with a florid face and large moustache, "There has been an accident on the road about twenty kilometers west of here. Two men who were in the vehicle appear to have struck their heads on the windscreen and wandered off into the bush in a daze".

"Oh, that is terrible. I had heard that there was some trouble", said Ashad, "I do hope you can find them".

"Well", said the sergeant, "We have two aircraft looking for them and police and SES volunteers on motorbikes but we have no sign of them yet. We were hoping that you might keep an eye out for them".

"Certainly sergeant, we will do our best. Do you want us to join the search party?"

"No sir. We have plenty of people looking. Just keep an eye out for anyone wandering around over this way", said the sergeant, "Is there anyone here with you Mr…?", slightly embarrassed.

"Brown, Alex Brown", lied Ashad. Fortunately his feature were regular enough and his complexion light enough to pass for a European, albeit one of mixed ancestry. "And yes, I have two helpers", he continued. He knew he had to acknowledge two helpers. In a small town like Marble Bar the police would know that two men regularly came into town for supplies. He just hoped that they did not know how big the supplies buy was.

"Thank you Mr Brown. As I said, just keep an eye out if you would"

"We will do so sergeant", his voice dripping with sincerity, "I do hope you find them soon or they will not last long in this heat".

"Thank you sir. That is all we can ask. Good day to you", said the sergeant tipping his hat and turning back towards the landcruiser.

Neither of the police had said anything about Banjo. Ashad, for obvious reasons, had not asked.

Both policemen got into the vehicle, the constable driving, and headed off down the entrance road. Ashad stood on the verandah watching them leave until they disappeared behind a sand dune. He then turned back into the house and went straight to Ben's room where he threw open the door.

"Untie him and get back to your training", he told the two gunmen.

One of the men, not the bruised one, knelt by Ben and using a small knife cut the ropes binding his wrists and ankles. Ben sat up and tore of the gag, ignoring the pain as he did so. He was about to ask Ashad what was to happen next but he had already disappeared with the two men, shutting the door behind them.

Ben sat on the floor deep in thought. Since they had taken Ibrahim away on the day that they were taken prisoner Ben had neither seen nor heard from him. Obviously he had not escaped but ben hoped that the terrorists had not killed him. Both Banjo and Ibrahim killed whilst working with him would be too much to bear.

Ibrahim, meanwhile, was free to enjoy the sights and pleasures of Bright Downs, such as they were. He joined the other men in physical exercises and was even provided with a rifle and allowed to practice his skills on the shooting range. The shooting range was however soon torn down when it became apparent that planes searching for the two men might see it and report it to the police. When he had first been handed a loaded AK47 he had thought that he might be able to shoot his way out and rescue Ben. It did not however take a genius to see that he was heavily outnumbered. He might be able to take down two or three but then the rest would surely kill him. No, it was best to wait for an opportunity.

Although he appeared to be trusted the trust was clearly not complete. He was free to carry a rifle and roam around the homestead but he was not given access to any of the vehicles. The keys were always carried by one of the other men or kept in Ashads study. He was also not given duty at the entrance watching post where he might alert a passing motorist.

Ibrahim mixed freely with the terrorists. He ate with them and prayed with them three times each day. Sometimes at night they invited him to play cards which he did, not wanting to arouse their suspicions. The other men would often talk of their hatred of the west and that they were going to punish the infidels. Ibrahim joined in the talk showing what he thought was an impressive acting ability. But none of the men spoke of how they were to achieve their glorious aims, possibly because they did not know.

He saw Ashad around the house and the shooting range from time to time and also ate most of his meals with him present. He saw how he related to his men and how ruthless he was. The man was without doubt a psychopath.

Ibrahim went everywhere and joined in all discussions to glean what information he could. He found that the terrorists had a total of five tray back four wheel drive vehicles. He also discovered a dump truck full of fertilizer hidden behind the aircraft hangar.

At night Ibrahim slept alone on an uncomfortably thin mattress on an iron bed in one of the workers quarters. It was usually the only time in the day that he was apart from the terrorists. He suspected that that was because Ashad had given instructions that he be watched surreptitiously. They still clearly did not trust him completely.

At night Ibrahim lay on his uncomfortable bed thinking about the men into whose company he had fallen. The terrorists were all medieval in their thinking and all seem prepared to die. Indeed, it seemed that most of them thought they would be dead sooner rather than later. And all believed that when they did die they would be granted fifty virgins. Ibrahim was a Muslim but did not believe that rubbish for a moment. Why would a good and beneficient god give virgins to violent men? And where would he get them from unless he manufactured them himself. Ibrahim knew enough of the World to know he couldn't get them from the corporeal World. There simply weren't enough unless he took the children!

As he lay awake at night he also thought of plans to extract himself and Steve from this mess. And he certainly would not leave Ben behind. He had come to respect the tall Australian and considered him a friend. A friend does not leave a friend to die! He would get himself and Ben out of here or die trying!

14

13 APRIL, 2014

Three days and I am still alive, thought Ben. His captives had fed and watered him and given him a bucket for the necessary bodily functions. The room stank but he lived, but for how much longer? The room was also stifling hot, there being no air conditioning. His comfort was anyway probably the least of his captors worries, and the least of his worries. He had to find a way out of here. Ibrahim had disappeared after they had come and got him that first day. Had they killed him? thought Ben. God, I hope not.

Two more times he had been dragged to Ashads study and tied before his desk. Two more times Ashad had asked questions. Two more times Ben had pleaded ignorance. Two more times they had beaten him until he felt that there was not an inch of his body left unmarked. He thought that even after the first time Ashad had no more reason to interrogate him but the man continued. Ben suspected that the interrogations continued for no other reason than Ashad liked to inflict pain. But he did not like to get his own hands dirty so he had his men do it for him. The man was truly a psychopath.

At the end of the last torture session Ashad had said, quite casually, as he was dragged from the room "Tomorrow you die Mr Wilde. I think it is time that the searchers discovered your body. But of course they will not discover Ibrahims body".

Oh no! thought Ben. They must have shot Ibrahim and of course could not risk his body being found with bullet holes in it. He had now lost two friends – Banjo and Ibrahim. Life certainly could not get any more miserable!

Interrupting his thought was a gentle tap on the door accompanied by a hissed "Ben, Ben". The door handle turned and there was Ibrahim, as large as life. Ben was about to exclaim his gratitude at seeing Ibrahim alive when Ibrahim pointedly raised a single figure to his lips in the universal signal for silence.

"Be very quiet Ben", he whispered, "They do not know I am here".

"Sure mate", Ben said equally quietly, "Where have you been and where's the door guard?"

"Unconscious in the broom closet", replied Ibrahim evenly, grinning, "But remember there is another outside of your window".

Ben went to the window and at first could see nothing outside. And then he saw the guard leaning against the wall to the right of the window. He returned to the door and shook Ibrahims hand.

"I don't know how you did it mate but, boy, am I glad to see you! I thought that you were dead! What do we do now", he whispered. He noticed that Ibrahim had two rifles slung over his right shoulder.

"Where did you get the second gun from?", he asked. One gun had obviously been taken from the guard now unconscious in the broom closet. Ibrahim handed Ben the spare gun which he slung over his own shoulder.

"I will explain later", whispered Ibrahim, "Put your boots on and then follow me and keep very quiet".

Ben quickly pulled on his socks and his elastic sided boots and signaled his readiness. He also found and donned his hat which the terrorists had not bothered to take from him. Ibrahim turned and starting to walk down the hall towards the side of the house. Ben followed.

"Can we steal a car?", whispered Ben.

"No, they have most of them out. And even if we could the watchers at the entrance would shoot us or at least raise the alarm. I am afraid we are going to have to walk out".

"We're a long way from nowhere mate", explained Ben, "Do you have any water?"

"Yes, I managed to find three flasks. We will just have to make do", said Ibrahim, showing the flasks he had strung over his shoulder on cords.

Ibrahim reached the back door and opening it peered around the frame.

"All clear", he whispered. The window guard was on the other side of the house and could not see them.

Ibrahim raced across the sand towards the sand dune at the back of the house, Ben hot on his heels. They scrambled up the steep slope to the top and down the other side.

"Which way do you think we should go?", asked Ibrahim, handing back control to Ben.

"Well", said Ben, sitting down on the soft sand, "If what Ashad said is correct they should be searching for us about twenty kilometers west of here. However, if we go west along the highway that is mostly open country. They will track us down in no time. We would be putting both ourselves and the search crew in danger. No point in heading east because there is only the NWR facility and that's about two hundred kilometers away. The Telfer gold mine is about one hundred and thirty kilometers to the southeast but I think that they might think we'll make for that and will be guarding the approaches. There is nothing at all to the north. So that leaves only the south. There is a station homestead about one hundred and twenty kilometers in that direction. I'm not sure how long the water will last but we'll just have to do our best"

"OK, south it is", agreed Ibrahim, and started walking in that direction.

"Hang on mate", said Ben, "They'll see our boot prints in the sand. They will know which direction we have gone. We'll have to try and cover them.

Together they found an old gum tree from which they broke off two branches. Being careful not to be seen they went back over the sand dune and almost to the back door. Using the leafy branches as brooms they backed towards the dune erasing their tracks as they went. They continued up the dune continually sweeping until they reached the top. Ben looked back down to where they had been. Their footprints were all but invisible. Clambering down the reverse side of the dune they continued walking, south into the desert.

15

13 APRIL, 2014

THE FIRST DAY of walking was brutal. Ben had estimated that the temperature was in excess of 40 degrees Celsius. They had dropped the rifles into the sand after only two hours. They were of no use to them now. And if the terrorists did catch up to them the rifles would be of little use against so many. But at least navigation was easy. All they had to do was cross each sand dune as they came to it at right angles and they would be heading south. But the sand dunes were themselves brutal, some up to thirty meters tall although the majority much lower. Nonetheless, their feet trod level ground for only fleeting moments in the valleys between dunes. The rest was a struggle through the loose sand up one side of a sand dune and then almost toppling down the other.

They could have made easier going on the track that led south from the homestead to the outstation some thirty kilometers distant but Ben knew the terrorists would be using that track to hunt them. They therefore kept at least two kilometers to the west of the track.

As they had walked Ibrahim had explained their miraculous escape. He explained how he had been accepted by the terrorists as a 'brother', even to the extent of being permitted to carry a gun. On the day that they had escaped he had made an excuse of being ill so as to be left alone at the house while the rest, with the exception of the two guards, went to the shooting range. He had approached the guard on Ben's door and greeted him and as the guard had turned away he had cold-cocked him with the butt of the rifle. The rest Ben knew.

Ibrahim also explained to Ben that he had discovered a total of five four wheel drive vehicles, three in general use and two hidden in the hangar. He had also discovered a large truck packed with fertilizer parked behind the hangar. Ibrahim did not know what the fertilizer was for but had figured that it could not be for anything good.

They had exhausted the three flasks of water by the early afternoon of the first day. In the unrelenting heat they had no choice but to keep rehydrating themselves. Now, approaching nightfall, they laboured onwards with aching legs, dry mouths and swollen tongues.

Approaching another sand dune Steve suddenly stopped. He had seen something and walked a few paces to his left to confirm it. Yes, it was a small bush tomato plant, often used by the Aborigines for bush tucker. Steve managed to pluck about twenty small berries from the plant and offered half to Ibrahim. Strangely enough, Ibrahim did not seem to be suffering as much as he was. Maybe it was the legacy of being born in a desert country?

"Bush tomatoes", rasped Ben, "They'll put some liquid back in you".

Ibrahim took them gratefully and wolfed them down in one go. Ben did the same. Not much, but better than nothing.

Ben knew they had to find water soon or they would die. The nearest source of water he knew of was a water bore at the Bright Downs outstation. At least there had been one marked on the map. Ben figured they had come about fifteen kilometers. Fifteen kilometers to go. Can we make it?

They staggered on. Up one dune, down the other side, and

up the next dune. A little further on Ben stopped again. He had stepped into what appeared to be a small, dry creek bed marked by a trail of pebbles in the loose sand. He dropped to his knees and began shoveling sand and pebbles aside with his hands.

"What are you doing?", asked Ibrahim with some concern.

"Creek bed. Water", gasped Ben.

Ibrahim understood immediately. He too fell to his knees and began shoveling with his hands. They had soon dug down about half a meter and Ben was losing hope. Then he felt the next handful of sand. It was moist! There must be water just a little further down.

They continued shoveling until the hole was almost three quarters of a meter deep. Water began to seep in from the sides. It was slow, but it was water! They sat back on their haunches and waited for the hole to fill. There was soon about ten centimeters of water in the bottom of the hole. Steve lowered in one of the water flasks and waited for it to fill. The water was a muddy brown colour but it was better than nothing. When the flask was full he handed it to Ibrahim. Whilst Ibrahim drank the whole flask in one joyous rush of relief Ben lowered a second flask into the water. That too was soon full and he lifted it to his lips, draining it in one long gulp. The water had now almost disappeared so Ben shoveled a few more handfuls of sand from the hole and waited for it to refill. They waited for about ten minutes while the water seeped into the hole. When there was enough in the bottom they refilled all three of the water flasks. They were now safe for a while longer.

Having replenished their water they recommenced their tiring slog. As they walked Ben veered slightly to the left. He knew that they had to find the track if they were to have any chance of finding the outstation.

The sun had set into the west with a crimson display when Ben fell forward into a sand dune. Turning onto his back he looked up at Ibrahim.

"I'm knackered mate", he said, "What say we camp here for the night?".

Ibrahim fell onto the sand beside Steve. That was answer enough. Within minutes both men were asleep.

The following morning they awoke tired and thirsty but somewhat refreshed.

Sitting up Steve said to Ibrahim, who had already awakened. "We'll walk today and see if we can keep walking tonight. Then we will sleep during the days, walk at night. It will be better that way as we'll avoid the worst of the sun".

Ibrahim muttered assent.

On and on they walked and scaled the sand dunes. By the early afternoon of the second day they had again exhausted their water supply. But Ben figured that they now had less than five kilometers to go to the outstation, and more water. A few hundred meters further on and Ben found he was suddenly walking along a two wheel track. The homestead to outstation track! He quickly ducked off the track and took cover behind a large spinifex clump, pulling Ibrahim down beside him.

"The track", gasped Ben, "We can't let them see us!". He pulled a small saltbush, roots and all, from the ground and went back and erased his boot marks from the track.

"We will keep the track on our left and see if we can follow it to the outstation", Ben said.

The men went on. Up one sand dune, down the other side, and back up the next. Three hours later they crested a sand dune and could see, about half a kilometer ahead, the outstation in a small, flat plain. The small building was situated in a small grove of desert oaks. Walking carefully, and keeping an ear out for engine noise, they walked towards the small, dilapidated structure. On getting close to the building they could see that the outstation was a single room shanty constructed of bush timber and corrugated iron. It was unoccupied. They bypassed the building at a distance of about thirty meters and headed eastwards towards the bore they could see about one hundred meters further on. The bore was capped by a large steel tripod atop which was a large revolving fan blade. At least the bore is still working, thought Ben. Adjacent to the windmill was a large corrugated iron tank with a pipe leading from the mill to the top of the tank. A little to the left of the tank was a cement stock trough. And the trough had water in it, albeit that it was slimy with algae. Ben went to the tank and hoisted himself up by the pipe. Peering over the edge he could see water pouring from the pipe into the tank. He cupped a hand under the outlet and bought some of the water to his lips. He took a tentative sip.

"OK", said Ben, "A little salty but drinkable".

Ibrahim handed up the flasks one at a time and Ben filled them from the outlet. Dropping to the ground he took one of the filled flasks and, putting it to his mouth, drained it. Ibrahim did the same with another of the flasks. Ben hoisted himself up with the pipe again and repeated the filling procedure.

"Right, that should last us a few more kilometers", he said, "Let's get out of here".

"I do not suppose that you can find us some more of those tomatoes", said Ibrahim, "I do not know about you but I am hungry".

"I'll see what I can do", muttered Ben.

Ben did not know it but inside the hut were two boxes of tinned food. They had not bothered to enter and search the hut. It would in any case have been fruitless as they had no can opener.

"Hey, I've got an idea Ibrahim. That wall that we found is only about eight kilometers southwest of here if I remember correctly. Maybe we should go there and hope that Michelle and her friends have started excavating. If they have then we're saved mate", said Ben with some excitement.

"And if there is no one there then we have not gone far out of our way", he added.

"Sounds good to me Ben", replied Ibrahim, "I am a little tired of walking".

"Good. Lets go then mate. I am pretty sure I can find the place again", said Ben with some enthusiasm.

Ben set of walking on a bearing a little to the west of their previous heading. Ibrahim trailed dutifully behind.

The entire distance from the outstation to the wall was dune country so Ben knew that they would have rough going. Nonetheless, with full water bottles they were relatively comfortable and they strode out with new purpose.

About five hours later they crested a final dune and looking down could see relatively recent tire tracks in the sandy valley below them. They had come a little too far to the west and were looking down on Bens tracks which stopped about three hundred meters short of the wall. Ben instantly surmised that there was no one at the wall or there would at the very least be more tracks. Nonetheless, he turned to the east, along the crest of the dune, towards the wall, closely followed by Ibrahim. Only about three hundred meters later and Ben was looking down on the wall and what remained of his excavation. He slipped gently down the side of the dune and sat on the wall, Ibrahim at his side.

"Well", said Ben, "Obviously no one here yet. Pity the original residents aren't at home. Maybe they'd invite us in for a cup of tea and a lie down", he laughed.

"Yes, it is a shame that no one is here but we had to try", said Ibrahim, "You did the right thing Ben", he added thinking Ben might be losing confidence.

"Yes, well, we tried but I suppose we'll just have to push on to the south", replied Ben, "Come on, let's go mate".

Together they kept walking, leaving the mysterious wall behind. Up a sand dune, down a sand dune, back up the next sand dune. About a kilometer later Ben grabbed Ibrahims arm.

"There mate!", he said excitedly pointing towards a clump of spinifex, "You said that you were hungry!".

Ibrahim could see nothing as Ben stalked towards the spinifex clump until a large lizard suddenly bolted from cover across

Ben's front. He immediately pivoted and darted off after it. There was a small hole in the base of the opposite sand dune down which the lizard darted. Ben immediately fell to his knees and began scooping the sand away from the hole. Ibrahim looked on in amazement. Ben suddenly exclaimed and lifted from his excavation the struggling lizard. Grabbing it by the head with one hand, the upper body with the other, Ben twisted his hands suddenly and broke its neck. The lizard hung lifeless from his hands.

"Dinner mate!", exclaimed Ben.

Ibrahim had a box of matches in his pocket and they soon had a small fire blazing. They let it die down until there was only coals, ashes and a few small flames and Ben threw the lizard whole onto what remained. The lizard sizzled, the internal fats causing the flames to rear briefly. Finally the grey-brown lizard began to turn black. Ben left it for another ten minutes and then using a couple of twigs flicked it from the fire.

"Eat and enjoy mate!", he said, "I've had it with the black fellows a few times and its not bad tucker".

Waiting for it to cool a little Ben showed Ibrahim how to peel the charcoaled skin off to get at the white meat beneath. Ben placed a morsel of the flesh in his mouth and chewed contentedly. Ibrahim did the same.

"What do you think mate?", asked Ben, "Not bad tucker eh?"

"A bit like a mixture of chicken and fish", said Ibrahim tactfully, "But not too bad".

They picked and ate the remainder of the flesh, leaving only the charred skin, bones and internal organs. Sated with water and a meal they rose from the ground and again set off to the south. They travelled for the rest of that day and on into the night. Finally, about five o'clock in the morning, Ibrahim fell face down into the sand and remained unmoving.

"I can see its time for some sleep", said Ben, "But we had better find some shade or the sun will bake us!"

Ibrahim staggered to his feet and together they staggered on for another five hundred meters, finally coming to a large desert oak.

"This will do", said Ben, and dropped to the ground under the tree. Ibrahim lay down beside him and they were both soon asleep. About fifty kilometers down, Ben thought before he fell asleep. Only seventy kilometers to go.

With the sun high in the sky Ben was awoken by engine noise. Not quite believing it he sat up and tried to tune his ears for the noise that had woken him. And then he heard it again. It sounded like a plane. Some distance off. He stood up and cast his eyes around the sky. There!, to the north he saw the glint of sun off something in the sky. It is a plane he thought joyfully. But then their situation came back to him. It might be a plane with his friends looking for him, or it might be the terrorists plane searching for them. He knew that they had a plane as he had seen it in the hangar that first day he had visited the homestead. He shook Ibrahim awake.

"Ibrahim, I think there is a plane heading this way. But it might be the terrorists so we had better hide". Quickly casting his eyes around he could however see nowhere to hide. Unless they buried themselves in the sand. The tree they had slept under would not shield them sufficiently from eyes in the sky. Then he had a better idea. It had the beauty of both confusing the terrorists and, if it was their friends, letting them know where they were.

"No, I have a better idea, Ibrahim", he said quickly, "We'll pretend that we are dead. That we died of thirst. Get down out in the open and pretend that you're a corpse!".

Ibrahim quickly scrambled out from under the tree and dropped to the sand about twenty meters away. Ben scrambled away from the tree and lay down about five meters from Ibrahim. Both of them were lying face down in the dirt, Ibrahim with his arms out from his sides and Ben with his outstretched arms above his head. Pretty good approximations of two blokes having fallen and died, thought Ben. Two blokes exhausted and dying of thirst eventually succumbing to the heat.

For nearly half an hour they lay in the baking sun. From the sound of the planes engine it sounded as though the pilot was doing a grid search, casting from east to west and back again. But the engine appeared to be getting louder. Without warning the plane passed directly overhead. They had been found!

The plane did a turn and once again passed directly overhead but at a lower altitude. Ben didn't think it could be much more than three hundred meters over their heads. Once again the plane turned and came back at an even lower altitude, this time slightly to the west. Before Ben could wonder what they were doing there was a stutter of gunfire and little fountains of sand appeared about five meters to Ben's left.

"It's the terrorists!", Ben whispered loud enough for Ibrahim to hear. Why he was whispering he didn't know. He could shout and they would not hear him up there.

"Try to look as though you're decomposing", he whispered again.

Ben heard a chuckle and then full throated laughter. The bastards were shooting at them and Ibrahim was laughing!

"Stay still", he hissed.

Again the plane made a pass and again there was a stutter of gunfire and small fountains of sand. This time the gunman in the plane had missed by an even greater margin.

The plane soared away, turned and came back again. This time it appeared to be passing directly over them. The stutter of gunfire again and fountains of sand kicked into the air. This time he had missed Ben by only a meter and Ibrahim by two meters. Crafty bastard, Ben thought. He had got the pilot to fly directly overhead and fired straight down.

Once again the plane turned and was then heading back towards them. This time as it passed overhead there were two loud explosions. Large columns of sand rose into the air and then plummeted down again, leaving two small craters in the sand. Much of the sand returned to Earth to settle on Ben and Ibrahim. One of the craters was about five meters to Ibrahim's left, the other the same distance to Ben's right. Now they're throwing bloody grenades at us, Ben thought!

The plane did another turn back towards them. What this time, he thought, bullets or grenades? There was however no gunfire and no explosions. And this time the plane did not turn. It kept going straight to the north, the engine noise gradually receding. When Ben was sure it had gone he sat up.

"Ok, they've gone mate. We were bloody lucky to survive that!", Ben said as Ibrahim also sat up, "Obviously they couldn't land to deal with us so they thought strafing us from the air was the way to go! Hopefully our ruse worked and they think that we are dead. I think that they probably bought it. Let's try to get back to sleep".

They both walked back to the tree and laid down in their old spots. Despite the excitement, they were both again asleep in seconds.

That evening they were awoken by the setting sun and the sudden drop in temperature. Still bleary eyed they struggled to their feet and set off. South. The light provided by a full moon was bright enough to see everything in shades of grey. They had little difficulty walking and, without the heat, drank less. They struggled on all of that night before Ben began looking around for a shady place to lie up for the day. Cresting yet another sand dune Ben thought he could see by the moonlight the answer, about three kilometers ahead across a broad sand plain. In the poor light it looked like a grouping of large rocks. They struggled onwards and did not reach the rocks until the sun had fully risen.

Running directly towards them out of the rocks was a dry stream. Ben figured that there might be a pool at the top so they struggled up the dry creek bed. The entire mass of stones appeared as though they had been dumped in the middle of the desert by a giant. Some rocks were the size of houses and the whole reached up to over fifty meters above the plain. Even the creek bed was a mass of boulders and smaller stones, often making them stumble.

About half way up the creek bed they were suddenly faced with a smooth wall of rock. This had been a waterfall, or would be when the creek had water. Seeking a way over the wall Ben discovered a series of fissures in the rock on the left side.

"Here mate", he said, "We can get up here. There might be water at the top".

Using the fissures for hand and foot holds Ben climbed the three meter wall. Ibrahim, coming behind him, also climbed. About half way up Ibrahim lost a foothold and pivoted to the side. Unable to brace himself with his hands his forehead slammed into the unyielding rock. Steve looked down, expecting him to fall, but Ibrahim regained his composure and continued the ascent. When he reached the top Steve saw that he had gashed his forehead on the rock and blood was trickling down his face.

"You all right, mate?", Ben enquired solicitously.

"Just a bit of a bump", said Ibrahim, "I am fine".

Turning away Ben saw what he had hoped to find. The water from long past floods had gouged a shallow depression in the rocks. The depression was half full of water. For it not to have evaporated in the heat Ben guessed that the pool was fed by a spring. It was also somewhat protected by the high stone walls around it which cast the pool in almost perpetual shade. He lay flat out on the edge of the pool and stuck his head under the water. It was so beautiful and cool! He lapped up some water with pleasure. This water was pure. An elixir! Ibrahim was on his knees and had splashed some water onto his face to remove the blood. He leaned back upright, smiling.

"Here Ibrahim, Let me take a look at your head mate. I don't want you passing out on me!", said Ben as he walked across to Ibrahim.

"I am fine Ben. Just a bit of a bump", replied Ibrahim.

"I'm sure you are mate but I'll take a quick look anyway", said Ben as he reached Ibrahim and tilted his head back with both hands. Ben saw immediately that Ibrahim had a jagged gash across his forehead but it did not look deep.

"Yeah, doesn't look to bad", said Ben, "How many fingers do you see?", he added raising his left hand with two fingers extended.

"Two Ben, only two", replied Ibrahim wearily.

"That's great mate. Just rememeber that if you feel dizzy or crook you must tell me. OK? I think you will have a really good bruise there"

Well, that's the water problem solved for now, thought Ben, as Ibrahim filled the containers. Hopefully we can make it to somewhere before it runs out again.

The small pool of water was closed in on three sides by smooth rock walls. The fourth side was the waterfall. On the rock faces Ben could see a number of aboriginal paintings. People, kangaroos, emus, turtles, snakes and the ubiquitous handprints. Also, high up on the right hand wall, was a carving of a flat roofed house with a single door and no windows. Exactly the same as the carving he and Michelle had discovered to the northwest. And to continue the comparison, carved above it were the concentric circles denoting shelter. The aborigines had clearly known of his ruins, and were not shy in advertising them, he thought.

"Lets cool off", said Ben, removing his shirt.

He slid into the water and felt the coolness envelop him. Although the water was less than a third of a meter deep it felt wonderfully decadent. Ibrahim quickly stripped off his shirt and joined him. Exiting the pool Ben crabbed over to an area of shade cast by one of the walls. He lay on his back staring up at the sky, wondering if he and Ibrahim would indeed get out of this mess. If he did he was going to see Ashad burn! About forty five kilometers to go he calculated. Ibrahim joined him in the shade and although both men spent some time looking up at the sky, both eventually faded into sleep. It was not the most comfortable of beds on the hard rock but both slept soundly.

Once again Ben was awoken by the onsetting coolness of the evening. He prodded Ibrahim who sat up with a jolt.

"Easy mate, we're OK", said Ben.

Without further ado both men got to their feet and, seeing again the splendid water, went down on their bellies at the pool edge and gorged themselves with water until they felt bloated. Then Ibrahim took the three water containers, now almost empty, and refilled them with the cool, sweet water.

Looking around they could see that they could not pass the rock faces and so lowered themselves back down the waterfall. They walked back down the creek bed and at the bottom turned right to round the rock pile. For a while they walked steadily over the flat ground of the plain. And then they came to the sand dunes again. They struggled over the dunes for about five kilometers and came again to a flat plain. This plain however seemed to go on forever, with no sand dunes in the distance. Sliding down the face of the last sand dune they found themselves standing on baked red clay. They had exited the desert proper. Nonetheless, they still had a long way to go.

All night they walked, taking the occasional small sip of water. The land changed slowly from barren red dirt with the occasional spinifex or saltbush to more heavily vegetated country. This was mulga country with gnarled trees reaching to twice the height of a man. In some places the vegetation became so dense that they had to barge their way through tangles of small branches.

Nearing dawn, Ben decided to stop. They now had a wealth of bushes to provide them with shade from the heat of the day. Ben drew up in a particularly shady spot, or would be shady when the sun rose, and lay down on the ground. Ibrahim joined him. Although both men tossed and turned somewhat on the rough ground they both eventually drifted off to sleep.

16
17 APRIL, 2014

IBRAHIM WAS AWOKEN by engine noise. He prodded Ben who started and sat up, blearily wiping the sleep from his eyes. He too could hear the sound of an engine. Probably those buggers in the plane come again to check on us, he thought. But then he noticed that this was not a hum but more of a growl. A car or four wheel drive, he thought. And the noise was coming from the south, not the north where the terrorists were.

Unbeknownst to either of them they had stopped the previous night only ten meters short of a rough bush track. The engine noise was a four wheel drive heading down the track, towards them.

Although Ben knew that they were now well beyond the boundary of Bright Downs station, he was still wary.

"Keep low", he whispered to Ibrahim, "It might be them looking for us".

Ibrahim did not need a qualification of who the 'them' might be. He lay down again flat on the ground. Ben also lay down but continued to look in the direction of the noise. Suddenly he saw a white four wheel drive heading towards where they lay. As it came closer he examined it and could see that it held a single person.

Closer still and he could see that the driver was a grey haired elderly man with a full grey beard. It was not the terrorists.

"Come on Ibrahim", yelled Ben, leaping to his feet, "Our ride just arrived!".

The two men ran forward and within paces found they were standing on a two wheel rutted track. The vehicle, now only five meters away, came to an abrupt stop. Ben ran to the drivers window.

The driver lowered the window and looked out at Ben with astonishment. "Where did you fellows spring from?", he asked. "No, don't tell me, you're those two fellows who were lost up north, right?"

"Yes, that's right", exclaimed Ben, "We've walked for flaming miles and we're just about buggered".

"Oh, I can imagine. I'll take you back to the homestead and get you some help. You fellows have obviously had a hard time.", said the driver.

"Thank you sir. You have saved our lives", said Ben gratefully.

"Don't mention it, least I can do. I'm George Clooney by the way", said the driver, "No, not the actor bloke. I had the name before him and am anyways much better looking", he added with a wry smile. "And you are?"

"Ben Wilde and Ibrahim Allawi", Ben offered, indicating himself and then Ibrahim.

"OK lads, jump up in here and I'll take you to the homestead. This is Clooney Downs station in case you're wondering".

Ben and Ibrahim darted around to the other side of the vehicle and scrambled into the cab, Ibrahim between George and Ben.

"There's a flask of water there on the floor if you're thirsty", offered George.

Steve found the flask and had a long drink before offering it to Ibrahim. Ibrahim also had a long drink and handed the flask back to Ben. The flask was now almost empty but Steve placed it back on the floor where he had found it.

"You blokes have certainly walked a long way", said George, "Over a hundred kilometers by my reckoning. You have certainly done very well to get this far".

"Feels more like five hundred k to us", said Ben weakly, "We're just grateful that you found us when you did. I don't think we could have gone on much further".

George did a three point turn on the rough track and headed back the way that he had come. An hour later he pulled up at a neat brick house surrounded by a lush garden, including roses. All three men exited the vehicle and, following George, went in through the small fence gate and up to the front door. George opened the door and ushered them in.

"Honey, I'm home", he called out, "And we've got visitors!".

George, Ben and Ibrahim had entered the house into a short hallway lined with what looked like family photographs. A grey haired, plump woman with an equally plump and rosy face appeared at the far end of the hall.

"Rose, Ben Wilde and Ibrahim", said George, unsure of Ibrahims last name, "Gentlemen, my wife Rose".

"Pleasure to meet you Mrs Clooney", said Ben and Ibrahim as one.

An hour later Ben and Ibrahim were showered and dressed in clean clothes borrowed from George. The shorts Ben was wearing were a bit loose in the waste but neither he nor Ibrahim had any complaints. They were sitting in what Mrs Clooney called the parlour wolfing down sandwiches and politely sipping tea. Mrs Clooney was sitting opposite the two men who were comfortably perched on beautiful padded chairs. George was in another room calling the Meekatharra police to come and pick up the lost ones. Having spoken to the Meekatharra sergeant he came back into the parlour.

"Meekatharra police are sending someone to pick you up", George said, "Should be here in about two hours".

Ben and Ibrahim spent the next two hours relaxing around

the house. Mrs Clooney seemed to pop up wherever they went, constantly offering sandwiches, cake and tea. Ben and Ibrahim accepted the majority of offers gratefully. Ben also asked to borrow the telephone to let everyone know that they were OK. He first rang the Major Minerals office.

"Major Minerals, how may I help you?"

"Hi Tiff, Ben here. Just calling to let you know we are OK".

"Oh, thank god! We thought you were dead!", said Tiffany, almost in tears.

"No, we're fine Tiff. We are at Clooney Downs station and are getting a lift into Meekatharra. We'll make our way down to Perth from there"

After several more assurances from Ben that they were OK, and an assurance from Tiffany that she would tell Tim and the rest of the staff the good news, Ben hung up. But not before he learnt that Mick was still searching for him and that Tiffany would let him know that they were OK when next he called in.

Ben had only one more call to make. His father had died twelve years before, his mother ten years after that so only his brother Greg was left. He picked up the telephone and dialed Gregs number from memory.

"Hello, Greg Wilde speaking", came a voice down the line.

"Hey, Greg, its Ben here just calling to let you know that I'm OK", said Ben

"Oh, thank God Ben. Your office told me you were missing and I feared the worst. Where are you?", said Greg.

"A place called Clooney Downs station. We're heading back to Meekatharra and should be back in Perth in a day or two. I'll come and see you then", said Ben.

"You do that mate. It'll be good to see you. Take care in the meanwhile", said Greg.

Ben hung up the telephone, now content that his loved ones knew that he was OK. He knew that Tiffany would call Ibrahims wife to tell her the good news.

About half an hour later than George had estimated a grey landcruiser pulled up at the front gate.

The man who had come to pick them up was however not a policeman. He explained that he was the Meekatharra mechanic and had completed the journey as a favor to the police, who would of course reimburse him for his time and fuel.

Thanking Mr and Mrs Clooney profusely, Ben and Ibrahim took their leave. It was a long trip back to Meekatharra and Frank, the mechanic, was a chatterbox. He talked almost nonstop and was amazed at their story of survival. However, Ben and Ibrahim, by unspoken agreement, said nothing of having been the captives of terrorists. That would be the province of the police.

Arriving at Meekatharra Frank took them straight to the small hospital. Ben was a little annoyed by the presumption as neither he nor Ibrahim had been seriously injured. Nonetheless, he knew it had to be done.

Both of the men were given a thorough examination by the local doctor. He pronounced that, other than a mild case of sunburn and Steves injuries from the beatings and Ibrahims head wound, they were both perfectly fit. Of course the doctor had heard the news of the missing men and assumed that the obvious injuries were the result of the car wreck. Grateful, Ben and Ibrahim left the hospital and went in search of the police. They found the police station only two doors up from the hospital in the small town. Entering the station they met a constable who, learning who they were, ushered them through to an office in the rear.

In the middle of the sparsely decorated room was a large desk behind which sat a sergeant of police.

"Gentlemen, so good to see you safe", he said, "I have already radioed Marble Bar to let them know of your miraculous return".

"Thank you Sir", said Ben, "But we have a serious matter to report".

"And what is that son", asked the older sergeant.

"We believe that everyone believes that we were injured in a car crash and wandered into the bush. Is that correct?"

"Yes Sir, that is as I understand it. You have a different version?"

"Yes we do", said Ben, "We were not involved in any car crash. We were captured by terrorists and held prisoner at Bright Downs station, from which we escaped".

"Whoah son, that is a serious accusation. Do you have anything to back that story up?"

"No", said Ben, "But Ibrahim here will confirm that that is what happened".

The sergeant turned his attention to Ibrahim who started "What Ben said is the truth. We were captured by about ten terrorists and held at Bright Downs. They killed Banjo and were going to put him in the vehicle and crash it to make it look like an accident".

"Well, there is a little something wrong with your story. Banjo, as you call him, was hauled from the wreck and is still alive. Last I heard he was in a coma at Royal Perth"

Royal Perth Hospital was one of the larger hospitals in Perth.

"Oh, that's wonderful", said Ben, a tear forming in his eye, "We thought that they had killed him"

"Well, they didn't, or he didn't die in the crash, one of the two", said the sergeant.

"Don't you believe us?", exclaimed Steve, "We are telling the truth!".

"That you might be son. But are you sure that you are not imagining it? You have been through a harrowing experience. And I notice you are both bearing wounds on your foreheads, consistent with a collision with a windscreen, for example?".

Ben knew that he was right. Both of them had cuts and bruises on their foreheads, Ben from the beatings and Ibrahim from his fall.

"Look, we know what happened", argued Ben, "Just send someone out there to check and you will see that our story is true.

But make sure that they are heavily armed – There is ten armed men out there!"

"We will certainly send someone out to check your story, have no concern. I will radio Marble Bar and have them do it as soon as possible", said the sergeant equitably, "Now I understand you have been checked by the doctor and are fit to travel?"

"Yes, we are. How can we get to Perth?", asked Ben, having given up on trying to convince the sergeant of the true story.

"Well, as luck would have it there is a plane leaving tonight. If you hurry you should be able to catch it", replied the sergeant.

Ben and Ibrahim thanked the sergeant and left the police station. They managed to catch a lift to the airport with a friendly local where they were able to book two seats on the flight to Perth. The plane boarded an hour later and as they relaxed back in their seats Ben worried that the police had not taken him seriously. Ben knew Ashad was planning something and the sooner he was banged up the better. You couldn't leave an animal like that wandering around loose.

17
18 APRIL, 2014

ASHAD WAS PLEASED. Pleased that his plans were still moving forward. Pleased that his men seemed to be performing well in training. The spying by that idiot geologist had been a problem, but a problem he had solved. The police seemed to have bought the story of a car crash without reservation. It was unfortunate that he had made an error with Ibrahim and the two men had escaped but it had turned out well in the end. As far as he knew they were still searching for the missing men. And when they did find them all they would have would be corpses. Granted that the corpses would have bullet holes in them but by then Ashad and his men would be long gone.

The escape of Wilde and the betrayal of Ibrahim had presented a significant problem. The men who had been on guard duty that day had both had to do the run of shame.

However, his men had since reported that they were both dead. He himself had not seen the bodies but he trusted his men not to lie to him. He had sent two of the men on an aerial search to the south. Fortunately, Tariq had learnt to pilot an aircraft during a brief visit to America. The rest of the men had combed the country around the homestead in the four wheel drives.

It had not taken him long to determine which way the escapees would go. At first they had been unable to discover any signs or tracks indicating their direction of flight. However, he had had his men scout further afield from the homestead and they had soon reported tracks on the sand dunes, heading south.

The aerial search had discovered the two men over fifty kilometers south of the homestead. No small feat he thought with some admiration. Not that it had done them any good. According to the two men in the plane it had appeared as though they had died of thirst. They had strafed them with an AK47 and dropped two hand grenades on them and the men in the plane were convinced that they were dead. Habeeb, the gunman in the plane, was convinced that he had put bullets into both of their already dead bodies. In addition, he was sure that the grenades would have finished the job. Good, thought Ashad, one less problem.

Ashad heard the radio crackle followed by some unintelligible words. The radio operator next door could however make out what was being said as he answered in brief statatco bursts. The call ended and Ashad awaited the operator to come and tell him the news. He was not disappointed. The operator appeared at the door and Ashad gestured for him to enter.

"Sir, a message from the watchers at the entry road. Two police vehicles are approaching with six men. What do you wish us to do?", asked the operator.

Six police? Coming here? That did not sound to Ashad like a routine visit. But nor did it sound like a full out assault. He would just have to bluff his way through.

"Get all of the men. Tell them that they are to load up all their sleeping gear and other equipment. Except leave two of the quarters as though they remain occupied. Then they must go down to the outstation with all of the vehicles bar one. And make sure you take the truck with the fertilizer with you. It must appear as though the station is deserted other than for myself and two others. But I want no one else to remain here other than myself. Go!", said Ashad in a fury.

Looking out the window Ashad could soon see men hurrying about. Four vehicles had been retrieved from the hangar and were now parked in front of the quarters. The men were hauling everything from the quarters, including mattresses, and throwing them into the backs of the four wheel drives. Other men were running through the house, ensuring that there was no incriminating evidence left. As they worked Ashad stepped out onto the verandah.

No sooner had the last vehicle, with all of his men, disappeared behind the sand dune behind the house than Ashad saw the first police vehicle emerge from behind the entryway sand dunes. Not wanting to be caught standing as though he was expecting them, Ashad quickly ducked back inside the house.

The two police four wheel drive vehicles pulled up in front of the house fence a few moments later. There were indeed six policemen in the vehicles, two in the front vehicle and four in the back. The two front riders were the sergeant and his constable from Marble Bar. The four men in the rear vehicle were four police from Port Hedland, drafted in for the occasion. The two Marble Bar officers exited their vehicle. The four police in the rear vehicle remained where they were. Those men in the second vehicle were obviously poised for a quick getaway should the situation turn nasty.

The sergeant rapped loudly on the screen door of the house. Ashad poked his head around from the adjacent room and went to the door.

"Good morning sergeant", he said, "A pleasure to see you again. Have you found those missing men?"

"Yes Sir, and that is why we are here. We have found them", replied the sergeant.

Ashad immediately thought that the search parties had found the mens bodies. And that would not look good if the bodies were full of bullet holes and blown up by hand grenades. Although there was no reason to suspect Ashad for the mens condition.

"Oh, that is such a shame", announced Ashad, "And where did you find the bodies?"

"Oh no sir, you misunderstand. The men we were searching for have turned up alive in Meekatharra. From what I have heard they are in reasonable condition and are not dead thanks be to god", said the sergeant.

Oh no!, thought Ashad. It was a raid. They had found that damned geologist and Ibrahim, who were not after all dead, and they had told their story. He now knew from the policemans words that the men had turned up alive and not been found as bullet riddled corpses in the desert. How could they still be alive when the men in the plane had been so certain? Had they accidentally strafed and killed two other unrelated men lost in the desert? No, impossible. Somehow they had survived and in the process had been able to fool his men. Those men would suffer for their incompetence.

He thought briefly to run but stayed his feet from betraying him. No, it can't be a raid. They would not have given us warning. He did notice however that the constable was caressing his holstered pistol nervously. No, I can brazen this out, he assured himself.

"Oh, that is marvelous news", said Ashad, "I had thought that those poor men had perished. But why have so many of you come to tell us the good news?".

"Well, both of the men claim that they were captured by you and held prisoners here", said the sergeant, with some embarrassment, "They also told us that there were ten heavily armed men here".

"Oh dear me no!", said Ashad, "Why would they say such a thing. I have captured and imprisoned no-one. And there is only myself and my two helpers here", he continued, wringing his hands.

"It is possible that the men were confused sir. I understand that both had head injuries. Nonetheless, we are obliged to check out their story. I believe that last time we visited you said that your name was Alex Brown. Might I see some identification to confirm that sir?"

"Certainly officer, please wait here".

Ashad left the two policemen standing on the verandah and entered the house, going straight to his study. He unlocked a small drawer on his desk and extracted a British passport. Fortunately, Ashad had several sets of fake documents, one in the name of Alex Brown. He returned to the verandah where the two police waited.

"Here sir", he said to the sergeant, handing him the passport.

The sergeant took the passport and closely examined it, particularly the photograph. It was indeed Ashad, aka Alex Brown.

"Thank you sir", handing back the passport to Ashad, "And I believe you said that you had two helpers here. Are they around?"

"Alas no, sergeant, they are out checking on the water bores. Perhaps if you came back tomorrow?".

"That won't be necessary Mr Brown. Can you tell me their names?", asked the sergeant.

"Certainly. Ralph Norrish and Peter Anders. I am afraid I do not have identification for them", replied Ashad.

"That is fine Mr Brown. Would it be OK if we had a look around? And then we will be finished with this matter", said the sergeant.

"Certainly officer. Go anywhere that you like. I think that you will however find that this is just a simple station homestead and the lost men are confused", said Ashad, "But please do tell me if you find any armed ruffians", he smiled.

Without a word the sergeant and the constable retreated to the second four wheel drive with the four men aboard. Through the drivers window the sergeant relayed some instructions to the men within and all four stepped down from the vehicle. Two of the men went to the workers quarters, two slogged across towards the hangar, and the sergeant and his constable returned to the verandah where Ashad awaited them.

"Please, gentlemen", said Ashad, ushering them through the front door. The police stepped around Ashad and entered the house. They then did a search of the house from one end to the other and discovered nothing other than a single occupied bedroom, an untidy kitchen, two unused spare bedrooms and a study. Interestingly, in the study they found a half finished bottle of whisky. This was a telling discovery for the sergeant as he knew that muslim terrorists did not drink alcohol. The rest of the house held no weapons, indications of terrorists, or a location where two men might have been imprisoned. The two policemen returned to the front door where Ashad waited. Ashad was happy to note that the constables hand no longer lingered near his holstered pistol. They walked over to the second vehicle where the other four policemen had gathered, having finished their inspection of the quarters and hangar.

"Nothing sarge", reported one of the four constables, "The hangar has only the Cessna plane and two of the quarters appear occupied. There are however no indications of anything untoward. We found no other indications of other men and we found no weapons".

The sergeant then retraced his steps to the verandah.

"I am sorry sir", he said, "Everything appears to be in order. Obviously the injuries the men sustained in the accident have confused them. I hope you understand that we have to check these things out. We will not trouble you again".

"Not to worry sergeant", said Ashad, "I fully understand. I just hope those poor men recover their wits soon".

"Thank you again sir for your trouble. We will be on our way", said the sergeant. With that he stepped down from the verandah and beckoned to the constable who was talking to the men in the other vehicle. The constable scuttled across and climbed into the drivers seat whilst the Sergeant made himself comfortable in the passenger seat. Both police vehicles had soon restarted their engines and before long had disappeared behind the sand dunes.

Well, that was close, thought Ashad as he watched them disappear. If he could he would kill the two men in the plane who had assured him that the troublesome two were dead. But he could not afford any further loss of men. He would reprimand them severely but they would get to live, for now. Although they would have some blisters after they had completed the run of shame, he thought with satisfaction.

The police had obviously decided that there was nothing amiss at Bright Downs. They had after all raided without warning expecting that if there was anything amiss then the surprise would find it out. But thanks to the sentries at the entrance road Ashad had had warning. But for those sentries the police would have discovered a lot more men, armed men at that!

Everything was as it should be, thought Ashad. Clearly, the police thought that Bright Downs posed no danger. Nonetheless, Ashad knew that the noose was tightening. He and his men would have to move quicker than he had hoped. So be it!

18

18 APRIL, 2014

THE MORNING AFTER the flight down from Meekatharra, Ben slept late. When he finally awoke, although he was not to know it, the police were visiting Bright Downs.

He believed he was owed a little consideration after the hell he had been through so it was not until after nine in the morning that he stepped through the doors of the Major Minerals offices. Tiffany saw him immediately and scampered around her desk to envelop him in a hug. Ben was instantly embarrassed. She was hugging him for comfort, for him, and to show her love whilst Ben thought only how nice it was to have her breasts pressed against him. He disentangled himself and held her at arms length.

"Oh Steve, I am so glad you are OK. We were all so worried", Tiffany gushed.

"Thank you Tiff, but as you can see I'm fine", said Ben, "Apart from a few cuts and bruises of course", he added.

For a moment Ben let Tiffany regain her composure before releasing her arms. She turned and resumed her seat behind the desk.

"Just so nice to see you back", she said, "We were really so worried!".

Ben nodded before turning away and stepping down the hall. He stopped at Tim's office and knocked briefly before opening the door.

"Morning Tim", he said, as Tim looked up from his desk.

"Oh, Ben. I am so glad to see you back in one piece mate. We thought we had lost you!", said Tim earnestly.

"No, as you can see I'm all OK and reporting for duty", smiled Ben.

"Look mate", said Tim with a serious expression, "You have been through a harrowing experience. Why don't you take a few days, a week, off".

"No, no Tim. I am fine, really. I just want to get back to work"

"Okay, if you are sure?", asked Tim.

"I'm sure", said Ben, "Although I'm going to see Banjo at the hospital this morning".

"You do that mate", said Tim, "Take all the time that you want. We have arranged for Banjo to have a private room at the hospital. Least we could do for the poor little bastard".

"Do you know what happened up there?", asked Ben, "I mean, what really happened?"

"Yeah, you got banged up in a prang and wandered into the bush", said Tim.

"No, that is not what happened", said Ben, and went on to explain in detail the true sequence of events.

"Well, that is bloody terrible", said Tim, "And what are the police doing about it?"

"Oh, they're going to visit the place", answered Ben, "But I don't think they believe us. They think we were traumatized by the accident and can't think straight. But I promise you it is the truth. I just hope that the cops find enough evidence to put the bastards away".

"I believe you mate. But I'm not sure there is anything we can do about it".

"Yes I know", said Ben, "I'm going back up there and by the

time I get there I hope the cops have got them banged up. If not, I will just steer well clear of the bastards. The cops will trip them up sooner or later".

"OK, if you are sure. And that reminds me. We got the results of the Global survey back and there's a boomer of an anomaly under your copper show. Possibly sulphides. I've already sent the young geo, Lance, to replace you and have organized for a drilling rig which should be on site tomorrow. However, if you're ready to go back to work you can go up and sit on the rig. I've also read your report and have noticed you have barely touched the western part of the lease because of a lack of access. Therefore, I think while you sit the rig I'll send a chopper up and Lance can do a helicopter-borne stream sediment survey off to the west. What do you think?", asked Tim.

"Sounds great", said Ben, "We can kill two birds with one stone. I'll fly out tomorrow and take Ibrahim with me. If he's Okay. I presume that Mick is still up there?".

"Yes he is", said Tim, "Nurse-maiding Lance and waiting for the rig".

"Terrific", said Ben, "I'm going to see Banjo now. I'll see you later".

With that Ben turned on his heel and left Tim's office and the offices of Major Minerals. He walked back to his apartment, retrieved his vehicle, and drove to Royal Perth Hospital.

Royal Perth Hospital was a huge institution spread over a block to the west of the city centre. Ben parked his battered landrover in the large car park and walked to the front door of the hospital. He stepped into the large foyer which was inhabited by a number of people seeking admittance for a variety of ills. A little girl scrunched onto a seat near the door cried piteously as her mother tried to comfort her. Steve walked past directly to the admissions desk, smiling at the little girl as he did so.

"I am looking for Bert Paterson", he told the girl behind the desk, "He was admitted about a week ago".

The girl looked down at a large ledger on her desk. She flipped a few pages until she found what she was looking for.

"Right. Mr Bert Paterson. Second floor, Ward C. Ask at the nursing station", she said officiously.

Ben mumbled his thanks and turned to the stairs. Taking them two at a time he ran up the stairs where he came to a long corridor. Affixed to the opposite wall was a small plaque indicating Ward C to the left. Ben followed the sign until he came to the nurses station, an island of counter ringed on three sides by access ways. A nurse stood behind the counter. He went up to the counter and asked the same question he had asked the girl below.

"Mr Paterson. Yes, he is in room 314. You do know he is comatose? He has been placed in an induced coma", said the nurse.

"Yes I do", said Ben, "I just want to look in on him".

"Fine. Go ahead. Down the corridor on the left and second to last door on your right", explained the nurse.

Steve walked down the corridor until he found the correct door. He walked in and was surprised to find not only Banjo but also Ibrahim sitting by his bed. Banjo looked to be peacefully asleep but the numerous wires and tubes leading to him indicated a more dire circumstance.

"Ibrahim, I wasn't expecting to find you here", said Ben.

"He is my friend", said Ibrahim simply, "Of course I had to visit him".

"How is he?", asked Ben, impressed by Ibrahims devotion.

"Well, as you can see, he remains in a coma. I have spoken to the doctor and he told me that when he was bought in they operated to relieve the pressure and bleeding on the brain. He has a depressed skull fracture but they believe he should make it through OK. They are just waiting for him to come out of the induced coma but they think it will probably be a couple of weeks. I think that they want to keep him comatose whilst the brain mends", said Ibrahim.

"Well, that's good. I think", said Ben, "Poor little bugger didn't deserve what happened to him".

"No he did not", said Ibrahim, "And we did not deserve what happened to us. But life goes on and we can only hope that the police caught those men".

"I wouldn't bet on it if I were you. I'm not sure that the police believe our story. If Banjo was awake he could confirm our story but sadly he is not. The cops wouldn't be able to dismiss three witnesses as easily as two. Mind you, when he does wake up the cops will have to move then".

"But that is preposterous", blustered Ibrahim, "They have two witnesses!".

"Yeah", said Ben, "But I think that they think that we are brain damaged just like poor Banjo here. Anyway, I am going back tomorrow. Are you going to take some time off?".

"No, of course not. I will be going back with you", said Ibrahim.

"Are you sure Ibrahim?", said Ben with concern, "After all, you deserve some time after what happened".

"You are not taking time off are you? Then neither will I", said Ibrahim.

"OK then", said Ben, "We'll fly to Port Hedland tomorrow and I'll organize a hire four wheel drive from there. After all, the company is down one vehicle now", he smiled.

19
19 APRIL, 2014

BEN AND IBRAHIM flew to Port Hedland the following morning. They picked up the vehicle Ben had hired at the terminal and then completed the two hour drive to Marble Bar. At arriving in town Ben drove straight to the police station. Entering the station, with Ibrahim trailing behind, Ben confronted the constable on duty at the front desk.

"I must speak with your sergeant", he said, brooking no delay.

"Certainly sir, and you are?", asked the constable.

"Wilde. Ben Wilde. And this is Ibrahim Allawi. He will know who we are", said Ben.

"Yes Mr Wilde. I know who you are as I was one of those who searched for you. I am so glad you turned up OK. Quite a hike you went on", said the constable with a shy smile, "I'll just see if sergeant Frost is in".

The constable disappeared into the back rooms and returned a moment later. "Go through Mr Wilde. He is expecting you".

Ben walked past the desk and turned into the sergeants office. The sergeant was sitting behind his rather rickety desk and looked up expectantly. Ben and Ibrahim sat in a pair of unsteady chairs before the desk.

"Good morning sergeant. You may remember me. I'm the bloke who was involved in the fictional car accident", said Ben determinably.

Sensing he was in for a difficult conversation Sergeant Frost replied pleasantly. "Certainly Mr Wilde. I fully understand your concerns. However, we have visited and inspected Bright Downs homestead and have been unable to find any evidence to support your story. I am not saying you are telling a lie – far from it. However, we found no men, apart from Mr Brown, no weapons and no indications of illegal activity. We even found a bottle of whisky and unless I am vastly mistaken Muslim terrorists don't partake of alcohol. Even if your story is true our hands are tied. We have no evidence of any wrongdoing".

"Well, that is just bullshit!", exploded Ben, "We were held captive, I was beaten, and they tried to kill Banjo!".

"Yes, so you say. But as I have said, we have no evidence. There is nothing we can do", said the sergeant.

Without saying another word Ben exploded from his chair and stalked from the office. He was at the front door of the police station when Sergeant Frost caught up to him.

"Believe me, Mr Wilde", he said, "I understand your anger. But please do not do anything rash or it will be you we will have to arrest".

"Oh, I won't sergeant", said Ben with some venom, "But sooner or later those bastards will shoot someone or blow something up and then you'll have to do something! In the meantime I'm going to give the damn place a wide berth". With that he stalked off to the nearby Ironclad Hotel. Ibrahim trailed after him, equally downcast.

Still furious he stormed into the hotel. And stopped dead when he saw Mick sitting alone at the bar. Even from behind, he would know that bulky form anywhere.

"Mick", he almost yelled, "How are you mate?"

Mick swivelled on his stool to see Ben standing in the doorway.

"Ben, you old bastard. Jeez its good to see you mate", Mick said with enthusiasm, "I was just drowning my sorrows thinking I'd get the blame for what happened. I thought the boss was gonna skin me for losing you! Thank God you turned up OK"

He lurched of his stool and caught Ben in a crushing hug. It was unlike Mick to show such emotion but Ben was a true mate. Then he saw Ibrahim standing behind Ben.

"Ib mate. It's good to see you too!', he enthused, crushing Ibrahim in a similar bone crunching hug.

"What are you doing here mate?", asked Ben.

"Waiting for young Lance to turn up today", said Mick as he released Ibrahim, "And the rig arrives here tomorrow. And Tim tells me we've got a chopper arriving at Blind Bluff the day after".

The publican standing behind the bar butted in at that point. "You must be the fellows who were lost in the desert", he said, "Drinks are on the house!".

"Thanks Dave", said Ben, "We'll have three beers thanks".

The publican pulled the beers and set them on the bar.

"Cheers!", said Mick, clinking his glass with Ben's and then Ibrahim's.

Ben proceeded to fill Mick in on what had happened to him and Ibrahim, and Banjo. Mick was at first shocked and then angry.

"Bloody bastards", he said, not for a moment doubting Ben's version of events, "And the cops can't touch them?"

"No, no evidence they say. I can see their point but it is still a bastard", said Ben, "But we'll just get on with our job and hope they screw up and the cops bang them up".

For much of the afternoon the three men remained at the bar swapping stories and laughing. Lance, the young geologist, finally fronted at about five o'clock. By that time, although they were not drunk, all three men were decidedly tipsy.

Nonetheless, on Lances arrival Ben immediately began poring over the results of the Blind Bluff geophysical survey. Lance had also bought the assay results for the samples collected by Ben.

The samples from Blind Bluff averaged nearly five percent copper and contained up to 42 grams per tonne silver and one and a half grams per tonne gold. The samples from the Bright desert gossan showed up to one and a half percent lead and half a percent zinc with a trace of copper. It was after all a true gossan and worthy of follow up. Ben knew that he would have to get the Global Geophysics boys back to do another IP survey.

Before the men turned in for the night Ben reiterated his story for Lance, who had not yet heard the truth. He then emphasized that if any of them came across men from Bright Downs they were to run like hell. None of them were to go near the bright desert prospect until the matter had been settled.

All four men had rooms at the Ironclad for the night. After a few more beers and dinner they all retired to their respective rooms, promising to get together in the morning.

The following morning after a hasty breakfast the four men mounted the two four wheel drives and drove out towards Blind Bluff. They left the vehicle that Lance had hired in Port Hedland at the hotel. In no rush they did not leave town until nine am. Steve knew that the drilling rig would not arrive in Marble Bar until that evening so they had time to survey the drilling site and plot where the drillholes would be before returning to town.

Driving the lead vehicle, Mick cruised past the turnoff to Blind Bluff. Ibrahim, driving the second vehicle, followed with no hesitation.

"Where you going mate", said Ben with some alarm, "The turnoff was back there".

"Yeah, I know", said Mick, "Just thought you might like to see where you had your 'accident'".

Ben said no more as the vehicle cruised down the good sealed road. And then he suddenly saw the overturned cruiser on the dirt on the right of the road. Mick pulled up next to it with Ibrahim directly behind. All four men stepped down to the ground.

Ben walked over to the crashed vehicle which lay forlornly on its side. He saw the dents in the cabin and the windscreen lying on the red earth. Most of the equipment that had been spilled from the tray had already been retrieved by Mick. He crouched down beside the windscreen.

"They did a good job by the looks of it", he said to the men grouped around him. "You can see where they bashed the windscreen to make it look like our heads had hit".

The blood on the windscreen had dried to a dark brown and resembled paint smears.

"I wonder where they got the blood from?", Ben queried curiously.

"Probably shot a roo", said Mick.

They had examined the rest of the vehicle closely but other than some dented panels, a smashed window and the windscreen, could see no serious damage. The back of the vehicle was buckled at an angle to the front but Steve thought that that was probably just a result of the way it was lying. He did not think that it meant important structural damage.

"Do you think she can be fixed?", Ben asked Mick.

"Yeah, I should think so. The chassis looks a little bent but that can be pulled back into line. That and a bit of panel beating and new windows and she should be fine", replied Mick.

"How are we going to get her back on her wheels?", asked Ben, "She's a bit too heavy for us to lift her".

"No worries mate. I've got an idea", replied Mick as he ran to his cruiser.

Mick returned from his vehicle with a stout coil of rope. He tied one end of the rope to a high chassis bar of the overturned vehicle and, having got his own vehicle into position, tied the other end to its towball.

"You and the other blokes push from the other side and I'll pull her from this side", said Mick to Ben.

Ben quickly organized Ibrahim and Lance to assist him with lifting the vehicle back onto its wheels. Ibrahim and Lance took holds on the tray of the overturned vehicle, Ben on the passenger window. The engine of Micks cruiser roared from the other side and they prepared to lift. Mick slowly pulled the vehicle forward until the rope was taught and Steve and the others bent their backs to lifting. Micks cruiser however took the majority of the weight and within seconds, and heralded by a dull crash, the vehicle was back upright on its wheels. Mick climbed down from the cab and came over to inspect the now upright cruiser. As they had already noted, the damage was limited to some dented panels and broken windows. There was also one tire that had been blown out in the crash. Ibrahim retrieved the spare from beneath the vehicle and set about changing the destroyed tire.

"OK, let's see if she starts", said Mick, leaping into the drivers seat. He turned the key which was still in the ignition. Other than a low grinding sound the engine remained silent.

"Must be flooded", said Mick stepping down from the vehicle after having popped the bonnet release.

He went around to the front of the vehicle and lifted the hood to inspect the engine. He then shouted to Ibrahim to bring the toolbox from his vehicle and on its arrival began tinkering with the engine. Whilst the others stood around looking lost he quickly bled the fuel lines and evacuated excess fuel from the system.

"Let's try her again", he said, climbing into the drivers seat. Again he turned the key and the motor roared to life.

"Piece of piss", he said, climbing down once again from the drivers seat, "I'll drive her back to the turnoff and we'll leave her there. We can run her into Port Hedland later for repairs".

Led by Ben the three vehicles turned back onto the road and headed west. When they reached the Blind Bluff turnoff Ben halted while Mick pulled the injured vehicle to the side of the road and shut it off. Leaping down from the cabin he joined Ben in the lead cruiser and they turned down the track towards their destination.

Arriving at Blind Bluff Ben first scouted the ground to make sure that the drill rig could gain access. Having confirmed that the country south from the track was flat, other than the bluff, and limited to only minor growth of spinifex and saltbush, Ben was happy that the drilling rig could easily drive across country to each drilling site.

Returning to the vehicles Ben had Lance lay out the map of the geophysical survey on the bonnet of his cruiser. Lance had bought the map with him from Perth. Ben closely examined the map which showed a large, elongate anomaly almost one kilometer in length. As Ben had suspected, the anomaly was oriented east – west and appeared to show a dip to the south. Nigel and his team had left a pile of pegs at the site so, Ben and Mick grabbing a handful each, they set out to mark where the drillholes would go.

Ben crossed the dry creek and walked over the bluff to the copper outcrop. He then retraced his steps, counting his paces as he went. At approximately one hundred meters south of the outcrop he used his pick to bang one of the stakes into the hard earth. Taking a large black marker pen from his shirt pocket he marked the white painted top of the peg with BBDD-1. This was shorthand for Blind Bluff Diamond Drillhole number 1.

Satisfied with the positioning Ben paced out to the west banging in a peg every eighty meters. He then did the same to the east, followed by Mick, with pegs at the same interval. He now had sited positions for eleven drillholes numbered BBDD-1 to BBDD-11. Each drillhole would be completed to a probable maximum depth of around two hundred meters making a total program of approximately two thousand, two hundred meters.

Returning to the camp site Ben found that Ibrahim and Lance had erected two large tents in their absence. These tents would form the core of a camp for the next month or so, whilst the drilling was being completed.

Having completed all that could be done until the drilling rig arrived, Ben dismissed his men, sending them back to Marble Bar to await the drilling rig. The men would pick up the damaged vehicle on the way and drive it to the town for later movement on to Port Hedland. Ben stayed alone at the newly established camp with his swag and a couple of tins of stew for dinner. The departing men had left him with a small box of supplies and one of the cruisers. Although Mick was concerned leaving Ben alone he had no qualms about staying out by himself. He had done it many times before and in fact liked being alone in the bush. He heated the stew over a small fire and ate with a fork directly from the cans. He then spread his swag on the ground about ten meters from the nearest tent. He could have slept in the tent but preferred to be outside under the stars. And he wasn't worried about the terrorists attacking him here. He was asleep in minutes.

20

20 APRIL, 2014

Ben had a dreamless night and was well rested when he awoke at six o'clock the following morning. With nothing to do he sat at the camp site drinking tea, boiled in the billy, until he heard the noise of engines approaching at about eight am. He was at first apprehensive, thinking that it might be the terrorists after all come to finish what they had started. He relaxed when he caught site of the first vehicle and saw that it was Micks cruiser with the Major Minerals logo emblazoned on the side door. Mick was followed by Lance's cruiser which in turn was followed by the large truck mounted drilling rig. That was in turn followed by another four wheel drive belonging to the drilling company and bearing that company's logo on the door which was in turn followed by a water truck.

Lances vehicle had on the back two two hundred liter drums of aviation fuel for the helicopter which would arrive later that day.

The four vehicles stopped just short of the camp and Ben wandered over to greet them. All of the men climbed down from their vehicles. Mick and Ibrahim from Micks cruiser, Lance from his, a large heavily built driver from the drilling rig truck, two men from the last cruiser, and the driver from the water truck.

One of the men from the cruiser was short in stature, barely five and a half feet, and thin with a thin, elfin face. Indeed, so short and lightweight was he that he could have passed for a jockey. He was the exact antithesis of a driller who were almost uniformly large, gruff men with muscles on muscles. This was Angus, the driller, with whom Ben had worked before.

"G'day Angus. Good trip out?", asked Ben jovially.

"Sure thing mate", said Angus, "And I've got a present for you". He did indeed have a cloth wrapped parcel in his hands. He handed the parcel to Ben without ceremony.

Steve did not unwrap the cloth because he already knew what was inside. The evening before he had left Perth he had taken the same parcel to Angus's house, knowing that he was the driller going up to Blind Bluff. Wrapped in the cloth was a Mauser pistol that his grandfather had taken from the body of a dead German officer in North Africa during the Second World War. His grandfather had returned to Australia with the pistol as a souvenir where he had acquired more bullets for the gun. The pistol, and bullets, had since been passed down to Ben's father and thence to himself.

Ben had asked Angus to bring the pistol north as he knew that he could not carry it on the plane. Ben had acceded to his request without qualm. It was good of him to have acted as courier as the pistol was unregistered and therefore illegal. He would not have been able to bring it north on a plane with the security in place for possible terrorist attacks. Ben thought it ironic that the pistol he had not been able to travel with because of terrorist threats may now be used to protect himself and his men from terrorists.

Ben had never fired a pistol or for that matter any firearm in his life. The pistol he had always sat in a box at the back top of the wardrobe, virtually forgotten. But if he was coming back into the lair of the snake, the terrorists, he wanted some protection. He walked casually back to his swag and put the wrapped pistol beneath it.

Turning back to Angus he said: "You and your boys ready to go then Angus?"

"Sure thing Ben. Just point us in the right direction", said Angus, "And show us where we can get water". Water was needed to cool the drill bit when the diamond drilling commenced.

"Follow me Angus and I'll show you where the first hole is", said Steve, and then to Mick, who was standing nearby: "Take one of the drillers and show him where that water bore is about five k west of here".

Ben and Angus set off across the dry creek bed and Ben showed Angus the peg denoting the first drillhole. Standing at the peg he explained that the drillhole was to be drilled at a sixty degree angle, pointing due north. He then pointed out how the drilling rig could easily drive across country to reach the site.

The two men returned to the camp and Angus quickly marshalled his men, with the exception of the one who had driven off with Mick to see the water bore. The driver of the drilling rig mounted up, did a tight turn and was soon heading down the track. After about one hundred meters he took a sharp left turn and headed off across country to the first drillhole site. One of the other drillers met him at the peg and began directing him to point in the correct direction. The drill rig positioned, both men then set about raising the drilling mast to the required angle of sixty degrees. They then attached the first drill rod to the mast and attached the hammer that would commence the drilling to that rod. The hammer was piece of steel pipe about one and a half meters long and fifteen centimeters in diameter with a drill bit attached at one end. Compressed air forced down the drilling rods caused a piston-like arrangement to force the drill bit to vibrate up and down, thus pulverizing the rock beneath. Compressed air fed down the drill tubes blasted the resultant dust and fine rock fragments to the surface.

Finally, having driven that vehicle across, they unloaded the cyclone from the drillers four wheel drive. The cyclone was a large drum-like piece of equipment through which chips of rock blasted by the air pressure from the drillhole cycled before falling into sample bags. They connected up the heavy duty reinforced rubber pipes to the collar of the drillhole and to the cyclone and they were ready to start.

Angus wandered across confidently to the drilling rig where he inspected the work of his offsiders. Satisfied that they had arranged everything correctly he switched on the motor that ran the rig and a second motor which pumped compressed air down the drill rods. The desert silence was suddenly drowned in a roar. Standing at the control panel mounted at the back of the truck and adjacent to the drillhole to be, Angus twisted a couple of dials and lowered a lever and the drill rods and hammer began to turn and lower. The rear end of the drilling rig was suddenly enveloped in a cloud of dust as the hammer began to bite and a hole to form. Dust and chips of rock were expelled by the air through the pipe and into the cyclone from where it dropped into a large plastic bag positioned by one of the drilling offsiders. Drill evaluation of the Blind Bluff prospect had commenced!

Ben stood to one side of the roaring drilling rig, now with a hard hat on his head, a dust mask over his mouth and nose, and ear plugs in his ears. Lance, the junior geologist, stood beside him similarly protected. So situated they watched as Mick and the other driller offsider returned from the water bore and pulled up next to the drilling rig.

As the drilling progressed, every meter the full bag would be removed from the cyclone to be replaced by another. The full bags were placed in a line about ten meters way from the drilling rig. As each bag was heaved into place Ben and Lance would squat down and closely examine the chips and dust with their hand lenses, each making notes in their notebooks. Ben had asked Lance to duplicate his work as he would later compare the two notebooks to see if the lad knew what he was doing. Lance knew that he was being tested and wore a continual frown as he examined the bags.

As the geologists examined the material bought up the hole, Mick, using a small length of hard plastic pipe, would spear through each bag of dust and chips, the material collected in the pipe being placed in calico bags for later assay. Ibrahim had been left to take care of the camp and to prepare lunch.

All morning the drilling rig roared as the hole deepened. By lunchtime the hole had penetrated to a depth of eighty meters, the dust and chips graduating from brown, weathered shale to grey, fresh shale. At eighty meters Angus stopped the rig. The sudden silence was almost deafening.

"Diamond from here on?", he yelled across to Ben.

"Yep Angus, change her over", yelled Ben in reply.

Before diamond drilling could commence Angus had to extract all of his drilling rods from the hole. This was a laborious process as each three meter rod had to be screwed loose and stacked on the rack as they were progressively drawn back up the hole. Finally, when all of the rods and hammer had been extracted they had to force hard plastic pipes down the hole to keep the rock in place when the diamond drilling commenced. When all was completed a diamond drill bit was attached to a rod and lowered down the drillhole. Once again they had to go through the laborious process in reverse, this time attaching a new rod as the bit was lowered. Finally, the drill bit rested on the bottom of the drillhole.

"Time for lunch boys", yelled Ben.

All of the men instantly dropped what they were doing and walked back to the camp some two hundred meters away. On arrival they discovered that Ibrahim had prepared a lunch fit for kings. Using the hot plate he had cooked each man a steak and several sausages to which he had added lettuce, tomatoes, onion and peppers. A loaf of bread, fresh from town that morning, sat on top of one of the bonnets. All of the men, hungry from the hard work, sat where they could to eat.

Mick was sitting close to Ben. "I know what Angus bought you mate. Do you think it's a good idea?", said Mick quietly.

Ben was not surprised that Angus had told Mick what was in the package. Angus was probably worried about Ben's state of mind.

"Look Mick', he said, "I know I probably shouldn't have but I didn't want to be defenseless with those idiots running around", he said.

"Fair enough mate. Just be careful OK", said Mick, looking Ben in the eyes.

"No worries mate", said Ben, appreciative of Micks concern.

The men were finishing the last of their lunch when all heard the whump! whump! whump! sound in the distance.

Chopper, thought Ben. He was proved right a minute later when the blue painted Bell Jet Ranger helicopter hovered into view. The helicopter circled the camp once and set down with a deafening thunder two hundred meters to the west. Ben walked over to greet the helicopter pilot.

As Ben neared the helicopter its blades slowly wound down until they were still. He walked up to the cabin and waited for the pilot to exit. After opening the door the pilot jumped down from the cabin and walked across to where Ben waited.

"You must be Ben Wilde unless I have the wrong address", the pilot smiled.

"Yeah, that's me. You've got the right place", answered Ben, "We've just had lunch. Would you like a bite?"

"Chuck Sanders", said the pilot extending his hand, "No, I'm OK. Had a sandwich on the way out. I am ready to go to work when you are".

"Great, I'll just get the boys", said Ben, turning to walk back to the camp. The pilot followed him with a kitbag and a swag that he had extracted from the small cargo hold of the helicopter. On arriving at the camp he asked Ben where he would be sleeping and was directed to one of the tents.

"Lance, Mick, you're both doing stream sediment sampling this arvo. Get your gear together", said Ben to the two men.

Ben was sending Mick out with Lance as he was experienced and would hopefully stop the young geologist from making a mistake. Mick had done stream sediment sampling on previous occasions with Ben. Mick got some water flasks, a sieve, a gold pan and an armful of sample bags. Lance retrieved a new notebook, an envelope of aerial photographs and his pick.

Stream sediment sampling was a fairly easy task. Lance would navigate using aerial photographs and would direct the helicopter pilot to land close to chosen creeks. He and Mick would then bolt from the idling helicopter to the creek, quickly sieve and bag a sample of the creek gravel, the fine fraction, and run back and board the helicopter. When airborne again Lance would write a brief note on the nature of the creek and rocks he had seen at the sample site. An easy job for a newbie geologist.

Lance and Mick were soon comfortably seated in the helicopter, Lance next to the pilot and Mick in the back. Both men had donned headphones and microphones so they could talk to the pilot. Chuck strolled back to the machine and within minutes had it airborne and heading away from the camp towards the west.

Ben and Ibrahim walked back to the drilling rig. With Mick gone, Ibrahim would take over his sampling job. Angus started the machines and with a few levers thrown the bit was soon grinding away at the rock eighty meters below. Although the bit ground slowly the rock was soft and Ben was pleased to see it progress faster than was normal.

Every couple of meters the drill core would be pulled to the surface and deposited in the aluminium trays that had been bought out from port Hedland by Lance. To start with the core was a solid tube of dark grey shale with the occasional glittering speck of a sulphide mineral. Ben was pleased to see that the bedding planes of the shale were almost at right angles to the core meaning that he had guessed correctly. When the drillhole reached the target they should pass through that too at right angles.

The drilling proceeded smoothly with Ben examining the core minutely and recording his findings in his notebook. As he did so Ibrahim was splitting the core and every meter retaining and bagging a half of the core for assay.

At a depth of ninety two and a half meters the core suddenly changed in appearance. The dark grey shale was gone to be replaced by massive sulphides. These sulphides were mainly the dull yellow iron sulphide, or pyrite. However, unevenly spread through the pyrite were numerous blebs and veinlets of a brighter yellow sulphide mineral. This was the mineral chalcopyrite, the ore of copper. You beauty, thought Ben. I knew it! Copper ore.

The drilling rig churned onwards, but at a slower pace in the harder sulphide ore. Finally, at one hundred and fifteen meters the core passed out of sulphide and back into the dark grey shale.

Ben had logged twenty-two and a half meters of sulphide ore, all with copper. He estimated that that length would assay an average of about ten percent copper. He had definitely discovered a significant copper orebody. Yippee!

Ben let the drilling continue through another fifteen meters of barren, dark grey shale. Seeing that there was no more mineralisation he decided to call a halt. Attracting Angus's attention by waving his arms he drew his hand across his throat in the universal signal. Stop!

Angus powered down the rig and finally killed the motors. Once again silence fell across the desert.

"Looks like you've found a good one", he said as Ben walked up to him. He too had seen the drillcore as it had been laid out.

"Yep, you bet", said Ben, "You are looking at one happy chappy!. I think we'll leave it for today and start the second hole tomorrow", he added.

It was too late to commence another drillhole, at least six

o'clock by Bens estimation. The men retreated to the camp as the sun began to sink in the west.

Ben had heard the helicopter return to the camp and land about half an hour previously. When the drilling crew with Ben and Ibrahim reached the camp Mick, Lance and Chuck had already started a fire and each had settled in with a can of beer except for Chuck who was drinking coke. Chuck could not afford to fly under the influence of alcohol or his licence might be withdrawn.

That night the men had another barbecue which was heartily enjoyed by all. Washed down with a couple of beers, except for Chuck, all of the men were content.

Throughout the meal and the chatter over beers after, Ben had been thinking. It's not right he thought. Here we are less than fifty kilometers from a gang of armed men and no-one was doing anything! Those men could be planning major carnage and there was nothing and no-one to stop them! Having made up his mind Ben wandered over to the tent in which Chuck, the pilot, was sleeping. Chuck had left the fire early claiming that he had things to do in his tent.

Angus had also retired to bed early pleading a long, tiring day at the controls of his machine. Mick, Ibrahim and the drillers offsiders were not far behind. All of the drill crew went to sleep in one of the tents whilst Mick and Ibrahim had their swags in the open air the same as Ben as was their habit.

"Knock, knock", said Ben, rustling the canvas flap at the entrance to the pilots tent.

"Yo, come in!", came a voice from inside.

Ben stepped into the tent to see Chuck divested of his clothes, standing only in a pair of boxer shorts.

"Oh, I'm so sorry", said Ben, embarrassed, "I'll come back later".

"Don't worry man! You're not gay are you?", laughed Chuck.

"No, of course not", said Ben, "I just wanted to ask a favour of you", he added.

"Ask away man. I'm all ears", said Chuck as he sat down on his as yet unrolled swag.

Ben remained standing and once again repeated his story. The capture of himself and Ibrahim, the attempted murder of Banjo, the staged vehicle crash, the beatings and finally their escape.

Chuck was visibly impressed. "Man, you have been through hell haven't you", he said, "And the police are doing nothing?".

"Well, apparently they can't because of lack of evidence", said Ben, "And I think that they think that Ibrahim and I were brain damaged from the supposed crash and imagined everything".

"Shit man", replied Chuck, "If this were the States the FBI would have rousted those bastards out of there by now".

"Yeah, well", said Ben, "Nobody has and no-one is going to. That's why I've come to you for a favour. I can't bear the thought of those terrorists on the loose so I want to spy on them and see what they're up to. If I can get some evidence then the police will have to act".

"Fair enough Ben. So what can I do to help?"

"I'm hoping you will fly me over the homestead, say tomorrow, to see if I can see anything damning. Will you do it for me?", pleaded Ben, "I don't want to put you in harm's way but I don't see what else I can do. And if you do I will pay for your time out of my own pocket".

"Listen Ben", said Chuck seriously, "I did two tours of duty flying choppers in Afghanistan for the marines. I've seen what those towelhead fuckers do. It will be my pleasure and honour to try to put a spanner in their works. If those fuckers were to do something on my watch I would never forgive myself. And don't worry about payment. I will just jiggle the logs a bit and no-one will know what we have been up to".

"Thanks Chuck. You have no idea how much I appreciate this", said Ben with feeling, "First thing tomorrow morning?"

"No worries buddy", said Chuck.

After wishing Chuck a good night Ben turned and left the

tent. He did not return to the campfire which had in any case been abandoned but instead went straight to his swag some distance away. He threw himself down on the swag and turned onto his back to watch the stars. It's been a bloody good day, he thought. It wasn't everyday that you found a potential multi-billion dollar mineral resource. He was even more cheered to think that he had taken steps to redress the situation with the terrorists. His plan was undoubtedly lousy, and would probably produce no positive result, but at least he was doing something. Cheered, he rolled onto his side and in minutes was asleep.

21

21 APRIL, 2014

ASHAD GAZED OUT his study window wearing a pensive expression. It had been three days since the police had visited and apparently gone away satisfied. However, he knew that it was only a matter of time before they put two and two together and came up with four. Perhaps the police would figure out that the geologist and Ibrahim were not brain damaged and that their stories must therefore be true. Or, if not, that meddlesome geologist might do something foolish that would place him and his men in jeopardy. He knew that he had to act before that happened.

Ashad had originally planned for the operation to take place another two weeks in the future. At that time the American President was scheduled to be visiting Canberra and he could kill two birds with one stone. Critically harm Australia and kill the American president at the same time. That was the original plan thought out in Riyadh. It now appeared that that opportunity would be denied him. Nonetheless, even without the Americans presence, his mission would still cause catastrophic harm to the American ally, Australia. The mission would go ahead now!

"Sameer", he called, knowing that his second in command was in the next room.

Desert Dreaming

Sameer quickly appeared in the doorway. "Yes Sir. What do you wish?", he said.

"Sameer, muster the men so I can address them. Forty minutes from now. The mission goes ahead tomorrow. I know it is a little early but we have no choice", said Ashad.

"Yes Sir", said Sameer, as he disappeared out of the doorway, and out of the house.

With the exception of the two men at the entry observation post, and one man at the NWR facility, most of the men were relaxing around the homestead. Sameer called Tariq from his quarters and instructed him to go and pick up the men at the entry observation post.

Most of the remaining men were also relaxing in their quarters except for two who had taken a walk to the aircraft hangar. Sameer quickly gathered them together and instructed them that there would be a meeting in forty minutes time.

Tariq returned from the entry observation post forty minutes later with the two observers in the front seat next to him. With all of the men gathered, except for the observer at the waste facility, Sameer instructed them to take seats in the large living room. There were not enough seats for all so some lounged against the walls. Many of them had AK47's slung over their shoulders.

Having heard the commotion of the gathering men Ashad emerged from his study after downing a reinforcing whisky. He went into the living room where all of the men looked to him expectantly.

"Men", he said in Arabic, "The time has arrived to act. We will leave here early tomorrow morning and the attack will take place that evening. I trust that you are all prepared?".

There was no answer from the cowed men so he continued. "You have all trained well and I am sure that you will perform well. Remember, we strike the infidels in the name of Allah. Praise be to Allah! Allahu Akbar! You all know what you must do so I will not repeat instructions. Some of you may die tomorrow and others will die later but remember, you will be martyrs and your souls will fly straight to paradise. Are there any questions?".

All of the men remained silent. If there had been a question none would be willing to be the first to speak.

Ashad looked around the room, trying to look deeply into each mans eyes. Most averted their gaze to find sudden interest in the floor or the ceiling.

"Good. Go and prepare yourselves. Make sure you have sufficient ammunition and your weapons are in good working order", said Ashad finally.

The following morning a convoy of five four wheel drives left the homestead and made their way out to the main NWR road. The sixth and last vehicle in the convoy was the large dump truck full of fertilizer. Ashad and Sameer rode in the lead vehicle, followed by the remaining nine men in the other five vehicles. One man rode alone in the fertilizer truck.

For two hours the convoy drove east before finally coming to the largely camouflaged entry into the small side track near the observation post set up to survey the facility. They drove down the track a short way before turning the vehicles around a large sand dune and parking. The vehicles would not be seen from the road in the unlikely event that some traveler passed by.

The truck could however not negotiate the loose sand behind the sand dune. It would have to be left in the open, visible from the road. Ashad just hoped that no lost tourist came driving down the road. He knew that there were no deliveries of radioactive waste due so the truck would not be seen by the convoy drivers.

Ashad dismounted from his vehicle and waited while the men gathered around. Satisfied that all were present and correct, and all carried their AK47's, Ashad set of the one kilometer to the observation post. Arriving at the dune on which the post sat Ashad signaled for the men to wait at the base. He alone scrambled up to the small tunnel and pit that was the post. There he found Mahommet.

Desert Dreaming

"Mahommet", he asked softly in Arabic, "Has there been any change?".

"No Sir. It is the same as always", anwered Mahommet, with some despair at not having been offered some variety in his lonesome task.

"Do the two hourly patrols always go the same way", asked Ashad.

"Yes Sir. Unfailingly. They always come straight across the compound and turn right behind the administration block".

"Good. Now go below to the other men and have some lunch. I will stay here to observe", said Ashad, "The attack takes place tonight".

Mahommet disappeared down the tunnel. Ashad could hear the low murmur of voices from below but he was confident that they could not be heard in the compound. He would not bother to berate the men. After all, some of them would probably die soon.

A half hour later Sameer bought a hunk of bread and a small block of cheese for Ashads lunch. Ashad took the food gratefully and sank into the bottom of the pit to eat. Sameer returned to the men. After having eaten, Ashad sat for hours watching the comings and goings of the men in the compound. At two o'clock in the afternoon he saw two men in army fatigues get into one of the humvees to commence their perimeter patrol. As advertised, the humvee came straight across the compound and turned right behind the administration building. At four o'clock he saw them repeat the exercise. At five minutes to four, before the last perimeter patrol, he saw the lieutenant stride across the compound to disappear behind the administration building. He is going to complete his daily radio report to base, thought Ashad. He could see the radio aerial atop the administration building.

At five o'clock Ashad descended the sand dune to the waiting men.

"Men, it is time to act!', he announced, "Sameer, take two men and cut through the fence this side of the administration block.

The cut will not be seen as it is behind the building. When the two soldiers do their circuit you are to cut them down as they come around the corner of the building. Mahommet, you take another man and get close to the front gate. The second you hear firing cut down the guards there. I will take the remainder of the men and cut a hole behind the mess building. Once again it will not be seen. When we hear you firing we will take care of the rest of the soldiers. We need not worry too much about the other men, they are unarmed".

Ashad was not concerned about the electric fence. Rubber handled tools and thick rubber gloves were great equalizers.

Sameer quickly selected two men and they set of around the end of the sand dune, keeping the administration building between themselves and the main compound.

Ashad led the remaining seven men on a circuitous route around the compound to the other side, always keeping the dunes between himself and the open compound. Mahommet and his selected man continued on towards the guarded gate.

Ashad saw that the sleeping quarters and mess building finished only three meters short of the fence. Realising that he could not be seen from within the compound, unless someone came around to the back of the buildings, Ashad went and crouched beside the fence. He beckoned the other men to join him and all ran over, bent double although there was no need.

"Abdul, cut the wire", he said to the man with the wire snips and rubber gloves. Although Ashad knew it was safe to cut the wire protected by the rubber, he himself was not going to take the risk.

Abdul knelt by the fence and quickly cut a square out of the wire about one meter tall and one meter wide. There was no blare of an alarm so the fence had not been monitored for breaks in the wire. Or, more likely, the current continued to flow in the unbroken wires above the cut.

Although the sun had already set there was plenty of light

from the full moon. His men had in any case been trained to fight in the dark.

"Quickly now, through the wire", hissed Ashad, "And keep silent".

One after the other his men passed through the gap, pushing their rifles ahead and squirming through after, being cautious not to touch the live wires on either side and above. Ashad was the last to enter the compound. He beckoned for the men to bend low to hear his whisper. "Other than the two men in the humvee, and the two at the gate, all of the soldiers are either in their quarters or in the mess. When you hear Sameers shots, be ready to run around the side and cut down the others as they answer the alarm".

Ashad retreated into silence and his men also remained silent. About twenty minutes later they heard engine noise as one of the humvees was started. A few minutes later there was the stutter of gunfire from the other side of the compound. That was quickly followed by gunfire and an explosion from the area of the front gate.

On cutting their way through the fence Sameer and his men had taken up positions about half way down the length of the administration block. Two remained standing whilst the third lay flat on the ground, his rifle extended. At six o'clock they heard the motor of the humvee start and two minutes later it poked its nose around the corner of the building. Sameer and his men held their fire until they saw the two humvee occupants sharing a joke as they drove. All three men opened fire almost as one and within seconds the two soldiers were dead, shot through many times. Running forward, and after a quick check to make sure the two men were indeed dead, the three terrorists bolted around the corner of the building to assist Ashad on the other side of the compound.

Mahommet and his man had found cover behind a small sand dune less than twenty meters from the front gate. On hearing Sameer start his assault, the two men stood as one and unleashed a torrent of fire at the small guard hut. The hut was constructed only of thin fibreboard and the bullets tore through it without losing any momentum. The two soldiers sitting on stools within were riddled with bullets with no time to return fire. They were both dead in seconds, never having had time to realize what was happening. In order to be sure one of the terrorists lobbed a hand grenade over the fence which, with a violent explosion, destroyed the small hut. The two men inside, already dead, were further shredded by flying shrapnel and splinters of wood. A thin trail of blood began to snake downwards across what had been the step into the hut. Unable to enter through the still locked gates, the two terrorists ran back towards the hole cut into the fence by Ashads party.

At the sound of the gunfire three of Ashads men ran around the end of the mess building into the open. The other two ran around the other end of the sleeping quarters. The five remaining soldiers, including the lieutenant, who had been watching a football match on the television in the mess, ran from the building at the sound of the gunfire. All were armed and seeking targets that they could not yet see. The three men at the end of the mess and the two men at the end of the sleeping quarters caught them in a crossfire. One of the soldiers was killed instantly and the others, including the lieutenant, went to ground, returning fire as they did so.

Three of Ashads men had run out into the open to get a better shot at the Australians. All three were immediately shot down and killed by the rapid fire of the Australian Austeyr rifles, blood spurting into the air. Meanwhile, one of the soldiers was hit in the arm causing him to drop his weapon. Another was hit in the leg and, although he continued to fire, his bullets sprayed wide.

"Do not kill the lieutenant!", Ashad shouted, "I need him!".

After the first three had been killed the remainder of Ashads men had taken cover behind the buildings, shooting around the corners. Sameer in the meantime had come running across the compound from the administration block. The soldiers, lying on the ground and shooting in two directions at Ashads men, did not hear them come from the opposite direction. Without hesitating, and without bothering to shoot, Sameers men ran up behind the Australians and clubbed them on their heads with rifle butts. The battle was over with the remaining four soldiers unconscious on the ground.

"Spread out!", screamed Ashad, "Find the rest and bring them here".

The remaining men spread out in pairs. Two went to the administration building, two to the tunnel entrance and two ran into the mess.

The two men who entered the mess found six men cowering behind overturned tables. These were the two cooks and the four drillers. They had been watching the football game with the soldiers.

"Out! Out! Out!" screamed one of the terrorists, gesturing towards the doorway with his rifle.

The six men slowly emerged from their hiding places and, thinking it prudent, one shot his hands above his head. The other five quickly followed suit. The two terrorists prodded the men with their rifles, hurrying them outside.

"Good", said Ashad as the men appeared, "Six down and six to go".

With gestures from the terrorists the six men sat on the hard ground, still with their hands raised.

"Watch them", said Ashad to the two armed men.

One of the terrorists came running back from the mouth of the tunnel.

"Sir", he said, "We think some of the men are down in the tunnel. What should we do".

"Just go down and bring them out", said Ashad with exasperation, "They are not armed".

The terrorist ran back to the tunnel and with his companion, and with some trepidation, began to walk down the broad roadway into the tunnel. Reaching the bottom they were pleased to see a large, well lit square cavern cut into the rock. They could not however see the missing four men.

"Come out", yelled one in badly accented English, "Come out and you will not be killed".

Slowly, like the men from the mess, the four hideaways emerged from their hiding places. Without being told they also raised their hands in the air when they saw the rifles. Gesturing with their rifles the terrorists shepherded the four men up the ramp and out into the moonlight. They soon joined their compatriots sitting in the dirt of the compound. Ashad directed two of the gunmen to guard the prisoners whilst the other two aided in the search for the two missing administrators. Just then one of the men ran back across the compound from the administration block.

"Sir, Sir", he yelped breathlessly as he approached, "We think there are men in the administration building. We could hear them talking. But they won't come out!".

Without answering Ashad strode across to the building, halting about ten meters in front.

"You men in there!', he yelled, "Come out now and you will be spared. If we have to come in after you then you will die!".

Ashads demand was at first met by silence. The front door then opened a crack and a white handkerchief stapled to a wooden ruler appeared in the narrow opening.

"Yes, come out and you will not be harmed", barked Ashad.

The door silently opened and two men stepped onto the threshold, one still grasping the makeshift flag of truce and the other with his hands raised.

"What do you intend doing to us", asked the older man with grey showing in his hair.

"To you, nothing", lied Ashad, "But we are going to destroy your facility used for disposing of the filth of the infidels". Ashad knew that the blast to come would kill all of the captives.

"Did you radio for help", he added, "Answer truthfully now and you will not be harmed".

"No, no we did not. We did not have time", said the older man.

"Good", said Ashad, "I would hate for things to become complicated forcing me to kill you", he smiled. Both men looked ashen but said nothing.

Ashad entered the building looking for a secure place to keep the captives. He found it quickly. A large conference room to the left of the entrance had a stout, lockable wooden door and no window. He exited the building and walked over to the huddled and guarded captives.

"Sameer, Take the captives and lock them in the conference room. Place a guard at the door", said Ashad.

The captives not having understood the Arabic stared blankly at the dirt. Sameer prodded them with his rifle and repeated the instructions in English. The conscious men carried the four unconscious soldiers as they shuffled into the building and into their prison.

"Two of these men are wounded", said the grey haired administrator, stopping in front of Ashad, "They need urgent medical attention".

"Apologies sir", said Ashad, "But as you can see we have no doctor here. They will just have to make do", grunted Ashad.

"At least let us have a first aid kit", pleaded the administrator, "There is one behind the desk in the foyer that has morphine".

Without speaking Ashad indicated for one of his men to retrieve the kit and give it to the prisoners. The man scuttled away on his errand. It made no difference to Ashad if the wounded received treatment or not. They were all going to die soon anyway. Nonetheless, some indication of compassion would keep the prisoners docile and compliant.

The captured men shuffled into the conference room bearing the unconscious soldiers and slumped onto the floor. The first aid kit was thrown in after them and the door was slammed shut.

One of the terrorists had found a set of keys in a drawer of the foyer desk and the door was locked. One of the terrorists took up a guard position to the side of the locked door.

"Sameer", barked Ashad, "Send six men to retrieve the vehicles and bring them here into the compound".

Sameer barked some rapid orders in Arabic and six men set off at a trot for the main gate and thence back along the road to the hidden vehicles.

Ashad prowled around the compound examining his new possession whilst he waited. He strode down into the tunnel and into the large cavern at the bottom. In the cavern he saw stockpiled in regimented lines numerous lead containers, each about one meter tall and two thirds of a meter in circumference, and each of which bore a label describing the contents. Ashad saw at once that the containers had been stacked in rows according to what they contained. Most of the containers were labeled as HLW – High Level Waste. This material had been sent here from nuclear reactors and included spent fuel rods. Some of the containers were labeled TRUW – Transuranic waste. Most of this material had been produced as a byproduct of the manufacture of nuclear weapons. Many of the containers contained plutonium. A number were also labeled as containing caesium. It was these last containers in which Ashad was most interested.

Ashad walked back up the ramp and out of the tunnel into the harsh sunlight. As he emerged from the tunnel the five four wheel drives and the truck carrying the fertilizer were entering the compound through the now unlocked main gate. Ashad stood watching as the vehicles parked on the hard earth of the compound.

"Sameer", called Ashad, "Have the truck park here next to the tunnel entrance".

Ashad had originally planned for the truck to be driven down into the cavern containing the waste but could see that the truck was too tall to negotiate the entrance roof.

Desert Dreaming

Sameer gave an approximation of a salute and walked over to the truck. The driver was still sitting in the truck awaiting further orders and with instructions from Sameer manoeuvred it so that it was parked at the top of the tunnel.

"There are three forklifts down in the cavern", said Ashad, "Have the men use them to stack the radioactive containers around the truck. Use mostly the containers marked 'caesium'. Also place two of those containers each, the caesium containers, on the backs of four of the vehicles".

Under instructions from Sameer three men ran down the tunnel and ramp to start the forklifts. Fortunately, all had keys in their ignitions. Equally fortunately, the waste containers had brackets welded to the sides that the forklifts could use to lift them. A few minutes after the men had entered the tunnel the first forklift emerged with a drum tightly clasped between its forks. Ashad was pleased to see the caesium symbol clearly labeled on its side. The forklift puttered over to the first of the four wheel drives and gently lowered the container onto its tray. A second forklift quickly followed and deposited its drum alongside the first.

Pleased that everything had gone to plan, and continued to go to plan, Ashad ambled over to the mess, leaving the men to their work. As he approached he could clearly hear the TV within continuing to broadcast the football game. It appeared as though the West Coast Eagles were beating Collingwood. Ashad entered the mess and stood looking for a moment at the TV. Seeing the control resting on a bench he turned the TV off.

Several partly finished cans of beer rested on a small coffee table in front of two comfortable lounges. There was also a half full glass of whisky. Ashad snatched up the glass and drank the contents in one gulp. He was a good Moslem, within limits. And those limits did not include denying himself Earthly pleasures. Indeed, back at the homestead he still had a half full bottle of whisky hidden in his study which none of his men knew about.

He sat down in one of the comfortable chairs and considered the situation.

He was in control of the nuclear waste disposal facility and had access to the radioactive materials that he wanted for the rest of the mission. His attack had not yet been discovered. He had lost three men but still had seven remaining. That thought reminded him. He rose from his chair and stepped outside.

"Sameer", he called, "We must bury our martyrs so their souls can go to paradise. Detail two men to do so in the sand dunes".

"Yes Sir", snapped Sameer, as he hastily cornered two of the men watching the loading of the trucks. These men grabbed shovels from the backs of their vehicles and marched out the gate and into the sand dunes. At the dune nearest the gate they rapidly commenced digging with sand flying from the shovels. There were soon three long holes, each about four feet deep.

The men returned to the compound and reverently hoisted one of their fallen comrades by the arms and legs.

"Wait", yelled Ashad, "They must be covered properly. Get some clean sheets from the quarters and wrap them decently".

The two men retreated to the quarters and swiftly emerged with bundles of white sheets. The sheets had been torn from the beds and were not strictly clean. Nonetheless, they would do. Returning to the bodies they wrapped each in a sheet until it resembled a mummy. Only then did they recommence ferrying of the now wrapped bodies out to the impromptu cemetery. Each corpse was then lowered reverently into one of the open graves. Two men then quickly shoveled the sand back into the waiting holes.

Ashad strode over to the site of the burials. In the absence of an Imam, it was his task to see that the men received a decent burial. Standing at the side of one of the now filled graves he mumbled some words that only he could hear and then impatiently directed the gravediggers back into the compound.

Four four wheel drives had now each been loaded with two

containers of radioactive waste. Each of the vehicles also carried a two hundred liter drum packed with fertilizer mixed with diesel. He directed five of the men who had been chosen for the next phase to mount three of the vehicles. The sixth chosen man had been killed in the attack so Ashad nominated Tariq to replace him. Tariq was in any case the only man remaining other than himself and Sameer. Tariq clambered into the passenger seat of one of the vehicles without demure.

"Allah be with you", he addressed the six men sitting patiently in their vehicles, "Go swiftly and deliver death to the unbelievers".

The three vehicles started and one by one did a sharp turn and drove to the compound gate. However, on passing through the gate instead of turning west onto the main road they turned east onto a rough dirt track. That track, Ashad knew, crossed the desert until it intersected with the Stuart Highway north of Alice Springs in the Northern Territory. Ashad knew that the track was passable as he had had two of his men reconnoitre it from the Stuart Highway end two months previously, before they had come to Bright Downs. Those same men had also positioned drums of fuel at strategic intervals along the track.

The three vehicles bumped off along the track before they disappeared behind the first sand dune.

It was already dark and Ashad knew that the men would have to camp within the hour but the further and quicker they moved away from the facility the better.

That night Ashad and Sameer ate food salvaged from the facility's mess. They gave their prisoners nothing, although Sameer did give them a five liter container of water. Ashad slept the night in one of the sleeping quarters, Sameer in one of the others. The guard on the prisoners was changed every two hours. As leader, Ashad was not usually expected to take a turn guarding but with only him and Sameer he had no choice. Ashad had thought of simply executing the prisoners but had decided that it was too messy and fraught with danger should one of the prisoners escape in the confusion.

The following day dawned bright and sunny. It would be another hot day typical of the desert. Ashad awoke bad tempered. The action was over and he would have to sit around for the next twenty four hours doing nothing. There was a light breeze from the west which however confirmed his decision. The three vehicles which had left the evening before had to put as much distance as possible between themselves and the facility and he had to give them time to do so. If he blew the facility too earlier he risked the six men being enveloped in a radioactive cloud being blown east from the facility. He had to give them at least a full day. That should put them at least two hundred kilometers to the east, hopefully out of range of any radioactive fallout.

Ashad was also bad tempered because, with no men remaining other than himself and Sameer, he would have to help with moving the waste containers to the truck and with guard duty. Both were beneath him but he had no choice. Curse those men for getting themselves killed!

Throughout the day either Ashad or Sameer used the forklift to move more waste containers whilst the other guarded the prisoners. By the late afternoon the fertilizer filled truck was closely surrounded by over one hundred waste containers stacked three deep and two high. When Ashad thought there was enough he retrieved the detonators and timing device from his vehicle and set about priming the truck bomb.

The truck was carrying over five tonnes of ammonium nitrate which had been covertly obtained from a number of sources. His men had then ensured that the fertilizer was mixed with diesel fuel which they had poured into the laden truck from buckets. Ashad was not an expert bomb maker but he had received some instruction and was sure that the bomb would work. Another of his men had also received some instruction in bomb making and he was sure that the mixture of fertilizer and diesel was correct.

Ashad connected three primers and detonators to the timing device. He was allowing for the circumstance that a detonator failed to go off. If one detonator failed then at least one of the other two would surely work. He set the timer atop the diesel soaked fertilizer and pushed the primers and detonators into the mixture as far as his arm would reach. He worked as quickly as he could as the acrid fumes from the fertilizer – diesel mixture burnt his eyes and nasal passages.

The timing device was of simple construction having been assembled by his bomb making expert. It comprised a simple alarm clock, a battery and a tripping mechanism which would ignite the detonators.

Finished arming the bomb Ashad climbed down from the truck. He knew that a bomb this size would obliterate the waste containers and create a large radioactive cloud. This was why he had given the other bomb carriers sufficient time to put distance between themselves and his much larger bomb. Ashad knew also that the coming blast would destroy all of the buildings at the site and almost certainly kill all of his prisoners. So be it! He had no sympathy for the infidels.

At two o'clock in the afternoon, with Sameer guarding the door, Ashad opened it and called into the room. "The army lieutenant. Come here now!"

The lieutenant, David Bryant, raised his head from where he was treating one of his wounded men. He gave Ashad a look of pure hatred but did not utter a word.

"Lieutenant", said Ashad reasonably, "I know you make a daily report by radio to your base. At what time do you make that call?"

Lieutenant Bryant remained silent.

"Sameer, shoot one of his men", growled Ashad.

"No, wait!", yelled Bryant leaping to his feet.

"The call. When?", demanded Ashad.

"Four o'clock", said Bryant dejectedly, his ashen face still a mask of hate.

"Good. I will return for you at five to four", said Ashad with satisfaction, slamming and locking the door.

During his reconnaissance Ashad had already seen the radio in the small room across the foyer.

At five to four Ashad again opened the door and gestured to the lieutenant who was standing, waiting. Ashad had drawn his pistol from his holster and waved it menacingly at the man. Bryant came to the doorway and exited whilst Sameer slammed and relocked the door. Bryant walked across the foyer to the radio room with Ashads pistol pressed to his back. Arriving in the radio room Ashad told him to sit which he did with some reluctance. Ashad then told him to turn on the radio.

"You are to say only this. Operations normal. No incidents to report. In your normal voice", said Ashad, "If I hear any hesitation from the person on the other end I will shoot you and then go and kill the rest of your compatriots. Do you understand?"

Bryant gave a small nod.

"Good. Go ahead", said Ashad.

Bryant made sure that the radio was on the correct frequency and spoke into the microphone. "Port Hedland Base, this is Alpha Two at NWR base. Do you copy?"

"Alpha Two. Reading you twenty – twenty. Go ahead", said a distinctly feminine voice.

"Port Hedland Base, Alpha Two. All operations normal. No incidents to report", said Bryant.

"OK Alpha Two. Speak to you tomorrow". The radio went silent.

"Well done", said Ashad, "You just saved yours and everyone else's lives".

Ashad directed Bryant back to the holding room and, when Sameer opened the door, shoved him inside. Sameer quickly slammed and relocked the door.

"I will relieve you on watch in two hours", Ashad said as he turned and left the building.

Through the remainder of the afternoon and through the night the two terrorists changed guard on the prisoners every two hours. Neither man got much sleep and the following morning both were tired and cranky.

Ashad woke for the final time at eight o'clock in the morning and instead of going to relieve Sameer, went straight to the truck bomb. Being careful to make sure he did it correctly he set the timer to go off in twenty minutes. He believed that that would be plenty of time to get clear of the radioactive cloud which would in any case drift to the east. He climbed down from the truck and went to retrieve Sameer.

"Sameer", he said, entering the administration building, "I have set the timer to go in twenty minutes. It is time that we made ourselves absent".

Both men jogged from the building and each climbed into the drivers seats of the two remaining four wheel drives, Sameer into the last vehicle;e containing drums of radioactive waste. They quickly started their engines and raced for the gate from the compound, Ashad leading the way. The facility would be destroyed in twenty minutes.

As they exited the gate and drove onto the main road Ashad saw a low flying helicopter heading directly towards them. For a brief moment he thought about stopping and trying to bring the machine down with rifle fire. Then he realized that the helicopter must be heading for the facility, possibly carrying government inspectors. Fine, when they landed they too would be engulfed in the blast.

22

23 APRIL, 2014

BEN WAS WOKEN by a steady whup! whup! whup! sound. He sat up groggily at first not comprehending what was happening. And then he realized. Shit!, Chuck is leaving without me, he thought. He quickly pulled on his shirt, shorts, socks and boots and raced back to where the helicopter had stood. As he neared he realized that Chuck was not leaving. Rather, he was simply moving the helicopter the one hundred meters to the fuel drums so he could refuel. Ben breathed a sigh of relief. The helicopter set down gently next to the drums and the rotors began to wind down. Chuck climbed down from the cabin and went to the nearest drum with a hand fuel pump poking out of the top. He did a few turns of the handle and a gush of aviation fuel splashed onto the ground. He was simply checking that the pump was working and that the fuel was clean.

"Morning Chuck", said Ben as he approached the helicopter, "I thought for a moment that you were leaving without me!".

"Hell no buddy. She was starting to run a bit dry so I'm just topping her up", replied Chuck.

Chuck placed the end of the hose from the pump into the opened fuel tank and began turning the pump handle. Steve could hear the fuel gushing into the helicopter. By that time Mick and Ibrahim had wandered over from the camp. Ben had yet to discuss his proposed excursion with them and wondered how they would take it.

"Listen boys", he said turning to his men, "Chuck is taking me for a bit of a ride this morning so I want you all just to stay here until I get back".

"Yeah, and where are you going mate?", said Mick suspiciously.

Ben saw no point in holding back. They would undoubtedly find out anyway.

"Look Mick", he said, "I'm just going to overfly Bright Downs to see if I can see anything suspicious".

"Fair enough. I can understand that", said Mick, "But I'm coming with you".

"As am I", butted in Ibrahim.

"No guys", said Ben, "I am not going to put any of you in harms way or get you in trouble. I do this alone, or more precisely with Chuck".

"No way man", said Mick, "You're my friend and it is my job to look after you. I'll never hear the end of it if I lose my geologist! Where you go, I go".

"I too am going", added Ibrahim, "You saved my life and I will not forget it".

"What do you mean?", protested Ben, "I didn't save your life! You saved mine!".

"Yes you did. In the desert. If you had not found the food and water I would surely have perished. And I just happened to save you so you could save me", said Ibrahim.

Ben just shook his head. He could see no point in protesting further as they would only hound him until they got their way. In any case, they were only going to be doing an innocent flyover. He nodded to signal his assent to their arguments.

Ben then retraced his steps back to the camp where he found Lance preparing for another days work.

"Hey, Lance", Ben said cheerfully, "Myself and Mick and Ibrahim are going to look at something to the east using the chopper. We shouldn't be long but I want you to stay here and sit the rig. OK?"

"Sure Ben", said lance, "You go and do what you have to do and I'll look after the drilling. Take care and have a good day".

Chuck had finished refueling the helicopter and he signaled that they could board. Mick and Ibrahim clambered into the rear seats while Ben turned to his swag. He returned to the helicopter a couple of minutes later with the mauser which he had loaded the night before.

"Whoah man", said Chuck, seeing the pistol in Ben's hand, "That's a nice piece of artillery. You not planning on shooting anyone, I hope?"

"No Chuck", Ben laughed, "I had just promised myself that I was never going anywhere near that place unless I could defend myself".

"Fair enough buddy", said Chuck, "You should be able to defend yourself good with that".

Ben climbed into the front passenger seat while Chuck walked around and climbed into the pilots seat. Mick and Ibrahim had already donned their headsets. Ben and Chuck quickly pulled theirs onto their heads and over their ears. Chuck started the motor and the blades started to rotate. They were soon up to full speed and Chuck eased the machine gently off the ground.

"OK, where to Ben", he said into their headphones.

"Due north to the NWR road, chuck a right and follow the road to the east", replied Ben.

Ben knew that the helicopter had a cruising speed of about 250 kilometers per hour. They should be over the homestead in less than twenty minutes. Ben soon saw the NWR road ahead, as did Chuck as the helicopter did a gentle bank to the right and began following the road.

"Listen everybody", said Ben, knowing that Mick and Ibrahim

could hear the conversation through the headphones, "We are just going to fly over to see what we can see. Chuck, if someone takes a shot at us you just get us the hell out of there!".

"Its OK Ben. I've got reinforcements back there anyway", laughed Chuck.

Ben glanced into the rear of the cabin thinking that by reinforcements Chuck probably meant Mick and Ibrahim. But what he saw was what looked to be an old lever action Winchester rifle nestled between the two rear seats, between Mick and Ibrahim. Mick smiled at him and stroked the rifle. Ben turned to stare back towards the front, momentarily dumbfounded.

"Do all chopper pilots carry weapons?", he asked innocently.

"Most of us do, yeah", answered Chuck, "I carry that because if ever I go down in the bush a long way from home I want to be able to hunt a roo or something to eat".

"Fair enough", said Ben, and left it at that.

A short time later the helicopter flew over the turnoff into Bright Downs homestead. Ben instructed Chuck to turn and the helicopter went into a tight bank, heading back the way it had come. Ben then directed Chuck to overfly where the entry observation post was. Flying low, only ten meters above the top of the sand dune, it passed over where the post had been. Now all that remained was the shallow hole in the sand. The tent and sleeping bags had gone. There was no sign of any men. Ben now directed Chuck to fly down the road towards the homestead.

"Gain a bit of altitude Chuck", Ben said, "I don't want to scare them into firing at us".

Chuck gained altitude until they were cruising at an altitude of about three hundred meters. Ben suddenly saw the red roof of the homestead ahead, nestled amongst the sand dunes. The helicopter flew on and passed directly over the building. Ben could see no-one on the ground and no sign of any vehicles.

"Fly over to the hangar there to the left will you Chuck. Just hover in front of it so I can see if there are any vehicles in there", said Ben.

Chuck did as he was asked and the helicopter was soon hovering in the open front of the hangar. Ben could see the small Cessna plane half in and half out of the hangar but no vehicles. On the way over he had also noted that the truck that Ibrahim had said was behind the hangar was no longer there.

"It looks as though they've all shot through", said Ben, "Perhaps they figured things were getting too hot for them". He was hopeful but still uncertain.

"Chuck, set down in front of the house. I'm going to have a look around", said Ben.

"Are you mad boss!", yelped Mick, "If they are there and they see you they'll blow your brains out! That's if you've got any!"

"Nonetheless", said Ben, "I have to see. Set her down Chuck, if you dare. I'll understand if you don't want to".

"No worries buddy. We'll have a quick look see and be out of there before you can say boo"

Chuck set the helicopter down about one hundred meters away from the house. He had increased the distance so he could cover Ben with his rifle as he approached the house. As Ben climbed down from the cabin Chuck asked Mick to pass his rifle forward. Mick did so and then scrambled down to stand beside Ben. Ben gave him a look and gestured for him to get back inside the helicopter. Mick stood his ground.

"Like I said boss. Where you go, I go".

Ben had the mauser in his hand wavering uncertainly. He thought now that he did not even know why he had bought the gun. He had never fired it before, or any gun for that matter. He did not even know if the weapon still worked. It was just as likely to blow up in his hand than shoot anything. Nonetheless, he held it forward as though it was a talisman against evil.

Seeing once again that it was pointless to argue Ben strode towards the house, Mick following close behind. On reaching

Desert Dreaming

the front door Ben gave it a gentle push and it swung open. It was only early morning and already Ben was sweating buckets. No wonder, he thought. I'm shit scared! He stepped inside the house, Mick following.

There was no sign of anybody in the house which was silent. Ben stepped forward pushing open doors as he went. Arriving at the kitchen he saw dirty dishes in the sink but still no sign of people. He quickly looked into the two remaining rooms and saw that they too were empty of people. The small bedroom where he had been held prisoner was much the same as he had left it except the bed and mattress were gone.

"It truly looks as though they've shot through", he said to Mick, trying unsuccessfully to hide his elation. If they had gone, hopefully back to the Middle East, his conscious was clear.

Ben trailed by Mick exited the front door and saw Chuck lying on the other side of the helicopter aiming his rifle back toward the house over the machines skids. Ibrahim remained sitting in the helicopter looking unconcerned. Ben and Mick trotted over to the helicopter.

"It looks as though there's no one here Chuck", gasped Ben on arrival, "I reckon that they've shot through".

"That's good man", said Chuck, "So back to camp?".

"Yep. Let's go", said Ben.

The three men climbed aboard the helicopter and Chuck fired up the engine. The whup! whup! whup! was almost silenced as they donned their headsets. Chuck lifted the machine gently off the ground and rotated it back to the west, towards the camp. However, as they gained altitude, Ben had a thought. What if the terrorists had not abandoned their plan, whatever it happened to be?

"Chuck", he said into the microphone, "Before we go back I just want to have a look at the entrance road where it meets the NWR road. Can you drop me there?"

"Sure thing Ben", said Chuck as he adjusted their heading

slightly to the northwest. The intersection of the homestead access road with the bitumised NWR road swiftly came into view.

"Don't set down too close to the intersection", said Ben, "I don't want your rotors to destroy any tracks".

Chuck did not answer but steered the machine for the sealed main road. He set the helicopter down on the road about one hundred meters to the west of the intersection. Ben quickly clambered out of the machine and, leaving the others remaining seated, bent low as he ran under the rotors back to the intersection. On arrival he could clearly see vehicle tracks in the sandy access road near where it met the main road. However, instead of turning west as he had half expected, the tracks turned to the right, towards the NWR facility. The tire tracks, deeply impressed into the sand, indicated that a number of vehicles had turned right at that point. The last set of tracks, overlaying the others, were of a broader tire, possibly belonging to a truck. Ben quickly ran back to the helicopter, again ducking low as he did, scrambled aboard and donned his headset.

"Chuck, Mick, Ibrahim", he said breathlessly, "When they left they didn't turn towards town. They turned towards the nuclear waste repository! I knew those bastards must be planning something! I think that they are going to attack the facility!"

"What do you want me to do then Ben", asked Chuck, "Radio the cops and let them know?"

"No, no!", answered Ben, "After my history they probably won't believe it anyway. Can you follow them?"

"Sure thing man. We are on our way", said Chuck as he pulled back on the collective and raised the helicopter from the ground. "I'll just follow the road shall I?"

Ben did not answer as Chuck was already following the road as it headed east.

"The facility is about two hundred kilometers away. How long will it take us to get there?"

"Less than an hour man", replied Chuck.

The helicopter hurtled through the air following the road at an altitude of about two hundred meters. Each man in the cabin sat in silence engrossed in their own thoughts. Although each man kept a lookout for strange vehicles they saw none for almost the entirety of the journey.

About fifty minutes later Ben could see the facility coming into view. In a cleared area surrounded by sand dunes the white buildings were visible for many miles. As they got closer a large truck loaded with what looked like fertilizer could be seen sitting in the compound. Ben could also see two four wheel drive vehicles passing through the gate back onto the tarmac road.

Flying over the entry gate they could see the remnants of a small hut that looked as if it had been blown to pieces. Chuck banked the helicopter over the compound and bought it in to land next to the large blue and rusted dump truck.

"That truck down there", said Ibrahim over the headphones, "It is the same one that was at the station!"

Stacked all around the truck were numerous grey containers. All of the men aboard the helicopter now feared the worst. There was no one about, the entrance hut had been destroyed, and the gates had been left open with two unknown vehicles just having left. Chuck quickly shut down the helicopter and all of the men yanked off their headsets and jumped down from the cabin. Ben and Chuck ran towards the administration block, Mick and Ibrahim to the mess and quarters.

23
23 APRIL, 2014

MICK RAN ALONG throwing open the doors of the quarters. All were empty. Coming to the end of the quarters block he glanced to his left and saw a body lying in the sand. It was the soldier killed in Ashads ambush, dragged there by Sameer. Mick ran over and knelt by the body but he swiftly saw that it was too late. The soldier was dead.

Ibrahim entered the mess and similarly saw no one, although there were partly drunk cans of beer sitting on a coffee table.

As they neared the administration block both Ben and Chuck could hear loud pounding noises. They skidded to a halt in the main doorway and immediately identified the sound as coming from a room to the left. They bolted to the left and stopped in front of the door on which the pounding was occurring. Fortunately, the key was still in the lock so Ben turned it and, despite some resistance from the other side, pushed it open. He saw a number of men, including two lying on the floor swathed in bandages. He also immediately saw what had been making the noise. The captive men had dismantled a large conference table and had been using the stout wooden legs to try to beat the stout wooden door down, albeit with only minimal success.

Desert Dreaming

"Who are you!", shouted a man dressed in the camouflage fatigues of a soldier.

Ben believed that he did not have the time to explain. He still had to see if the terrorists were still here, possibly hiding. He turned and ran from the room leaving Chuck to explain the situation. Exiting the building he saw again the second hand dump truck parked in the middle of the compound. He also quickly realized that the containers stacked around it contained radioactive waste. He bolted to the truck and clambered up the rungs welded to its side. At the top he saw that the truck was nearly full of fertilizer and what smelt like diesel. Perched atop the fertilizer was a black box with what looked like a clock and wires leading to it from the fertilizer.

It's a fucking bomb, Ben thought. And with the radioactive waste they had been planning on producing a huge radioactive cloud.

"Mick, Ibrahim", he yelled, "Get over here. We've got a huge problem!"

Mick was the first to arrive and came to a halt below where Ben perched on the rim of the truck.

"Mick!", said Ben, "They've turned this truck into a huge bomb with the fertilizer. There's a timer up here but I can't see when its primed to blow. That must have been them we saw leaving so we probably don't have long".

"Well, let's get everybody a safe distance away and let it blow", said Mick, "After all, the government can afford to replace the buildings".

"We can't. When it goes its going to blow those drums and create a huge radioactive cloud that might drift across to Alice Springs, maybe even Adelaide. We can't move the drums of waste in time so we'll have to move the truck!"

Ben clambered down from the truck and ran around to the drivers door. Wrenching the door open he saw what he had hoped not to see. There were no keys in the ignition!

"We're fucked", he said to Mick who had joined him, "There's no keys!"

"Not to worry boss", said Mick with a grin, "I knew my misspent youth would come in handy". With that he clambered into the drivers seat and with his head bent below the dashboard began tearing wires from their mounts. He found the two wires he wanted and twisted them together. The engine immediately roared into life.

"That's terrific Mick", yelled Ben over the engine noise, "Now Ibrahim, go and get some of the blokes in there to help us to move those drums from the front of the truck".

Ibrahim ran to the administration block to get the required help. Ben and Mick began wrestling the drums aside. Fortunately, there were only seven drums positioned in front of the truck. By the time Ibrahim returned with four men to help all of the necessary drums had been safely moved aside. Ben leapt into the drivers seat.

"Mick. Get everyone as far away from here as possible – She could go at any time! I'm going to try and drive it out of here".

Ben thrust the gears into first and with a touch of the accelerator the truck moved forward. As he turned it to head back towards the gate he saw that Mick and Ibrahim had mustered Chuck and the former prisoners and were hurrying them towards the gate, the two wounded soldiers being carried by four of the facility workers. The men had mostly reached the gate when one turned to look back and saw that the truck, and bomb, was heading straight towards them. With a shout of alarm all were alerted and they quickly split off to the sides, running into the sand dunes beyond the gate.

Ben drove as fast as he dared, expecting to be immolated at any second. He passed through the gate and, to make sure, drove the truck another five hundred meters down the main road before bringing it to a stop. Ben did not bother to turn off the engine or set the park brake. Instead, he jumped down from the cabin and ran for a nearby sand dune. He ran up the dune and clearing the top threw himself down the far side, landing and sliding in the loose sand.

Mick and Ibrahim had been running alongside the far side of the sand dune and soon joined him lying down just below the crest.

Ben had expected it to be just like the movies. The hero moves the bomb and just as he gets a safe distance away it blows, throwing him to the ground shaken but not injured. The truck however refused to explode. It sat there in the middle of the road, its engine still idling.

"Looks like she must have been on a long timer", said Mick after a while, "Or else she's a d…."

Just then the timer ticked over and the truck blew up in a deafening roar. Even though they were behind the sand dune the three men felt the pressure wave as it rolled them violently to the base of the dune and covered them with sand. After the roar there was dead silence, broken only by dull thuds as pieces of the truck returned to Earth.

The three men laid inert and deafened where they had been thrown, and did not move for several minutes. Ben finally sat up shaking the sand from his clothes and using his hand to brush it from his hair. Cautiously he crawled back up to the top of what remained of the sand dune. On reaching the top he stared out over where the road had been.

The explosion had created a crater almost fifty meters in diameter and several meters deep. Small wisps of smoke eddied upwards from the broken earth. The road where the truck had come to rest had disappeared. The truck had also disappeared, although about one hundred meters to the west Steve could see what he was sure was the engine. Small ripped and twisted remnants of the trucks panels could be seen at some distance lying on the sand.

A wide circle of vegetation had also been scythed down by

shrapnel from the explosion, almost to the ground. Ben could easily see that if the bomb had been left where it was it would have destroyed the entire facility.

Ben, Mick and Ibrahim ambled back along what remained of the road towards the gate where all of the others had gathered. Half way along on their journey Ibrahim began laughing uproariously.

"What's got into you Ib, Mate", asked Mick, sounding confused.

Tears were streaming down Ibrahims cheeks. "I lived in Iraq during and after the war", he said, trying to stifle the laughter, "I saw many explosions. But I have never seen such a big explosion that did so little damage. If the terrorists in Iraq had been able to place that bomb in a market place they would have been well pleased!" He continued laughing, but more quietly.

At the gate the three men were welcomed by the others. Several men crowded forward trying to shake Ben's hand and showering him with congratulations and thanks. Embarrassed, Ben finally came face to face with a soldier in camouflage fatigues with two pips on his shoulders. The man faced Steve squarely and thrust out his hand to be shaken.

"Lieutenant David Bryant", he said, "And who is the man who just saved our lives?"

"Ben Wilde, Lieutenant. And in case you are wondering why we are here we had suspicions about those men who attacked you and came here to see what they were doing. I am sorry we were too late".

"David please, and may I call you Ben?", asked David.

"Sure David", answered Ben.

"I am glad you showed up when you did. You saved all of our lives. If you had gotten here earlier there would have been nothing you could have done. There was about a dozen of them and they were well armed".

"Sure, but nonetheless, I feel some guilt. I should have known".

"For the final time. You saved our lives and prevented a

disaster. I have never seen anyone do anything as brave as what you just did"

Ben looked at his toes sheepishly.

"Anyway", continued the lieutenant, "We are going to have some breakfast. We have not had any food and very little water for over a day and a half. But first I have to radio the base and let them know what has happened."

Seeing that the others were re-entering the compound, Ben and David followed. Ben began laughing almost at once. He had seen that every window in the administration block facing the road had been blown out.

"Look's like I didn't park far enough away', he laughed, "I'm going to owe the government some new windows".

David laughed too.

The first thing to be seen to was the dead men. Led by the lieutenant a party discovered the two soldiers murdered in the humvee behind the administration building. The men carried the bodies to the foyer of the administration building where they were reverently laid on the floor. The body from beside the sleeping quarters was laid next to them along with the two bodies from what remained of the guard shack. Another man had found some clean sheets which he draped over the abused bodies.

Whilst the bodies were being tended to the two wounded men were carried into two of the sleeping quarters and laid on beds. The two wounded were conscious and in good spirits. It did not appear as though there wounds were too serious and that they would make full recoveries.

All of the tired men entered the mess except lieutenant Bryant. He had gone back to the administration block to radio his superiors. Most of the other men went immediately to a large wash basin to wash the blood from the dead off their hands.

The two cooks, although they too were worn out from their ordeal, immediately commenced cooking breakfasts of bacon and eggs with plenty of toast and coffee. Although he was probably the least hungry there, Ben was served first. Having finished making his radio call in the administration building, David arrived and sat across from him at the long table as Ben was finishing his breakfast.

"Luckily the terrorists did not destroy the radio. I guess that they figured that we would all be dead and so there was no need. So I've spoken to base", David said, "They are sending a plane with a doctor to treat my wounded and another eight men to take over the duty here. They should get here in about an hour. There's an airstrip just to the east of the compound. I guess that they will be closely followed by the investigators, army intelligence, Federal police, ASIO. I have also unlocked the armoury and given several of the fitter men rifles in case the terrorists come back. The bastards stole our weapons".

Looking out the wide door of the mess Ben could indeed see several men walking around with Austeyr automatic rifles slung over their shoulders.

"David", said Ben, still chewing a piece of toast, "You said that there were about a dozen attackers. When we flew in we saw two open back four wheel drives leaving, heading towards Marble Bar. There were no men in the backs and there was no way that that many men could have fitted into the front of the two vehicles. Do you have any idea where the other men might have got to?"

"No. I think we killed three when they attacked but that still leaves nine or ten. I've got no idea where they might have got to but they are certainly not here. The three we killed they either took with them or buried somewhere close by".

"Did you see any vehicles", asked Ben.

"No, we didn't, at least not to start with. I think they cut through the fence to attack us. Except for the guard hut at the entrance which I think they attacked from outside. But one of the drillers thought he heard several vehicles being driven into the compound the same night after we were attacked".

"So. We are missing a number of terrorists. And we know they had at least five four wheel drives so there's three of them missing too. It's possible that they left earlier to drive back to Bright Downs or Marble Bar. We should get the police to block the road!", he added hurriedly.

"It's taken care of Ben", said David, "My base were calling the Marble Bar police to put up a road block on the NWR road as soon as possible".

"Well, I hope they haven't already slipped through the net", said Ben despondently.

Having finished breakfast Ben wandered back out into the compound. He was pleased to see that the helicopter was undamaged, having been protected from the blast by the administration building. The workers had commenced moving the nuclear waste containers back down into the bunker using the forklifts.

Ben next went in search of the site administrator. He found the elderly man in the mess sitting on one of the lounges, he legs splayed out before him and looking thoroughly dejected.

"Sir", said Ben, "I am sorry to trouble you but can you tell if any of the radioactive waste is missing?"

"Sorry sonny", said the administrator, "But we won't know until we have done a thorough inventory. And that will take days if not weeks".

Disappointed, Ben thanked him and left the mess.

Out of curiosity, Ben went to take another look at the blast crater. He passed through the gate and went and stood on the edge of the crater. Incredible, he thought. I could have been atomized. Ben puffed out his chest thinking how brave he had been. Or stupid, he thought, as his chest collapsed.

Walking back to the gate Ben idly noted that there was a track veering off to the east. Looking closer he could see from the tracks in the loose sand that several vehicles had turned that way. Recently.

That's it!, he thought. They didn't go west, they went east! He ran back to the compound where he found Chuck checking over his helicopter.

"Chuck!", he gasped, "The rest of the terrorists went east. I've just seen their tracks!"

"What do you want me to do Ben? Do you want me to radio it in?"

"No. I'll get Lieutenant Bryant to do that. But I think we should go after them".

"Are you sure Ben? Surely the police or army can do that".

"No! These arseholes might be at least a day ahead. Follow them by four wheel drive and they'll never catch them. And I don't think either the police or army have any helicopters up here. They'd have to come up from Perth. And that would be at least one, probably two days. By that time they could have reached the Stuart Highway and disappeared! No, we have to go and maybe see if we can delay them. God knows what evil they have in mind!"

"Fair enough. I noticed on the way in that there's an airstrip to the east of here and I thought I saw some fuel drums. I'll just move the machine over there and refuel her".

Chuck climbed into the helicopter cabin and within minutes had the rotors turning. Shortly after he lifted off and flew the short distance to the airstrip where he set it down. Ben went in search of Mick and Ibrahim to tell them what he had planned. He found them both in the mess watching a rugby match on the TV and drinking cokes.

"Boys", said Ben, "I think the terrorists went to the east of here along a track. I'm going to chase them down and see if I can hold them up until the police or army get there".

"Hear that Ib", said Mick, "Looks like we're going for another chopper ride".

Before Ben could reply that they weren't needed, Mick gave him a deliberate frown. He knew when he was beaten.

While Chuck was refueling the helicopter, Ben heard the drone of an approaching aircraft. Mick and Ibrahim already had their heads in the air looking for the approaching plane. Ben saw it first heading in from the west. The plane flew over and banked on its approach to the gravel airstrip. It touched down with puffs of dust and taxied to where Chuck had just finished refueling.

Some of the other men in the compound also saw what was happening. Three of them jumped into their parked vehicles and raced off to the airstrip. Ben put up his hand to halt the last vehicle and beg the driver for a lift. The worker was glad to oblige and Ben piled into the passenger seat, Mick and Ibrahim hoisting themselves into the rear tray.

Arriving at the airstrip there were men already exiting the plane. First came eight soldiers, led by a lieutenant, who clambered into the backs of the first two vehicles and headed off towards the compound. Two of the soldiers had been carrying black plastic packages. Body bags, thought Ben.

Following the soldiers was an elderly man dressed in jeans and a flannel shirt. He was the doctor, called in from a day off from his duties in Port Hedland.

The doctor was followed by two army officers in full uniform. One was a colonel, the other a major. While the man who had given them a lift ferried the doctor to the compound, Ben walked over to introduce himself to the officers. He walked directly up to the colonel and thrust out his hand.

"Ben Wilde", Ben said confidently, "It was me and my men who discovered what had happened here. I am sorry we were too late to save the soldiers who were killed".

"Mr Wilde. Colonel James. And this is major Hennessy. Lieutenant Bryant has already explained some of what you did on the radio. I thank you", said the colonel.

"My pleasure", said Ben formally, "As I say we are sorry we did not get here sooner. However, I believe that some of the attackers have escaped into the desert. We should get after them!"

"Not to worry Mr Wilde. The Marble Bar police have already set up a road block on the entrance road. They won't get far!"

"No, no. You misunderstand", pleaded Ben, "I mean that some of them have escaped east into the desert".

"What makes you think that?", queried the colonel seriously.

"I've seen tracks leading onto the track that goes to the east. It runs just to the south of the airstrip here".

"Show me these tracks", demanded the colonel.

Left without a vehicle, Ben led the two officers back towards the compound gate. Mick and Ibrahim trailed behind. Arriving at the turnoff of the track from the main road Steve pointed to the clearly visible vehicle tracks. The colonel remained standing while the major crouched down for a closer look.

"These tracks could have been made by anyone", said the major, "It might even have been the facility workers playing around".

"I don't think so", insisted Ben, "They are very fresh. And we know that the terrorists had access to at least five four wheel drives. We saw only two leaving the facility!"

"Nonetheless", said the colonel reasonably, "There is nothing to the east other than desert. They went west and we will catch them!"

"No, I don't think that they did!", said Ben heatedly, "I am sure that they have gone east".

"Well, Mr Wilde, I know that they have cctv here so let us look at the film and see what it tells us shall we?", said the colonel reasonably.

Ben nodded his agreement and with the major and colonel walked back to the administration block where lieutenant Bryant was waiting.

"Lieutenant", said the colonel, "We need to have a look at the cctv to see what happened. Can you organize that?"

"Certainly sir. It is in the administration block here. Come right this way", answered David.

The four men entered the block and with David in the lead entered a small room behind the reception area. This room contained several computer monitors and what Ben took to be the cctv machine. David sat at one of the computer monitors and rapidly entered some commands. The screen came alive, divided into three to show three separate images. One part showed the area directly in front of the administration block, one showed the tunnel from above and the third displayed only static.

"As you can see we have three cameras", said David, "Or at least we did but the one at the gate looks like it was destroyed during the attack. I see that they threw a grenade into the box at the gate and shrapnel probably took out the camera".

"I understand", said the colonel, "And it doesn't look as though the camera at the tunnel will be of much use so can we just have the camera out front and replay from when the attack commenced?"

"Certainly sir", said David as he typed some more commands into the machine. The static filled image and the image of the tunnel disappeared to be replaced by a single image of the area to the front of the administration block.

"The attack commenced at about five thirty pm the day before yesterday so I'll rewind to then", David added as he pressed more keys.

The image immediately blurred and went out to be replaced a few seconds later by the same image taken two days previously. At first there was nothing on the image other than the administration block forecourt and the mess and quarters across the way. Then men could be seen running from behind the mess and five men in army camouflage, including David, burst from the mess.

"I am sorry that there is no sound", whispered David apologetically.

The vision continued showing three of the attacking men cut down by gunfire whilst one of the soldiers was also killed and two wounded. As the battle raged the camera showed Sameer and his men creeping up behind the soldiers and clubbing them on their heads.

"That was horrid!" said Ben, "And I don't mean to be rude or disrespectful but can you fast forward to when they leave. I think that is what we are most interested in".

"Certainly Ben", said David, once again typing instructions into the machine after noting that there was no countermand from his superiors.

The image suddenly fast forwarded showing men being captured and then moved into the administration block, Vehicles arriving from somewhere off screen to the left, and then terrorists moving backward and forward and using forklifts to pile cannisters around the truck and into four of the four wheel drives. The image finally showed several of the terrorists climbing into the four wheel drives.

"Stop her right there if you don't mind David. And go forward at normal speed", asked Ben. Ben had however seen enough to know that the camera would not show which way the vehicles had turned after leaving the compound. The camera at the administration block did not cover the gate. The gate camera would have helped but unfortunately that had been destroyed. Nonetheless, he had to see to make sure.

Once again David quickly typed some commands and the film slowed down to normal pace. Terrorists continued climbing into three of the cruisers until there was two men in each vehicle. Ben could see Ashad in the background directing the men. Bastard! He thought. I hope you rot in hell. Then each of the vehicles began to move until they were all in line heading towards the gate. Then one by one the cruisers moved off to the left side of the image and disappeared. There was no telling if they turned left or right when they reached the tarmac.

"Shit!", said Ben, "We can't tell which way they went but I'm sure it was east, into the desert. And you all saw the drums of radioactive waste on each vehicle and the drum in the middle which is probably a bomb. They are obviously on their way to do evil somewhere!"

"You are undoubtedly right Mr Wilde", said the colonel, "I mean right in everything except their direction of travel. I think they went west, not east. If they went into the desert they could be weeks tooling around out there. And they obviously don't have the fuel to go far. No, they went west. And it looks as though they left soon after the attack which is about forty hours ago so they could be in Perth by now!"

"No, I am sure that they went east", Ben almost shouted, "You must do something before they create a catastrophe"

"No, Mr Wilde. They went west. But I will certainly do something. I will alert police Australia wide to be on the lookout for them. We can't have them completing whatever they are planning. We will soon scoop them up".

"But sir", said Ben reasonably, "They could still slip through. Are you going to have police stop every four wheel drive? And I saw no readable number plates. They will disguise the drums in the back before they reach civilization. You must pursue them into the desert!"

"As I have said Mr Wilde, I do not think that they went east. I do not have the assets to cover everything but whether they went east or west they will not get far", said the colonel.

With that the colonel turned and strode from the room followed by the major. David simply shrugged and looked embarrassed. Fuming and mumbling to himself Ben followed the officers out of the building.

As he left the building the colonel turned to him and said "Mr Wilde. When the investigators get here, and that should be in six or seven hours, they will want to speak to you. Please don't go anywhere".

With that both officers turned away and walked away into the compound. Ben and his concerns had been dismissed. Part way through their walk the colonel turned around and looked at Ben who had not moved.

Screw you, thought Ben as he turned back to the helicopter. No one else wants to do anything so its left to me.

Arriving back at the helicopter of which Chuck was doing a pre-flight inspection, Ben spoke to Mick.

"Mick, we might be gone for a while so someone has to let Lance know what's happened and where we are. Can you go and ask one of the facility workers if he will go to Blind Bluff and fill Lance in? But tell him to tell Lance that we're just staying the night here. Nothing has happened. I don't want to worry the boy"

"Sure thing boss", said Mick, as he turned and trotted back to the compound. He returned, panting, five minutes later.

"One of the boys is going to drive over to see Lance", Mick said, "I've given him a bit of a mud map".

"Terrific", said Steve, "Are we right to go Chuck?"

"Sure thing. Jump in boys and buckle up. Chuck airlines will be airborne in two minutes".

24

23 APRIL, 2014

AFTER LEAVING THE compound and seeing the helicopter fly in Ashad had driven about five kilometers down the road before pulling over to the side. The road from the facility was dead straight so, although he could no longer see it, he knew exactly where it was. Sameer pulled in behind him. Ashad wanted to see the blast but be far enough away to avoid the immediate effects of the radioactive cloud. As the wind was blowing to the east he was well clear and could quickly retreat further to the west if the wind changed. He climbed down from his four wheel drive and was joined by Sammeer, both men peering back down the road to the east. Ashad was counting down the timer in his head.

With about five minutes to go Ashad thought he saw something on the road in the distance. He grabbed the binoculars sitting on the passenger seat and trained them on whatever it was. Focusing them he could soon make out what it was. It was the truck! The bomb! The people in the helicopter must somehow have moved it! As he watched the truck came to a halt and a figure jumped from the cabin and began to run to the side. Ashad focused on the fleeing figure and got an impression of khaki shorts and shirt and dark hair. Could that possibly be that interfering geologist? The figure bounded over a sand dune and disappeared.

Ashad remained watching, not believing that his plans had gone wrong. He stared at the truck through the binoculars as if to will it to reverse back into the compound.

The explosion when it came almost blinded him. There was an intense burst of light and, as he tore his eyes from the binoculars, he saw an immense column of fire, sand and rock blossom into the air. Even at that distance they could feel the stiff breeze of the shock wave.

Even Sameer perceived that something had gone awry, even though at that distance he could not have seen the truck.

"Sir, it looks as though the blast was too far to the left. Do you think the truck could have rolled out of the compound".

"No you fool. It was moved, I think by that bastard geologist we should have killed!"

Without further ado Ashad leapt back into his vehicle. He was seething as he started the motor and pulled back out onto the road. Sameer had also pulled back onto the road and had gone around in front of Ashad. He would lead for the remainder of the drive.

As he drove Ashads temper slowly cooled. After all, six of his men were still on the road on their way to their destinies. The primary part of the mission was still functioning. And then the meaning of what he had seen became clear. If they had stopped the bomb then they would almost certainly have radioed to the police or army what had happened. There would as a consequence almost certainly be a roadblock on the road he was travelling. He should have destroyed the damn radio!

Ashads immediate reaction was to signal Sameer to stop so they could make new plans. Indeed, his hand had already flicked the headlight switch before he could think further. Sameer however drove on unheeding.

Ashad thought more deeply about the problem. The original

plan had been for Ashad and Sameer to head towards Marble Bar and then South to Perth. In Perth Ashad would get the first flight out of Australia to Riyadh. Sameer would wait until Ashad was airborne and then detonate his bomb, with its radioactive waste, in the centre of the city. Sameer had actually pleaded with Ashad to be able to immolate himself for the cause. Another man was supposed to accompany Sameer but he had been killed at the compound.

If Ashad let Sameer continue on to the road block then the police would think that they had discovered all of their plans. A single bomber on his way to cause destruction at some undisclosed location, the rest of the men scattered to make their way out of the country. Surely that would be what the police would think. Sameers capture would therefore divert suspicion from the six men headed to the east. It might also provide a diversion for Ashad to escape. So be it, thought Ashad. I will let him carry on to his destruction while I escape. After all, he had wanted to sacrifice himself for the cause.

Settled with his decision, Ashad drove on, Sameer several car lengths in front. When they reached the turnoff to the homestead two hours later Ashad turned in. He knew that Sameer, if he became aware of his absence, would think that he had gone back to the homestead to clean up any remaining incriminating evidence.

Ninety kilometers further along the road, and twenty kilometers to the east of Marble Bar the two local policeman had set up a roadblock. The roadblock consisted solely of their four wheel drive vehicle parked obliquely across the road, barring passage. The roadblock had been set up less than half a kilometer beyond a bend in the road in heavily forested country so Sameer was not aware of its presence until he was almost upon it. He thought briefly about making a run for it and then decided that he could not go back the way he came and could not get around the road block so it was better to try to brazen his way through.

Sameer pulled up about ten meters short of the police vehicle and switched off his motor. One of the police, a young constable, walked up to the drivers window.

"Please step down from the vehicle sir, there has been an incident and we need to search your vehicle", said the constable.

Sameer knew instantly that he was in trouble. The police would certainly find the weapons he should have disposed of and the two drums of radioactive waste in the back. He opened the door and stepped down from the vehicle. Standing on the ground and reaching back inside as though for his wallet or papers his hand closed on the Austeyr rifle he had stolen lying on the passenger floor. The constable standing directly behind him had however seen what he was reaching for.

"Drop it!", he yelled, "Drop it or I will shoot!". He had already withdrawn his pistol from its holster.

Unable to bring the rifle to bear Sameer threw himself backwards onto the young constable. The constable toppled backwards and Sameer fell with him. The pistol flew from the constables hand and landed a short distance away. Sameer was scrabbling across the ground towards it when a shot rang out. The shot took Sameer in the throat and blood fountained into the air. He dropped flat on his face with only a few seconds of life remaining.

The young constable scrabbled to his feet and retrieved his weapon. His sergeant was standing about five meters away, his hand, holding his pistol, still extended.

"Thanks sarge", said the constable with feeling, "You saved my bacon there!"

"No problems son, though I think I'm going to have to go back to the academy", said the sergeant.

"Why do you say that sarge. You saved my life!"

"Because, son, you are supposed to aim for centre mass and my bullet took him in the throat, That's why!"

Unaware of Sameers fate Ashad had arrived at the homestead and parked his four wheel drive by the small garden gate. He walked up the dry sandy path and in through the front door, which had been left unlocked. He walked to his study where he retrieved a satellite telephone and his half bottle of whisky.

Ashad then went to the kitchen to salvage what food supplies that he could. He did not know what was going to happen but thought that he had better prepare for all eventualities. He found a few tins of beans and stew, a loaf of bread and several packets of dry biscuits. These he hastily packed in a cardboard box and took them outside where he loaded them into the back of his vehicle. He knew that there remained in the house refrigerator a number of cuts of meat but these were useless to him as he had no way of keeping them refrigerated and fresh. In any case he did not expect that he would be out of contact with civilization for long.

He then went back into the kitchen where he picked up a box of matches from beside the gas stove. Going back to the study he grabbed a number of papers and maps which had been lying on his desk, crumpled them up, and threw them in a corner of the room. Beating it against the floor, he broke a wooden chair to pieces which he threw on the pile of paper. Satisfied, he struck a match and held it against a sheet of the crumpled paper until it caught. He then stalked from the room and back to his vehicle.

Sitting in the four wheel drive Ashad remained unmoving. He was not going anywhere until he was sure that the fire had taken hold. Looking through the window into his study he could see red and orange flames dancing. The flames soon took hold and a few minutes later flames were visible in other rooms and shooting from the roof eaves. He turned on the ignition and drove away.

There had been no need to destroy the house. It held nothing that would incriminate him or lead the police to him. However, after the failure of his explosion at the facility, he had felt a burning need to destroy something. The house would have to do.

Ashad knew that there was nowhere to escape to either to the north or east. There were no roads to the north and the east was barred to him by the NWR facility which would now be on full alert. The west was barred to him by the police. But he knew that there was an outstation to the south from which there might be tracks that would take him further south or west, avoiding any searchers. He had not been to the outstation but two of his men had and had described its situation.

Leaving the burning homestead behind he found the rough sand track that led to the outstation. He turned on to it and began the journey south, to his salvation. The track was seldom travelled and was therefore rough and often covered with drifts of sand. On a number of occasions the track led up and over sand dunes. Several times his wheels spun uselessly trying to find traction to climb the dunes. Slipping and sliding he eventually found his way over all of them and continued south.

Ashad finally arrived at the outstation, a crumbling wood and corrugated iron building situated in a small grove of desert oak trees. He drove a circuit around the building looking for tracks leading away. However, other than the track he had come in on, there were none visible.

He parked the four wheel drive in front of the outstation building and climbed down. The front door of the building comprised planks nailed to cross pieces and suspended on hinges of rope. He pushed the door open and walked inside. The whole outstation comprised a single room about three meters square. The furniture was two old rusted steel spring beds, one with a torn and dirty mattress, and a rickety wooden table made from bush timber. There were no chairs or other furniture but in one corner were two old and weathered wooden crates. Walking over Ashad saw that the crates contained a frypan, billy, miscellaneous cooking and eating equipment and a number of tins of food together with a jar of coffee and another of sugar. All were covered in a thick film of red dust and may have been there for many years.

Ashad stalked back outside. There must be a track going somewhere, he thought. He walked around the hut to see if he could see a track he had not been able to see from the vehicle.

Nothing! He walked about fifty meters from the hut and did another circuit. Still nothing! Not yet ready to admit defeat he walked two hundred meters from the humpy and completed a final circuit. As he did his circuits he unknowingly passed over boot prints that had been made less than a week before. These were Ben's and Ibrahims tracks made when they had passed this way. Now he had to admit defeat. There were no tracks leading out other than the track from the homestead.

What was he to do? If he went back to the homestead the police would inevitably trap him. He was trapped with no way back or forward. He sat down in the shade of a desert oak to think.

He had it! He would wait here until the police had given up the search. It might take a few weeks but there seemed to be plenty of food in the hut. Hopefully it was still edible. If the police came here looking for him he would hear them long before they arrived and would hide until they left. He could hide, but what about the vehicle? And what about water?

He had seen the large windmill when he had driven in. He walked over and was pleased to see that it was pumping. He climbed the side of the tank and took a cupped handful of water from the outlet pipe. Taking a sip he noted that, although a little salty, it was drinkable.

During his circuits of the site he had seen a large sand dune about two hundred meters south of the hut. He walked back to the dune and saw that with some care he could drive the vehicle behind the dune where it would be out of sight. Running back to the hut he climbed in the four wheel drive and drove it slowly towards the sand dune where he turned left to take it around the back. Almost there, but still visible from the hut, the vehicle became bogged. He retrieved a shovel from the back of the vehicle and began to shovel away the loose sand. The wheels were soon free and he drove the vehicle the rest of the way until he could no longer see the hut.

Climbing from the vehicle Ashad walked back to the tree grove where he broke a branch from one of the desert oaks. Carefully walking backwards he used the branch as a broom to obliterate his tire tracks. When he got to the spot where he had had to dig to free the vehicle he used the shovel to fill the hole back in. He then used his makeshift broom to sweep over where the hole had been.

Back at the vehicle he retrieved the satellite telephone, his whisky and an Austeyr rifle he had stolen. He walked further along the back of the sand dune and then climbed over the top. Sliding down the other side he once again used the branch to smooth over his tracks and the long furrows he had made in the sand.

Back at the hut he decided that he was making a mistake. If the police came here they would surely see that someone had been living in the hut. There was nothing for it. He would have to camp behind the dune, hidden with the vehicle.

Ashad entered the hut and lifted the box of foodstuffs. This he carried around the dune and placed in the tray of his four wheel drive. Then he went back for the second box. Returning a last time to the hut he looked to see if he had left any sign of his presence. He carefully blew dust across the two blank spaces where the boxes had sat. Finally, he circled the hut with his branch removing any sign of his bootprints, and Steve's and Ibrahim's which he had finally seen. So his nemesis had come this way when he escaped, he thought. A pity that his men had not found the escapees here. If they had his plan would have gone flawlessly and he would now be motoring towards Perth. He would kill that interfering geologist if ever he came across him!

Ashad found a sleeping bag in the footwell of the four wheel drive. With the soft sand it should make a comfortable bed. He also had food and water. A quick inspection of the tinned food also showed that he had choice. Tinned beans, tinned stew, tinned beans or tinned stew. There were also a few tins of canned peaches and one of canned pear halves.

It was the afternoon of the next day when the police came. He was lying on the sleeping bag when he heard the far off drone of an engine. Taking the rifle he crawled to the top of the sand dune and looked down upon the hut. About five minutes later a police four wheel drive occupied by four men emerged from between the sand dunes. That vehicle was followed by an army humvee with six soldiers aboard. Both vehicles pulled to a halt in front of the hut.

Peering down the barrel of the rifle Ashad thought that he could probably shoot a few of them as they emerged from their vehicles. But they vastly outnumbered him and would kill him eventually. And he was not ready to die yet. He continued looking along the rifle as two policemen entered the hut and the others milled around outside.

Three of the soldiers wandered around the clearing, there eyes glued to the ground looking for tracks. They won't find any, Ashad smiled to himself.

"No one here", he heard one of the policemen say, "And it doesn't look as though anybody has been here in a good while although we did see those fresh tracks on the way in".

"Yeah, but that was probably one of the men having a deco around the station. There is certainly no one here now", said another of the policemen.

Without looking further afield all of the police and soldiers got back into their vehicles. The engines started and within a few minutes both vehicles had disappeared back the way they had come, as though they had never been there. Ashad breathed a sigh of relief.

For five days and nights Ashad camped behind the sand dune, eating tinned stew and baked beans. He dared not take up residence in the hut in case the police or soldiers returned.

On the fourth day at the out station he sat quietly behind the sand dune waiting for the ever present satellite telephone to ring. His six men travelling east had left with firm instructions that they were to call him on the fifth day after they had left the facility. By that time Ashad had hoped that the men would be at or near Alice

Springs in the centre of the continent and he would be in Perth. All day he listened for the sound of an incoming call. There was none. All the next day he did the same in the event that his men had misinterpreted his instructions. Still no call! He checked the telephone to see if it remained charged. It was.

Ashad had to believe that his men had either perished in the desert or had been captured. All of his plans had come to nought! And now he was alone and trapped.

On the sixth day, early in the morning, Ashad decided he should take a look at the homestead to see if the authorities had abandoned it. He knew that they would have descended on the homestead, or what remained of it, as soon as they had received word of the attack. Starting his vehicle he drove carefully along the track until he reckoned he was about five kilometers short of the homestead. At this distance he did not believe they would have heard any engine noise. He hiked the remaining five kilometers carrying only a small container of water and the Austeyr rifle.

Reaching the last sand dune before the homestead he climbed it and at the top looked out upon a scene of devastation. The homestead had burnt in its entirety to the ground. All that remained were scatterings of charcoal and ash and the blackened and buckled sheets of corrugated iron that had once comprised the roof. Three men in blue overalls were carefully wading through the wreckage. At times they would lift a sheet of iron or prod a pile of ash with a stick. Probably looking for what remains of my body, thought Ashad.

Looking towards the hangar he saw two police four wheel drives and the light plane which had been pulled out onto the airstrip. It appeared as though they had converted the hangar into a camp site. Two men sat in the shade of the hangar, one with a cigarette dangling from his lips. So, the police were still here and looked as though they would remain for some time, looking for clues to his disappearance.

Ashad knew that the police would be looking for him

specifically. The interfering geologist had seen him and would have provided them with a description. Although that description would be a bit dated – With no hot water or razor Ashad was quickly cultivating a beard. The scar above his eye was however a dead giveaway.

Ashad slid down the back of the sand dune and began walking back to where he had parked the four wheel drive. He was weary and dejected but still hopeful he could find his way out of this situation. Arriving at the vehicle he mounted, did a three point turn, and drove back towards the outstation.

Arriving at the outstation he pulled up in front of the small hut. Maybe I can make a new way out of here, he sat thinking. He could not go east, that way was only desert. He could not go north, that way was blocked by the police. That left only the south or west. To go south meant crossing dozens if not hundreds of sand dunes. That way was therefore impossible and left only the west. If he travelled west he would be travelling parallel to the sand dunes and would not have to cross them.

Putting the engine into gear he turned the four wheel drive to the west, facing a gap between the two nearest sand dunes. He drove in that direction until he had entered the relatively flat valley between the dunes. This is not too hard, he thought, bouncing across the uneven sand and spinifex clumps. However, about five hundred meters to the west he encountered a large pile of sand dumped between the two dunes. With the gears in four wheel drive he made a run at the mass of sand and had made it about half way to the top before the vehicle came to a halt. With the vehicle tilted upwards at about thirty degrees he continued applying accelerator with loose sand spraying to the sides and the rear. The vehicle was soon bogged to its axles. He could no longer go forward. However, with the slope assisting him, he found that he could retreat backwards. Back on the flat he turned the four wheel drive around and headed back the way he had came. Nearing the hut he veered to the north, passed the end of that sand dune, and entered the valley to the north of the one he had just been attempting. Once again, about five hundred meters in, he encountered an impassable mound of sand. It was as though god had, with a huge sand bucket, deliberately placed sand to spite him. He did not attempt to drive over this mound but once again retreated to his camp site near the hut.

He could not get away. At least not until the police and army had become bored and abandoned the homestead and road to Marble Bar.

Ashad knew that he was a dead man walking. If he did get out of his current predicament and somehow made it back to the Middle East he would be killed. His superiors did not take kindly to failures. His uncle was one of those superiors but he would not hesitate to sign Ashads death warrant. Family honour demanded it. He could go back under an assumed name but that would mean never again being able to associate with his friends or associates. It would also mean never again seeing his two small sons or his wife. He was a dead man!

It was all the fault of that infidel Wilde, he was convinced. With his interference he has killed me as surely as if he had driven a stake through my heart! Filled with hatred he made up his mind. With rationing he had enough food to last almost another two weeks. He would stay where he was and when he could escape he would track the man down and kill him! He has taken my life, and so I will take his. A fair exchange!

25

23 APRIL, 2014

THE HELICOPTER HUMMED over the desert at a speed in excess of two hundred kilometers per hour and at an altitude of about five hundred meters. At that height the desert looked like a vast yellow sea, complete with giant yellow waves. Although it would frighten most, Ben thought it looked beautiful.

They had landed once on the faint track to see if there were any signs of vehicles having passed. Ben had bolted out onto the track where he had seen fresh tire tracks embedded in the soft sand. Running back to the machine he had given Chuck a thumbs up sign through the perspex window. Once again donning the headphones and microphone he had confirmed what he had seen.

"Fresh tire tracks. Two, maybe three vehicles heading east', he had said.

At about one hundred kilometers east of the facility the track had veered to the north to skirt a large salt lake. The white salt had shimmered in the midday sun, almost blinding the men in the helicopter.

At two hundred kilometers to the east Chuck had spoken into his microphone. "Ben, we are about two hundred k out. Do you want to continue?". His voice sounded doubtful.

"Yes, yes I do Chuck. Can you give it another hundred k? Do you have the range for that?"

"Sure thing Ben. Yeah, I've got plenty of fuel for that distance and to get us back".

When Ben had spoken he had glanced into the rear seats where Mick and Ibrahim sat. Ibrahim sat stoically looking out of his window. Mick was asleep, his chin resting on his chest and snoring softly. He had taken off his headphones so he would not be roused by their voices. Ben could not believe it. Here they were, heading into possible danger, and Mick was sleeping! What kind of men was he associated with? One who laughed while being shot at and another who slept while heading into possible danger!

At about two hundred and fifty kilometers from the facility Ben, looking ahead, saw a range of low hills in the distance. At the same time he saw the sun wink off something on the floor of the desert. Continuing to look where he had seen the flash of light the helicopter drew closer. Suddenly Ben shouted into the microphone. "There Chuck, about ten kilometers ahead! I can see one, two, no three four wheel drives on the track! Heading east".

"Got you Ben. I see them", replied Chuck, "Now that we have caught them what do you want to do? Remember, we only have my rifle and your peashooter".

"Can you get ahead of them, maybe on the other side of those hills? And can you do it without them seeing or hearing us?"

"Sure I can buddy. I'll just loop out and come at the hills from the other direction. They'll never know we are here", said Chuck, "Boy, this is like Afghanistan all over again. Dropping troops behind the enemy!"

As he spoke Chuck was already executing a turn to the right which would take them well away from the track and the vehicles on it. At about ten kilometers to the south he turned to the left so they were paralleling the track at that distance. Having then passed over the hills he turned again towards the north and finally settled the helicopter onto the track to the east of a small hill.

Anybody coming through the hills would not see the machine until they were almost upon it.

With the slight bump of the landing Mick sprang awake. Quickly looking around and then donning the headphones he said "I take it that we are wherever we were going. Is that right boss?".

Ben quickly explained the situation for Micks benefit as Chuck shut down the machine. When the rotors had come to a stop they all climbed down and stood on the red earth that had replaced the yellow sand that they had been flying over for so long.

"I'm not sure what we can do", said Ben, "We only have two weapons and all of the men in those vehicles have to be presumed to be fully armed. Nonetheless, I am going to do whatever I can to at least hold them up until the police or army get here. First, however, I'm going up on that hill to make sure we've got the right blokes. Chuck, I noticed that you have a pair of binoculars there in the back. Do you mind if I borrow them?"

"Go for it buddy. And I'll come for the walk with you".

Ben reached into the back seats of the helicopter, his hand emerging grasping a pair of binoculars. He and Chuck set off walking to the small hill about two hundred meters away, leaving Mick and Ibrahim squatting down in the shade thrown by the helicopter. Ben scrambled up the slope of the hill and threw himself down on his belly at the top. Chuck followed him. At first Ben could see nothing other than more low red hills to his front. Then, about two kilometers away, a four wheel drive poked its nose around from behind one of the small hills.

As the vehicles came closer Ben raised the binoculars to his eyes. With some manipulation of the focus the front vehicle suddenly leapt into view as though it was only five meters away. Ben panned the glasses up to look into the cabin. He saw two faces, one he did not know, the other he did. The second face was sporting two fading black eyes and a bent nose. It was his friend from the homestead whom he had kicked in the face.

"It's them", he hissed to Chuck beside him, "I recognize at least one of them from the homestead!".

"OK, but what do we do now? I suppose I could try to hole their radiators or shoot out their tires and then bugger off in the chopper?". He sounded uncertain.

"Well, let's go back to the chopper and get the police or army on the radio. Get them here as soon as possible!", said Ben.

Chuck did not answer but wiggled back from his position until he could stand without being seen. Ben did likewise and then the two men ran back to the helicopter where Mick and Ibrahim waited. Without pause chuck and Ben both quickly took their seats in the machine. Taking the hint, Mick and Ibrahim quickly regained their seats. Chuck quickly had the helicopter airborne again and keeping only a few meters above the dirt turned hard to the right, away for the track. When they were several kilometers to the south Ben looked back behind the machine to where they had just been. The lead vehicle was just rounding the small hill he and Chuck had climbed. He did not believe that they had been seen.

Having avoided discovery Chuck keyed his microphone to contact the Port Hedland airport tower. Ben had also donned a set of headphones and microphone. Chuck radioed the Port Hedland airport tower and asked them to relay him through to the nearby army base. He was soon talking to a sergeant who, on hearing the reason for the call, passed him through to a captain.

"Captain, this is Chuck Sanders piloting a helicopter for Major Minerals. We believe we have found half a dozen of the terrorists you are looking for about two hundred and fifty kilometers east of the NWR facility. I suggest you send some troops out here pronto".

"Two hundred and fifty kilometers? That puts you smack bang in the middle of the desert. I am not doubting you about the terrorists but if we send troops in humvees it will be at least two, probably three days before they get to you. And we have no helicopters so they would have to come up from Perth. Once again we are talking two to three days before they could get to you".

Although the captain had said the opposite, Ben believed from the sound of the mans voice that he did indeed doubt their report. And in two to three days the terrorists would be out of the desert and have a number of tracks to choose from. They could easily be lost with no hope of finding them again. In three days they could even be in Alice Springs from where they could disappear. Despite what the colonel had said about the police keeping an eye out for them.

"Understood Captain. Please though send troops as soon as you can so they do not get away. Chuck Sanders signing off".

Chuck pressed a switch and terminated the connection. He also was clearly not pleased with how the conversation had gone. Ben was now concerned with how the four of them might be able to at least delay the six terrorists.

"Chuck. The army aren't going to be able to help and in a day, certainly two, these arseholes may have disappeared. I suggest we fly on ahead and set an ambush. Who is with me? I'll go with the majority", said Ben.

Chuck replied first. "I'm not sure what we can do but I'm your man. I haven't had this much fun since Afghanistan!"

"I will go where you go Ben", said Ibrahim.

"Well, it looks like I'm outvoted", said Mick dolefully, "I'm in because someone has to look after your sorry arse".

Ben knew that Mick was only joking. He knew that Mick would do anything for him. Nonetheless, he was gratified by the show of support.

"OK", said Ben, "Can you take us on about one hundred k. That should be where they'll camp for the night".

"No problem", replied Chuck, "Although that is getting close to my fuel range limit".

They flew on across the red soil plains. The yellow sand and sand dunes had disappeared for the moment. At about seventy kilometers out they began flying across another range of low hills.

At eighty kilometers Ben looked down and saw a glimmer of sunlight reflecting off something way back towards the north.

"Chuck, there's something down there. About where the track should be at ten o'clock".

Chuck banked the helicopter to the left and decreased altitude as they neared the track. Getting closer Ben saw what had caused the reflected light. A small pool of water was situated at the base of a small cliff. The track ran past the water only ten meters away. The pool itself was surrounded by a small copse of gum and mulga trees. A perfect camping spot.

"Chuck. I'll bet my last cent that they'll camp by that pool tonight. Can you set us down about one kilometer beyond".

Chuck did as asked and soon set the helicopter down gently on the red earth just the eastern side of the low hills. The landing site was about one and a half kilometers to the east of the pool. The machine quickly wound down and they all climbed out.

"Well, we're going to have a bit of a wait guys. Just relax while I see if I can come up with a plan", said Ben.

The men all sank down gratefully to sit on the dirt in the shade of a small gum tree.

"I'm starving" said Mick, "Don't suppose you've got any food Chuck?"

"Yeah, I think I've got a few muesli bars and a couple of tins of beans for emergencies. I'll just get them".

"No need", said Ibrahim standing, "I have come prepared".

Ibrahim had been carrying a small haversack slung across his shoulder the entire day. Ben had of course seen it but had not questioned it. Now Ibrahim dug into it and came out with a large loaf of bread, a block of cheese and three large salamis. He had looted the mess at the NWR facility before leaving, knowing that food might be required at some time. Mick tore of a hunk of bread and broke of a ragged lump of cheese off the offered foods. He then broke one of the salamis in half, wrapped the broken bread around the salami and cheese, and began eating hungrily. Soon all four men were eating comfortably in the shade.

"OK guys, I have a plan", said Ben at the end of the impromptu picnic, "We wait till they go to sleep, Wake them up with mine and Chucks guns, tie them up and wait for the army. Not much of a plan but what do you think?"

"Yeah, why not", said Mick, "We can probably do that without screwing it up".

Chuck and Ibrahim kept their opinions to themselves but nodded acquiescence.

"You guys laze about here", quipped Ben, "I'm going to see if I can find a place to spy on them when they get here". Ben knew that it would be at least four or five hours before the terrorists could cover the ground that the helicopter had in less than half an hour.

Ben wandered west along the track idly noting, as all good geologists do, the geology as he walked. Mostly shale and sandstone, he saw, with at least one thin seam of conglomerate. These must be the Proterozoic sediments that had been mapped in this region. Not much potential for mineralisation but he would have to think about it. He thought it would be quite pleasant to work out here.

Ben reached a small hill overlooking the pool in seemingly no time. He did not however descend for a closer look. He did not want to leave tracks that might be seen by the terrorists. The small hill was in any case ideally located to study the putative camp site. Satisfied, Ben wandered back towards the helicopter. There was no point in waiting around in the savage sun for the next four hours.

Arriving back at the machine Ben saw that Mick was again asleep, stretched out on the red soil in the shade of a gum tree. Ibrahim also lay on his back staring at the branches of the gum tree over his head. Chuck was propped sitting by the trees trunk reading a book he had obviously kept hidden in his machine. Ben sat on the other side of the tree from Chuck.

For three hours the men sat or lay, occasionally engaging in desultory conversation. When Ben had calculated three hours had passed he rose to his feet.

"I'm just going back to see if they're coming along", he said.

"I'll come with you", said Ibrahim, rising to his feet.

The two men walked to the west leaving Mick and Chuck sprawled under the tree. On reaching the hill they climbed to the top where Ben lay himself flat on the ground. Ibrahim joined him.

For three quarters of an hour they saw nothing. Then Ben saw a tell tale plume of dust in the distance.

"They're coming", he whispered to Ibrahim. Why do I keep whispering when no one can possibly hear me?, he thought angrily to himself. All of this stress must be getting to me!

They watched the dust plume as it steadily grew larger. About five minutes after seeing the dust Ben could just make out the first of the vehicles beneath it. The vehicles were obviously making slow going over the rough track, averaging less than twenty kilometers per hour. About fifteen minutes later the three vehicles entered the small grove of trees and came to a halt. Six men descended from the vehicles. Two men stripped off their shirts and jumped into the shallow waterhole for a rough bath. The other men unroped tarpaulins that covered the trays of each of the vehicles and began unloading swags and other camping equipment. The men were talking and joking with each other but other than a low murmur Ben could hear nothing of what they were saying. Not that it would have helped if he could as all were talking in Arabic. Nonetheless, they were clearly camping for the night.

Having unloaded their camping equipment the four men disappeared into the bush to the north of their camp. A few minutes later they reappeared rolling two large grey drums. They were drums of diesel fuel. Having arrived at the vehicles one of the men retrieved a hand pump from one of the vehicles whilst another removed the bung on the drum. The men soon had the pump inserted into the drum and began pumping fuel into the vehicles.

Ben softly cursed himself as an idiot. Of course they had previously set up fuel dumps. They could not cross over two thousand kilometers to the next service station without fuel dumps, even if they had long range fuel tanks. If Ben had more closely examined the site earlier he would have discovered the drums. He could have emptied them onto the earth and the terrorists would have been stranded without fuel. They probably had another fuel dump further to the east but they did not have enough range with the helicopter to reach it. Ben had let an opportunity to deal with the terrorists without confronting them slip through his fingers. Idiot!

Ben and Ibrahim watched the men a short time longer as they rolled out their swags and got a campfire going. Then they carefully retreated from the hilltop and walked back to the helicopter. On arrival they saw Chuck still reading his book in the setting sun and Mick pacing to and fro like a caged animal.

"Where the hell have you buggers been. I've been worried sick that you'd gone and got yourselves shot!", Mick said.

"Calm down Mick", said Ben, "We've just been up to check on the competition. They've arrived and are making camp where I thought they would". He mentioned nothing about the fuel dump as it was of no consequence to their current situation.

"Tonight", he continued, "We'll wait until they're asleep, wander in and stick Chucks and my guns under their noses, tie them up and call the cops".

"OK, sounds good", said Mick, "I think".

For the next two hours they sat under the shade waiting for the sun to go down completely. They had another meal provided by Ibrahim's bag of loot from the facility. At about eight o'clock Ben stirred them and they all began the walk to the terrorists camp. Luckily it was a full moon with good vision for up to one hundred meters. Arriving at the hill they all scrambled up and lay at the top, practically invisible from the camp below. The terrorists were all still awake and talking softly. They settled in to wait for them to go to sleep.

At about half past eight five of the terrorists settled into their swags and soon seemed to be sound asleep. The men on the hill could actually hear some snores coming from below. However, one terrorist remained awake patrolling around the perimeter of the camp. He had one of the looted Austeyr rifles slung over his shoulder. After a while he settled to sit with his back to a large gum tree, but remained awake. Even in the middle of the desert, they had set a guard!

What do we do now, thought Ben. We can't just wander down there or he'll fill us full of holes!

"It looks like we've got a problem chaps", he whispered to the other three, "We can't wander down there with a guard on duty".

"Well", whispered Chuck casually, "We'll just have to take care of the guard".

"And how do we do that? If we shoot him it will wake the others. Or are we going to dong him over the head with a rock?", whispered Ben.

"Neither", said Ibrahim, "I have come prepared". There was a rustle of cloth and Ibrahim drew a knife from where it had been hidden beneath his shorts. The knife was about six inches long with a wickedly serrated edge.

"Where the fuck did you get that", hissed Mick.

"I liberated it from the mess at the facility", said Ibrahim, "I thought it might come in handy and I have been proved right".

"What, Are you suggesting I go down there and slit his throat?", whispered Ben incredulously.

"No. I will go down and slit his throat", replied Ibrahim casually.

"What. You can't do that! I can't allow you to put yourself in danger! And I can't ask you to kill someone! To become a murderer! I won't allow it!"

"Ben. This is no problem for me", said Ibrahim calmly, "These men are animals. They have already killed and plan to kill more. I have killed before and these animals won't bother my conscience".

Ben was dumbfounded. Ibrahim was a murderer? The man he had befriended had killed other people? He could not fathom it.

"Please Ben", Ibrahim continued, "Let me do this. I will be striking a blow for freedom and for my new country".

"You've killed before?", Ben asked incredulously, "Where? When? Why?"

"When I was in Iraq, after the war, I and my family saved an American serviceman. He had lost contact with his patrol and was lost. We took him in, fed him and returned him to his base. My neighbor, a member of the Sunni militia, heard what we had done and was going to tell his brothers. They would have come and slaughtered my family. I did the only thing I could. I took a knife, snuck into his house, and slit his throat. The next day I and my family fled Iraq".

"Well Ibrahim. I never knew. I am so sorry for the shit you've had to go through", said Ben with sincerity, "Since you seem to be the best equipped, and are happy to do it, you go and silence him. Chuck and I will come and cover you with our guns. Mick, you stay up here and keep watch".

Ben, Ibrahim and Chuck silently made their way down the back of the hill. At the bottom they skirted left to round the hill back towards the camp. Treading silently, and being careful to avoid twigs and loose rocks, they entered the small grove of trees. If Ben remembered correctly, the guard was sitting with his back to a tree facing away from them as they approached. With a tug of his sleeve and a pointed finger Ben indicated to Chuck that he was to go to the left and cover the sleeping men. He would stay close to Ibrahim. Ahead, in the semi-dark, Ben saw the large tree against which the guard was resting. He indicated the tree to Ibrahim who seemed to understand what was required. He replied with a gentle nod.

The tree, whilst covering their approach, now presented a

problem. Ibrahim could not reach the guard without stepping around the tree and into the mans view. Ben and Ibrahim sank to crouches behind the tree, less than two meters from the armed guard. With no other option they waited to see what might develop.

After crouching uncomfortably for an interminable five minutes they heard movement from the other side of the tree. The guard was standing up. Before either man could react the guard had stepped around the tree, on the way to relieve himself, and seen both of them. As the man opened his mouth to shout, and his weapon started coming up, Ibrahim wrapped his left arm around his throat blocking his air supply. There was a soft gasp and shuffling on the earth as both men fought for ascendancy, although the sounds were not loud enough to wake the sleeping men. Without warning Ibrahim adjusted his grip, moving his arm up to cover the other mans mouth. Then his right hand reached out and back, the held knife coming forward and cleanly slicing the guards throat. There was a second soft gasp and the pattering sound of spurting blood hitting the ground and the tree trunk. Ibrahim released his left arm and the body fell to the ground, lifeless.

One of the terrorists was however a light sleeper. Something had disturbed him and as he sat up in his swag he saw two dark shadows under the nearest tree. He reached for his AK47 lying beside his bunk but as he bought the weapon to bear the top of his head disappeared in a spray of blood, brain and bone. The sight was followed a millisecond later by the crack of a high powered rifle shot. He sunk back soundlessly into his now soiled bedding.

With the crack of the gunshot the remaining four terrorists sat bolt upright in their beds. Chuck was already running forward from his position twenty meters away as was Steve from behind the tree. Two of the terrorists were aimlessly reaching for their weapons when Chuck slid to a halt five meters away and shouted. "Don't move! Move and you die!"

One of the two men reaching for weapons dropped his rifle as though scalded. The second continued to raise his AK47 until a second shot crashed out, the slug burying itself in his swag between his legs. Chuck had fired the shot and Ben had pulled the trigger on his pistol at the same time. He had heard nothing but a muted click from the pistol.

"Lie face down on your bedding! Face down! Do not move", Chuck shouted.

Defeated, the four remaining men, including the potential hero, turned to their sides and then lay face down.

Chuck had now advanced to stand over the man at the end of the line of swags. Without warning he swung the butt of his rifle down and hit the man squarely at the base of the skull with a barely audible thunk! He walked to the next man and repeated the process. The remaining two men had by now realized what was happening. Each of them stared imploringly up at Chuck as in turn he used the rifle butt to hit them at the base of the skull. All four men were now unconscious.

Seeing Ben's puzzled expression he explained "They're easier to tie up if they're unconscious".

Ibrahim had bought a length of rope from the helicopter. Cutting lengths with his killing knife he quickly bound each mans hands behind their backs. He also tied their legs together. Between them Ben and Ibrahim then dragged each of the four men to two trees near the campfire. With the excess rope Ibrahim lashed two of the men to each tree. The dead man on the swag they dragged to join his also deceased compatriot behind the tree.

Ben and Ibrahim picked up the terrorists AK47's and looted Austeyr rifles and placed them in the cabin of one of the four wheel drives.

"Ibrahim. That was incredible what you just did!", said Ben with feeling, "I owe you big time!"

"Now that we have them secure I'll run back to the chopper and get Mick", he continued.

"Don't worry boss, I'm right here", said Mick, stepping out from behind a tree, "You didn't think I'd miss the fun did you?"

Ben knew it was pointless to chastise Mick for not following instructions so he did not bother. Instead he said "My gun didn't fire. Right at the crucial moment and the damn thing wouldn't fire!"

"Here, let me have a look", said Chuck.

He took the pistol from Ben and walked across to one of the terrorist vehicles and turned on the interior light. For several minutes he examined the weapon, opening the slide and peering intently into the chamber. Suddenly he laughed. "You know why it didn't fire? Somebody has filed the firing pin down. She was never going to work!"

Ben realized what had happened. His grandfather, having returned from the war with the pistol as a souvenir, had probably later filed the firing pin so there could be no accidents. Thanks granddad, he thought, you almost got me bloody killed!

Ben picked up a torch from next to one of the swags and walked across to the nearest four wheel drive and threw back the tarpaulin that had already been untied. Sitting in the tray of the vehicle were two grey containers similar to those he had seen at the Nuclear Waste Repository. Switching on the torch he could see that they were marked with the radiation hazard symbol and the designation 'Cs'. Between the two drums was a third drum which he knew was filled with diesel-soaked ammonium nitrate. Ben went to the other two vehicles and found the same.

"It looks as though they were planning to blow something up and spread a lot of radiation around", he said to anyone who was listening. "Chuck", he continued, "We better go back to the chopper and radio the army about this. They'll have someone there on night watch. Can you two fellows guard this lot while we're gone?", referring to Mick and Ibrahim.

"Sure thing boss. They ain't going anywhere", said Mick.

Leaving Mick and Ibrahim with Chucks and the terrorists

rifles, Ben and Chuck set off on the walk back to the Helicopter. The moon still brightly lit the track and the going was easy, almost peaceful, thought Ben. Back at the machine Chuck climbed in and fired up the electronics before calling the Port Hedland airport and asking to be transferred to the army base. He was soon put through, again to a sergeant, who transferred him to a lieutenant, the senior night officer. Chuck gave the shocked lieutenant a quick précis of what had happened and what they had found and asked him to contact his commanding officer soonest. Before signing off he gave the young officer their grid coordinates and his own call sign.

"The lieutenant was going to phone his boss at home straight away", Chuck told Ben, "I think we'll get some pretty prompt action this time".

Ben and Chuck arrived back at the terrorists camp to find Mick wielding Chucks rifle and keeping a steady eye on the still unconscious men tied to the two trees. Ibrahim had washed the blood off his arms and hands and had restarted the fire. He was busy heating cans of stew looted from the terrorists supplies and the billy was bubbling. He poured the boiling water into four clean mugs he had located into each of which he had previously put a heaped teaspoon of coffee. He handed each of his three friends a mug, keeping the cracked mug for himself.

"Well", said Ben as he entered the camp, "We may as well stay here tonight. At least there is food and some swags we can use. We'll take turns guarding the prisoners, Chuck and I will go first and we'll change every two hours. How's that sound?"

There were no objections so the men settled down to a meal of tinned stew and sipping their coffees. After the meal Ibrahim and Mick threw themselves down on two of the recently vacated swags, although not the one that was now covered in blood and brain matter. It had been a long and stressful day and both men were soon asleep. Ben retrieved one of the Austeyr rifles from the four wheel drive and Chuck was once again armed with his rifle.

They sat side by side at the campfire, sipping their coffees and watching the terrorists. Through the night the four men rotated shifts, two hours on and two hours off. At various times during the night the terrorists awoke but would say nothing, merely staring sullenly at their captors.

Morning came and all the men were awake, as well as their four captives. For the first time one of the captives spoke, pleading that he needed to use the toilet. A second also ended his silence to say that he too needed the toilet. Each of the terrorists was then released one at a time to complete their business. Staring down the muzzles of four rifles they were not about to attempt anything heroic. They were all then retied and lashed firmly to the trees.

Ben had thought that they might have to wait there for at least another day but at about ten o'clock in the morning he heard the distant whup! whup! whup! of an approaching helicopter. Looking in the direction of the noise, to the west, not one but two helicopters materialized out of the heat haze. As they came into land at a nearby clearing Ben saw that the two helicopters were painted blue and white. They were not army. Who might this be?, he thought.

Immediately upon landing six men emerged from the helicopters, five of whom were wearing army greens. So they were army. Four of the men in army greens carried Austeyr rifles. The two pilots of the machines stayed where they were.

As the men walked towards the camp Ben saw that one of the soldiers, the one not carrying a rifle, was the major he had met at the NWR facility. The sixth man was dressed in blue jeans, a pale blue shirt and what looked like new boots.

The major stopped in front of Ben and extended his hand. "Mr Wilde, Major Hennessy. You may remember me from the faciltiy", he said as they shook hands, "It appears that you have been having quite an adventure". Seeing Ben still looking at the helicopters he added "We commandeered the helicopters from a firm that services the offshore drilling rigs. Our helicopters won't get to Port Hedland until later today".

They walked across to where the bound prisoners sat, now being guarded by the four soldiers. The man in the clean casual clothes trailed behind. On nearing the prisoners the major stopped and turned to the casually dressed man.

"I am so sorry, a bit remiss of me", he said, "Ben Wilde, this is Mr Dance, Mr Dance, Ben Wilde. Mr Dance is an agent with ASIO. Flew up to Port Hedland yesterday".

Ben and the agent shook hands.

"I am so sorry for what you have been through", said Dance, "We should have realized something was in the wind but we did not have a clue, I'm afraid to say".

Major Johnson interrupted. "So you have four prisoners here, and I understand that there are two deceased?".

"That's correct", said Ben, leading them to where the two corpses lay behind the tree. In the heat of the Australian sun they were already starting to decompose and smell.

"Well, Mr Wilde, I don't know what to say. If we were to hand you over to the police I have no doubt that they would charge you with murder. Personally, I think you should get a medal", said the ASIO officer. Ben looked at him aghast as he added "I am however fairly confident that neither of those things will happen. The police will never know what happened here. And you will never get a medal because what happened here – didn't".

"Are you saying that you are going to sweep all this under the carpet?", Ben asked incredulously.

"That is exactly what I am saying. We will not compromise Australian security or unnecessarily frighten the Australian public. The dead men will be disposed of and I daresay the live ones here will probably be shipped to the Yanks at Guantanamo to enjoy some water boarding. You and your companions will be asked to sign a national security document saying you will never talk of this matter. To anyone. Ever. Are we clear?"

Ben nodded in acquiescence. Mick, Ibrahim and Chuck, who had gathered near to listen in on the conversation, also nodded.

"But what about the dead soldiers? You can't dismiss them!", said Ben with renewed determination.

"Those poor, unfortunate men died in a tragic training accident. Their families will be taken care of".

Stunned, Ben just nodded again. He then realized that he had better show the ASIO man the rest of the story. He took the ASIO man and the major to the closest four wheel drive and showed the weapons stowed on the seats. He then showed them the drums of radioactive waste and primitive bomb in the back of the vehicle. A quick tour down the line of vehicles showed that each carried radioactive waste and a bomb. The ASIO man then went and squatted down in front of the bound prisoners. He began talking to them, in Arabic. Two of the prisoners remained silent, one grunted a few responses, and the fourth seemed to be suffering from verbal diarrhea. He yammered at the man questioning him whilst the others looked at him with expressions of contempt. After a few minutes of this mostly one sided discussion the ASIO officer returned to where Ben still stood with his men and the major.

"At least one of the boys is a bit talkative", he said, "Seems he wanted to gloat although they hadn't achieved anything, other than killing those poor soldiers. They were on a mission for Allah and were prepared to die for him. Others will come to complete the mission. Yaddah, yaddah, yaddah. Apparently, one vehicle each was bound for Sydney, Melbourne and Canberra. They were going to drive into the centres of those cities like country yokels come to visit the big smoke and then blow their bombs and immolate themselves. Dozens, if not hundreds of people would have been killed and radioactive dust spread over the cities. It would have been an unparalleled disaster. You truly deserve our thanks and much more Mr Wilde. And the rest of you men too of course".

Ben simply shrugged. The major walked over to one of his men and began talking quietly to him. Having received his instructions the soldier walked to one of the four wheel drives where he grabbed a shovel out of the tray. He then walked about ten meters away to a clear space and began digging a hole.

"What are you digging holes for", Ben called to the major.

"We have to bury the corpses you made, don't we?"

"I thought you'd be taking them back for identification or autopsies or something".

"Don't worry, we'll take photos before we bury them. And I don't think we need autopsies do you? One slit throat and one guy with the top of his head blown off? Remember, this didn't happen! Oh, and I'd like to congratulate your guy who did the throat. Nice job".

Ibrahim, who had heard all of the exchange, blushed and found something interesting to look at in the dirt at his feet.

"OK, you have everything under control here so we are leaving if that's OK?", said Ben uncertainly, addressing the major and Mr Dance.

"Sure Mr Wilde. You go. But we will be calling upon you all later for complete interviews and debriefing. And to sign a non-disclosure document", said Mr Dance "I understand that you are working out near a place called Blind Bluff, is that correct?", he continued.

Saying nothing further, other than a nod to confirm the majors query, Ben turned and started to trudge up the track towards their helicopter followed by the others. Ten minutes later they were all seated in the machine and a few minutes after that they were airborne, heading west.

26

24 APRIL, 2014

Ben and his men arrived back at the Blind Bluff campsite weary from their adventure but also strangely elated at their success. True, they had killed two men but Ben was not concerned. To him, the dead men had been rabid dogs who had had to be put down. They had after all killed innocent people and were planning on killing a lot more. Ben had no compassion for them and he doubted that any of the others did. Ibrahim and Chuck had actually done the killing but they appeared to be the same as always, even exchanging jokes on the journey back.

Now comes the hard part, thought Ben. The part where I have to start telling lies.

Dismounting from the helicopter they all saw that the camp was deserted. All of the men who had been left at the camp would of course be over at the drilling rig. Without hesitation Ben headed towards where he had seen the rig on the flight in. Mick and Ibrahim followed whilst Chuck stayed with his machine.

Arriving at the drilling rig, which was spewing out clouds of dust, Ben saw Angus at the controls, his two men moving drilling rods and Lance bent over bags of drill chips. Ben walked over to Lance who hadn't seen them arrive. Tapping the young geologist on the shoulder he said "How goes it Lance? Get many holes done yet?"

"Oh, Ben. I didn't see you coming. Yeah we've completed another two and this is BBDD-4 we're on now. Where have you guys been? I was starting to worry. A bloke came from the NWR facility yesterday and said that you had been delayed. Delayed doing what?".

"Sorry Lance. We went to the NWR site but there was nothing happening. I know we shouldn't have but we stayed the night there and returned late this morning".

"Oh, good. I'm glad to see that all of your worries were for nothing. Mind you, we had a visit from the police this morning. They questioned all of us and told us to be careful. Apparently there's a madman with a gun about here somewhere".

"Well, that is a bit concerning. Take their advice and be careful but for now it's full steam ahead. I want you to go back to the camp and take the chopper out with Chuck to finish that stream sediment sampling. I'll take care of things here".

Lance nodded, picked up his notebook, and trotted back towards the camp. Ben turned to Mick and Ibrahim who had been standing behind him.

"Ibrahim, can you go back with Lance and help with the stream sediment sampling. Mick, you stay and help me here".

Ibrahim trotted off in Lances wake and Mick began sampling the piles of drill chips, a job that had been allowed to lapse for the past two days.

Ben walked over to where the second drillhole, BBDD-2, had been drilled and where the core trays still lay. On inspecting the core he saw at once that this drillhole too had intersected massive sulphide mineralisation. About thirty-three meters he quickly calculated. The core trays at drillhole number BBDD-3 told a similar story. However, the massive sulphides intersected there were almost fifty-seven meters thick. They had definitely discovered a substantial copper orebody. His bosses would be overjoyed and would certainly overlook his absence from the site for two days.

Ben returned to drillhole number BBDD-4 where the drilling rig was still completing the percussion precollar before diamond drilling could commence. He set to describing the chips where Lance had left off.

For the remainder of the day Ben worked at what he was good at – Geology. He had had an adventure and done his bit to save the World but he was glad to retreat to the work he knew so well. From now on he would leave the adventures to others. He was already excited in anticipation of what the diamond drilling would reveal in this fourth drillhole. However, by the arrival of dusk the drilling had still not reached the target depth of the mineralisation and he had to call it a day. Angus shut down the machine and he, his three helpers, Ben and Mick traipsed over the bluff back to the camp. The helicopter had returned from its day of work about an hour previous and Chuck, Ibrahim and Lance were seated by the campfire deep in conversation. Ben hoped that Chuck and Ibrahim were not telling Lance anything he shouldn't know.

As each of the men wandered into the camp Ibrahim got up from his seat and handed him a cold beer.

As Ben sank into his comfortable deckchair he heard the sound of engine approaching. He immediately sprang back up and looked north along the track. Instantly he saw a station wagon – type four wheel drive approaching followed by two flat bed trucks carrying what looked like front end loaders. Steve walked over to where the vehicles would stop, curious about what new surprise the day had bought. As the first vehicle closed Ben could see that the driver was Michelle. She bought the four wheel drive to a halt, the trucks stopping behind her.

"Hello Ben", she said as she stepped down from the driver's seat, "Fancy meeting you out here".

"Michelle! Well, this is a pleasant surprise. What brings you to my humble abode?"

"After you showed me your ruins I put a proposal to the museum and UWA that it should be excavated and examined. It is so unusual and there is absolutely no record anywhere of anyone building out here so I believed it should be followed up. As a result the museum has given me the time and some money to start work. And the UWA has loaned me some assistants to help", Michelle said gesturing to the three young people in the vehicle behind her.

The three people in the vehicle, two women and one man, all stepped down onto the baked earth and gathered behind Michelle. The drivers of the trucks had also stepped down and drifted over.

"Steve, this is Tammy, Susan and Vince, all archaeology students at UWA, the University of Western Australia. The big guy is Tug, he drives one of the front end loaders, the other driver is Mack. Guys, this is Ben Wilde the geologist I told you about who found the ruins".

Tammy, Susan and Vince were all in their early twenties with earnest faces doing little to hide their excitement on being on a real archaeological dig. The driver loader named Tug looked on with a small grin curving his mouth. Mack stood motionless, frowning to himself. They all murmured their hellos as did Ben.

"Do you mind if we camp with you tonight?", asked Michelle, "Only its getting dark so I don't think we'll make the site tonight".

"Certainly. My pleasure. Make yourselves at home", said Ben, "I'll have Ibrahim whip you up a meal since it is his turn to cook. In the meantime would anybody like a drink?", he added, waving his beer can as if by way of demonstration.

All of them opted for the beer. Ben waved to Ibrahim who bought over six more cans. Ben introduced Ibrahim to the new arrivals and said "Come over and I'll introduce you to the rest of the crew".

Mick, Chuck, Lance, Angus and his three men were seated by the campfire drinking beer, except for chuck who was once again drinking coke. Ben introduced Michelle and her people and found them seats, in many instances packing cases and drums. Ibrahim hoisted the barbecue plate onto the fire and set about preparing a salad. When the barbecue plate had heated and the steaks added the air was soon thick with the smell of roasting meat.

"You have quite a setup here Ben", said Michelle, "Almost a home away from home".

"Well, in most ways it is home for me. I don't really feel complete unless I can see the stars and eat food cooked on an open fire".

"You are a strange one aren't you", Michelle said. Leaning in closer to Ben who she was seated beside she whispered "I can see I'll have to get to know you better".

What does that mean, thought Ben. Am I getting the come on? God, I hope so!

The evening went well with the new arrivals to enliven the atmosphere. Ben and Michelle spent most of the time talking together, usually in low voices so they couldn't be overheard by the others. Mick spent the evening trying to charm Susan who must have been at least ten years his junior. His charm must however have failed as at about ten o'clock he retired to his swag, alone. Ibrahim spent much of the evening deep in conversation with Tug, the front end loader driver. The other front end loader driver, Mack, sat by himself and did not join in any of the conversations.

Ben finally turned in at about eleven o'clock, the others all marching off to their swags at the same time.

The following morning Ben woke at about five thirty. In deference to the ladies he had gone to bed the previous night fully clothed in his normal uniform of shorts and short sleeved shirt. He had of course removed his boots. He sat and then stood, stretching his arms into the air to yawn and greet the dawn. For a moment he thought he was the first awake until he looked across to the campfire and saw Michelle already sitting there drinking a mug of coffee and staring at him quizzically.

"Morning Ben. How are you this fine day?"

"Fine Michelle. And you? I hope you slept well".

Desert Dreaming

"Like a baby", she said, "And I'm keen to get to work today".

"What exactly are you going to do?", asked Ben.

"We bought the front end loaders to clear a road into the site from the track. Then we are going to use them to clear as much sand as possible to see what's there. It will take a while but I'm very excited about what we may find".

"I bet", said Ben, "Do you mind if I visit you down there in a few days? See how its going?"

"I would be disappointed if you didn't", she smiled.

The rest of the men and women were soon up and gathered around the campfire. All helped themselves to coffee from the billy and Ibrahim cooked a breakfast of bacon and eggs. Each person made their own toast.

Michelle and her people left the camp at about half past seven leaving a small cloud of dust hanging in the air and marking their progress. Ben watched their progress until they had disappeared.

"You've got it bad don't you mate?", said Mick sneaking up behind him.

"Got it bad? What do you mean 'Got it bad'?"

"You and Michelle. I saw the way you two were last night, whispering together. And this morning. It's OK though mate. You have my approval. She's a real cracker that one!"

Ben just shook his head although he was blushing. Am I that transparent? Still, there was no doubting that he liked her and hoped to get to know her better. He would have to see what he could arrange.

For the next two weeks Ben 'sat' the drilling rig. He completed all of the planned drillholes and was pleased to find that all of them intersected mineralisation except for two. He had indeed discovered an important orebody. While he was sitting the rig Chuck and Lance continued with the stream sediment survey. After one week they had finished their work so Ben dismissed Chuck and sent Lance back to Perth. Before Chuck left Ben warned him again about saying anything about what had happened and said he would look forward to working with him again, next time without terrorists!

During the two weeks one or two of Michelles students passed through the camp four times on errands to Marble Bar or Port Hedland or to get supplies. Michelle, however, never made another appearance. And nor did Ben get the time to visit her at the dig.

During the stay at Blind Bluff the police visited again about three days after Michelle had left the camp. They were still searching for a gunman, they said, and warned Ben's men to be careful.

Four days after Michelle had left the camp they had still more visitors in the form of the major, Mr Dance and a third man who was introduced as Mr Simons, another ASIO agent. It was lunchtime when the humvee drew up, driven by a private soldier. All of the men, including the drillers, were in the camp enjoying their meal. Ben greeted the major and Mr Dance and was introduced to Mr Simons.

"I guess you want our statements", said Ben perfunctorily, but out of hearing of the others.

"Yes Mr Wilde, we do. We thought we would save you the trouble of a trip to Port Hedland and it is convenient for us as most of you are here. We will interview Mr Sanders later in Port Hedland. Please believe me when I say that you are under no suspicion. This is simply to rule a line under the affair", said Mr Dance.

"But since this is confidential do you think you can get rid of those other men who were not involved?"

"Sure, wait here", said Ben.

Ben walked back to the campfire where Angus and his men were finishing lunch.

"Angus, These blokes are from the army and Department of Defence. They want to talk to us about some army exercises they're planning on doing around here", he lied, "Why don't you and your mates get back to the drilling and we'll be out later".

Desert Dreaming

"No worries mate. We'll get onto it".

Angus and his men finished the last scraps of their lunch and trotted off across the bluff to the drilling rig.

"OK", said Mr Dance walking up to Ben, "I know this looks like a bit of an inquisition but we have to interview you one at a time. Can we use one of these tents?"

Ben gave his permission to use a tent as a makeshift interview room and the two ASIO agents invited Ibrahim to join them inside. Ben, Mick and the major sat on the seats by the campfire drinking coffee and exchanging small talk. The two agents had Ibrahim for about half an hour before replacing him with Mick. After another half an hour the agents released Mick and asked for Ben. When Ben entered the tent the two men were seated on chairs facing an empty chair intended for him. He sat. There was a recording device sitting on the tent floor between the two agents. The agents quickly ran through with Ben his version of the events of that fateful day. When? Who? Why? How? Steve answered truthfully giving a full account of everything he had seen and done. Seemingly satisfied, one of the agents turned off the recording machine.

"As expected", said Mr Dance, "All of your stories corroborate and are consistent with what we now know. When the transcript has been typed you will be sent a copy to sign and return. Otherwise we will not trouble you further".

"So, can I take it you have caught all of them?", asked Ben.

"Well, no. There's the rub", said Mr Dance, "We have three killed at the facility, we found their graves, two you killed and four you captured, and one shot dead by the police at the road block near Marble Bar. That makes a total of ten. However, you say that on that day you saw two vehicles heading west away from the facility. The man killed at the road block had one. That means that there is one vehicle and presumably at least one man still missing. The police and army are still doing patrols but so far we have no clue as to where he might have got to. We have searched all of the known roads and tracks and there is no sign of him, or them. We believe after talking to the men that you captured that the missing man might be their leader. So please be careful if any strangers should turn up here".

Well, thought Ben, so it isn't quite over. There is still at least one madman out there. And it looked as though the escapee might be that psychopath Ashad. Whichever was the case, it was no longer his concern. Ben farewelled the major and the ASIO men who drove off into the setting sun.

When the two weeks were up, and the drilling had been completed, Ben decided he would take a break from work and go and see Michelle. Perhaps they would let him help out on the dig? He phoned the Perth office and was willingly given one weeks leave by Tim. Ben packed up what remained of the camp and drove south to the site of his discovery. Mick and Ibrahim returned to Perth.

27

9 MARCH, 2014

It had been almost two and a half weeks since Ashad had taken refuge at the outstation. He was down to his last one or two days of food. He had however supplemented his food supply by shooting a kangaroo which had come in to drink at the trough adjacent to the well.

The kangaroo had arrived at dusk six days previously and Ashad would not have seen it if he hadn't climbed the sand dune to look down at the hut to see if there had been any new visitors. The kangaroo had bounded in small hops over a dune and down to the trough. She had been followed by a much smaller kangaroo, probably her joey. Ashad had taken the shot with the looted Austeyr rifle from almost two hundred meters away and was pleased to see the adult kangaroo drop almost instantly into the trough, shot through the lungs. At the sound of the shot the joey had bounded a few meters away and then turned to look back to his mother, now dead. When Ashad had walked over to retrieve his kill the joey was still standing dumbly, staring at his mother and wondering why she did not move. He had shooed the joey away and dragged the carcass back to his camp where he had butchered it with the hunting knife always kept in a pouch at his hip. However, despite his best efforts the meat soon turned rancid in the sun and he got only three meals out of the carcass.

Six days later and Ashad was again on top of the sand dune looking down at the hut. He knew he should be doing something else but he did not know if it was safe yet and he did not know where the geologist Wilde was. Killing Wilde was the only constant on his mind. Wilde had destroyed his life so he would destroy his if it was the last thing he did. The thirst for revenge was like an incurable disease in him. Nothing would cure that disease short of Wilde's death.

He was sure that the men he had sent to the east had failed. He had had no contact from them at all and he should have done by now if they were still alive and free. They were either dead or captured he had concluded.

Perched on top of the dune looking idly around his self-made prison Ashad heard the sound of engines approaching. Sliding down the dune fractionally so he would not be seen he looked over the top to where the track entered the small grove of trees. A few minutes later he saw one, then two, no three battered four wheel drives come into view and stop by the shack. Six men stepped down from the vehicles, two from each, some stretching, the others looking idly around the area of the hut.

What do we have here, thought Ashad. They are not police and certainly not army. Who were these men invading his sanctuary?

Ashad watched carefully as the men unloaded swags and other camping equipment from the vehicles. Two of the men carried long, flexible pouches from one of the vehicles, pouches that Ashad guessed contained rifles. One of the men walked into the hut and exited moments later with a look of disgust on his face. He made some comment to the other men, most of whom laughed.

These men are definitely not authorities, Ashad thought. They are probably tourists or hunters seeking some excitement. Perhaps I should make myself known, he thought. They will be able to tell me what is going on at the homestead and on the main road.

His mind made up, Ashad lifted himself to his feet, slid down the side of the sand dune and sauntered over to where the men were gathered. One of the men saw him as he approached. "Who the hell are you?", he shouted, "Sneaking up on us like that!".

"Apologies gentlemen", said Ashad, "But my name is Alex Brown, I am the owner of the station on which you are trespassing". Ashad had decided that it was best to take a tough stance with these interlopers.

"Oh, so sorry mate", said the man who had first spoken, "We would have asked permission to come onto your property but when we came past the homestead it had been burnt down and there was no one around. We figured that the place was abandoned".

Well, that answers one of my questions thought Ashad. The authorities had obviously finished sifting the ashes at the homestead.

"My name is Artie", said the group spokesman, "This here is Charlie, Tex, Allan, Slug and Junior", he continued nodding in turn to each of the other five men. "We came up here from Perth to have a look at the country and maybe do a bit of hunting. But if we're not welcome we'll leave".

"No, you are fine", said Ashad, "You are welcome to camp here and shoot some kangaroos if you want. I have been camping here myself since the homestead burnt down".

"Yeah, sorry about that mate. Must have been a bit of a shock seeing your home burn down. We won't be any trouble and if you need a hand with anything just let us know. In the meantime we were going to have a cuppa. Care for one?"

As they scattered in search of firewood and got the billy, tea and coffee together, Ashad examined the men more closely. Most of the men appeared to be in their late thirties or forties except for two. One was the spokesman, Artie, who with a balding head and the remaining hair mostly grey appeared to be in his early sixties. He was clearly the leader of the group. The other, the one he thought was referred to as Junior, was in his early twenties.

Three of the middle aged men had hardened looks and with their tattoos looked like they had probably done prison time.

"So, Alex – You don't mind if I call you Alex do you?", asked Artie.

Ashad just shook his head. He did not care what they called him, as long as it was not Anwar Ashad.

"So, Alex, how come you're camping way down here instead of up at the homestead".

"Ah. Well, you see, waking up every morning to see the destruction was depressing. So I moved down here until I could determine what to do", Ashad lied.

"But you're not camping in the hut are you? Where is your camp?"

"Oh, behind that sand dune. No, I wasn't going to camp in there with the fleas and rats".

Artie laughed. "Can't say I blame you mate!"

The men soon had a fire going, the billy boiled and tea and coffee prepared. Ashad opted for a mug of coffee. His own coffee had run out six days before. The seven men sat around the fire chatting amiably.

"Was the road very busy on the way across from Marble Bar?", Ashad asked Artie casually.

"No. Pretty empty. We did see two army jeeps though didn't we boys?"

The other men nodded or murmured assent. So the army were still on the hunt, thought Ashad. Good luck to them – they won't find anything.

For the rest of that afternoon the men sat around drinking beers from a large car fridge. Ashad retreated to his own camp to contemplate his options at about four o'clock, but only after receiving an invitation from Artie to return for dinner. He returned to the mens camp at about five thirty and readily accepted a beer that was thrust into his hand. He did not actually like beer, preferring whisky, but did not want to make the men suspicious.

From what he had read of Australia before embarking on his mission, he had gathered that all Australian men drank beer.

Sitting down on a camp chair near the fire he listened to what the men were talking about. The primary subject of discussion appeared to be about the Aboriginal people. It was clear that the men had no love of their darker skinned brethren, calling them abo's, boongs, niggers and coons.

"I take it from the conversation that you men are no lovers of Aborigines", Ashad said ingeniously.

"You take it right!", said Artie with venom, "They're lazy, stinking, thieving savages! What do you think of them Alex?"

Deciding it best to stay in the mens good books Ashad said "No, I cannot stand them. Like you said, savages".

The new arrivals stayed on the subject of Aborigines, and their hatred of the race. Ashad slowly teased out of them that they were all members of an organization called the White Australia Movement, WHAM for short. As Ashad kept confirming his hatred for the race the other men became bolder in their statements, believing they were with a like-thinking friend. After a meal of steak and beans prepared by the men, and two more beers, the other men had become decidedly drunk and rowdy having been drinking all afternoon. Any guarding of their language or thoughts disappeared.

"We're going to blow the bastards up!", said Junior suddenly.

"Hush Junior", said Artie sternly, "We're going to do no such thing".

"Yes we are!", said one of the men. The one called Slug, Ashad thought.

"So, it seems you are planning some mayhem", said Ashad, "Tell me where and maybe I'll join you".

Artie could see that the game was up. He may as well tell the truth since Alex seemed to be on their side.

"A woman from the museum and some students are doing an archaeological dig about eight kilometers southwest of here", he said, "From what we can gather from our spy they believe they have found an ancient coon city. With buildings and everything. Can you imagine black savages building a city? Of course not! So we're going to destroy it before the boongs get uppity. Now, are you going to turn us in Mr Brown", he continued suspiciously.

"No. Of course not! I will even help you", said Ashad still trying to play the part of helpful neighbor. Besides, if he stuck with them perhaps he could get his hands on some of the explosives they planned to use. "But how do you know all this?"

"We have a spy in their camp", said Artie, "He's one of their loader drivers, Mack, and he rung us a couple of days ago. Apparently they have found all kinds of shit which to them indicates that the abo's had a sophisticated society thousands of years ago. Can you believe that rot!", he added viciously. "And apparently that bloody geologist that found the thing is there helping them".

"Geologist?", asked Ashad, suddenly very interested, "Do you know his name?"

"Yeah, Williams? No, Wilde!, that's it. Why, do you know him".

"No, I have never had the pleasure", lied Ashad. He was secretly overjoyed. So that was where his enemy was. Only eight kilometers away!

The conversation for the rest of the evening turned to more mundane matters such as football, cricket, the government and even the stock exchange. Ashad finally said his goodnights as the visitors began collapsing into their swags in drunken stupors. He was none to sober himself after the unaccustomed beers. He said goodnight to Artie last, promising to become a fully paid up member of WHAM.

Walking uncertainly back to his own camp Ashad was thinking furiously. I could walk to the dig area tonight, find Wilde, and shoot him. It would probably take about five hours to walk over the dunes but he knew he could make it. Trying to shake off the alcohol he fought to think more sensibly. No, he thought, eight kilometers southwest was not accurate enough. He could pass on the other side of a sand dune less than one hundred meters from the diggers camp and miss it. His visitors clearly had a more accurate way of finding his quarry. Besides, if he could get a vehicle there it would give him a better chance of escape, and the drunken racists might just provide a distraction. He would wait till morning to hear their plans.

The following morning Ashad awoke early and walked across to the newcomers camp. The men were just beginning to stir, some clearly with monster hangovers. Artie, however, looked as bright eyed as usual.

"Good morning Artie", said Ashad, "I trust you slept well?".

"Morning Alex. Yeah, slept like a log. These bastards snoring don't help though", he added with a grin.

"So what is on your agenda today?", asked Ashad casually.

"Today? Today we're going to see if we can bush bash a way through to the abo site".

"Well. Good luck. I have already tried to make a road through to the west but with little success I'm afraid".

"Not to worry mate. With all of these big strong lads we'll get it done. Do you want to come along for a look see?"

Ashad wanted nothing more than to see, and kill, Ben Wilde. Instead he said "Sure, I will come. As you can see I don't have anything better to do".

The men, and Ashad, had a rather burnt breakfast of bacon and eggs with toast and coffee. Ashad nonetheless appreciated it given the rather limited and monotonous food he had been eating. At about eight o'clock, after a word from Artie, the men mounted up and drove their three four wheel drives to the west. Ashad rode with Artie in the lead vehicle. The other five men shared the other two trailing vehicles. They entered between the same two sand dunes that Ashad had previously first tried to use as his road to the west and similarly came to the large mound of sand. Artie put his foot down on the accelerator intending to take the mound at speed. However, about half way up the tires began to spin uselessly, in the same manner as Ashads had. Artie dismounted.

"OK guys. Time for some work. Get the shovels and dig me out", he said.

The men retrieved shovels from the backs of the vehicles and four of them began to dig the sand away from Arties wheels. They then went forward from the vehicle and tossed aside small mountains of sand, attempting to lower the level of the slope. Finished with the road making the men stepped back to see if it had been effective. Artie got back into the driver's seat and, with Ashad still sitting in the passenger seat, easily reversed back down the slope. He reversed up to about fifty meters from the slope and put his foot down, sending the four wheel drive hurtling towards the mound of sand. The vehicle at first made good progress until the slope and the clinging sand began to bite. However, it just managed to reach the top of the mound and then coast down the other side. The men looked on and several clapped as they saw the effort had been successful.

Four of the other men retreated to their vehicles and one tied a length of rope to the front of the second vehicle before running the other end across the sand mound to tie it to the tow ball of Arties vehicle. He then stood on top of the mound giving signals to both Artie and the vehicle to be towed. Artie slowly took up the strain on the rope whilst his towee slowly crept forward. With both engines pulling the second vehicle easily cleared the mound. The same process was then repeated for the third vehicle. During the remainder of the journey the same process had to be repeated twice more.

The following vehicles could probably have crested the sand mounds in the same manner as the first but the men seemed intent on their chosen method of towing. In addition, Ashad believed that the other two vehicles motors weren't as strong as the lead vehicles. In any case, they were making a decent road towards his quarry.

Since the sand dunes ran east – west the vehicles were at first funneled to the west when they wanted to head to the southwest. As a result whenever they came to a low area of the southern dune, or the southern dune disappeared, they would veer to the south.

Nearly two hours after leaving the camp they finally arrived adjacent to the archaeological site. There spy at the site had used a satellite telephone to give the men the sites coordinates that he had gotten from a hand held GPS. Artie also had a hand held GPS which he consulted regularly during the drive.

Artie finally stopped the lead vehicle in the lee of a large sand dune and dismounted. The other two vehicles also stopped and their occupants dismounted. Ashad looked around curiously. He could see no sign of any digging activity. Indeed, there was no sign of any other people ever having been where he now stood. He could however hear faint engine noise which was obviously not coming from their vehicles which had been switched off.

Artie could see that Ashad was confused. "Just the other side of this dune I think Alex. We'll climb up and have a look see". Artie pulled a set of binoculars from behind the drivers seat.

Led by Artie the five other men scrambled up the side of the steep sand dune. Ashad followed in the rear. Arriving at the top Ashad found the other six men lying on the ground staring down into the next valley. He joined them to look down upon the archaeological site.

About one hundred meters away two front end loaders were scooping up sand and running it to a dump further to the south. He could also see what appeared to be seven stone buildings in a large depression dug by the loaders. The buildings were all square in shape and comprised of a fawn coloured rock only one or two shades darker than the surrounding sand. He could also see open doorways in three of the buildings. There were four people down in the depression around the buildings shoveling sand or examining the building facades. One appeared to be a man, and three women.

A fifth figure stepped into view through one of the doorways. This figure was a man with dark hair dressed in khaki shorts and a short sleeved khaki shirt. Ashad grabbed the binoculars from Artie and focused on the man. It was Ben Wilde, without a doubt! He continued to examine him under magnification as he went to talk to one of the women.

If I had my rifle I could end this now, thought Ashad. But he had not bought the rifle, not wanting his companions to know he was armed and certainly not with an Australian army weapon. But now I know where he is. And next time I will have my rifle!

"When do you plan to blow this up", Ashad quietly asked Artie.

"Not yet mate. We don't want to blow this up only to find they've dug up some more do we? No, we'll be waiting for at least a few days until we get word from Mack that they've finished. And we don't want to kill anyone, just make sure that this abomination goes away".

With that the men retreated from the dune top back down to their vehicles, Ashad following. All of the men climbed aboard the four wheel drives and after some maneuvering headed back the way that they had come. Ashad travelled in silence, planning his revenge.

28

9 MARCH, 2014

"**Oh Michelle, this** is incredible!", exclaimed Ben, "You have made incredible progress in such a short time!"

"It is though isn't it. And how are you today?"

After finishing the drilling and packing up the remainder of the camp Ben had driven straight down to what he thought of as the 'house site'. On arriving at the rough track he had made into the sand dunes he had found that it had been graded to a rough but serviceable road. Following the road he had eventually driven downhill into what could only be described as a quarry. Huge quantities of sand had been moved to produce a depression two to three meters deep, eighty meters long and thirty meters wide. Many thousands of tons of sand had been moved.

In the middle of the excavation were seven stone buildings all of which were about two and a half meters tall and five meters on each side. Each of the buildings was flat topped with no apparent roof and all were arranged in a semicircle with about three meters between buildings. Each of the buildings also had a single open doorway but no windows. The doorways all pointed towards the centre of the semicircle. Several of the buildings were still largely full of sand.

Ben had parked his cruiser and was wandering around in awe between the buildings. He saw that with most of the sand removed the ground underfoot was compressed brown clay.

"How did you get so much done so quickly?"

"Well, it's only loose sand and is easily removed. The loaders just cruise along slowly with their buckets lowered to scoop out the sand. The moment a loader even gently bumps something a bit more solid they retreat and clean up around it. Then myself and the kids use shovels to scoop out the remaining sand. That's how we've managed to excavate so quickly".

"Incredible", said Ben again, shaking his head, "And so what have you learnt? Who built this?"

"I am pretty certain that it was built by the Aborigines. Oh, I know what you're thinking, how could stone age tribal people build something so incredible? Well, the evidence is here and I'll show you".

As Michelle spoke she led the way through the narrow doorway into one of the buildings. Inside, all of the sand had been removed revealing a brown clay floor similar to the ground outside. The walls were made of blocks of sandstone each about one meter long and half a meter thick but no two blocks were exactly the same size. Looking closer Ben could see that the blocks appeared to have been mortared together with clay. The interior of the single room was unadorned other than with what appeared to be faded paintings on the walls near what would have been the roof.

"You see the paintings. They are definitely Aboriginal. Unfortunately only parts survive where the sand didn't reach. Lower down, where the wall was covered by sand, the sand probably acted liked sand paper, scrubbing the surface clean. Of course all the building were full of sand but we think that the top half meter or so was only covered when the roofs collapsed. As you can see none of the building have roofs any more. Such a shame!", said Michelle.

Looking closer Ben could see that the badly faded paintings

showed the top half of a kangaroo, a turtle and most of a fish. The red, white and yellow painting was definitely in the Aboriginal style.

"Yep, I can see the painting is Aboriginal. But the Aborigines could have taken this over when the builders left for whatever reason".

"True", said Michelle, "But we have other evidence. I firmly believe that this place was built by Aborigines".

"Do you see the notches at the top of the walls Ben?", continued Michelle.

Ben looked up and could indeed see notches about ten centimeters across and the same deep carved in the tops of the walls at about one meter intervals. He could guess for himself what they were for. They must be notches that had held beams or rafters which in turn had supported the roof which was now entirely absent. He nodded to Michelle to indicate that he had seen that of which she spoke.

"We think that they supported wooden rafters which in turn supported about ten centimeter thick slabs of sandstone which had formed the roof. We found fragments of those slabs in all of the buildings. Remember those fragments you found on your first visit? Several slabs had remnants of what looked like a bitumen coating, probably to waterproof them".

Interesting, thought Ben. I'll have to tell my mates in the petroleum industry. If the builders used tar they must have obtained it from some natural seepage somewhere in the area. And if there was tar seepage, there would be a good chance that there would be oil at depth. Although Ben believed that there was no real potential for oil in this area.

Turning back to the doorway Michelle asked "See anything unusual about the door Ben?"

Steve examined the doorway. "Other than there isn't one, no. I presume if it was wood it would have rotted away long since".

"Look closer at the doorway. Tell me what you see".

"Nothing?"

"Exactly, nothing. If you look at the sides you can see there is absolutely nowhere that a hinge or even a bit of rope to support the door could have been attached. There were no doors. We believe that this was a truly open society with no barriers between members".

"I see what you mean. OK, what's your other evidence? And have you been able to tell how old the place is?"

Although the site was fascinating and hinted at an interesting history, Ben was still not convinced that it was Aboriginal.

"Oh, that is the really exciting news we only got back yesterday. We found some charcoal in the remnants of a fireplace in one of the other houses and I sent it down to Perth to get carbon dated. It came back yesterday with a date nine thousand, six hundred years before present! Over nine thousand years! The people who lived here did so when civilization was only just starting to awaken in Europe!"

"That is incredible! We know that the aborigines have been here for around forty thousand years but to think that they might have built civilized buildings", said Ben with some doubt.

"Sorry, that sounded terrible. It seems to imply that the nomadic Aborigines who built nothing weren't civilized. That isn't what I meant", Ben added quickly.

"I know Ben. But it is amazing to think that people we thought of as primitive nomads might actually have built a city. Well, not a city exactly, more like a small village. But the amazement still holds! You must remember that when the British first found the stone ruins of Great Zimbabwe in Rhodesia, now Zimbabwe, they believed that it must have been built by a vanished civilisation. They could not believe that such structures could have been built by tribal black Africans. But they were!"

"Come with me", said Michelle, suddenly grabbing Ben by the hand.

She led him out of the house and over to a small tent that had been erected in the bottom of the depression. Entering the tent Ben saw that it contained only a rough wooden table and a small stool on which sat Susan, one of the students.

"Oh, Hi Ben. Nice to see you. Is Mick with you?", said Susan, turning on the stool.

Mick must have made more of an impression than I'd thought, thought Ben wryly.

Looking down Ben could see several stone artifacts arranged on the table. A large rounded block of rock looked to have been a hammer. The signs of impacts in the artifacts centre were obvious. A second object was a eight inch length of hard chert rock which had been fashioned to a chisel point at one end. Fractures and erosion at the other end indicated that it had been hit repeatedly with another rock, possibly the adjacent hammer. There was a third piece that also had the form of a chisel and there at the end of the table were two rough gold nuggets. Ben did a quick estimation and calculated that one nugget weighed about seventeen ounces, the other about nine ounces.

"Marvellous aren't they", said Michelle, "We discovered all of the tools in one of the houses. You can clearly see that they are of Aboriginal manufacture".

"But what of the gold?", said Ben incredulously, "Where in hell did you get that from? And the gold is certainly not Aboriginal. There has never been any evidence to suggest that the Aborigines were ever interested in gold. Even though they must have seen the stuff lying about the place"

"We found one nugget in each of two houses", said Michelle, "And I do think it was picked up by Aborigines, probably from the goldfields to the west of here. They may just have found the colour fascinating and bought it back here as a curiosity".

"Look, don't get me wrong Michelle. I love the Aboriginal people but I can't see how they could have possibly built something so..., so precise. They did not have the technology. They had no metal tools. I mean, they didn't even get around to inventing the wheel!"

"I understand your doubts Ben, I really do. But look at the facts. We have Aboriginal tools, we have Aboriginal paintings and we have Aboriginal carvings, remember those carvings for 'shelter' we saw that first day. Well that's repeated on all of the other houses. And the clincher is that someone was living in these buildings more than nine thousand years ago! It can't have been wayward Europeans or even Asians. Nine thousand years ago they were only just starting to get their own acts together! And the only people who were ever known to have lived here nine thousand years ago were the Aborigines! And how could they have done it without metal tools? Well, as you've seen that sandstone is very porous and quite soft. I mean you wouldn't want to bang your head against it, it would certainly leave a bruise, but you can actually carve it quite easily. We know, we've tried. And each of those blocks could easily be lifted by four strong men like yourself".

"OK", said Ben, thinking furiously, and strangely thrilled by her reference to his supposed strength, "Then where did they get the stone from?"

"Ah, that I can show you", said Michelle, once again grabbing him by the hand and leading him out of the tent.

Michelle set off at a brisk pace walking to the east, still holding his hand. Ben felt strangely excited by the continued bodily contact. She certainly must like him!

They walked across the excavation and up the eastern lip. For another four hundred meters they walked, crossing two sand dunes on the way. Having descended from the last dune Michelle walked another hundred meters and stopped.

"There you go", she said, "Their quarry!"

Ben looked around and saw that they were standing on flat ground. There was no excavation in sight. He was about to question Michelles use of the word quarry when she went on as if she had read his mind.

"I know it doesn't look like what you think of as a quarry but it is. One of my students found it when going for a walk. We think there was once a hill of sandstone here and they simply carved it away to ground level".

Ben looked more closely at the ground and saw that although there were drifts of sand much of the ground was actually the same sandstone that had been used in the buildings. The sandstone surface was perfectly flat other than a couple of projections of the rock through sand. On looking at those projections closer Ben saw that they were actually squared off blocks of sandstone. He crouched beside one of the blocks and looking even more closely saw that it had been broken off along its bedding plane, a natural weakness formed when the sediment had been deposited. He could see that it would be quite easy to break the rock along those bedding planes to give perfectly flat surfaces. Careful chiseling could then have created the other flat planes at right angles.

Not quite defeated, Ben asked his final question "OK, you pretty much have me convinced except for one very important point, and this pertains to whoever did the building. Why build a town in the middle of the desert? It doesn't make sense".

"Ah, there again I can help you", said Michelle, "I don't believe that this was always desert. If you look at satellite imagery you can see the faint trace of something that may have been a river just to the south. We actually used a hand auger to drill a shallow hole into the 'river' and at five meters deep we discovered black mud and two meters deeper we found gravel. So I am pretty sure the river existed. And I believe that this whole area might once have been a forest. During the excavation we have found pieces of what we believe are partly fossilised rotten wood. So I believe that before the climate changed this might have been a Garden of Eden.".

"I have one last thing to show you that will blow your mind, come with me", Michelle continued excitedly, tugging Ben by the hand back towards the excavation.

Arriving back at the village Michelle took Steve to another tent beside the first that he had visited. This tent though was substantially larger. Undoing the flaps that covered the entrance she led him inside. Ben was shocked by what he saw lying on the canvas tent floor. Three almost complete skeletons lying side by side. The skeletons were in good condition and seemed to be missing only a few bones, mostly fine bones from the fingers and toes. The skeletons had however been discolored to a pale coffee tone.

"We found these almost by accident", said Michelle, "Tug was completing a run with his loader to the south when he bumped into something a bit more solid. When we cleared away the sand we discovered an almost complete rectangular plate of sandstone about one and a half meters by half a meter by ten centimeters thick. Curious, we dug beneath it and at a depth of about two feet discovered the first skeleton. We subsequently found two other broken sandstone plates nearby and digging beneath those we found the other two skeletons. It was an Aboriginal cemetery!"

"OK, sure, it was a cemetery. But an Aboriginal cemetery?"

"Listen Ben, as part of my uni degree a did a one year course in osteology so I know a little about skeletons. You can see that all of these skulls have pronounced brows, an elongate brain case and jutting chins. Features typical of Aboriginal Australians. These three people were an Aboriginal man about fifty years old, an Aboriginal woman probably in her forties and a young male probably in his late teens. There is no doubt. We are in any case getting a professional osteologist up here to confirm it".

"OK, I surrender", said Ben throwing his hands into the air theatrically, "You have made an amazing discovery of a previously unknown Aboriginal society. Your discovery will change Australian history. But I have one final question. Why here? Surely there must have been better places that they could have built?".

Desert Dreaming

"Ah!, Once again I can help you with your problem. Come with me!"

Michelle once again grabbed Ben's hand and led him from the tent. Retaining her hold on his hand this time she led him to the south. On the way Steve saw three shallow pits excavated in the red soil. These would have been the shallow graves from which the three skeletons had been excavated. Michelle carried on leading him by the hand over three sand dunes before stopping.

"There, do you see it?", Michelle asked.

Ben looked forward and for a moment could see nothing unusual. Then his gaze drifted to the left and he saw an outcrop of red rock with what looked like a deep pit or cave in the centre of the outcrop. Reluctantly releasing Michelles hand Ben strolled across to have a closer look. On arriving at the outcrop he saw that it was in fact ochre, a clay formed by the weathering of iron-rich rocks. And the ochre was a brilliant red colour. The hole in the centre was about two meters by one meter and descended for only one meter, the bottom being covered by sand. Tool marks could clearly be seen on the walls of the pit.

"I'll be damned", exclaimed Ben, "An ochre mine!"

"Yes, I thought you would be interested as it's in your line of work. Vince was taking a walk down here when he saw the outcrop of ochre and lying nearby he found what we think is an Aboriginal stone axe. When we came down here and dug around a bit we found the entrance to the mine. The mine had been completely filled in and obscured by the sand. We had quite a lot of fun digging it out, I can tell you! We think it goes down a considerable depth below the sand".

"So you see", continued Michelle, "These people were miners. And they mined red ochre which is much prized by the Aborigines all over Australia. This tribe would have been the BHP Billiton of their day", she laughed.

"You truly have made a remarkable discovery", said Ben with some awe.

"Your discovery too", reminded Michelle, "If it hadn't been for you none of this would have come to light".

Ben was pleased but a little embarrassed by her words. Nonetheless, his innocent adventure into the desert had started the chain of events that had led to all of this.

"It is an amazing discovery", repeated Michelle, "But don't expect that Aboriginal towns will start popping up all over Australia. I think that this was an anomaly. The Aboriginal people were true nomads, they did not grow crops and nor did they keep domesticated livestock. They had to move around to find their food. I think that what happened is that one day some bright spark thought 'I'm sick to death of all of this traipsing around the bush. I am going to stay in one spot. There looks like there is a lot of food around here so I think I'll just stay put!'. And that is what the tribe did. They built stone buildings to make it permanent. But it was doomed to failure. They would have killed off all of the game in the area and eaten all of the berries and roots and so forth until one day they discovered that they were starving and couldn't stay here anymore. So they left to become true nomads again. They may have continued to live here for a few months of each year, maybe in the winter or during the wet, but they had to keep going away to find new food sources. And then the climate began to change and their little town became entirely untenable".

"It's a bit like Atlantis, isn't it?", mused Ben, "I mean Atlantis was supposedly a city that sank into the sea. This was a town that sank into a sea of sand".

"Yes. Yes it is. But when I say that I think this was an anomaly it doesn't lessen the sites importance. It showed that the Aboriginal people were capable of building. If they had been able to get a handle on growing crops and raising livestock then when Captain Cook arrived here, instead of finding mostly naked 'savages', he might have found sophisticated towns, possibly even cities! Then the history of Australia would have been entirely different".

"Why do you think the modern Aborigines call this area bad or poison ground?", asked Ben seriously.

"I have given that some thought", said Michelle, "I think that when the town failed it became a sort of embarrassment. I think that the Aborigines did not want to be reminded of their failure so they essentially declared the place off limits. And that taboo has carried down to this day".

With the sun beginning to sink in the west in a blaze of orange, Ben and Michelle made their way back to the teams camp. Perched on the lip of the excavation adjacent to the entry road the camp had several tents and even a bucket shower rigged up on poles and shielded by a length of canvas. Each of the workers at the site had their own pup tent and there were larger tents for supplies and one which functioned as a cookhouse. Ben of course would continue to sleep outside, under the stars.

Ben could not believe his luck. He was here working on an exciting project which would change history. And, more importantly, he was working with a woman he suspected that he was starting to fall in love with! Ben pitched in and worked at the site for his week of leave and then, reluctant to leave either the work or Michelle, he applied for and was granted another weeks leave.

29

18 MARCH, 2014

All of the team at the dig got on well together with the exception of one. Mack, one of the loader drivers, did his work but rarely exchanged more than two words with any of the others. He usually ate his evening meal in silence and retired to his tent while the others were still chatting and laughing. Ben had tried to draw him out but more often than not was responded to with mumbles, silence and sometimes even hostile glares. He could not figure the man out.

One evening after dinner the crew were sitting around talking and laughing when, without a word, Mack left the side of the camp fire. However, instead of heading directly for his tent Ben saw that he made a detour to the equipment tent and when he came out he was carrying one of the satellite telephones. And then, instead of retiring to his tent to talk with a loved one, he walked out into the darkness.

Ben stood from his chair but was then conflicted about what he should do. The man was acting strangely and taking the telephone to make a phone call out in the dark was definitely strange. But he couldn't spy on the man, could he? His actions might after all be entirely innocent. But why go to such trouble to make a private phone call that he could make in his own tent? Ben's mind was made up. He would see what Mack was up to and if it was innocent he wouldn't breathe a word to anyone. He padded away from his chair and from the cheerful glow of the fire in the direction Mack had gone. The soft sand muted any sound his boots might have made.

Creeping forward Ben heard the murmur of a voice ahead, around the brow of a sand dune. He could not however make out what was being said. Silently creeping forward he suddenly saw Mack silhouetted against the soft light thrown by the moon and stars and could now hear what he was saying. He could not hear the other end of the conversation but the intention was clear.

"… think they have found everything here. Seven buildings in all"

"I'm leaving tomorrow Artie. I've pleaded work back in town"

"No!, blow the bloody place tomorrow night!"

"Ten o'clock usually. Blow it any time after twelve and they'll all be sound asleep. By the time they get out of their tents you'll be long gone".

"No, you'll be perfectly safe. These people know nothing"

"When you get back to the outstation get out of there soonest. Before the police put up roadblocks"

"Bye Artie, see you in the Port".

Realising that the telephone call had finished, Ben quietly retraced his steps before Mack was alerted. He wandered over to the camp fire as though he had just returned from a call of nature and sat in his chair. Mack reappeared into the light less than a minute later and after replacing the telephone in the equipment tent, went to his own tent.

"You all right Ben. You look like you've seen a ghost", said Michelle with concern.

"No, I'm fine Michelle. Perhaps something I ate. I think I'll turn in".

With that Ben got back up from the chair and wandered over

to his swag placed some distance away from the camp fire and tents. His mind was in a quandary. Someone was planning on blowing some place up, probably this place!. But why? The site had no strategic or monetary value. Why destroy it? Ah well, it takes all sorts he thought. Some people were just bent on mayhem but not if he could do something about it. He should know that after what he had experienced only a couple of weeks before. He drifted off to sleep thinking about what he could do about it.

The following morning, over breakfast, Ben told Michelle he had an errand to run in Marble Bar. He would be back that night. In reality he was intending to go to the police there and tell them what he had learnt. And this time they had better believe him! He did not tell Michelle what he had heard the previous night, or what he intended, as he did not want to worry her.

Straight after breakfast Ben was on the road back to Marble Bar. He drove past Blind Bluff, turned onto the NWR road and was in Marble Bar by ten o'clock in the morning. He drove straight to the police station and accosted the young constable behind the counter.

"I must speak with the sergeant straight away. Is he in?"

"Yes sir. Mr Wilde isn't it? I'll just get him", said the constable.

The constable retreated into the back rooms and returned a couple of minutes later with the sergeant in tow.

"Mr Wilde", said the sergeant, "I suppose you have come for your apology".

Steve was confused. "Apology? What apology? No, I have come on another matter".

"Ah, I see. I do owe you an apology though. We thought you had taken a knock to the head but you were right about there being something fishy at Bright Downs. You probably heard that we shot the bastard dead? At first the army told us that there were a couple of madmen shooting up the NWR facility. Later they changed it to say there was only one man. You told us that there was about a dozen of them. Now, I might be just a dumb copper but I know bullshit when I hear it. That four wheel drive we stopped had two drums of nuclear waste aboard. The bloke that had it didn't hold up the facility by himself and he didn't go up to the gate and ask for a couple of drums! I think the army have pulled the blinds down over this one and a lot more happened than what we were told!".

The police had clearly not been told the whole story of what had happened at the NWR facility or the aftermath. It seemed as though they had been told that there was only a single crazed gunman from Bright Downs, apart from the man that they themselves had shot. Ben was not going to enlighten the sergeant. Particularly as it would mean him spending time in prison for divulging state secrets!

"I thank you sergeant. I really couldn't say what happened although I'm glad its over. But this is another matter". Ben then proceeded to give the sergeant the details of the telephone call he had overheard, and his suspicions. He finished by saying that the bombers were at the Bright Downs outstation because he had heard Mack refer to it in the telephone call.

"Well, I'm not going to make the same mistake I made last time. Me and the constable will go out there right now".

"Do you mind if I tag along sergeant? I won't get in your way".

"I can't see why not Mr Wilde. But you stay well back and if it looks as though there's going to be trouble then you skedaddle, OK?"

"Sure thing sergeant. I will keep well out of the way"

The sergeant instructed the constable to get the police four wheel drive and all three men left the building together. The constable ducked around the back of the building to get the vehicle as Ben climbed into his. The Police four wheel drive soon appeared around the corner and, after picking up the sergeant, both vehicles were soon heading east, towards Bright Downs, with Ben following the police vehicle. Two hours later passing the homestead Ben saw that it had been reduced to a pile of charcoal and buckled and rusting tin. The room where he had been held a prisoner had entirely disappeared.

The two vehicles bumped down the track towards the outstation and on arriving saw three vehicles parked there with six men milling about. They had obviously heard the vehicles coming but were uncertain what to do. Brazen out their presence or try to make a run for it?

The police four wheel drive had been leading and it parked next to the first of the three vehicles already there. Steve parked about fifty meters back blocking the entrance road and remained seated in his cruiser.

The two policemen emerged from their vehicle.

"Good morning gentlemen", said the sergeant, "I am the sergeant of police from Marble Bar. May I ask what you fellows are doing down here?"

"Good morning officer. Nice to see the boys in blue about. We're just down here camping and doing a bit of hunting. Is there a problem?", said Artie.

"You might say that sir. Some information has come to light and I am afraid that we are going to have to search your vehicles".

The men standing close by all suddenly took on aggressive stances and expressions. They clearly did not like the idea of a search. They relaxed a little when they saw how the constable was caressing the butt of his holstered revolver.

"There is no need for that sergeant. What you see is what we have. We've got nothing to hide. Do we boys?"

There were several unintelligible grunts from Arties friends.

"I am afraid I must insist sir. Guard my back constable"

The sergeant walked across to the nearest four wheel drive and opened the front passenger door. Seeing nothing alarming other than two rifles he closed the door and opened the rear door. Once again he saw nothing to give alarm and closing the door moved on to the next vehicle.

The sergeant moved from vehicle to vehicle, searching each

in turn. The constable stood watching the other men, his hand still caressing his revolver butt. The men looked on angrily. Artie looked grey and as though he was about to have a heart attack.

The sergeant found nothing until he reached the third vehicle. This vehicle was a trayback and on pulling back the covering tarpaulin he was confronted by four identical wooden boxes. Clearly stenciled on the lid of each of the boxes was the word 'explosives'. Using a handy shovel he prised open the lid of one of the boxes and when he turned back towards the men he had in his hand a stick of gelignite.

"Pretty unfair hunting to be using gelignite don't you think gentlemen? Do you have a permit for these explosives?"

"No. No we don't", said Artie tiredly. He could see that the game was up.

"Ah, well. That is illegal don't you gentlemen know. We are going to have to confiscate this and take you all in for questioning. Constable, get identification from each of these gentlemen. I will cover you".

The constable went around to each of the men nervously requesting identification. One by one the men reluctantly pulled wallets and produced driving licences. The constable noted down the details of each licence in his notebook.

"Now gentlemen, we have a problem. As you can no doubt see, you outnumber us three to one. At the moment you are all coming into Marble bar to assist us with our enquiries. However, if you decide to bolt you will be caught before you reach either Port Hedland or Newman and then you will be thrown in a cell", said the sergeant, "Constable, I note that there are two rifles in the first vehicle. Please fetch them and place them in our vehicle. The gelignite is in the back of the third vehicle so please gather that evidence and place it in the back of our vehicle. But carefully lad, I don't want to have to post your remains back to your folks!". "You, Mr...", pointing at Artie.

"Rasmusson, Arthur Rasmusson", said Artie sulkily.

"Mr Rasmusson, you will be joining the constable and I in our vehicle. Now pack up your equipment and let us go".

The men sullenly went about gathering up their swags and other camping equipment and throwing it without care into the vehicles. The constable gathered the two rifles and placed them on the rear seat of the police vehicle. He then took the wooden boxes of gelignite one at a time and placed them carefully in the rear of the police vehicle.

After exchanging a quiet word with the constable the sergeant marched across to where Ben still sat in his vehicle.

"Mr Wilde. It seems we owe you our thanks again. I have no doubt that they will behave and follow us into Marble Bar. Thank you again".

"What will they be charged with?", asked Ben.

"Certainly possession of illegal explosives, possibly conspiracy to commit a terrorist act", answered the sergeant. He nodded to Ben and walked back to the constable.

Five minutes later the WHAM camp site had been dismantled and cleaned up and the five vehicles left the clearing on the way back to the homestead and Marble Bar. Ben, however, was planning on turning off on the Blind Bluff road and returning to the dig.

Who would have believed it, thought Ben as he drove. In less than a month and I have helped to foil two terrorist plots. Maybe someone should write a book about me!

Ashad watched the parade of vehicles as they left. He had seen the whole confrontation from his perch atop the sand dune above his camp. In the more than a week he had been with the WHAM people he still spent most of the time alone in his own camp. He had joined the other men only for meals, and then only because his own food supply was running low. He had no doubt that the men had been arrested because of their plot to blow up the Aboriginal site. During questioning at least one of them was bound to mention him. That would cause severe complications. He had to get out of here and act now!

Desert Dreaming

When he had been watching he had clearly seen the geologist Wilde waiting in his vehicle. He had been tempted to slide back down to his camp, retrieve his rifle and blow him away. However, if he had missed he would have had two police and possibly six other men down on him. Even if he hadn't missed he would almost certainly have been either shot or arrested. It had been too risky. So he had simply watched, seething with hatred for the man who had destroyed his life. And now he had done it again! To another group of people. He simply did not know when to stop interfering. Well, his interfering days were almost over. As he sat observing he decided that tomorrow was the day he would move, for better or for worst.

In the meantime he had to move in case one of the WHAM men told of the owner of Bright Downs station being at the outstation. It would not take much for the police to put two and two together and come looking for him. He decided that he would move to the location overlooking the dig that he had visited with the WHAM men. He had no concerns about getting through. The WHAM vehicles had flattened and compressed the sand making negotiation of the sand mounds almost easy. He packed up the few items from his small camp and placed them in the four wheel drive. He then drove to the first sand mound and easily negotiated it. Stopping the vehicle on the other side He went back over his tracks, obliterating them with a branch from a desert oak. He was about to move on when a thought occurred to him. When he had left the homestead he had destroyed the house. Perhaps that was his signature? He retrieved a box of matches from the vehicle and walked back to the hut that comprised the outstation. With a few small twigs he was soon able to get a blaze going in one corner of the hut. The dry timbers soon caught fire and by the time he had walked the five hundred meters back to the vehicle the structure was fully ablaze. He climbed into the drivers seat and continued his journey.

30

20 MARCH, 2014

Ben was shoveling sand from one of the newly discovered stone buildings when the police arrived. Hearing the motor straining as it negotiated the steep descent Ben stepped out into the daylight to see who had come to visit. The four wheel drive pulled up on the other side of the building and Ben went around to greet the visitors. The sergeant and his constable were just exiting the vehicle as Ben rounded the buildings corner.

"Mr Wilde. Good to see you", boomed the sergeant, "I had heard about this place but I didn't quite believe it. It truly is incredible!"

"Sergeant. Nice of you to pay us a visit. Is there anything I can do for you?"

"Well, its more along the lines of what we can do for you", said the sergeant, "As you know we arrested those men yesterday. It turns out that they're from a race hate group called the White Australia Movement, WHAM for short. We are fairly certain that they were planning on blowing up this site but it will be difficult to prove. We do however have them for illegal possession of explosives and it turns out that one of their rifles wasn't registered so we have them for that too. We also found some marijuana on one of the men so we'll probably hit him for possession. At least some of them will almost certainly do jail time".

"Well, I am glad to hear that. I suppose it also explains why they were intent on destroying this place. They wouldn't have wanted the Aborigines to receive any credit".

"No, they wouldn't. But that is not all that we discovered. Apparently there was another man camped near to them at the outstation, a man calling himself Alex Brown and purporting to be the owner of Bright Downs. Clearly, he must have been one of those terrorists that didn't exist", said the sergeant sarcastically.

"Oh, that's great. He is the man that the army still thought was missing. Did you find him and arrest him?".

"No, we didn't. We have just come from there and we found where he had been camping behind a sand dune. But no sign of him or his vehicle. And it looks like he torched the outstation hut before he left. That is why we have come to see you. To warn you. He is possibly still in the area and the outstation is only eight kilometers from here as the crow flies. Please keep a look out and be careful".

"Do you know what this bloke looked like?", asked Ben, with no real interest.

"We do. From the descriptions those men gave he was of European appearance although with a deep tan. Dark hair. The most distinguishing features however appear to be a broken nose and a scar above his left eye in the shape of the numeral 7".

"Ashad!", exclaimed Ben, "He was the leader of the terrorists! I would know that bastard that had me beaten anywhere!"

"Ah ha! Well that does explain a lot. Anyhow, we have let the army know and they are sending out some people to search. In the meantime, just be careful in case he hasn't left the area and comes this way".

"Sure sergeant. We will do. Now, I was just going to have lunch. Would you care to join us?"

"Thought you'd never ask", said the sergeant with a large smile.

Ben gave the interested policemen a brief tour of the site and then led them up the rise to the camp. Today, instead of sandwiches or tinned stew, one of the crew had decided to cook sausages and baked potatoes. Ben could smell the appetizing aroma of the cooking meat as he approached the camp. All of the crew were already there, including Michelle. The only absentee was Mack who had loaded his machine that morning and left for Port Hedland.

The police had a fine early lunch of sausages, baked potatoes, salad and freshly baked rolls and chatted amiably with the crew. They did not however enlighten anyone else as to the reason for their visit, leaving that to Ben. Ben remained silent on the subject, not wanting to alarm his friends. He would see to it that they came to no harm. The police left at about two o'clock, waving to their new friends as they drove away.

After lunch Ben returned to his job of shoveling the sand from a newly discovered building. Michelle also came to the same building to see what Ben's excavating had uncovered. Ben was standing on a mound of sand at the doorway when Michelle grasped his hand to pull herself up the mound and out of the building. Suddenly, there was a loud crack! And blood exploded into the air. Michelle collapsed back into the building pulling Ben with her, yelping as she did so. Both collapsed onto the still sandy floor inside the building.

Pulling himself up onto his hands and knees Ben saw immediately that Michelle was bleeding from a wound on her upper arm. Although she was moaning gently she did not yell or cry. Ben closely inspected her bare arm and saw that she had been shot, the bullet taking a chunk of flesh out of her bicep. The wound was about an inch deep and over two inches long. It appeared as though the bullet had passed straight through the muscle of her arm. Although not life threatening, it must have been painful.

Desert Dreaming

Ben called out for Susan who had been working nearby. "Susan, Come here quickly. Michelle has been shot!"

Susan poked her head in the doorway only seconds later and saw Ben applying a rough bandage to Michelles arm, the bandage comprising strips from his torn shirt.

"What on Earth is happening Ben", said Susan quickly, "She can't have been shot! I thought I heard something but it can't have been a gun, not out here."

"Well she has! Get the first aid kit and have someone call the police and flying doctor! We must get her to hospital!"

"Ben", said Michelle gently, "I don't need the flying doc. Someone can run me into town to the first aid post. Yes, it hurts like hell but I don't think I am going to bleed to death".

"OK, if you are sure. Susan, get the first aid kit and bandage this properly and then drive her into Marble Bar. I'm going after whoever did this!"

Ben already knew who the villain was. Ashad! It had to be! He was going to hunt him down and kill him for what he had done to the woman that he loved.

"Ben! Don't be silly. He will just shoot you! Let the police handle it. Please?", begged Michelle.

"Michelle. By the time the police get here he will be long gone. No, I am going after the bastard. Don't worry, I'll take care".

Without another word Ben turned and strode away towards the camp, leaving the love of his life in Susan's care.

It had indeed been Ashad who had loosed the shot. Perched on his vantage point atop the sand dune he had seen Ben at work and then seen him turn his back to him. Lining up the centre of Ben's back he had taken the shot from a distance of one hundred and fifty meters. And he was certain that he had been successful. He had seen a brief spray of blood and Wilde collapse into the hut that he was excavating. And when he had shot the kangaroo with the Austeyr from a similar distance at the outstation the shot had gone exactly where he had aimed, right in the centre of the animals chest. He had killed Wilde and satisfied his need for revenge. Now he had only to ensure that he survived the outcome. He turned from the dune top and slid down the opposite side to his vehicle.

Ashad had of course been mistaken in his assumption. Firstly, the constant jolting of the rifle in the footwell of the four wheel drive had minutely jarred the sights from a true alignment. Enough so that when he had shot the bullet had passed only a hairsbreadth over Ben's right shoulder. He had also not seen Michelle. He had therefore concluded that the spray of blood he had seen must have come from Wilde.

Trotting into the campsite Ben went first to his swag where he retrieved a new shirt from his kitbag. He then ran to the kitchen tent where he grabbed the first weapon he could see, a vicious looking carving knife. He also picked up a full water bottle on a long strap.

Ben left the camp and ran back to where he thought the shot had come from. It was a large sand dune and he believed that the sniper must have been lying atop it. He scrambled quickly up the side and on reaching the top cast around for any sign. He soon saw it about ten meters away. The sand had been disturbed, probably by someone lying down and with their arms extended. He also saw clear tracks leading down the other side of the dune.

Ben quickly scrambled down the side of the sand dune and at the bottom found vehicle tracks deeply impressed into the soft sand. He was also sure he could hear engine noise. Looking to the right he was just in time to see the cabin of a four wheel drive disappear behind the next sand dune. He took off after it at a run. The vehicle carrying Ashad started about three hundred meters ahead of Ben and as he started to run it slowly dawned on him. Until now he had been fuelled by anger, forgetting all other considerations. But now he saw the situation for what it was. He was chasing a man armed with a gun whilst he had only a butchers knife. Knife versus gun was not a fair contest. He slowed to a walk and then stopped completely. He was not going to give up but nor was he going to commit suicide. What to do?

Thinking quickly Ben realized that Ashad must be returning to the outstation. If he didn't catch him soon then he would disappear. He realized that he could probably catch up with Ashad as the vehicle was forced to weave between the sand dunes at less than ten kilometers per hour whilst he could travel over the sand dunes, in a straight line.

He knew what he had to do. It would be risky but so be it. He knew without doubt that Ashad had come to the dig for a single purpose. To kill him. Why else would he fire just one shot, apparently at him, and then run? He would use that blind thirst for revenge to his own advantage.

Ben set off again at a run. However, instead of following Ashads wheel marks he ran due northeast, directly towards the outstation, navigating by the sun. He went over a sand dune, down into a valley and over another sand dune. Ten minutes later he was sweating with the exertion but had again arrived on Ashads wheel tracks. But he was certain that these tracks had been made on the way in. Ashad had yet to arrive back here. He quickly cast around looking for the best place to set his plan in motion. Then he saw about two hundred meters ahead that the track turned sharply to the left to skirt the large sand dune currently on his left. He ran to the bend in the track and stood facing back the way that he had come. With Ashad heading towards him he would surely be seen. That was what he wanted. He stood and waited.

Ben heard the engine noises first and then two minutes later saw the four wheel drive heading towards him. Ashad must also have seen him as the vehicle came to a sudden stop about three hundred meters from where he stood.

"Hey Ashad, you arsehole!", he yelled, uncertain that Ashad could even hear him, "You fucking missed!"

The four wheel drive started moving again making the maximum pace it could through the clinging sand. Ben raced around the corner of the sand dune until the vehicle had disappeared. He then ran across the tracks and up the side of the next sand dune to the north. At the top he stopped and waited.

Ashad came around the bend in the road a couple of minutes later, Ben standing about thirty meters above it and to the north.

"Hey dickhead!", Ben yelled, "You are as fucking hopeless at assassination as you are at being a terrorist mastermind!"

Ben saw Ashads eyes flick up to look at him. Seconds later he was sliding and tumbling down the far side of the dune. He ran across the flat valley and up the next sand dune. Looking down into the next valley he could see vehicle tracks. He ran down the sand dune, across the tracks, and up the next sand dune to the north. He halted at the top and waited for Ashad to appear again. This time he had to wait over five minutes before Ashad appeared below him in his vehicle.

"Wanker! You've got a car and you still can't keep up!"

Once again he saw Ashads eyes flick up towards him. Once again he fled down the far side of the sand dune. This time he stopped at the bottom and waited. He was not disappointed. He heard a car door slam. Ashad had realized that he could not catch him with the vehicle and was coming after him on foot. Ben slid down the dune, scrambled up the next sand dune, over the top, and up the next. He then lay down behind a clump of spinifex to watch.

A few minutes later he saw Ashads head and then his whole body appear at the top of the next sand dune over, the position he had been only a few minutes before. Ben saw that he was carrying in one hand a rifle. He did not appear to be carrying water. Good!

Ben stood up from his cover. "Hey, Ashad. Do you really think a prick like you can catch me?"

Ben immediately ducked and slid down the far side of the dune. As he was sliding he heard the sharp crack of the rifle discharging. Ashad had taken a hurried shot at where he had been standing only moments before. Ben ran as fast as he could over another three sand dunes, putting some distance between him and his pursuer. He climbed the fourth sand dune and stopped on the top, once again taking cover behind a clump of spinifex.

About eight minutes later Ashads head and body appeared atop the third sand dune. It had taken him longer this time. He was already slowing down.

"Moron!", yelled Ben, standing up, "You must be getting thirsty!"

"Yes Wilde, I am. But I will soon be drinking your blood", yelled Ashad.

Once again Ben ducked and slid down the reverse side of the dune and once again a bullet accompanied by a loud crack parted the air where he had just been standing.

For five hours Ben played his game and although Ashad unloosed a number of wild shots none struck home. On one occasion Ben had felt something tug at his shirt as he dived for cover. He would later find two neat holes through the shirt at the front and rear. Luckily it had been flapping away from his body when the bullet had passed through.

It was a hot day, over thirty eight degrees, one hundred degrees in the old money. Ben regularly took small sips from his water bottle but even so his tongue was starting to feel swollen and heavy and his lips were cracking. How must Ashad be feeling with no water?

Of course Ashad could have retreated on his own steps to his vehicle for water but Ben believed that his thirst for vengeance was too strong. He believed that Ashad would continue with the pursuit to a bitter end.

Ben had once again bypassed three sand dunes and was waiting for Ashad to appear. He waited for five minutes and there was nothing. Ten minutes – nothing. Twenty minutes – nothing. Ben finally slid over the top of the sand dune and climbed the one he had left twenty minutes before. He peered over the top of the dune into the valley below. There was nothing. He went back to the next dune and repeated the exercise. This time looking down he saw Ashad spread-eagled on the sand about half way up. For five minutes he stayed hidden looking down but Ashad did not move. Finally, emboldened, Ben descended the dune about twenty meters to the left of Ashad all the way to the bottom and quietly walked up behind where Ashad lay. Walking quietly was easy in a terrain that had only soft sand and scant vegetation. Reaching Ashads body Ben quickly stooped and snatched the rifle from Ashads outflung right hand. Ashad groaned and turned his head to look back at Ben. His lips were cracked and his eyes bloodshot. Clearly, the lack of water combined with carrying a heavy rifle had taken its toll.

Ben pointed the rifle at his fallen adversary as Ashad rolled over and pulled himself to a sitting position.

"Well, Ashad, it ends here. You just weren't good enough"

"You destroyed my mission and my life infidel", Ashad croaked, "Allah will make sure that you rot in hell".

As he spoke Ashad reached for the pistol holstered at his side. Ben had not even seen it and at first wondered what his adversary was doing. Two shots rang out almost as one. Ben felt a gust of wind caress his neck. Ashad grew a third eye and the back of his head disappeared in an explosion of blood, bone and brain. He slumped back onto the sand, lifeless.

Ben looked down at the corpse. He was filled with conflicting emotions, elation and shame. He had killed a man. No, not a man, he thought. An animal. He was an animal who had killed other innocents. Although the comparison with animals was unfair since Ben loved all animals and they did not need to be tarred with the same brush as this homicidal maniac. He had deserved to die. Ben let out a deep breath and sank onto the sand.

Snapping out of his lethargy Ben set to work. With his hands alone he scooped out a shallow trench in the loose sand of the dune. A half hour later the trench was about two feet deep, six feet long and two feet wide. It would have to do. Grunting with the effort he rolled Ashads body into the shallow grave. The rifle and the pistol followed. He then swiftly covered the grave with the loose sand he had excavated. Finally, he tore spinifex from a nearby clump, piercing his hands, and used it to obliterate the grave. If some curious soul followed his and Ashads footprints then they would discover nothing.

The sun was setting in the west as Ben set out to walk back to camp. Instead of setting out the way he had come, over the sand dunes, he followed the valley between two sand dunes directly into the setting sun. He knew that this route would take him back to the dig access road where he would turn south towards the camp.

Three hours later, at about nine o'clock, Ben finally stumbled into the camp to the confusion of those sitting around the camp fire. He went directly to one of the water containers and took a long drink, letting the water overflow his mouth and cascade down onto his chest.

"Where in hell have you been mate? We've been worried sick. We thought you'd been shot. We heard several shots a long way off during the day", said Tug.

"Sorry for worrying you all. I chased him but all that I found was his abandoned vehicle. It looks as though he set off into the desert, poor bastard".

"Well, the cops were here and they went off to the outstation to see if they could get him at that end. We haven't heard anything. And Michelle has been taken to the hospital in Port Hedland. The docs reckon its only a flesh wound and she should be fine", said Tug.

Ben exchanged a few words with the rest of the crew and then begged their understanding as he was tired and wanted only to go to bed. Taking the water container with him Ben went to his swag and lay down. Laying on his back staring up at the stars Ben wondered what would become of him. He wasn't worried about legal repercussions. He was confident that Ashads body would never be found. He was worried about his state of mind. He had killed a man. Did that make him a murderer? He knew that he was now a changed man, but for better or worse? He hoped for the better. He finally drifted off knowing that, yes, he had killed a man, but that man had been an animal who thought naught of killing innocents. Surely the World was a better place with him no longer in it?

31
23 NOVEMBER, 2014

THE DAY WAS sunny and the temperature mild. It had been six months since Ben's adventure with Ashad and nearly four months since he had been back to the Aboriginal village. But he was back with a completely recovered and healed Michelle, his wife to be.

Ben had proposed only a week previous after a dinner date in Perth. Because he was by nature old fashioned Steve had actually gone down on one knee in the restaurant. He had pulled a small jewel box from his pocket and opened it, letting Michelle see the one carat Argyle pink diamond within. Michelle had accepted without hesitation, laughing and crying at the same time. All of the patrons and staff of the restaurant had laughed and applauded. At that moment he had been the happiest man on the planet.

Ben was driving his own beat up landrover as they coasted down the newly graded road between the NWR road, through Blind Bluff, to the Aboriginal village. Michelle sat in the passenger seat staring out the window and smiling secretly to herself. Approaching the village they passed beneath a large sign mounted on two large steel posts. Painted on the sign in black letters on a white background was the word 'Julkurrji', the name that had been given to the village.

"You came up with the name didn't you?", asked Ben.

"Yes I did. And it was accepted by everyone. Julkurrji is the local Aboriginal word meaning 'dreamtime'. I thought it was appropriate", said Michelle.

Driving on a little further they came to where the camp site had been. The camp was now gone to be replaced by a simple timber and fibreboard building with wraparound verandahs and a corrugated iron roof. A small sign mounted on wooden posts in front of the building read 'Ranger'. This would be the home and office of two Aboriginal rangers who would be based there full time. The rangers would of course be drawn from Jacks people. Behind the rangers quarters was a large gravel parking area which was almost full of vehicles from Mercedes and BMWs to beaten up sedans and four wheel drives. There were also several vans bearing the logos of prominent TV stations. Clearly, the guests had arrived.

On the other side of the road from the rangers quarters was a large cleared area. Steve had seen the plans so he knew that this was where the concession would be built. The concession would sell drinks, chocolates, sandwiches, pies, souvenirs and Aboriginal paintings to the tourists. The concession would be staffed by Aborigines from the Mandandanja community and all of the profits would flow to that community.

Driving beyond the rangers quarters and down a shallow incline they came at last to the village. The sand had been entirely cleared and the ancient village sat on compacted brown clay. A small area to the north of the village had been cordoned off for parking for dignitaries. As discoverers of the village he and Michelle qualified just this once as very important persons. There were five other vehicles in the parking lot and Steve pulled in next to the last and cut the engine. Of the six vehicles now in that special parking lot his was by far the cheapest and dirtiest.

Ben and Michelle climbed down from the four wheel drive and walked across to the village. Six of the houses remained exactly as they had discovered them. The seventh, however, had been restored to its former glory. It now had a new sandstone roof complete with a coating of tar for weatherproofing. Walking inside they saw vibrant aboriginal paintings covering all of the walls. Painted by an Aboriginal woman from Mandandanja the paintings were of most of the animals native to Australia, including, Ben saw, budgerigars, frogs and even tiny honey ants.

"Its beautiful isn't it", said Michelle.

"It certainly is. They have done a wonderful job", said Ben.

Walking back out through the open doorway they were confronted by Mick, his arm wrapped possessively around Susans waist.

"G'day boss. Glad to see you could make it", Mick boomed.

"G'day Mick, Susan. Wouldn't have missed it for the World!". Ben caught Mick in a bear hug and then gave Susan a light peck on her cheek. Michelle also hugged Mick and kissed Susan.

"Bloody good about Blind Bluff wasn't it. Eleven million tons!", crowed Mick.

After the drama with Ashad, Ben had returned to Blind Bluff to supervise further drilling assisted by Lance. At times they had had up to three drilling rigs working at once. When they had finally done the calculations they had discovered that Blind Bluff was a tabular shaped orebody containing eleven point two million tons of 7.9% copper, 2.6 grams per ton gold and 72 grams per ton silver. The in-ground value of the resource was measured in billions! Major minerals was currently seeking financiers to fund the development of the mine.

"You do remember that we're drilling Bright Desert next week, don't you?", added Mick.

Ben did remember. He, Mick and Ibrahim were going to commence drilling of the Bright Desert prospect. Although the company had been concentrating on Blind Bluff, Global

Geophysics had been sent to do an IP survey at Bright Desert. The survey had produced another anomaly and it had been decided to test drill it.

"Hello Ben", said another voice, "It is good to see you". It was Ibrahim, standing behind Mick and Susan. Ben gave him a hug and turned to the tall statuesque woman by his side. She was wearing a dark green headscarf and was smiling impishly.

"And this is my wife Laila", added Ibrahim proudly.

Ben was uncertain of the protocol of dealing with Muslim women so simply took her hand and gave it a light shake. She in turn pulled Ben towards herself and gave him a hug and brushing kisses on both cheeks. She stood back, a dazzling smile revealing brilliant white teeth.

"Ibrahim has told me so much about you. I feel that I have known you for ages", she explained, "Ibrahim is so proud to be working with a man like you. I know you saved his life".

Ben blushed. Michelle hugged Ibrahim and Laila in turn.

As a group they headed off across the cleared area towards where a makeshift stage had been erected.

"Hey! Mr Wilde. Ben", cried a high voice.

Ben turned and saw Banjo running towards him. Standing behind him, smiling indulgently, was his uncle Jack. As he came closer Ben saw that Banjo was glowing with good health, his eyes clear and all of his movements normal. He was however still wearing a large white bandage wrapped around his head like a compressed turban.

"Oh, Banjo! So good to see you mate! I see that they have finally let you out of the hospital", said Ben.

"They had to mate. Nothing wrong with me!"

Although Banjo was a little shy about such things Ben gave him a huge hug. He was at first a little stiff but then started giggling as he pulled away. Michelle stepped forward and, although she had never met him before, also gave Banjo a hug. If it could have been seen beneath his black skin, Banjo would have turned a delightful shade of pink. Then Mick, Susan, Ibrahim and Laila all gave Banjo a hug and he turned red beneath the black.

"I take it the government people have been to see you Banjo", said Ben.

"Yeah, they did", said Banjo, "I signed a bit of paper and apparently what happened didn't happen! But there you go!"

"By the way Banjo, we're going to be working out near Bright Downs next week. Care to sign on again?", said Ben.

"You betcha boss! I'm keen for some work and I don't mind working out there now that those bastards have gone!"

The group then walked across to where Frank stood gazing about himself, apparently with approval.

"Ben", he said, as Ben stepped up, "And Michelle. I want to thank you for returning some dignity to my people. Now everyone knows that we weren't just grub-eating savages!". He shook Ben heartily by the hand.

"It has been our pleasure Frank", said Michelle, enveloping him in a hug, "This has all been a truly wonderful experience".

They were interrupted by the crackle of loudspeakers that had been set up around the site.

"Ladies and gentlemen, welcome to Julkurrji!", boomed a masculine voice, "We are gathered here today to open this truly marvelous site which casts an entirely new light on the history of the Aboriginal people".

Ben looked towards the temporary stage and saw that the speaker was the Australian Minister for Aboriginal affairs. As the voice droned on Ben saw that sitting behind the minister on the stage were the Prime Minister, Premier of Western Australia, Governor General and two well known national Aboriginal leaders. The two black faces were essential to the proceedings. One could hardly open a major Aboriginal site using only white faces!

As the voice droned on Ben looked at the five hundred or so people gathered around, their attentions riveted to the stage. Complexions varied from milky white to the deepest black. Some were dressed in suits, complete with ties, and elegant dresses. The majority however were dressed in jeans and T-shirts or other casual clothes, a few even in shorts. At least three TV cameras were pointed towards the stage.

To the south of the village was a large tent which had been positioned as a temporary concession selling drinks and snacks to the visitors. Just beyond that Ben could see three slabs of sandstone lying on the ground. These were the Aboriginal graves where the three skeletons he had seen had been reinterred.

Looking back towards the stage Ben saw four men, all dressed in dark suits, to the left and right of the stage. Several of those men appeared to be wearing earpieces. Security detail for the Prime Minister, he thought. They were probably worried that Ashad might still be in the area and out to cause mayhem. He alone knew that Ashad would never cause mayhem again. Ben looked to the north. About six kilometers in that direction Ashad was mouldering in a shallow grave.

Ben was wrong. Only two days after he had buried Ashad the mother dingo and her pup that he had seen about two weeks before had smelt appetizing aromas seeping from the sand on the side of a sand dune. They had been joined by a large male dingo. When the male dug down through the sand he had found meat. It was starting to turn but was still edible. Ashads corpse had been dragged from the shallow grave, the flesh stripped from his bones and his bones broken and crushed by powerful jaws. Even the shattered skull had been crushed in the mothers jaws. The rifle and pistol had been left where they lay. The dingos had no use for them. For three days they had feasted until all that remained were some skeletal fragments, none bigger than a matchbox, and scattered and blood stained remanants of clothing. If the authorities were to now find what remained of the skeleton they would have no choice but to determine that an unidentified person had died in the desert, and the remains eaten by dingos. If such a discovery was made then they would certainly find the pistol and rifle and conclude that the remains were those of the terrorist leader. It was in a fashion poetic justice. A rabid dog had planned to kill innocent Australians, and he had in turn been consumed by Australian dogs. A man who had lived his life as a piece of shit had been turned into dog shit on his death. That is justice!

While Ben had been thinking the Minister had given a brief speech, to be followed by the Premier, the Prime Minister and one of the Aboriginal leaders. The Minister for Aboriginal Affairs once again took the microphone.

"And now I would like to welcome Dr Michelle Michaels who, with Mr Ben Wilde, were responsible for discovering this treasure. Perhaps Dr Michaels might explain to you all a little more about the site and its significance. Dr Michaels!".

By this time Michelle had made her way onto the stage. Now Ben new why that morning she had insisted on wearing a sleek black dress more suitable for a boardroom. She had been expecting this.

As Michelle began talking into the microphone he again tuned out. He loved nothing better that listening to Michelles voice but he had heard all that she would say many times. Once again he studied the people around him. Black and white conversing and laughing together. Why could not all of the World be like that? What led to the creation of racists and bigots like Ashad? Unfortunately, he knew that he would never know. He was just happy that he had done his bit and Ashad no longer posed a threat to innocent people.

That night, when all of the visitors had gone, Ben and Michelle retired to their joined swags in one of the ancient buildings. As the sites discoverers they had been granted permission to spend one last night in the village. The only other people remaining in the village were two Aboriginal rangers. For dinner they ate sandwiches that they had prepared that morning and drank water direct from a bottle. Ben lay on his back on the swag staring up at the stars. They had camped in one of the buildings without a repaired roof. Michelle lay next to him with her head on his shoulder.

"What are you thinking sweetheart?", asked Michelle dreamily.

"Me? I'm thinking that it has been a very eventful half year. I got into some trouble with some very bad people, I found a major orebody, I helped to discover a previously unknown Aboriginal civilization and, most importantly, I discovered the girl of my dreams".

Michelle kissed him gently on the cheek. She too had had some significant adventures, and had been shot! But she too had discovered the love of her life. She believed that she knew exactly what Ben was feeling.

Ben continued staring up at the stars. It had certainly been an adventurous time. On the negative side he had been kidnapped, beaten, threatened with death and shot at. And he had killed a man. On the positive side he had found the girl of his dreams, changed Australian history and found a significant orebody. Most importantly his friends were all OK, Michelle was OK and he was OK. All in all, everything had worked out pretty well in the end.

The following morning Ben and Michelle loaded up Bens landrover and were soon driving down the road away from the village. They had only gone about one kilometer when Ben, who was driving, saw a dingo on the side of a sand dune immediately to his right. He slowed down and stopped and pointed out the waiting dingo to Michelle. The dingo was simply standing and did not appear to be troubled by their presence at all. As Ben looked closely at the animal he could have sworn that it winked at him and then smiled. Ben was astounded but in a feeling of solidarity winked back at the dingo which then turned away and trotted over the dune. Ben drove on with a huge smile on his face – He was convinced that he and the dingo shared a secret.